RIVER FRONT

An American twentieth-century story of
children moving up from desperate poverty
on city streets to corporate boardrooms
in spite of depression and war.

JAMES W. COLMEY

Order this book online at www.trafford.com
or email orders@trafford.com

Most Trafford titles are also available at major online book retailers.

Note for Librarians: A cataloguing record for this book is available from Library
and Archives Canada at www.collectionscanada.ca/amicus/index-e.html

Printed in Victoria, BC, Canada.

ISBN: 978-1-4251-6663-2 (soft)
ISBN: 978-1-4251-6664-9 (hard)
ISBN: 978-1-4251-6665-6 (ebook)

*Our mission is to efficiently provide the world's finest, most comprehensive
book publishing service, enabling every author to experience success.
To find out how to publish your book, your way, and have it available
worldwide, visit us online at www.trafford.com/10510*

Trafford rev. 9/8/2009

 www.trafford.com

North America & international
toll-free: 1 888 232 4444 (USA & Canada)
phone: 250 383 6864 ♦ fax: 812 355 4082

This book is dedicated to my wife, Betty,
who has been so important to my life in
our sixty-five years of marriage.

ACKNOWLEDGMENTS

The characters and story of this novel are entirely fictional, but the author strived to be accurate in using settings such as historical events, cities, military bases, battles, and statistics.

My wife, Betty Colmey, was a partner in the original writing of this novel. My three children, Betsy Lee, Cynthia Bosson, and John Colmey, gave me wise advice and assisted in editing this book. My son-in-law, Larry Lee, did the design and art work for the book cover.

In addition to the author's personal experiences, the following people offered advice and counsel: Major Kenneth Tidwell, United States Army; Captain Frank Liberato, United States Navy Air Corps; Sergeant Major George Smith, United States Marine Corps, and Colonel Hal Roach, United States Marine Corps.

FOREWORD

Blinding streaks of lightning and frightening thunder raging across the United States of America, then deafening silence-- that's the way the Great Economic Depression felt as it began in 1929.

The Depression of the 1930s was like a roaring flood, crushing everything in its way. One worker in four lost his job or business. Government support programs such as welfare, unemployment, social security, or bank insurance did not exist.

The culture of the time had one "breadwinner" and one "homemaker." When the "breadwinner" lost a job or business, a family would instantly lose its total income. In a common struggle for survival, destitute families from all walks of life typically moved together into the deteriorated areas on the Mississippi River front in St. Louis, Missouri, and in other cities.

Buildings in the river front neighborhood above the century-old St. Louis levee had been hurriedly rebuilt after St. Louis's Great Flood in 1844 and Great Fire in 1849. In the 1920s these buildings were declared uninhabitable and had been scheduled for demolition. Instead, in the 1930s they became shared dwellings for uprooted families, drifters, and prostitutes. Some people survived, and some did not.

Children cannot choose the time and place of their childhood.

Their neighborhoods, along with the sensed security of a parent, form the boundaries of their experiences. That's the way it was for children living on the St. Louis river front in 1930. This novel is a story of the lives of three of these children.

PART ONE

1930-1941: THE GREAT ECONOMIC DEPRESSION

WHEN YOU GO THROUGH DEEP
WATERS AND GREAT
TROUBLES, I WILL BE WITH
YOU. WHEN YOU GO
THROUGH RIVERS OF DIFFICULTY,
YOU WILL NOT DROWN.

Isaiah 43:2
The Living Bible

THERE IS HISTORY IN ALL MEN'S LIVES.

Henry IV, Part two, Act III, Scene I
William Shakespeare

1

MATT, JACK, RICK

MATT

Bill came home late that night. At half-past nine Matt was already asleep. Elizabeth was worried because her husband always called when he was going to be late. She felt relieved when she heard the car enter the drive. It was strange that he didn't come in right away, but she was glad he was home. She started to get ready for bed.

A few minutes later, a loud bang came from the garage, and Elizabeth ran to the back door shouting, "Bill, are you all right!"

No answer. Confused and fearful, she scrambled toward the garage. The car was in the drive; the garage door was shut. Throwing the door open, she froze in her steps before letting out an animal-like scream that woke the neighbors. What she saw would remain etched in her memory forever: a body, with no appearance of a head, lay on the floor in a pool of blood.

"Bill!" she shrieked.

*   *   *

Almost a year later in September 1930, Elizabeth awoke with the sun coming in the window. She lay quietly, not wanting to wake her six-year-old son, Matt. They were bone tired and desperately in need of sleep. Their one-room flat was hot and humid, and its one window offered little relief. Elizabeth and Matt had spent their first night in their river front home sleeping together on a mattress without sheets in the midst of a dozen boxes and a pile of clothes.

Elizabeth never imagined that circumstances would force Matt and her to move from their large eight-room home. They had lived on an acre hillside in one of the most prestigious St. Louis suburbs, but now here they were in the inner city of St. Louis in a one-room flat near the Mississippi River.

Matt was understandably upset when Elizabeth told him that he would be living in one room with his mother and that he wouldn't be able to see his friends in his former neighborhood again. He asked angrily, "Mom, why did Daddy kill himself?"

"We won't talk about it now, Matt," Elizabeth Simmons told her son kindly but firmly.

Matt kicked the mattress on the floor. "Okay, but I'm not going to live here."

Annoyed by his attitude, Elizabeth rebuked him sharply, "Matt, this is our new home, and we will just have to get used to it."

"It's only a dirty ole room."

"It's better than most places people live in on the river front."

"Mom, why did we have to come here?" Matt asked as he started to cry.

"I don't like it either, Sweetheart, but our money is almost gone. This is the best place that I could find for two dollars a week. It'll have to do."

Elizabeth drew her son close. She knew how much Matt missed his father. Even though Bill had been gone almost a year, Matt could not or would not accept that his Daddy was gone. Bill was a good man, and he had been devoted to Matt, always giving him the time and attention love demands.

Elizabeth had dreaded the day when her son would have to face the reality of their new life. Matt no longer fought back tears as she held him close, as much to comfort herself as him.

*   *   *

Elizabeth was a beautiful woman with auburn hair and green eyes. She had confidence in her ability, loved life and wasn't afraid of it, even when it had come crashing down on her. Even so, she was still confused and full of self-incrimination.

"What did I do wrong?" she asked herself.

She concluded that she had done nothing wrong. Her thoughts then accused her husband. "Bill, you had no darn business leaving me with this mess." Back and forth in her mind: guilt . . . anger . . . guilt . . . anger. Bill's tragic suicide had left Elizabeth physically and mentally exhausted. She desperately wondered what was happening and knew that she had to sort it out once and for all, or lose her mind.

When she remembered that terrible night, everything was a blur. The tragedy had happened so quickly. Matt had been sleeping soundly in his upper floor bedroom while Elizabeth remembered trying to answer questions from the police, coroner, and funeral director. In the morning she had sent a telegram to her parents in Illinois, explaining that Matt would be coming to stay with them for a while. She had hastily packed a suitcase and managed to get Matt on the train. Then, the funeral.

Elizabeth remembered very little of the actual service, but she could not forget the great sense of relief that had come over her when Charlie Thorpe, Bill's close friend and lawyer, had come up to her afterward to assure her that he would help her through the days ahead. He had told her to refer all questions to him.

*   *   *

Ten days later Elizabeth decided to go talk to Charlie Thorpe. She kept wondering, what was it that had put so much pressure on Bill? What was their financial situation now? She knew Charlie would have some answers.

As she entered his law office, Charlie met her at the door. "Would you like coffee?"

"Thank you, Charlie." She paused. "I really need to know what happened to Bill."

"You may already know most of what I can tell you."

Elizabeth sat up in her chair and looked at Charlie with pleading eyes. "If you have time, please tell me the whole story."

"I'll take the time."

Elizabeth was grateful. She pulled her dress straight and settled back in her chair prepared to listen.

Charlie started from the beginning. "As you know, Bill used the money from his mother's estate to purchase your home and the florist business in Webster Groves. He did well, and his business was growing. He reviewed his expansion plans with me, and I told him that I thought his strategy was sound."

Elizabeth nodded. "Yes, he talked with me about his plans."

"Unfortunately, several unexpected things happened within a short period of time," Charlie explained. "Bill could have handled any one of them, but no one could have financially survived all of them at once."

"Of course I read the papers and heard wild rumors about economic disaster, but I didn't think it could affect us."

"That's what Bill thought, but he was blind-sided . . . ."

Elizabeth started to cry, but quickly regained her composure.

Charlie hesitated, sat back in his chair, and paused before continuing, "Your house had only a small mortgage, and Bill decided to take advantage of the expanding stock market. He put a larger mortgage on the house and invested most of the money in stocks. Investors were making a lot of money that way."

"Then, as you know, the stock market crashed. Bill tried to sell his stocks, but he was too late. His Singer Sewing Machine stock dropped from thirty dollars a share to four dollars a share in a matter of a few days."

Elizabeth leaned forward, stunned. As she began to realize what had happened, her voice faded in disbelief. "Bill told me that he always kept savings in the bank to protect the business and our home."

"He did. He had sufficient savings in the bank."

"What happened?"

"Bill went to the bank to withdraw his savings but discovered that the bank was closed. He told me about his terrible experience outside the bank that day. When he arrived at the bank, a crowd of people were standing outside. Some were crying; others were shouting angrily, and some just stood staring in disbelief. They were told that the bank was going through bankruptcy proceedings and that everyone would have to wait months before they would know what portion of their savings, if any, would be returned to them.

"What could Bill have done?"

"Very little, Elizabeth. His accountant also told him he would need additional cash for the business because customer orders were falling off. Bill probably started to consider alternatives."

"I know that Bill had gone to his real estate agent to sell his business. His agent told him that most businesses were closing, and with the Depression deepening, no one wanted to buy a business."

Elizabeth began to cry as she thought how desperate Bill must have felt.

Charlie got up and carefully poured her a glass of water. "Do you really want to hear more?"

"Please go on. I need to understand."

"The heavy impact of the Depression must have been too great for Bill to bear. His savings, stocks, and business were all gone. He probably thought about selling your home and trying to find a job. I found out what Bill must have learned, that housing values had fallen below the amount of your mortgage.

"Why didn't he talk to me?"

"I don't know."

After a long silence between them, Charlie added, "Bill worked so hard to build up his business and provide a nice home for you and Matt. To lose it all so quickly . . . well, it must have been overwhelming."

Elizabeth sobbed softly, blotting the tears with her handkerchief.

Charlie sat quietly waiting. Finally, he said, "I'm sorry, Elizabeth. Bill was a wonderful person and my closest friend. I feel terrible telling you these things."

"I'll always be grateful that you did."

*   *   *

Seven months later, Charlie Thorpe called Elizabeth back to his law office after resolving the legal problems of her estate. He summarized his conclusions, "I was able to recover enough money from your estate to cover funeral expenses and leave you with this small check. You'll need to leave your home by the end of the week. I've written a reference letter for you that may be helpful. I've a friend who manages the Jefferson Hotel downtown, and he may be able to find some work for you. And, by the way, you owe me nothing for my legal services."

"Thank you, Charlie. You're a dear friend."

Elizabeth's other friends were not in a position to offer her more help. She was on her own. Charlie's letter was all Elizabeth needed in order to see Mr. O'Hare at the Jefferson Hotel. When she entered his office and he pulled back a chair for her, she sensed immediately that he was a kind man.

"Charlie called me, so I've been expecting you, Mrs. Simmons."

"Thank you for seeing me."

The plush office gave Elizabeth false hope. Mr. O'Hare got right to the point. "I'm afraid I don't have good news for you. With your background and experience, the one job opening that we have is quite different from work that you're qualified to expect."

"I need work, Mr. O'Hare. If you have anything, please tell me, and let me decide," Elizabeth replied.

"I'm embarrassed to tell you that the job opening is for a floor maid with low pay and hours that are disgraceful, but I have to manage a hotel that won't go bankrupt in this Depression."

"When can I start, Mr. O'Hare?" asked Elizabeth without further questions or hesitation. "I do understand your thoughtfulness, but my son and I have to eat."

"All right, Mrs. Simmons. I'll call the personnel office and tell them to expect you."

When Elizabeth arrived at the personnel office, a woman met her saying, "Floor maids work six days a week, ten hours a day, at a rate of fifteen cents an hour. You can start Monday."

*　　*　　*

That was how Elizabeth and Matt found themselves on the river front. They began to unpack the boxes in their one-room flat and fold their clothes, carefully placing them in neat stacks on the bare wooden floor. Elizabeth wiped the sweat from Matt's brow.

"Mom, what's going to happen tomorrow?" Matt asked.

"Tomorrow is Monday. You start at Jefferson Elementary School, and I go to work."

"I don't want to go, Mom. I'm kind of . . ." he struggled to get the words out, ". . . kind of scared."

9

"You know what?" Elizabeth smiled. "I'm kind of scared, too, but no matter what happens, we won't shoot ourselves."

"We can make it together, Mom," said Matt, clinging tightly to his mother for desperately-needed reassurance.

JACK

In September 1930, six-year-old Blackjack Pershing LeGault, known by everyone but his father as Jack, lived in the storeroom of a speakeasy on the St. Louis river front. Since he had never had a decent place to live and had always been poorly fed and clothed, Jack had not been immediately affected by America's Depression. Blackjack LeGault was an undernourished boy who was devoted to his father, Louie.

Three years earlier Louie and his son Blackjack had arrived in St. Louis penniless. They had walked aimlessly into the Blue Rhine Restaurant owned by Hans Krueger. Needing to camouflage his illegal beer, Hans had told Louie that he and his son could live in the storeroom and work for a dollar a week and have food from the restaurant.

After Prohibition in 1920, Hans had struggled to keep his business going without the bar. In 1927 he made the right connections to obtain bootlegged beer. After moving his family out, he converted their upstairs living quarters into a speakeasy with six private rooms and a dance hall, where he sold the illegal beer. He served meals on the first floor and hid the beer in the storeroom where Louie LeGault and his son lived.

*   *   *

Blackjack's father, Louie, had quit school when he was twelve to live with his Grandpa Piney. They had lived in the

Ozark Mountains, trapping animals along the rivers for their fur pelts. Like their ancestors before them, they would go into Ste. Genevieve, Missouri, to replenish their supplies and sell their pelts. A nearby salt springs provided the salt to preserve meat and hides.

Louie was responsible for preparing pelts and smoking fish and venison. By the time Louie was fourteen, he could shoot a deer or squirrel with one rifle shot. Grandpa Piney always reminded Louie never to kill an animal except for food or a pelt.

Growing up in the Ozarks was a great life for Louie, but after the turn of the century, the trapping environment and market for furs was changing. Trappers no longer had the wilderness to themselves. People were moving into the Ozark region to farm and develop lead mines. Families were building cabins along the rivers. Trading posts in Ste. Genevieve were closing, and furs had to be shipped to St. Louis.

One day, when Piney was eighty years old and close to death, he gave Louie a pouch with thirty-nine quarter eagle gold coins, telling him, "These coins have been passed on from one LeGault to another for over a hundred years."

"Ya kept them all these years, Piney?"

"My father told me not to use the coins just 'cause yer hungry or need a drink. Only use 'em when there's no other way for ya to survive. Add some coins when ya can."

"Piney, let me take ya to Ste. Genevieve for the winter."

"No, Louie. I ain't goin'. I wanna hear the river splashing over the stone bed. LeGaults should die and be buried in the forest."

Louie gave his grandfather broth and sips of whisky to keep him comfortable until he died peacefully in his sleep. Louie buried him where Piney had buried his father. At the graveside, Louie repeated the prayer that the Sisters of St. Joseph had taught him, "Holy Mary, Mother of God, pray for us sinners." He added, "Please take care of Grandpa Piney. He tried to do good."

During the next two days between drunken sleeps, Louie downed two bottles of whiskey that were in the cabin. When the whiskey was gone, he turned to broth. While he was recovering, a young man walked up and greeted him, "I'm Jimmy Andersen. I bought the Douglas homestead on the plateau above here that comes down to the river."

"I'm Louie LeGault. I hunt and fish here."

"You can hunt and fish all ya want on my land," said Jimmy. "I can't farm the side of the mountain or the river."

The pioneering period of the French trappers in the Ozark Mountains was over. Louie hunted and trapped for two more years with less success each year. One fall day Louie took the long walk to Ste. Genevieve, taking everything he owned including traps, rifles, furs, knives, and his gold coins. He sold everything and added ten gold coins to the deer skin pouch that Piney had given him. Louie had one hundred eighteen dollars more that he put into another pouch.

Louie woke early the next morning and walked toward the river. Passing the Ste. Genevieve Cemetery, he knew that only one LeGault had been buried there, his Grandma Annabel LeGault. There were no other grave markers in remembrance of LeGaults who had lived in the Ozark Mountains. Louie never knew his grandma, but Piney had talked about her as they would sit watching their evening campfires burn out.

An idea flashed into Louie's mind. He carefully cut out a square of grass in front of his grandma's sandstone marker and removed dirt to three knife lengths deep. He placed Piney's deerskin pouch with the forty-nine gold coins into the hole, pushed the dirt back, and replaced the patch of grass. Then he walked the mile or so down to the river landing where barges stopped overnight to obtain supplies.

When Louie reached the river landing, a barge captain was hollering, "My damned deckhand took off, and I'm shorthanded. Will anyone make the trip to St. Louis for passage, food, and a dollar?"

Louie shouted, "I'll make the trip."

"How soon can you board?"

"Less than an hour."

Louie did what he was told, and the trip up the Mississippi was uneventful. When they docked in St. Louis, he aimlessly wandered around the city and found himself outside a recruiting office, where a sergeant asked him, "You here to enlist?"

"What happens if I do?"

"If you sign up, you'll be in the army for three years. You'll have hard work, food, and a place to sleep. Sometimes you'll have a weekend leave. Once a year you'll have a longer leave. Pay'll be twenty dollars a month. The army decides what you do, and you do it. Wanna sign up?"

"Sure."

"Sign this application," continued the sergeant. "Be here tomorrow morning."

"What about my dollars?"

"Spend 'em, put 'em in the bank, or eat 'em," was the sarcastic reply. "That's not army business."

"Where's the bank?"

"Down the street."

Louie found the bank and spoke with a banker, Mr. Rohde, "I got a hundred dollars. Can ya save it for me?"

After opening a savings account, Mr. Rohde said, "Mr. LeGault, keep this card--it has your account number on it. If you're not in St. Louis, other banks can get your money for you."

Louie thanked Mr. Rohde and kept his other eighteen dollars in his pouch. He had no idea what the army was all about, but the first step to survival was to have a place to sleep and food to eat. The thought of killing men instead of animals never entered his mind, but he took his new life seriously and learned everything he could. At his first visit to the firing range, he hit the center of the target from all firing positions and was assigned to the infantry.

Louie's army division went to France, where two life-changing incidents occurred. The first came on the battlefield. When German machine guns and rifle fire were killing soldiers beside him, Louie decided that he must somehow get behind the enemy gunners to stop their killing. Without orders, he managed to crawl slowly behind the dangerous enemy trenches. Each time a German fired, the sharp sound of a rifle or machine gun would ring out. Simultaneously, Louie would shoot the enemy soldier that had fired. Over a period of two hours, Louie was able to close down two machine gun nests and kill over twenty enemy riflemen. The Germans retreated, and the Americans overran their trenches.

When the American soldiers found Louie, his company captain asked, "What the hell are you doing here?"

"Shootin'," answered Louie as he joined his platoon.

The captain reported Louie's bravery, and later General Pershing and a French General personally awarded Louie several medals.

Louie's second life-changing incident occurred as World War I concluded. While celebrating the Allied Army victory, Louie and other soldiers were out on the town drinking. Louie overheard someone at the next table say that many of their enlistments wouldn't be renewed. Since Louie spoke fluent French, and villagers idolized him as a hero who had received the French medal, he contemplated the possibility of accepting an offer to remain in France to work in a vineyard. The next day Louie discussed his idea with his sergeant and was told to report to a public relations officer, Colonel LeBeau.

Louie saluted as he entered Colonel LeBeau's office. The Colonel returned the salute and told Louie to be at ease.

In an unmilitary fashion, the Colonel rose from his chair in front of the American flag. He walked around his desk and put his hand on Louie's shoulder. "Private LeGault, your heroic actions have endeared you to the French people. Since the war ended, some of our soldiers have been creating negative images of America. By staying in France you might help change that image. Your request is granted."

"Thank you, sir."

As Louie left, he wondered what "endeared" meant.

*   *   *

Louie worked in a French vineyard for several months, where he met Monet, a beautiful, wide-eyed seventeen-year-old girl. She guessed that Louie needed companionship, and she had it to give. Monet would follow Louie into the vineyard where she would find him alone, nudge her body into him, and chatter away. She became bolder, and Louie became more receptive. One evening Monet suggested that they go to Louie's room to be alone and share some wine. He could not believe that this was happening to him.

Monet quietly and gently led Louie, who had never been with a woman, into the acts of love. First, she slowly undressed herself and then him. Monet was soft and beautiful. Louie was lean and hard. As they came into each other, they experienced an exploding new world.

For the next few months, they met secretly in Louie's room each evening. Their overpowering enjoyment of each other seemed to have no end. They abandoned any thought of consequences.

As suddenly as it had started, their dream world was over. Monet's mother discovered that her daughter was pregnant. After a painful consultation with all the parties involved, the family determined that Monet would marry Louie and move away from the village. Monet's father would send them money every month until Louie could find work in the city.

Louie found a job working in a bar in exchange for an upstairs room that would be their home. Their infatuation with each other continued until the baby came. They named their baby boy Blackjack Pershing LeGault, after the American general of the army. By this time, Louie was making a meager living.

When Blackjack was three, Monet started to pay attention to men who were aroused by just seeing her walk down the street. She left with one of those men who made an offer that she couldn't resist. Louie's life was shattered. Now his only plan was to protect Blackjack and to return to St. Louis.

*　　*　　*

Louie and Blackjack had been content living in the storeroom of the Blue Rhine speakeasy. They had food, shelter, and each other. Today Louie had heard that six-year-old children were supposed to go to school. He called to his son, "I've got somethin' to tell ya, Blackjack."

"Ain't ya ready to eat, Louie? I got the potatoes boilin'."

Louie decided that talk of school could wait and answered, "I gotta carry out these two boxes first."

"Hurry. I'm ready to dish 'em."

After they'd eaten, Louie said, "Blackjack, ya start school in the mornin'."

"Why?"

"Ya hav'ta learn to read to survive."

"Who'll clean this room and boil potatoes?"

Louie pulled his son to him and said softly and confidently, "Ya gotta suck in yer gut an' do it."

"We can do it," said Blackjack as he stood up straight, sucking in his little belly. "Can't we, Louie?"

"Sure we can," said Louie proudly.

They had little else, but they had each other. When things got tough, they got tougher. Blackjack was emotionally secure with his father, but right now he wished he had his mother, even though he could barely remember her.

"Will ya tell me again about my mama, Louie?"

Louie loved to tell Blackjack about Monet as much as Blackjack wanted to hear about her. Reminiscing kept this part of his life alive. Memories of Monet became common bedtime stories for the little boy, and his father always told them with heartfelt tenderness.

"Your mama's name was Monet," started Louie. "She was the most gentle and beautiful lady in all of France. She was like a dainty, shivering fawn in the forest."

Blackjack would be sleeping before Louie finished. He'd

gently cover his son, wondering how their lives would unfold as his son grew to manhood.

RICK

In September 1930, six-year-old Richard Emil Bauman, known as Rick, lived in the St. Louis river front neighborhood in a former carriage house that his father, Emil, and his mother, Maria, had converted into their home. Rick was strong and self-reliant. Tonight he was in the alley waiting for his father while his mother was cooking a special meal. Tomorrow Rick would start school.

Maria was a woman of resolve, who faced life with a quiet determination and acceptance. For meals, she prepared available food. Moments when others might rest or feel bored, she would scrub the floor, knit sweaters, or darn socks. Maria always did something with the time that was hers.

*   *   *

Maria found special pleasure in reviewing events in her life. Her greatest blessing was finding her home in America. Her move was really two miracles exploding into one in an unimaginable way. Every night she silently thanked Jesus, knowing that there was no other explanation.

When Maria Brodowski left Poland ten years before, she barely had enough money for steerage passage to America. She had arrived totally dependent on a letter that offered her employment in New York City as a nanny.

Maria had met Emil Bauman on the ship coming to America. He told Maria that he was going to St. Louis, Missouri, where his cousin had work for him. They had doubts about their future but reassured each other as they met daily.

Emil was pleased that Maria could speak the German language. English words were still difficult for them, and Emil could not speak Polish. Their comfort and confidence in each other continued to grow. One evening, in a boldness that surprised him, Emil asked, "Maria, let's marry and go to St. Louis together?"

Maria astonished herself by her hasty answer, "Ya."

The evening their ship entered New York harbor, Emil and Maria were holding hands as they leaned forward against the ship's rail. The New York and New Jersey skylines, with lights twinkling like stars on a clear night, enveloped them. The orange colors of the sunset ahead of them were fading and a new moon was rising behind them. It was magical.

Before them rose the Statue of Liberty, that priceless gift from France to America. The beauty of the crowned lady with the flaming torch gave them a sense of awe as she warmly welcomed them, and this whole scene made them feel as if they were living in the midst of a miracle. Emil put his arm around Maria and pulled her close to him as the passion of the moment surged through them.

When they arrived in America in 1922, Emil was forty-six, and Maria was thirty-seven. Emil had told Maria about his career as a cabinetmaker in Germany, but he would not elaborate on the details of his past. Maria also skipped painful details about her life in Poland, but she did tell Emil that her parents had died when she was six. She had lived and gone to school at a convent until she was fourteen.

Maria arrived at Ellis Island with only a basket of clothes and a clock that had been in her family for generations. Emil had sufficient money for railroad tickets and to get established in St. Louis, so they stayed in New York City only long enough to get married. Although their marriage was one of convenience, there would be time for passion later.

Maria thought pleasantly, 'No panic ever again--maybe sad days and hard days, but not panic." Emil always had answers, even when there didn't appear to be any.

'What else could it be but a miracle?' thought Maria.

Sitting for over twenty-four hours on hard coach seats with coal soot seeping in through the train windows made the Baumans' trip to St. Louis extremely tiring. They were surprised at how big America was.

Finally, their train arrived at St. Louis' Union Station where eighty trains were continuously coming and going. The rushing crowds of strangers frightened the Baumans. After Emil found a room for them to stay, he sought out his cousin, who helped him find work as a carpenter's helper.

A few months later, Emil arrived home and excitedly picked Maria up by the waist and told her that he had purchased a business. Emil explained that he had borrowed money from the bank and used his savings to buy an ice and coal delivery business that included a small parcel of land, a carriage building, and a horse and wagon.

At one time the carriage building had been used for three horses and wagons. Having only one horse and wagon provided extra space where they could live. Maria loved the horse named "Sweetie."

Proudly helping Maria into their wagon, Emil took her for a ride along the Mississippi River past the big cobblestone levee. As they reached Eads Bridge, Emil stopped the wagon to watch a barge churn by them. The two-level bridge reached all the way across the great river, the upper level of the bridge for carriages and automobiles and the lower level for trains. As they held hands, once again Emil and Maria felt that same awesome energy they had experienced gazing at the Statute of Liberty.

Before they moved into their home, Emil renovated the carriage building by constructing a wall between their living quarters and the stable. He built a wood floor in their home, as well as several pieces of furniture.

Since they could not afford to install city electricity and sewage, they had cold water, kerosene lamps, and a privy behind their home. Maria stitched two large sheets together, filled them with straw to make their bedding. Emil bought a used, all-purpose cast iron range that used coal for cooking and heating. Maria had never imagined having a home of her own, but now she did.

In the summer Emil would load his wagon with hundred-pound pieces of ice packed in sawdust. Customers would put a cardboard sign in their window signaling Emil how much ice they wanted. He would cut the right size piece of ice and, using ice tongs, would put the ice on his leather-covered shoulder and carry it to the customer's ice box.

In the winter Emil would deliver fifty-pound gunny sacks of coal to families using pot belly stoves for heat. Large coal companies only delivered to homes with furnaces where a ton of coal was shoveled down a chute into a basement coal bin. They did not compete for Emil's customers.

Emil's ice delivery route was in a poor area along the river front. He made friends with his customers and took time to give children chips of ice and an opportunity to pet Sweetie. Sometimes customers were not able to pay, but he still left ice or coal. Usually payments would be caught up at a later date.

A few months after they had moved into their home, Maria proudly announced to Emil that she was going to have a baby, "Maybe a son for you, Emil, to help with Sweetie when you come home at night."

"That will be good, Maria."

The baby was born on July 4, 1924. Maria had struggled through a long labor but was ready to have her baby by the time the doctor arrived. The baby boy cried as the doctor gave him a spank and handed him to Emil.

Tears came to Emil's eyes as he cleaned and wrapped his son in a clean towel and gently laid him in the cradle he had made. Emil observed quietly that the otherwise healthy baby boy had no left hand. Only small finger nubs had grown at the end of his left wrist. The doctor had too much to do to talk about the missing hand, so Emil slipped out into the backyard. Leaning against the back door, all he could do was ask himself, "Why? Why?"

The doctor carefully placed the baby in Maria's arms as she smiled serenely and proudly. Looking for Emil, the doctor went outside. "Emil, you've got to pull yourself together. Maria doesn't know about the missing hand. She's had a hard time and won't be able to have another baby. She needs sleep, and she needs you to be there for her."

"I'll help her."

After giving Emil instructions, the doctor left in his horse and carriage. Emil controlled his emotions and washed Maria's forehead with a wet cloth.

Maria spoke first, "Emil, a fine son for you."

"Thank you, Maria," said Emil. "Doctor says to keep the baby wrapped, and you should rest."

Smiling contentedly, Maria did exactly as Emil had asked.

While Maria and the baby slept, Emil cleaned the room and buried the waste in the back lot. Later, when the baby started to cry for Maria to nurse him, Emil desperately searched for words to tell his wife about their son's deformity.

"Maria, our son has a problem."

"What?"

Emil gently pulled back the corner of the cover and showed Maria the missing hand. Tears poured down her cheeks. Emil looked sadly at Maria without speaking. Maria continued to sob quietly as she nursed her baby. They named their son, Emil Ulrick Bauman, but they would call him "Rick," because it was more American.

When the Great Depression came, Emil saw it as a new challenge rather than a disaster. He had faced many setbacks in his life and had learned to accept them for what they were: a time to adjust and work harder. In 1929 Emil made his second big financial decision since arriving in St. Louis. With trucks taking over the work of horses, Emil knew that he had to sell Sweetie while horses still had value.

Emil had almost completed the loan payments on the carriage property, and with a new loan from the bank, he bought a truck.

Now came the difficult task of saying goodbye to Sweetie who had been part of the Bauman' life since Emil and Maria had moved into their carriage home before Rick was born. The next day, when a truck came and hauled Sweetie away, Rick and Maria just stood and cried.

Emil took two chairs to the back lot that evening to be with his young son and patiently explained why a man must do hard things. Many times Rick wondered where Sweetie had gone, but he never asked. Emil was glad he had not.

*   *   *

When Maria heard Emil and Rick coming in for dinner, she quit thinking of past years. She had to hurry because the family always sat down at the table as Maria's clock from Poland was chiming their eight o'clock dinner hour. The clock was small and plain, but the soft, pleasant chimes were reassuring to the family.

This evening was special. For the past year, Emil and Maria had created anticipation in their son's mind about going to school. Now Rick would actually start school. Maria prayed silently and made the sign of the cross before the family began to eat. Emil did not participate in this ritual, but he always respected Maria's resolute feeling about this moment at the beginning of their meal.

"Tomorrow you go to school, Rick."

"I know Papa, but it doesn't seem real."

Emil responded, "America means free! School means free! Mama and I came to America to be free."

"I know Papa."

Rick did not fully understand about "free" and "school," but he loved his parents, and they knew what was best for him. After dinner Rick climbed into the loft and went to sleep.

Emil was determined to raise his son to become a good man.

Rick had reached a step on the way to that goal. He was ready to go to school and learn to read. Emil knew that there were some things he and Maria could not teach Rick, but Maria nurtured and loved Rick, and Emil taught him to solve problems and to face reality.

Maria sensed that this special evening was important to Emil, and she took advantage of it. When they were in bed, she pulled herself close to him and felt his warm quivering response that had been missing in recent months. Though their passion was reserved, their loving took away tensions.

"You're a good man, Emil, and your son will be a good man," whispered Maria. "I love you."

"I love you too," responded Emil as he fell asleep.

2

Jefferson Elementary School

Like other first graders, Matt, Jack, and Rick were nervous when they arrived at Jefferson Elementary School located on the south edge of their deteriorated neighborhood. During the Depression, some families lived as squatters with no legal residence, and children often dropped out of school.

The playground was filled with excited children. A few older boys were playing mumble-peg with their pocket knives; others were playing marbles. Girls were playing tag or just visiting.

The first graders entered their room and took seats, row by row, until all thirty desks were filled. The teacher, Miss Goerner, had her desk located below a picture of George Washington. An American flag was in the front corner of the room. Behind the back wall was a cloakroom.

Miss Goerner said, "As I read your name, please come to the front of the room and tell us what name you'd like to be called and something about yourself, like how many brothers and sisters you have."

When Miss Goerner called Mary Ellen Jackson's name, she came forward and said, "I like to be called Mary Ellen. I have a brother and two sisters." She was a pretty girl with long, blond hair and clear blue eyes. Children noticed that she had two different-sized shoes, one for her regular foot and one for her smaller foot, as a result of the dreaded disease polio.

Miss Goerner called Matthew William Simmons. A tall, redheaded boy came forward and said, "I have no brothers and sisters, and I like to be called Matt." His leather boots came to his knees. No one else had such nice boots.

Next, Miss Goerner called Blackjack Pershing LeGault, who moved quickly to the front and said, "I don't got nobody but Louie. I like to be called Jack." He was thin with dark eyes and coal black hair combed straight back. His short pants and shirt were dirty. He was not wearing socks, and the toe of one shoe had a large hole.

Miss Goerner continued with Emil Ulrick Bauman. He was a strong boy with dark, curly hair and brown eyes. He stood and said, "I'm called Rick, and I don't have brothers or sisters." Then, on an impulse, Rick raised his left arm, showing everyone that he did not have a hand, and said loudly for emphasis, "I never had a left hand, and I don't know why. I don't want to talk about it anymore." He wanted this part of his introduction to be over, since children on the playground had already troubled him by asking questions.

Soon Miss Goerner had called all the names.

As a brief orientation, Miss Goerner told her class, "Always use the separate boys' and girls' entrances for toilets at your end of the basement. At noon you can take your lunch to the basement cafeteria."

Even though the Depression had begun less than a year ago, it had already taken a heavy toll. The children's eyes seemed to reflect the despair and hunger in their lives, and each child seemed confused with thoughts that he or she could not unscramble at this time.

Their long, tense first day was finally over.

*   *   *

Hilga Goerner, a tall, slender woman, came to school each day in a newly washed and ironed dress. Some children were in her class for two years, but they did learn to read.

This was a hard year for Hilga. She had always lived with her mother, who had died a few weeks before school started. Hilga thought about the time when she had almost married. According to school board policy, she would lose her teaching position if she had married and become pregnant. Without her salary, the boy she was to marry would not have been able to support both Hilga and her mother, so they didn't marry.

*   *   *

Time went by quickly for the new first graders, and their anxieties about attending school disappeared. In November Miss Goerner tested each child's progress. She called Matt, Jack, Rick, Mary Ellen, and Ruth to her desk. They were to study assignments together in the cloakroom, moving ahead of the other children.

Miss Goerner had guessed that she would be selecting Matt, Rick, Mary Ellen, and Ruth, but she had never expected Jack to be with them. By the fourth week, she had realized that he was an unusual little boy. She had never seen a child try so hard to learn, and his efforts showed results. Soon these five children became close friends and spent more time together at lunch and on the playground.

One day Ruth spoke to the advanced reading group and to Miss Goerner, "My family is moving, so I won't be coming back to school. Papa lost his job and told us that the only thing he knew to do was to move to the river."

Ruth Alger was a pretty girl, and when she walked across the room, there was a spring in her step that made her light brown hair bounce. Her pleasant smile was contagious. Now Ruth would be gone.

Children received vaccinations for small pox, but there were no vaccines for other infectious diseases such as polio, diphtheria, measles, chicken pox, scarlet fever, and whooping cough. Epidemics were frequent and dangerous.

The weather was turning cold, and a measles epidemic hit St. Louis. A large, red quarantine sign hung on the front door of each sick person's home warning people: MEASLES, DO NOT ENTER. The epidemic began with a few children, but before long nearly everyone in the school had had their turn with the measles.

During the Depression, officials made little or no effort in depressed areas to enforce the compulsory education laws. In prior years a truant officer would go to the home of each child who had dropped out of school, in order to find out why. Seven children had dropped out of Miss Goerner's class, and only one new child had been added. Although Miss Goerner could teach fewer pupils more effectively, she was always disappointed that children dropped out.

Mary Ellen was one of those who had measles. Walking to school in the snow was particularly difficult for her, and Rick helped her in bad weather. Snow was on the ground in February, and Mary Ellen had not been to school for ten days. Rick kept watching the weather. When the snow melted and Mary Ellen had still not come to school, Rick went to her home to find out why.

When Mary Ellen's mother saw Rick at the door, she burst into tears. Frightened, Rick asked, "What's wrong, Mrs. Jackson?" She reached down and held Rick to her, and didn't say anything.

"What happened?" Rick pursued.

"Mary Ellen was sick with scarlet fever. We sat with her last Wednesday night, but she kept getting weaker. She died in her sleep, Rick."

"How can that be?" questioned Rick in disbelief.

"Doctor Bryer said she just wasn't strong enough to overcome both measles and scarlet fever in one winter."

Rick was traumatized and simply wandered around for over an hour before he went home.

"What happened, Rick?" asked Maria when he arrived.

"I didn't know that children died, but my friend Mary Ellen did. I thought only really old people died."

"That's usually the way, but death can come to any one of us," Maria said sadly, hurting for her young son.

"How can that be?" cried Rick, rushing outside to shed the tears that he had been holding off.

His mother followed. "Rick honey, please come back in where it's warm, and we can talk." Rick came back in, sat down on the bed with Maria, and cried himself to sleep in the warmth of her arms.

The three boys continued to study in the cloakroom. One day Miss Goerner asked them, "Would you stay after school once a week for special study time with me?"

They all agreed.

On the last day of school Miss Goerner told the boys that she was going to give each of them a double promotion.

"What's a double promotion," asked Rick.

"You read so well that you are going to skip grade two and start grade three next fall."

"Wow!" said Jack.

Miss Goerner smiled, "I have another surprise for you."

"What?" asked Matt.

"Here are three books for you to borrow this summer. If you exchange them, you'll each have three books to read."

They thanked Miss Goerner and left for home.

3

Scott

In the summer of 1932 Matt, Jack, and Rick met on the levee when they had finished their chores. Jack was the last to arrive, shouting, "Let's go down to the water and see the boats!"

"Okay," answered Matt as he started walking.

Walking down the steep cobblestone levee to the river to watch the barges up close was great excitement. They had stopped running down the slippery levee ever since Matt had a bad fall that had broken the Mickey Mouse wristwatch his father had given him.

The boys were competitive, but each had different skills. On the top of the levee was a pile of debris where they'd play "King of the Hill." Jack was usually pushed off first. Then there would be a tough struggle between Rick and Matt. Jack was the quickest when playing tag and would duck and dodge until Rick and Matt ganged up on him.

Today they were in a mood to explore along the river.

"How can that river change so fast?" asked Matt. "Only a couple months ago most of the levee was under water."

"Louie says floods cause the river to come up."

"But where do floods come from?"

"There are a lot of things we don't know," said Rick. "Papa says school can teach us."

"We learned to read," said Jack.

Rick stopped and looked up, "We're under Eads bridge."

They were in awe that the bridge was so high. As they stood there staring at the bridge, a boy came up behind them. "Ya'd better stay outa that river." They looked up and saw a tall black boy about their age.

"What do you mean?" asked Jack.

"Andy jumped into the river when he was playing last summer," answered the boy. "He was carried down that damn river so fast that I couldn't catch him."

"What's your name?" asked Matt.

"Dred Scott Lincoln, but just call me Scott."

"Who's Andy?" asked Jack.

"My little brother."

"What happened to him?" asked Rick.

"He floated away like a driftwood log and then just disappeared in that damn muddy river," answered Scott. "Mama says he's dead, and we ain't gonna see him again. I shouldn't have brought him down here when he was so little. Now I come here a lot to think about Andy and try to keep other kids out of that damn river."

Rick muttered, almost to himself, "My friend Mary Ellen died, and I couldn't do anything about it."

"My Daddy died," added Matt.

"We don't have brothers and sisters," said Rick. "Do you have other brothers and sisters, Scott?"

"Two big sisters, but I miss Andy."

They assured Scott that they would never jump in that damn river. Walking home, the three boys were silent as they continued to think about Andy.

In the weeks that followed, Scott often joined them in their summer games. He was quick and strong. When they got tired of playing, they would sit on the levee and watch "rich kids" go up the gang plank to take a trip up the river on the paddlewheel boat called *The President*. When the boat was out of sight, the boys would climb to the top of the levee near the elevated tracks and wait for a train. When they waved their arms wildly, the man in the cab of the steam engine would almost always blow his whistle and wave back at them.

When the summer was over, the four boys began to talk about going back to school.

"Did you read your last book again, Jack?" asked Matt.

"Yes, that makes two times for each book."

"They were good books," Rick added.

"Where did you get the books?" asked Scott.

"Our teacher let us read them during the summer."

"Where do you live, Scott?" asked Matt.

Scott pointed, "Down that way."

"That's near Jefferson School," said Matt. "Why don't you go to our school?"

Scott, showing his surprise at the question, answered, "I can't go to a white kids' school."

"Why?" asked Rick.

"Papa says it's the law," said Scott. "I thought everyone knew that black kids couldn't go to school with white kids."

"Seems like a dumb law in a free country," said Rick. "Guess we won't see much of you 'til next summer."

"Guess not," said Scott.

*   *   *

"Hi, Granny," called Scott when he returned home.

"Been lookin' fer ya," greeted his grandma, who was sitting in her rocker watching the river.

"Granny, did you use ta be a slave?"

"Long time ago."

"How was it?"

"It wuz bad."

"I got it bad," said Scott, "and I ain't a slave."

"Scott, baby, you doesn't know what bad is."

"What's bad then?"

Rocking back and forth on the dusty river bank, she did not answer right away. Sitting peacefully in her rocking chair was how she wanted to spend her last days. In the evening she just liked to listen to the emerging night sounds. She had asked Scott's father, Abraham Lincoln, to build their shanty close to the river, so she could watch the river boats and barges. He had agreed against his better judgment. She was proud of her son-in-law for changing his name to Abraham Lincoln and for naming his son, Dred Scott Lincoln, after men who had fought slavery.

Granny was barefoot and dressed in one of her two ankle-length gowns made from old sheets. Her shrunken body was tired, and her hair had been thin and white for years, but she was comfortable with her life now. Through the years she had understood more and more how good it was to be free. Nevertheless, she was sympathetic to the conditions that pained and discouraged her grandchildren. She thought, 'If'n I don't tell Scott now, I mightn't get another chance.'

"Have you got some time to sit and hear me, Scott?"

"Yes, Granny," answered Scott, who was sure that his eighty-eight-year-old grandmother had some important things to say. He sat down quietly on the hard, dusty ground with his feet crossed, ready to listen.

"Fer me, it started to be bad when I wuz seven years old, and we wuz moved to St. Louis," said Granny. "Before that, me and Mama lived in a little cabin on Masta Ingram's cotton plantation. Mama worked in the kitchen and not in the cotton fields like most slaves. Masta Ingram, a tall, shy man with wavy hair, wuz good to us. Mama wuz sixteen when I wuz born in 1844. Folks said that she wuz the prettiest girl they'd ever seen."

"What happened, Granny?"

"One day, Masta Ingram come to see us and told me to go play, as he did sometimes. When Masta Ingram left, I come back to the cabin. Mama was on her bed sobbin' away. She told me we wuz going to St. Louis. At sunrise we rode in a wagon to the big Mississippi River and wuz put on a boat in a room with other slaves."

"I wuz crying and scared and asked Mama what wuz hapnin'. All she said wuz we wuz leavin'. Some years later she told me that ole Miz Ingram told Masta that she wouldn't have a little slave girl around there lookin' anything like Masta Ingram. Masta told Mama he wuz gonna hav'ta sell me, but Mama said she begged Masta not to send me away alone. Finally, he said he'd sell us both in St. Louis, so we wouldn't show up in west Tennessee again."

"In St. Louis we wuz put in a dirty basement room with bars on the high windows. There was a slop can in the corner that stunk up the whole place. After a week or so, they took a bunch of us to the ole Court House."

"I know that place," said Scott.

Granny continued, "It wuz noisy and scary. White men crowded around us slaves. I wuz so little that I could hardly see the sky, just sweaty heads and shoulders. When it wuz our turn at the auction, they put Mama and me up high by ourselves where everyone could see us. When I looked down at all those staring men, I wanted to cry. Mama had told me not to cry, and I didn't."

"Two men wanted to buy us. One wuz a heavy, rough lookin' man in dirty clothes. The other man looked nice, and I hoped he'd buy us. I smiled at him whenever he looked at me. The bad man finally said, 'I'll bid higher if I don't have to take the baby bitch.' The auctioneer told him the owner said to sell 'em together."

"Then the bad man walked off, and the other man took us to his carriage. He told us that his name wuz Mr. Green and not to talk unless we wuz spoken to. No one spoke. When we got to his big brick house, he walked us to a back room with two beds and a small table with a wash dish. He left us and said, 'Mrs. Green will be by after a bit.' In the two years that we lived there, we tried to never say nothin' to Mr. Green."

"Directly, we heard a big key turn with a clunk, and Miz Green come into our room. She wuz a small, plain lookin' woman with hair piled up like a big, brown ball on top of her head. She had small eye glasses pinched to her nose. She never smiled-- probably never had a happy thought in her whole life. She wore a pretty stone on a long black dress buttoned tight at her neck, and she laced her black shoes above her ankles."

"Miz Green put food and a pitcher of water on the table. She told us to use the slop jar in the corner, and she'd show us where to empty it in the mornin'. She stared us over pretty good. Then she turned on her heels and left, slammin' the door and turnin' the big key. Mama hugged me for a long time. We wuz tired and scared."

"We got up early and cleaned the best we could and waited. Around midmorning Miz Green turned the key and clomped into our room. She asked us our names, and we spoke for the first time. She almost seemed surprised that we could speak. When Mama told her our names wuz Mabel and Nadine, she shouted at Mama that her name wuz to be Lizzie. Later we found out Miz Green's name wuz Mabel."

"She took us to the washroom that wuz between our room and the main house. My work wuz washin' and ironin', and I wuzn't never to go into the main house. I wuz only seven years ole, and I wuz 'fraid I couldn't do all the work, and then I'd get sold. Mama cleaned, cooked, and served meals. She'd help me whenever she could."

"We never once wuz out of that house. Mostly talked to ourselves, but we had each other. In the evenin's, Mama told stories. We'd sing songs and sometimes dance around 'til we wuz dizzy. I loved mama more than my own life.

"Then Mr. Green died, and Miz Green sold the big house." On the day she sold it, we wuz locked in our room. The next day three men came and told us they were takin' me to Miz Green's new house, and Mama wuz goin' some place else. My heart wuz broke. I never saw or heard from Mama again."

"I'm sorry, Granny," said Scott interrupting Granny's story. "I don't want someone takin' my mama."

Granny reassured him, "They won't, Scott, 'cause President Abraham Lincoln and the big war freed us. Life can be bad at times, and ya hav'ta accept what happens."

"I will, Granny."

"Nice people made things better for me, Scott. When I wuz freed, I found a church, married, and had your Mama. Your Grandpa wuz a good man. He's gone, but I got you."

"I'm glad you told me, Granny."

"Scott, you gotta work hard and make things better for others 'cause you're smart. And, always remember that I love you."

"I love you too, Granny," whispered Scott as he kissed his grandma and helped her up from her rocker.

Darkness had come over the river. The moon began to rise, and a sliver of yellow was forming on the river like an artist's first brush stroke.

4

Summer 1933: Hard Times

"Let's walk along the river," Matt suggested as the boys sat on the levee.

"To look at swirling water?" Jack shrugged indifferently.

Rick started to walk, "Let's go, anyway."

They walked a mile or so until they came to a squalid complex of homeless families who had chosen to stay together on the river bank rather than sleep in a city alley. Black and white, farm and city folks had drifted together. Fragile, one-room shelters usually had a doorway and a window opening that the squatters covered with a piece of cloth or cardboard. Utilities were frightfully inadequate or nonexistent.

The river was rising, and the boys saw families who had torn down their shacks and carried what they could with them to escape the flood waters.

Suddenly Rick called loudly, "There's Ruth Alger!"

"Are you sure?" Matt asked skeptically.

They hurried over to a shack a little above the flood level. They saw their friend Ruth, who had been in the advanced reading group with them in first grade, and called, "Hi, Ruth!"

Ruth greeted them with a tired smile.

"What are you doing here, Ruth?" asked Matt.

"This is where we moved when I left school. Papa bought some posts and roofing, and he found some old boards and boxes to build our place. It's better than most around here."

"Where are your Mama and Papa?"

"They go away every day to look for work. Mostly they get a dollar or two for food. Come in."

They went into the shack and saw a small, potbelly stove tightly surrounded by cots with a blanket folded neatly on each. Ruth's little sister, Joy, was lying on a cot. Her brother, Joey, was on the dirt floor pretending that a piece of driftwood was a truck. The skinny Alger children, dressed only in dirty underwear, made their suffering painfully obvious.

A few days later the boys went back to take some gifts to Ruth. Rick took a cabbage from his mother's garden. Jack took some old clothes that he had outgrown. Matt took apples that his mother had let him buy with her church money. As they walked, they saw an empty space and thought that Ruth might be gone. They were relieved when they heard Ruth's loud voice, "Here I am, boys."

Debris was piled near the front of the Alger home where the river had started to fall back. Ruth explained what had happened, "The river was almost to our door when it stopped rising during the night. Papa woke all of us when he was sure it was going down. We all kneeled down and thanked God for not making us have to move."

They talked until Joy got hungry and restless. They left and told Ruth that they'd be back. They climbed up to the road on top of the levee where they saw Scott carrying some boards.

Jack asked, "Where are you going?"

"To an old building near the bridge. Papa said it'd be better than here. He's getting more work now."

"Where'd you get the boards?" Rick asked.

"River flooded us out. We had to tear our shack down and

bring our stuff up to the road. That's when Papa decided to move. I'm taking the boards to our new home to build shelves."

"Can we help you?"

"Sure could use some help. If you can come with me, we'll carry all these boards in one trip."

When they got everything moved, Scott's mother thanked them and gave them each a glass of water. Going home they didn't say much, but they were glad to be able to help their friends.

*   *   *

Later that summer the three boys were looking for odd jobs. Once at the Farmer's Market, they worked all day and got nine apples. They each ate an apple and decided to take the rest of the apples to Ruth.

When they arrived at Ruth's home, a tired-looking black woman was in the doorway. At first the boys were confused and thought they were at the wrong place. But Rick took courage and asked, "Where's the family that used to live here?"

"I don't know," answered the woman.

"What happened to them?"

"The Mista got a job, but I don't know where they moved. They wuz the nicest white folk I ever knowd. My Ben wuz a hod carrier until there wasn't work for him. Since then we've been livin' on the streets beggin' for work or food. Usually all we'd get wuz soup in the church line. I woke one night last week, and my baby Loua wuz dead in my arms. We had to bury her in the river. We wuz desperate!"

"Yesterday we decided to walk along here and ask folk if they knew of a place to stay. We asked here, and the Mista says, 'We're moving out today. You can have this place.' Didn't ask a dime. Now we got a chance again."

The boys went away glad for Ruth, but sad that they might not see her again. They decided to go by and see Scott. They found him just sitting in the street.

"Something wrong, Scott?"

"Granny died. Things won't be the same."

The boys didn't know anything else to do, so they left their apples for Scott's family.

"Thanks. They'll be awful pleased to have 'em."

As the boys walked home, they began to realize how quickly things could change. They thought, 'Sometimes you can't do anything about it. Things just happen.'

5

Repeal of Prohibition

The Bauman, Simmons, and LeGault families all felt the impact of the repeal of Prohibition. Their lives changed dramatically. In unique ways, they felt the tensions and trauma of major economic adjustments.

BAUMAN FAMILY

Emil Bauman was a pragmatist. He faced life head on and saw new situations as they were. He had the insight to be able to see ahead and sense necessary changes. Even poor people were buying used refrigerators, and soon he would have fewer ice customers. The coal business was not good either. Emil was barely making his bank payments.

Maria noticed that Emil was acting differently and asked, "Emil, is something wrong?"

"Business isn't good. I'll get a longer route."

"We have a nice home and enough to eat."

The last thing Emil wanted to tell Maria was that he would

have to sell their home. Since his ice business finished before his coal business started, he was spending his free time looking for other work. He went to the St. Louis Dairy Company and the Kroger Baking Company and asked about driving a home delivery truck. He was told that since they were now selling milk and bread in stores, their companies were no longer delivering to homes.

At fifty-six years, age was against Emil. In November he went to see his cousin to ask for help, but Hugo just shrugged his shoulders. Emil's face showed his disappointment, so Hugo added an encouraging word, "Rumors have it that Prohibition will be repealed. Nobody knows, but it could mean more jobs someday."

When the Twenty-first Amendment to the Constitution in 1920 shut down the breweries, people lost their jobs in St. Louis. Anheuser-Busch barely managed to survive as a business, but the company was able to keep some skilled workers by making cereal and cattle feed.

Congress repealed Prohibition in December 1933, and rumors became stronger that Anheuser-Busch would reopen its brewery and employ more people. Emil went to see his cousin again in January 1934, and Hugo encouraged him, "Hiring has started. Maybe there'll be a job for you."

In February Emil was late with his bank payment for the first time. In March he missed a payment. He explained the situation to his banker, who was sympathetic but warned Emil of the seriousness of not making payments. The warning was not necessary--Emil had been thinking about it for months.

In April Emil went back to Hugo. This time Hugo told him, "I think there is a chance, Emil. Come with me."

Cousin Hugo had been with Anheuser-Busch for more than twenty years and was well respected as a skilled, hardworking master craftsman. On the basis of Emil's delivery experience in the river front neighborhood and on Hugo's recommendation, the beer company hired Emil. Starting on May 1, he would drive a truck making beer deliveries to bars and restaurants.

Emil hurried to the bank and explained that he would be able to make up payments missed in June and July. From July forward he would not miss a payment. The bank approved the agreement on the basis of his responsible payment history.

The Baumans sat down to eat that evening at the usual time, when Maria's clock struck eight, but Rick sensed that his father had something special to say. Maria felt it, too, and asked, "Do you have something to tell us, Emil?"

"I no longer have an ice and coal business."

"What will you do, Emil?" asked Maria visibly shaken.

Emil quickly explained that he would be driving a truck for Anheuser-Busch. He would sell his truck to help pay the missing bank payments and walk to work. Rick would not forget the importance of bank payments.

That night, after Rick had gone to sleep, Maria said, "The long walk will be hard, Emil. Can't you keep the truck?"

"The truck has to go. We'll save to buy a car."

Emil thought to himself, 'Now Maria can keep her home.' Maria, feeling Emil's elation and relief, snuggled into him, and they made love.

*   *   *

SIMMONS FAMILY

The Simmons family also felt the effects of Prohibition.

"Sadie Johnson, the housekeeping supervisor at the Jefferson Hotel, came by and said, "Elizabeth, you're to go to the Personnel Office."

"Is anything wrong?" asked Elizabeth as she shut the door to the room that she had completed cleaning.

"You've been doing a fine job. Don't worry about it."

Having just finished cleaning all of her rooms, Elizabeth was dripping wet. She hurried to the employees' restroom to rinse her face and brush her hair before going to the Personnel Office.

Personnel Director Tom Flarity explained, "With the repeal of Prohibition, we are now able to serve wine and cocktails at the Jefferson Hotel, and the restaurant will be open longer hours. Salesmen and others will be entertaining their guests in our Rathskeller Restaurant instead of at a speakeasy. Would you be interested in working as a receptionist and cashier?"

Elizabeth's green eyes sparkled, and she did not hesitate to show her enthusiasm, "I had experience doing that kind of work while I was at the University of Illinois."

"You'll do well, Elizabeth," said Mr. Flarity. "On Monday through Friday you'll start at two in the afternoon and work until nine-thirty. On Saturday and Sunday, you'll come in at four-thirty in the afternoon and work until nine."

"Those hours would be fine," said Elizabeth, concealing her concern about Matt.

Mr. Flarity continued, "Calley Carr will take the early shift. She has been in her position for the past eleven years and will answer your questions."

"I know Calley. She's a lovely person."

"You may need some new clothes. I'm sure that you'll be an attractive addition to the restaurant."

"I have some nice clothes that I haven't been able to wear."

"Your pay will be increased from fifteen to sixty cents an hour."

"When do I start?"

"April 1."

"Thank you, Mr. Flarity. I won't let you down,"

When Elizabeth arrived home that evening, Matt was not there as he usually was. She began to have second thoughts, 'Matt will have to be alone until ten at night.' Before her thoughts wandered further, Matt arrived out of breath.

"Matt, where've you been?" Elizabeth scolded.

"I left my sweater on the levee and ran to get it."

"You've got to be more careful. Wash up, and set the table. I've something serious to talk over with you."

"What?"

"Wait until we sit down to eat."

When they sat down, Elizabeth explained her new position and then said, "You're almost ten years old, Matt, and you're going to have to be more responsible. You must eat, do your homework, and be in bed before I get home. This new job will give us the extra money we need for clothes and savings."

After Elizabeth had started her new job, she realized how nice it was to greet visitors instead of working alone. Mr. O'Hare came by and asked, "How do you like your new position, Elizabeth?"

"I couldn't be more pleased. If you had anything to do with it, I want to thank you." She suspected that he had.

Mr. O'Hare responded with a smile, "Mr. Flarity makes these decisions. I think he made an excellent choice."

Elizabeth had been concerned about walking home late in the evening, but with the additional pay, she would be able to pay streetcar fare and shorten her long walk.

*   *   *

LeGAULT FAMILY

In January Hans Kruger called Louie into his small office and said, "Louie, we gotta talk."

"What about?"

"That damn Prohibition is gone. We're going to make the Blue Rhine into a big business."

"Like ya always said ya wanted to do."

Hans continued, "The Blue Rhine is going to be a grand place. The family restaurant and bar will be on the first floor. On the second floor we'll have tables, music, another bar, and the dance floor. I can already hear my Music Werke with its bell box and 20-inch disks. Can you picture it, Louie? Customers will sing and dance, just like old times in Berlin."

Louie did not respond, so Hans continued, "Starting in February, we'll work longer hours. It'll be harder for both of us, but we can do it. I'll pay you a dollar a week more."

Louie agreed.

That evening Louie proudly told his son, "Things are gonna be better for us. Hans is making the Blue Rhine bigger."

"How will it help us?"

"I'll get an extra dollar a week."

"What are you going to do with the extra dollar?"

"Save it."

"Can Matt and Rick come to see you now that beer is legal?"

"Sure. Bring 'em by the back door, but don't let 'em inside."

Hans completed the renovation of the Blue Rhine in June, and just before the grand opening, he asked Louie to come into his office. Louie sat down uncomfortably on the new office furniture.

"What do you think, Louie?"

"It's swell," answered Louie sitting stiffly in a red leather chair that still had the smell of new furniture.

"Tomorrow we open the doors to the public. The Anheuser-Busch sales manager will be here to cut that red and white ribbon that I showed you yesterday."

"That's what ya always wanted, Hans."

"There's one problem, Louie. I need more storage space."

"Blackjack and I can crowd up and give ya more space." Louie saw the problem: he was it!

"I'm afraid that won't do, Louie. I'll need all the space and can't have you serving anymore. The place has to have some schmaltz with young girls in pretty dresses. You'll have to leave tomorrow."

Louie did not respond but headed quickly to his storeroom

home where he and Blackjack had lived for more than six years. Not since Monet left him had he had such a sick and empty feeling. As a young man, he remembered wounded animals in the forest. All they looked for was a place to hide. Now he was wounded and wanted to hide.

When Blackjack came home, Louie said, "We've gotta talk."

"What about?"

"We move out in the morning," answered Louie looking at the floor instead of at his son.

"Why?" asked Blackjack, almost falling into a chair.

"Hans don't want us no more."

"What'll we do?"

"I figured the first step. With the dollars I've saved, we'll buy a tent and carry our stuff down near the river."

"What then?"

Louie's mind wandered, and he thought to himself, 'If only President Roosevelt hadn't vetoed the soldiers' bonus.' Then Louie answered, "I don't know. Yer ten years old now, and ya don't need no more school. I don't wanna talk now."

"Okay, Louie."

Blackjack went to his cot to reflect on the shocking news, thinking, 'How could Hans do that?' They didn't talk until morning, while they carried out Louie's plan.

*   *   *

Rick came home upset after he heard about Jack's trouble.

"What's wrong, Rick?" asked Maria sensing Rick's anxiety.

"My friend, Jack, says he can't go to school anymore."

"Why?"

"His father lost his job."

"You talk to Papa," consoled Maria.

That evening, after Emil had washed up, Maria said, "You need to talk with Rick."

Emil did not say anything but motioned for Rick to take their chairs outside. Rick explained what had happened.

"Where are they staying?"

"They're in a tent on the river."

"That's bad. I'll think about it tonight."

At the breakfast table Emil said, "Rick, I'll talk to Jack's father, if he'll come here tonight about seven."

When Louie and Jack arrived at the Bauman home that evening, Emil was out near the garden with a couple of chairs. Louie went out back, and the boys stayed in the house. Emil thought, 'What's bad for Rick is bad for me.'

Emil had decided to learn what kind of man Louie was. They shared a love for their sons and took time to talk. Louie explained why he had to leave the Blue Rhine Restaurant and about his early life in the Ozark Mountains.

Louie spoke briefly about the battle in France that had resulted in his medals, and the villagers' request to have him stay in France. Louie seldom talked about his war experiences, but Emil showed an intense interest in the battle and asked detailed questions.

There was a pause in their talk, and they sat quietly.

Emil remembered that battle clearly but did not tell Louie. He now realized what had happened to his German comrades in their trench that day in France. Emil had observed that when each soldier near him fired a shot, that one would drop dead. Emil quit firing! He had always felt guilty about not continuing to fire his rifle, but now he knew that his action had saved his life. A dead soldier cannot help his fellow soldiers. This new discovery lifted the guilt that had haunted him for years.

Emil thought to himself, 'How strange that the same men who tried to kill each other are now trying to help one another. A few months ago I thought that I might lose my home. Somehow, I'll help Louie. Helping is part of being free.'

When the conversation started again, Louie confided to Emil his plan to go to Ste. Genevieve where he would recover his gold coins and bring them back with him. Then he and Blackjack would be able to find work and a place to live.

"What'll you do tomorrow, Louie?"

"I'll go back to our tent by the river and decide."

"You come here tomorrow, Louie. "

"Much obliged, Emil."

The next day, with Rick's help, Louie and Jack moved the LeGualt belongings into the Bauman's garage.

When Emil came home, Louie told him, "I'm goin' to Ste. Genevieve tomorrow. Can ya take care of Blackjack?"

"Sure. How long will you be gone?"

"Maybe two weeks."

In the morning Louie went down to the Mississippi levee where the barges docked. He had given eight dollars to Blackjack and had kept the twelve dollars left from his savings. He was fortunate to obtain a ride on a barge that day. He would receive free passage and food for his work.

Louie got off the barge at Ste. Genevieve and walked the mile or so uphill to town. He was glad to see some friends in town, but was sad to hear that his friend, Jean Baptiste, had died.

Early the next morning, Louie walked to the cemetery and found his Grandma's grave and started digging with his knife. Without his coins he and Blackjack would have no place to go. He dug slowly, then faster. He dug to the depth that he had buried the coins but still did not find the deerskin pouch. He was desperate!

Digging deeper, inch by inch, he watched every piece of dirt as it turned up. He went down another three inches before he struck something that he slowly uncovered--the deerskin pouch with the forty-nine small gold coins.

Louie sat back exhausted but relieved. He put the pouch around his neck and buttoned his shirt. Fear came over him again. Someone might pass by and alarm the town that he had been digging in a grave. He quickly filled the hole and left.

That night Louie thought about his conversation with Emil.

He had told Louie about coming to America but had not talked about Germany. Louie guessed that Emil had been a soldier and that they may have fought against each other. He wondered why men fight and then help. His only conclusion was that each man knows what he has to do, and he does it, sometimes without knowing why. War experiences haunted Louie as they did Emil.

Two days later Louie was pleased to get on a barge back to St. Louis. As soon as the barge docked, Louie walked to the bank and asked for Mr. Rohde, who had helped him years before. Mr. Rohde was now the bank president, and his secretary did not think he would see this dirty, poorly dressed man.

Mr. Rohde remembered Louie and surprised his secretary by his greeting. "Louie, it's good to see you after all these years. Tell me what's happened to you."

"Thank you, Mr. Rohde. I need help again," said Louie as he sat down in one of the leather chairs across from Mr. Rohde's desk. Louie wondered to himself, 'Why does this chair feel good, when the same chair in Hans' office felt so bad? Maybe because Hans wasn't a real friend.'

Thinking about years back when he could take more time with customers, Mr. Rohde thought, 'When you're too engaged to know your customers personally, you're too busy.'

Louie told Mr. Rohde briefly what had happened to him in France and showed him one of his coins.

Mr. Rohde explained, "Our cashiers can't give you money for your gold coin at the counter because President Roosevelt took the United States off the gold standard two months ago. But now gold has a greater value, and collectors will pay more for an old gold coin. Go and have it appraised."

"What's appraised?"

"An estimate of how much the coin is worth. Here is the name and address of a reliable man who can tell you how much money someone should give you for your gold coins."

Louie followed Mr. Rohde's advice and went to the address that he had been given and showed the man two of his coins.

The coin dealer said, "Collectors will buy a quarter eagle gold coin for a hundred dollars, but it'll be hard to find a buyer in this Depression. I'll buy your two coins for seventy-five dollars each."

Louie sold his two coins and walked to the Bauman home.

When Emil arrived home that night, the men went out of the house with their two chairs. Louie explained what had happened in the past twelve days, including his visit to the bank and the coin dealer.

"You did good, Louie, but don't carry your coins with you. Mr. Rohde can tell you how to get a locked box in the bank."

"Thanks, Emil, I will. Now I'll find a place to live."

Emil was satisfied that Louie was responsible and deserving. He would try to think about where Louie might find a job, and in the meantime, he suggested, "Stay here while you look for work."

"Much obliged."

Louie started looking for work the next day. He thought how lucky he was to have a friend like Emil Bauman. A week went by and no work. Then Louie had an idea. "Emil, let me help ya put in a toilet in yer house while I'm here. I've the money now for the stuff ya need, and I can help ya build it while Blackjack and I live and eat at yer home."

"Together we can make Maria happy," Emil replied, knowing he did not have money for fixtures and pipes, and needed someone to help. He remembered a German proverb: when one helps another, both are stronger.

By the middle of July the inside toilet was nearly finished. It did not include the bathtub that Emil had always wanted, but space was left for the washtub to fit in the new bathroom. The old sheet that used to hide the washtub could now come down.

The next day Emil had an idea, 'Louie knows and loves animals, and the Clydesdale horses at the Anheuser-Busch stable are the finest in the world. Emil went to the horse barn to ask if there might be work for Louie. Superintendent Gerhardt said,

"There is a job to feed and water the horses. How did you know about the Clydesdales?"

"I heard some of the men talking."

"Mr. August Busch Jr. gave the Clydesdales to his father to commemorate the first bottle of post-Prohibition beer brewed in St. Louis. Pulling their big red, white, and gold beer wagon, they delivered a case of beer to former Governor Smith of New York and a case to President Roosevelt at the White House in gratitude for their leadership in getting Prohibition repealed."

"That's really something."

"Has Mr. LeGault had any experience as a security guard?"

"He was a security guard for the Blue Rhine Restaurant."

Mr. Gerhardt said, "Good, I know Hans' place. Send Mr. LeGault over, and let me talk with him. We do need a night watchman who understands horses better than the last guy."

Superintendent Gerhardt interviewed Louie the next day and told him, "You can start to work on the first of August caring for the horses at night. You'll be paid a dollar a day and work seven days a week. When the horses are on tour, you'll get time off with pay."

Louie responded, "Thanks, I'll take good care of them beautiful horses."

The next day, Louie and Blackjack moved to a cold-water flat with two rooms. Sitting on their folding chairs in their new home, Blackjack commented, "Louie, let's not eat potatoes now that you have a paying job."

"No more potatoes," Louie agreed with a smile.

6

1934-1937: Summer Adventures

At the end of each school year, the boys would stop and see Miss Goerner. They expected her to have something for them to do during the summer, and she had never disappointed them.

Vacation time in 1936, Miss Goerner challenged the boys, "I've something new for you to do."

"What is it?"

"This summer you should go to the St. Louis Public Library and find books for yourselves. Can someone take you?"

"My mother'll take us," answered Matt.

"After the first time, you can go alone."

"Then we can get all kinds of books," said Rick.

As Miss Goerner was packing her things to take home for the summer, she was momentarily haunted by thoughts of children hurt and fallen before they had a chance in life, like Ruth Alger and Mary Ellen Jackson, who would have been excellent students. She thought of other students at Jefferson Elementary School who had suffered with polio, measles, whooping cough, diphtheria, scarlet fever, chicken pox, and mumps. Her thoughts then turned to her positive teaching experiences. As with all good teachers, outstanding students like Matt, Jack, and Rick motivated her, and she was pleased when they returned to visit long after they had left her first grade class. She was always happy to see them and to find some way to encourage them in their studies.

*   *   *

Elizabeth was glad to take the boys to the library. As they approached the St. Louis Public Library, Rick leaned backwards and shouted, "Stop! Look way up there at the letters cut in the stones."

Elizabeth read the words:

> I choose free libraries as the best agencies for
> improving the masses of people, because they
> give nothing for nothing. They only help those who
> help themselves. They never pauperize. A taste for
> reading drives out lower tastes.
> — ANDREW CARNEGIE

"What does that mean, Mom?" asked Matt.

"Mr. Carnegie had a lot of money, and he gave libraries to cities for people to use for free. He believed that if people would read books, they'd stay out of trouble and have a better life."

The reading room was so quiet they were afraid their shoes would squeak. They could hardly believe how many books there were. The librarian showed the boys how to obtain and use a library card, and then she took them to the shelves with books for boys their age. Each of them selected a book.

When Rick got home, he breathlessly told his parents about the wonderful free library. Emil and Maria asked Rick to take them there, and before long, they were going to the library themselves and finding interesting books to read.

*   *   *

St. Louis had baseball fever in August of 1934, and the city dubbed their famous team the "Gas House Gang."

"With Pepper Martin, Dizzy Dean, and Joe Medwick on the same team, I don't see how they can ever lose," said Jack.

"The Cardinal Gas House Gang will win the Pennant and the World Series," agreed Matt.

Rick added, "Pepper Martin keeps his race car in a repair garage near here, and sometimes the guys say he's there. Why don't we look for the place?"

"I think I know where it is," said Matt. "Lets go."

They found the garage, and Pepper Martin was sitting on his racing car talking to other men. He had the baseball team's logo of a red cardinal sitting on a baseball bat painted on his white car.

Jack whispered, "He looks like any other guy."

"Yes, but he's not," Matt whispered back.

The boys were sitting with their legs crossed on the garage floor near the door. They knew they would be chased away if they got in the way, but they were close enough to listen.

*   *   *

One morning, while they were listening to the ball game at the Farmer's Market, they heard that a vendor had not been able to sell all of his muskmelons. He told them that if they would put the remaining melons back in his truck, while he continued to sell, he would give them each a dime. They worked hard for two hours. They were tired but pleased.

Matt asked, "Why don't we use our dimes to go to Sportsman's Park and watch the Cardinals play? Mom says a streetcar only costs a nickel each way."

Jack and Rick both thought that was a good idea.

Their parents, with some concern, agreed to let them go.

Elizabeth told Matt that they could buy three tokens for a dime. They would have an extra token if they got lost.

Men could not afford to buy baseball tickets during the Depression. To get a home crowd, boys under fourteen could go to ball games free with a "Knothole Gang Member" card given out at the public library. There were usually more boys sitting in the Knothole Gang section than there were people in the rest of the ballpark. The boys' noisy cheers encouraged ball players, which brought about a friendship unique in baseball history between the players and the boys.

For Matt, Jack, and Rick, their first ride on the street car was an experience they would never forget. The streetcar conductor told them how to transfer from the Manchester car to the Grand Avenue car, which would take them to Sportsman's Park. The boys got off the streetcar at the ballpark stop and started walking. They had chosen a special game--Dizzy Dean would be pitching against Carl Hubbell of the Giants, and Joe Medwick would be throwing a dozen balls to the Knothole Gang.

As they walked to the ballpark, they noticed folks waving signs to get people to park in their yards for only a quarter instead of fifty cents, the cost of parking in the Sportsman's Park lot. Suddenly, Rick yelled, "Stop fellows, we need to help this guy."

Matt and Jack did not know what Rick was talking about until he explained, "That poor fellow over there in the wheel chair is having a hard time directing the cars into his yard. Other people are out in the street waving to the cars, and he has to stay back in his yard."

They went over to help him.

"Thanks, boys. I'd appreciate your assistance," said Angelo Sarno, the man in the wheel chair.

They went out to the edge of the street to wave at the cars and hold up the card that said, "PARK FOR A QUARTER." Soon the yard was filled with cars, and Mr. Sarno gave them each a nickel.

At the stadium they climbed the ramp, following the rest of the boys. The three friends found seats about twenty or so rows back. Matt, Jack, and Rick sat mesmerized as they watched players warming up by throwing balls back and forth to each other, and as they studied the beautiful green grass and the carefully cut dirt running paths.

On the radio the players had not seemed real; now they did. The Cardinal players wore white uniforms with a picture of a cardinal perched on a bat, like the one on Pepper Martin's race car. On the other side of the field, the New York Giants wore dull gray uniforms.

All at once, thousands of boys in the Knothole Gang jumped up shouting and screaming. At first Matt, Rick, and Jack did not understand what was happening. Then they saw him . . . "Ducky Wucky" Joe Medwick was coming over toward their section with a box of baseballs. He pretended to throw several times before actually throwing balls for the boys to catch.

As one ball came toward the three boys, everyone started to push and shove as they moved toward the ball. Rick climbed up on his seat, reached above the other boys, and caught the ball with his one hand. He fell and bruised himself but held onto his prize. Matt and Jack were so excited they couldn't stop shouting.

After all the excitement, the game finally started. In what seemed like a moment, it was the last half of the ninth inning. With the two great pitchers, Dizzy Dean and Carl Hubbell, neither team had scored. Pepper Martin was able to beat out a bunt with his great speed. The boys were still screaming when he stole second base and then third base. Joe Medwick bunted. Martin was almost to the home plate before a player got to the ball. Martin plowed into the catcher and scored.

The game was over, but the screaming continued until Martin, Medwick and Dizzy Dean waved their caps to the Knothole Gang and finally disappeared into the dugout.

That night their parents listened intently to their sons tell about their wonderful experience, knowing how important the game had been to them.

*   *   *

Late one summer the boys were walking to the library when Matt said, "Let's walk farther."

"What for?" asked Jack.

"Why not?" asked Rick.

"Okay," said Jack knowing that he was overruled.

They walked past the post office to Union Station.

"Let's go in and see the trains," said Matt.

As they walked in the door and started down the long flight of steps to the main floor, Jack shouted, "Wow!"

On the main floor they walked along the high, black iron fence that protected the track entrances. Trains were backing into the station, and others were pulling out. Smoke belched loudly from the locomotives, and train wheels made a clanging noise as they rolled in or out of the station. Screeching sounds came from trains as they braked to stop. Men with red caps were rushing to carry suitcases. Looking down the tracks, they saw a man running to get on a train.

Matt said, "This must be the world's biggest train station."

As they got to the last track, they saw an older lady standing by two suitcases and two hat boxes. The Red Caps were all busy, and Rick said, "Let's help her."

They carried her things to a car that was waiting for her. The lady stunned them by giving each of them a half dollar. As they stood amazed at their good luck, a big policeman with a blue uniform with a silver badge said in a gruff voice, "You're not to carry suitcases. That's a job for Red Caps."

As they walked home, Rick said, "Some laws are stupid. Why can't a boy help a nice lady carry her suitcases?"

Jack figured, "I guess that's just the way it is."

Matt said, "When I grow up, I'm going to be a lawyer and find out why the laws are the way they are."

Walking back, they tried to decide what excited them more,

the trains or the most money that they had ever made in one day.

*   *   *

Usually the boys found worthwhile things to do, but they sometimes got into trouble. With only one window and temperatures sometimes above a hundred degrees, the heat inside their homes was miserable. For this reason, on summer evenings Matt and Jack would meet on the high, open steps of the Old Court House. Louie worked all night, but Elizabeth would get home by ten o'clock. Matt knew that he had better be home before ten.

One night Matt saw someone that he knew and called, "Hey, Greg, come over here."

"What are you little kids doing out here?" asked Greg, who was a few years older than the boys but still going to Jefferson Elementary School.

"Nothing. Just sitting," shrugged Jack.

Greg said, "I'm going over to the red-light district and have some fun. Wanna come?"

"I don't think so," Matt answered.

"Aw, come on. Let's see what Greg is up to," said Jack.

"Okay," said Matt reluctantly.

Greg took them to an old wooden three-story building near Eads Bridge, close to where Scott lived. Except for a small red light at the end of the building, everything was dark. They walked up a creaky, wooden stairway to the third floor where a new moon did not even begin to light the dark, open corridor.

"I'm not so sure about this," Matt whispered to Jack.

"Ouch!" Jack yelled, as he tripped on a broken board. Several doors opened. The door beside them opened into a room with a single light bulb hanging from the ceiling and a bed with a dirty mattress. A woman was standing at the door.

Greg spoke, "You interested in our money?"

Matt and Jack were scared and shaking.

"Give me a quarter and come in for a show."

"Sorry, no money," Greg said, as he started running.

Greg got away, but Matt and Jack did not know what was happening as the woman grabbed them. Two other women from the next rooms came over to help. They stripped the boys of their clothes down to their BVD underwear and whacked each of them a few times with an old piece of rubber hose.

"Now you little bastards get the hell outta here!"

Matt and Jack were upset and didn't even tell Rick about their experience. Jack told Louie that he had gotten his black eye when he fell on his way home. Matt was glad his mother had not noticed the bump on the back of his head. He didn't want to lie to her.

*　　*　　*

The boys would go to Sportsman's Park whenever they could to see the Cardinals or Browns play and to help Mr. Sarno park cars. Even when no game was scheduled, Rick would make frequent trips to visit and work with Mr. Sarno, who always gave him nickels for streetcar fare.

When Rick arrived, he would shout, "Hi, Mr. Sarno. What are you working on today?"

Mr. Sarno was always busy working in his backyard garden or watering down the dust in his front yard where the cars would park for ball games. He kept his arms strong, and Rick marveled at the things he could do in his wheel chair.

Mr. Sarno had built wooden frame planters that he had filled full of dirt for his vegetable garden. With the dirt in the planters waist high off the ground, he could work in his garden in his wheel chair. He liked to plant seeds each spring and see the little plants grow, bloom, and bear fruit. He told Rick that as a young man he had planned to work for the railroad until he had saved enough money to buy a vegetable farm.

Rick liked to help Mr. Sarno in his garden or just sit on the porch with him while he told railroad stories. Mr. Sarno had worked for the Missouri Pacific Railroad until he broke his back. He spent the rest of his life in a wheel chair. He had no children, and his wife had left him after he was hurt.

"How did you get hurt?" Rick asked one day.

Mr. Sarno pulled a stained, worn letter from his wallet and said, "Here's a letter that will tell you better than I can."

> Dear Mr. Sarno:
>
> We understand that you alertly observed a broken iron rod being dragged along the track, and warning the engineer to slow the train, you prevented the possible derailment of one of our trains coming into St. Louis. An accident like that could have cost a loss of lives and property.
>
> It is regrettable that you fell and injured yourself as you leaned out to signal the warning with your lantern.
>
> You have my deepest gratitude for your courageous action.
>
> Daniel Evans, Manager
> Missouri Pacific Railroad

"Gee!" said Rick, as Mr. Sarno folded the letter and carefully placed it back in his wallet. "I don't really know how to say this, but I'm sure proud of you."

"I'm proud to have you as my friend too, Rick."

*   *   *

While walking home one day, Jack asked, "What are you going to do tomorrow?"

"Nothing. Just clean the room for Mom," shrugged Matt.

"Helping Mama with her cabbage plants," added Rick.

"Cabbages?" questioned Matt.

"Mama has a small cabbage patch," answered Rick.

"My grandpa lives on a farm and plants things, but I didn't know that you could farm in the city," said Matt.

"You can, and Mama does," said Rick impatiently.

"Why don't we dig up your back lot and plant cabbages?" Jack suggested. "The ones your mother grows are really good."

"What would we do with all those cabbages?" asked Matt.

"Sell 'em," said Rick, aroused by the idea. "I think Jack's right. Let's go talk to Mama; she'll help us."

When they got to the Bauman home, beaming with enthusiasm, Rick spoke to his mother, "Mama, we need lots of little cabbage plants. Will you help us?"

"Of course," Maria replied.

She had always wanted to plant more cabbages. Maria was a quiet person who smiled often, but seldom laughed out loud. When the boys rushed out with one small spade, she burst into loud laughter. She knew they would be back soon to learn about serious farming. Soon they were back, discouraged by their first hurried attempt.

"Rick, talk to Papa about a plow."

"What's a plow?"

Before Maria could answer, Matt said, "That's what my Grandpa McClaren uses for his garden. There's a junkyard a few blocks from here. I'll bet we can find one."

"I'll bet you can," Maria encouraged them with a smile.

Off the boys went and found a rusted hand plow with a loose wheel and a broken right handle that they could buy for sixty cents. Matt had two dimes, Rick a dime, and Jack three nickels. Needing to sell something and seeing disappointment in the boys' faces, the owner of the junkyard told them that they could have the plow for their forty-five cents.

Emil looked at the plow when he got home and said, almost to himself, "It's not good, but it can be fixed."

Three days later the boys had their plow, and Emil had expanded Maria's seed bed for the hundreds of Dutch Flathead cabbage seedlings the boys needed. Matt led the plowing effort. In six weeks of hard work after school and on weekends, the boys had plowed the lot and had it ready for planting. Maria had more than enough seedlings for them to plant.

The boys put the small plants into the ground and weeded them all summer. The sixty-by-thirty-foot lot, where horses had previously exercised, had manure-rich soil. The boys planted fourteen rows with thirty cabbages in each row, just as Maria had told them to do.

By late August almost four hundred heads of cabbage that were larger than those they had seen in the Farmer's Market covered the lot. At three cents a pound, their cabbages, averaging nine pounds each, could be sold for over a hundred dollars.

Maria explained how to add value to their cabbages by making sauerkraut. Taking the semicircular knife that she had brought in her basket from Poland, she showed them how to core and shred the cabbage. With salt and crocks for the sauerkraut, Maria showed them how to put first a layer of cabbage, then a layer of salt. For the final step, she showed them how to tamp the sauerkraut with a wooden press. In no time the layers of sauerkraut had reached the top of her crocks.

Maria told them, "In six weeks you'll each have two crocks of sauerkraut for your dinners. You can sell the other cabbages."

Each time Rick went to Mr. Sarno's, he would carry a cabbage in a gunny sack that he could sell for seven cents a pound while he helped Mr. Sarno sell his vegetables. Rick increased his profit and saved customers the drive to the Farmer's Market.

*　　*　　*

The boys graduated from eighth grade a month before their thirteenth birthdays.

Matt had wavy, red hair and was taller than the other boys. He was neat and precise. His leadership qualities were as natural to him as a sheepdog's innate ability to head and control sheep. Matt did not strive, but he was comfortable with himself and excelled in opportunities that life offered.

Louie had shaped Jack's personality a great deal. He was self-reliant and tended to make reactive decisions rather than rely on philosophical or culturally oriented long-term goals. Jack was thin and medium in height. Like the LeGaults before him, he was mentally and physically tough. His facial features were soft and attractive like his mother's, but his straight, black hair and steely, dark eyes surely must have originated with his Great-Great Grandma Morning Star.

Rick was a strong, heavyset boy, taller than Jack, but not as tall as Matt. His dark, curly hair never seemed to need a comb. Rick was more sensitive and enterprising than either Matt or Jack. He was a born entrepreneur, envisioning ideas that tended to draw criticism when he spoke about them. He was learning to keep his thoughts to himself until it was time to act.

Jack, Matt, and Rick were inseparable companions. They went farther and farther from the river front. Matt had taken the initiative the day they discovered Forest Park.

"What are we going to do today?" asked Jack as they sat on the Mississippi River levee one morning watching barges drift by.

"Why not go exploring?" suggested Matt.

"Like Lewis and Clark going up the Missouri River to where it ended thousands of miles from here?" Jack teased.

"Explore what?" Rick asked.

"We've never walked farther than Union Station."

"We'll just see more buildings."

"Maybe Matt's right," Jack said. "Real explorers didn't know what they'd see; they just went."

The boys finally agreed that it was a good idea.

After they walked a couple of miles past the Union Station, Jack looked back. "It's mostly the same thing. Why keep going?"

Matt answered, "Columbus kept going when the sailors thought that there was nothing but more ocean. Maybe there is something more than just buildings."

So they kept walking until they came to a wide road named "Kingshighway." The boys crossed and started to walk down a green, grassy slope with trees.

Jack pointed and said, "There's a river."

"No, that's a lake," Rick said, "I remember the map of St. Louis that I studied in the library. This must be Forest Park."

They walked around the lake and found a park bench. They sat quietly for awhile, looking at things that they had never seen before. Squirrels were chasing each other from tree to tree. Different colored birds were chirping and singing. A swan was swimming on the lake.

"I didn't know that birds could swim," Rick commented.

"Ducks and swans can swim as well as fly," said Matt as he walked to the lake and took a picture of the swan with his mother's camera. Then he spoke to a young man walking by, "Would you take a picture of us on this park bench?"

"Sure, why not?" the man answered as he came over and took the picture. Matt thanked him.

Except for two ladies on the other side of the lake, the boys were alone on their park bench. This was a new and quieting experience for them after noisy city streets. They agreed that even though reading in the library about things was fun, seeing them was better. The idea of exploring appealed to them.

"There wouldn't be a St. Louis if that French explorer, Pierre Laclede Liguest, hadn't landed here in 1763," said Jack.

"What else should we explore?" asked Matt.

"We could use streetcars," suggested Rick.

From that time on they would take streetcar rides after they had finished their work. One day they stayed on the Manchester streetcar to the end of the line. It went by the Scully Steel Mills, through the city of Maplewood, then across a long railroad trestle that crossed a deep ravine to Webster Groves, and then on to Kirkwood before turning around to go back.

They learned to use transfers and found the Forest Park Highlands Amusement Park with ferris wheels and all sorts of rides. They watched people ride but didn't have money to ride themselves. Once St. Louis Dairy Company had a promotion called, "Milk Bottle Cap Day." Boys and girls could have a free ride for five bottle caps. Matt's mother got bottle caps at the restaurant where she worked, and with those bottle caps they rode on most of the rides. Matt took the airplane ride more than any other ride at Forest Park Highlands and decided that he wanted to be an airplane pilot instead of a lawyer.

When they wandered through the Forest Park Zoo, they were surprised by how many animals, birds, and snakes there were from all over the world. They visited the Art Museum, Jefferson Memorial Museum, and Shaw's Garden. At Fairgrounds Park some boys helped them learn to swim. They thought that St. Louis was the best city in the whole world.

*   *   *

The day before Matt, Jack, and Rick were to begin at Central High School, the next step in their education, they met on the levee. They never tired of watching activities on the Mississippi River front.

Jack suggested, "Let's make a blood pact that we'll help each other do something good for St. Louis when we grow up."

"Okay, but what good thing are we going to do?" said Matt.

"Just let it happen," said Jack.

"Okay by me," Rick thoughtfully replied. "I'd like to meet on this levee or at our park bench whenever we can for the rest of our lives, to see how we are doing and what we can do better."

Jack cut his finger with his pocket knife. Rick followed.

"Why blood?" said Matt, lukewarm about the cutting.

"Louie said American Indians used to seal a pact that way."

"I'm not an Indian," Matt replied as he cut his finger.

Blood drops emerged on their cut fingers as they agreed on words to use for the pact.

"We, Rick, Matt, and Jack, swear on this blood pact that we'll stick together and do something good for St. Louis."

When they carefully put their fingers together, merging the blood drops, they could not possibly have known how their friendship would change their lives and St. Louis forever.

*   *   *

In the fall of 1937 Matt, Jack, and Rick climbed up the front steps of Central High School. When they entered the large hallway, Matt said, "We're the new kids again just like when we first started Jefferson Elementary School."

They did not take classes together in high school, but they remained close friends and continued to meet when they could. On the first Saturday after completing their freshman year in 1938, the boys took sandwiches to their park bench.

"Louie says he thinks he can get me a job," said Jack.

Matt said, "Grandpa McClaren had a stroke, so I'll go over to Gladesville, Illinois to help."

Rick added, "I'll be taking care of my cabbages."

7

Summer 1938: Jack, Matt, Rick

JACK

"Good news, Blackjack."

"What's the good news?"

"I got ya a job."

"What doing?"

"Wait until I catch my breath and wash up."

"I'll start cooking the eggs," said Blackjack, who was ready to cook breakfast when Louie got home in the morning.

As they sat down to breakfast, Louie blurted out, "You can work in the horse barn for seven dollars a week."

"Great. When do I start?"

"This evenin'. We'll get that barn as sparklin' as a fast moving mountain stream in a spring rain."

Louie had waited a long time for the day when he could work with his son. Blackjack worked hard and did well.

One morning walking home from work, Louie said, "More good news, Blackjack."

"What?"

"The Clydesdales will be on tour in July."

"Why's that good. You'll get paid, but I won't."

"They'll pay ya the first week while we clean the place. I've got an idea for the other weeks."

"What?"

"We'll go to the Ozark Mountains. I'll show ya where Grandpa Piney and I used to trap. I've been savin' for the trip."

"How much have you saved?"

"A little over a thousand dollars, includin' my veteran's bonus that I finally got."

"Louie, put the money in the bank. It's not safe here."

"It's as safe as a squirrel in a hollow tree."

"We should take it to the bank anyway. Especially if we leave this place for three weeks."

"We'll put it in the bank. You can help me do things now that ya got yer education. Sometimes I wish I'd had more."

Louie put nine hundred dollars in the bank and kept the rest for their trip. In July they were on a Mississippi River barge to Ste. Genevieve. The trip was a dream come true for Louie, and Jack was glad to be able to see the Ozark Mountains that Louie kept talking about.

When the barge tied up at Ste. Genevieve, Blackjack was disappointed. All he could see were a few old houses.

"Is this Ste. Genevieve? I thought it was a nice town."

"This landing ain't the town. When it kept floodin' down here, the people moved the town to the top of the bluff."

Louie and Jack worked the rest of the day on the barge doing the chores required for their passage, but early the next morning they started climbing up the bluff to Ste. Genevieve.

"What do we do when we get up there, Louie?"

"We'll visit around town and buy what we need."

"Where'll we stay?"

"We'll get far enough by dark to find a place to camp."

"Can we get to your river by dark, Louie?"

"Blackjack, the walk takes days."

"Days?"

"I bought our boots last month so they'd be broken in before we started this walk," said Louie, remembering his long walk with Piney when he was six years old.

In Ste. Genevieve, Louie purchased a rifle, two knives, backpacks, and two canvas water bags. A little past noon they started up the gravel road out of town and crossed the new highway. A few hours later they were camping in the mountains.

When Jack started to rinse his face, Louie put his hand on the water bag and warned, "Only use water to drink."

"Why?"

"That water may have to last us a couple more days."

"Are you kidding?"

"No. You've got to learn how to survive in the forest."

Blackjack had other questions but decided this was not the time to ask them. Besides, his feet hurt, and he was tired. They ate smoked sausage and bread.

At daybreak they started walking. Finally, Louie came to the St. Francis River. About a mile or so down the river, they came to a campground with a lodge and a stable.

"You never told me about this place, Louie. You told me that St. Francis River was in a wilderness."

"I reckon things can change."

Louie was upset, but he found the lodge owner and asked, "Are there camps up and down the river?"

"No," said Derk Samuelson as he shook hands with Louie. "You'll find some smaller places upstream, but as you go down the St. Francis River from here, the land is too rugged for safe use. My campers ride our horses on a trail up the river and then go into the foothills. They don't go into the rugged areas downstream. How far did you plan to go?"

"Probably another half day, maybe fifteen or so miles."

"That's craggy country down there. It's dangerous walking, and you can get lost if you leave the river.

"Much obliged, but I know the area. Who owns the land along the river downstream?"

"I think Jimmy Andersen still owns it. He farms on a piece of the plateau that was originally part of the old Douglas homestead. You won't bother him because folks say he lives alone and sticks to his cornfield and hog lot."

Louie thanked Derk again for filling their water bags, and off they went. After a difficult walk, Louie found the spot where he wanted to stay. They finished the last of the sausage and most of the bread. Blackjack went to sleep almost the instant he lay down, but Louie didn't go to sleep so quickly. Memories of Grandpa Piney drifted happily through his mind.

As the sun came up, Jack woke up complaining, "We don't have food or water; what are we going do now?"

"There's water at a spring near here, and we're gonna eat fish for breakfast," answered Louie as he stood and stretched.

"What do you do for a fishing pole?"

Louie didn't bother to answer. He pulled some line from his pack and tied on some hooks. They walked along the river until Louie found the spot where he had fished as a boy. He took out his knife and dug in the ground until he found worms, baited the hooks and threw the line into a pool in the river. Blackjack had his doubts but said nothing. In about an hour Louie had caught his fish and cleaned it.

"How are you going to cook the fish?"

"You can eat the fish raw, but we'll cook it on our fire."

Louie started a fire, and when the burning embers were just right, he pushed a stick through the fish and turned it slowly. Blackjack was surprised at how good the fish tasted.

Leaning back to enjoy his breakfast, Blackjack asked, "Did you used to live here with Grandpa Piney all the time?"

"I did until he died."

"Why didn't you live with your mama and papa?"

"They drowned in a Mississippi flood when I was a baby."

"How'd you learn to read?"

"Piney never learned to read and wished he had, so for six

winters he had me live in a fur trader's cabin in Ste. Genevieve and go to school with the Sisters of St. Joseph."

"Why did you quit school?"

"Piney wanted me to learn how to survive and not get myself drowned or killed." Louie gave him a friendly boot. "Off your butt; we got things to do."

"What?"

"We're goin' huntin' in the morning."

They walked down the river about five miles to a spot that Louie remembered. "We're campin' here tonight."

"I'm hungry, Louie."

"There's a pretty good fishin' hole about a quarter of a mile upstream. You go catch a fish, and I'll get the camp fire ready."

Blackjack was not confident, but he was hungry. He had watched Louie closely that morning. As the sun set, Blackjack had caught his fish. He cleaned it like Louie had done and proudly took it back to their camp.

"You did good. I wasn't sure we'd eat tonight."

As soon as they had eaten, Louie said, "Time to hit the sack 'cause we gotta be up before daylight."

"What are we going to do?"

"Shoot us a deer, if we're lucky. Deer used to drink near here early in the morning before they'd go back into the hills. While you were gone, I found tracks. We need to be hidden in the brush an hour before they are likely to come."

Before daybreak they sat quietly waiting until an older doe and a young buck came down to drink. Louie killed the young buck. He gutted it, and they carried the split carcass back to camp.

"What do we do now, Louie? This meat will rot before we can eat more than two meals."

"Not if we salt and smoke it."

Louie cut the venison into strips and salted them on both sides and put them on a long rack that he had prepared earlier. After building a fire, Louie took two strips of meat that he had not salted and cooked them on a stick in the fire. When they had finished eating, and their fire had turned to smoking coals, Louie moved the rack of salted meat over it.

As they sat quietly by the smoldering camp fire, Jack asked, "How did Grandpa Piney come to this spot?"

"He was born here."

"How? There are no doctors out here."

"If you listen, I'll tell you."

Jack settled back and listened attentively as Louie told his story:

> Piney was born while his father was living here on the river with an Osage Indian woman named Morning Star. While his father was trappin', Morning Star cared for him and taught him how to survive in the wilderness. She taught him about nuts, fruits, seeds, mushrooms, herbs, and roots--all that. He learned to build fires and to smoke fish and venison. Grandpa Piney told me he loved his mother. He stayed in camp with her until he was eleven years old. Then one day his father and mother left him alone.
>
> Ten days later his father returned without Morning Star and told Piney that she'd gone to live with her people and wouldn't be back. Piney told me that he ran into the woods and hid behind a blackberry bush and cried. He didn't return until it was time for him to make the evenin' fire.
>
> Piney and his father trapped together for ten years until his father died of gangrene that he'd got in a wound from a broken leg. Piney said he wrapped him in a deerskin blanket and dragged him to the ridge above here, a place I call 'Piney's Ridge.' He buried his father there and covered his grave with rocks to keep animals away.

A few years after he buried his father, Grandpa Piney married my Grandma Annabel, who lived in Ste. Genevieve and worked as a dressmaker; they had one son, my father. When my father was grown, he married, and soon after, I was born.

My Mama and Papa took a canoe down the Mississippi River at flood stage, and no one ever heard from 'em again. They had left me with Grandma Annabel 'cause I was only three years old. I lived with her until she died when I was six. Then I went with Grandpa Piney on the river.

As they started to get to sleep on their blankets, Jack said, "Thanks for telling me, Louie; I always wondered."

Louie spent three tedious days teaching Blackjack how to fire the rifle accurately and quickly. Finally, Blackjack shot his first rabbit, and he proudly said, "Now I can shoot as well as you."

"We'll test you tomorrow."

The next day they went hunting and found a squirrel in a tree. Blackjack shot, and the squirrel scampered away. Later Louie shot a squirrel and cooked it for dinner.

"You'll need to learn more about the rifle, Blackjack."

"Will you teach me?"

"We'll start tomorrow right after breakfast."

Blackjack thought they would go out into the woods again, but instead, Louie spread their canvas, took the rifle completely apart, cleaned it, and put it back together.

Blackjack asked, "Do you think that I can learn to do that?"

"You'll have to if you live in the forest."

Jack worked most of the day taking the rifle apart and putting it back together. The next morning he went out alone to hunt, and after two failed shots, he killed a squirrel.

When he returned, Louie greeted him, "That's more like it, Blackjack. Tomorrow we don't hunt or eat meat."

"If we don't eat meat, what are we going to eat?"

"There's more to be found in the forest than meat."

The next morning they walked up into the mountains where Louie showed Blackjack different herbs, berries, and roots. Some were safe to eat, and others were poisonous. By this time Blackjack was excited by what he was learning and paid close attention to Louie without asking silly questions.

As they sat down at their campfire that night, Louie said, "Tomorrow we have ta go back."

Blackjack was disappointed and understood why Louie had missed the forest and river. While they were in the Ozarks, Louie drank only a portion of a bottle of bourbon that he had brought. Louie handed the bottle to Blackjack. "A shot of bourbon'll ease the let down of leavin'." Blackjack had a shot of the whiskey, and Louie finished the bottle.

Early the next morning they filled their water bags, packed their smoked meat, and headed for Ste. Genevieve. They stopped at the River Ranch Lodge and visited with Derk Samuelson. Louie gave him some smoked venison and asked, "Can you store our stuff until next summer?"

"Sure," answered Derk, who had taken a liking to Louie. "Here are some biscuits that you can use on your trip."

"Much obliged."

In a few days they were back at the horse barn, and Jack got a permanent job offer. That night they had a long talk, and Louie said, "Why don't you quit school and take this job?"

"I really want to finish high school. Can we get by again on the ten dollars a week that you make?"

"Yeah, I guess." Louie did not understand what they taught in high school but hoped it would help his son.

MATT

Grandma McClaren met Matt at the train station at Effingham, Illinois, with her cheery voice, "Hello, Matt!"

"Where is Grandpa?" asked Matt.

"His stroke a few months ago keeps him at home."

" I can help this summer."

"Is that the only bag you have?"

"Yes, Ma'am."

"I have a surprise for you, Matt. We now have a truck. Our horse is too old to pull the wagon."

"Can you drive it yourself?"

"Yes, and I'm glad it's a Model A instead of a Model T Ford, so I don't have to crank it."

As he approached the truck, Matt asked, "Will you teach me to drive this summer?"

"How about right now? Get into the driver's seat, and I'll tell you what to do."

"Are you sure?" asked Matt, not believing his ears.

"You'll have to drive the eggs to town each Friday."

Matt climbed into the driver's seat, and after a few bumpy starts and some over steering, he got the knack of it. He drove on the gravel roads to the McClaren farm.

"Hi, Grandpa. I see they can't keep a good man down."

"No, Matt, but they can sure slow him down. You're as tall as I am. How old are you?"

"Fourteen this month."

"My goodness," Grandma said, "As big as you are and still have years to grow."

Grandpa McClaren said, "I'm glad you're here. We've a lot of work, and I can't do it anymore."

"Come, Matt," Grandma said as she walked to the door. "Let me show you around before we have supper."

"How many hens do you have now?" asked Matt as they opened the gate to the chicken yard.

"Before he had his stroke, Grandpa built a larger hen house, and we now have forty laying hens and two roosters," answered Grandma proudly. "The fence needs fixing to keep the hens from getting out and laying their eggs in the field."

"Were you able to get your garden planted?"

"Yes, Matt, but it needs weeding."

"That's where I'll start tomorrow Grandma."

Grandma reached down quickly and grabbed a chicken and said, "I'll fry this one for supper to celebrate your coming, Matt."

The next morning, Matt weeded the garden. When Grandma McClaren finished working in the kitchen, she called, "Let's get some driving practice."

"Swell," Matt answered as he left the garden.

The first two weeks Grandma McClaren rode with Matt when he drove to town. Then Matt went alone, so Grandma could do her chores.

Matt worked hard during the next two months. Using Grandpa's scythe and hand mower, he put the yard back in shape. He kept the garden weeded, mended the fence and set a trap that caught the weasel that had been eating eggs. Grandma bought field corn for the chickens, and Matt put it through the sheller and grinder to get the right size feed for growing chicks.

At the end of the summer, Matt was surprised by how fast the little chicks and vegetables had grown and by how many jars of vegetables they had stored for winter.

One evening Grandpa McClaren said, "I've decided to sell the farm, Matt."

"You'll miss it after all these years, Grandpa."

"Yes, but it's time. Grandma wanted me to sell it two years ago, but I kept putting it off."

"Is there someone in Gladesville who'll buy the farm?"

"A young couple, Ben and Joan Turnbull, want to buy it. They own twenty acres next to our farm that they've paid for with their town jobs and hay crop."

"This would be a nice place for them," said Grandma. "If they buy it, they'll have their larger pasture in addition to the house and chickens."

"Where'll you move, Grandpa?" asked Matt.

"We'll stay with one of Grandma's friends in Effingham."

When it was time for Matt to return to St. Louis, Grandpa McClaren tried to get into the truck and ride to the station, but he couldn't.

Matt encouraged him, "Next summer you can ride in the truck with me, Grandpa."

"I'm going to try hard to do that. Thanks for coming."

* * *

Elizabeth missed Matt, but she found that living alone had given her an opportunity to reflect on the future. She had been unable to save enough for Matt to go to college, and he was only three years away from high school graduation.

In Elizabeth's new position as receptionist at the Rathskeller Restaurant, she had offers of dates. Most of the time they were one-time visitors. Elizabeth shrugged them off in a casual way. Once she had dated a regular customer several times and was fond of him. It might have led to something serious, but she discovered that he was married.

In August Elizabeth heard that Mr. O'Hare's wife had become ill, and he had taken her to the hospital. Mr. O'Hare had mentioned his wife and daughter with a great deal of pride. Elizabeth sent a card. A few days later Mr. O'Hare thanked her and said that Mrs. O'Hare was back home.

* * *

Elizabeth greeted Matt with a big hug when he arrived home from Gladesville. "Matt, I can't wait to hear about your summer. How are Grandma and Grandpa doing?"

"Grandma's doing fine, but Grandpa isn't so good."

"Was he getting any better during the summer?"

"I don't think so, but he did make one decision that I think will help. He's decided to sell the farm. He has a buyer, and I think it'll work out."

"When will the sale take place?"

"Sometime late next summer. Guess what, Mom?"

"I can't guess. What is it?"

"I learned to drive."

"But you don't even have a driver's license," Elizabeth said with a note of alarm in her voice.

"They don't pay too much attention to driver's licenses in farm country. I needed to drive eggs to town every Friday."

"I know you were a big help," said Elizabeth as she got up and walked over to the stove to heat some hot cocoa.

Matt followed his mother across the room and whispered in her ear, "Guess what I decided to do this year at school?"

"Study, I hope," kidded Elizabeth.

"I've decided to play football."

"Are you sure that's a good idea, Matt?"

"It's something I've always wanted to do, and I catch the ball better than anyone."

Brushing a tear or two aside, Elizabeth turned to Matt and said, "I want you to live your own life, so go right ahead."

"Thanks, Mom," replied Matt as he kissed his mother.

RICK

"Did you hear somebody honking in the alley, Mama?"

"I did hear a honk. We'd better check."

In the alley they saw Emil in an automobile. "Get in our new car," he laughed.

Emil was not usually this frivolous. He had saved thirty-five dollars and had bought a 1926 automobile made by the Moon Motor Car Company in St. Louis.

Maria was pleased and said, "Now you can ride to work, Emil."

"Can I drive, Papa?" Rick asked.

"You'll have to wait until you're sixteen, Rick, but you can practice in the alley. I'll fasten a leather strap on the steering wheel for you to use with your left wrist when you shift gears."

"Both of you climb into the car," said Emil, pleased that they were happy. He remembered driving his truck home when Maria and Rick had cried because he'd sold Sweetie.

Maria climbed into the front seat, and Rick got in the back. As they rode they saw new places that they hadn't seen before. Rick noticed that parking lots were scattered all over St. Louis because cars had replaced horses. Since Rick did not have enough money, he had dismissed the idea of owning a parking lot.

Rick spent more time working alone in his cabbage patch in the summer of 1938 because Matt and Jack were not able to work with him. It was a big job, but he did it.

One afternoon Rick said, "Mama, I've finished my work, and I'm going to see Mr. Sarno."

"Try to get back early, Rick. When you're late, Papa gets worried."

Mr. Sarno was not on the porch or in his garden when Rick arrived. Rick knocked, and Mr. Sarno called, "Come in."

"How are you feeling?" Rick asked as he walked in.

"Not too good, Rick. I get out of breath when I work too long in the garden. But I really need the garden crop."

"I'll take care of the garden, Mr. Sarno. Can you come to the back porch and watch?"

"Yes, I'd like that. I've always been able to take care of the garden, but this year I don't seem strong enough."

Rick wheeled Mr. Sarno to the back porch where he could watch Rick work. Mr. Sarno always planted four dozen tomato plants, and he needed to have them ready to sell by the end of the summer. He planted vegetables for himself too. Rick sometimes traded his cabbages for Mr. Sarno's vegetables.

Working alone in his cabbage patch that summer, Rick thought to himself, 'What makes one business transaction worth more than another? Cabbages sell for three cents a pound at the Farmer's Market and seven cents near the ballpark. Changing cabbages to sauerkraut increases their value. A man can make more money by looking for a good location or by changing his product from one form to another.'

Business thoughts consumed much of Rick's free time. Emil would help Rick solve problems, but when Rick had an idea that seemed impractical, his father showed little interest. His mother encouraged him, though, even if Rick's plan did not appear to have any value. She believed that Rick would soon be able to use some of his business plans.

Rick thought about the unused property opposite the alley from their home--another carriage house and an old horse lot like the Bauman's lot. No one was using the property, and Rick wondered who owned it.

One morning he asked, "Mama, do you know who owns the lot across the alley?"

"No, Rick, but you can ask at the factory building."

He walked over to the factory and asked the receptionist if he could speak with the owner of the property. She told him that the owner did not work in the building, but she gave Rick the owner's name and address.

One afternoon Rick went to visit Scott at his home near Eads Bridge. His house was a wooden addition to a deteriorated tenement building that had been built after the Great St. Louis Fire in 1849. Similar buildings took all of the land, except for narrow alleys where families visited or hung clothes to dry. As bad as it was, his house was a lot better than his family's river shanty. Since only black folks lived in this area, he and Scott would usually go to the levee to visit to avoid the attention of curious neighbors.

Scott greeted Rick warmly and said proudly, "Last June I graduated from the eighth grade like you did last year, and I'll go to Vashon High School this fall. I'm the first in my family to go to high school. Where are Jack and Matt?"

"Matt's helping his Grandpa in Illinois, and Jack has a job with his father."

When Rick's cabbages were ready to sell, Emil asked Rick to come out behind the house one evening to talk.

"Rick, I have a way to help you sell your cabbages."

"How?"

"When you're ready with your cabbages, you load them in the car, and I'll drive them to your friend's house to sell."

"Great."

"I've been wanting to meet your friend."

A week later they packed the car with cabbages and drove them to Mr. Sarno's house. Emil visited with Angelo Sarno while Rick was selling his cabbages and Mr. Sarno's tomatoes.

Shortly before school started, Rick sat on the porch with Mr. Sarno and asked, "Will you be okay this winter?"

"As long as I stay in the house."

As Rick started to leave, Mr. Sarno asked, "Would you write down your full name and address on this paper."

"Sure." As he wrote, Rick thought it curious that Mr. Sarno wanted Rick's full name, but he didn't say anything. As he left, Rick said over his shoulder, "I'll be here to park cars for the Saturday and Sunday ball games this fall."

ON THE LEVEE

On the day before school started in 1938, the boys met on the levee. They had a lot to talk about since they hadn't been together throughout most of the summer.

Matt said, "I'm going to play football."

"Doesn't that take a lot of time?" asked Rick.

"Yes, but I really like football."

"What do you like about it?"

"Catching the ball and running."

Jack said, "I'd like to play, but those big fellows would kill me. What was the best part of your summer, Matt?"

"Learning to drive."

Rick was more impressed by Matt's story of driving a truck than he was about football and said, "Papa got an automobile, but I can't drive except in the alley. He drove my cabbages to Mr. Sarno's, and I made more money."

Matt explained, "I couldn't drive in St. Louis even if Mom had a car, but boys drive in farm country."

Jack told them about his trip to the Ozark Mountains.

Matt asked, "How many animals did you shoot?"

"Louie wouldn't let me shoot any animals unless we ate them, but we shot squirrels, rabbits, and one deer. I was shooting better after I practiced, but I never saw Louie miss. We caught fish when we needed them to eat. I brought some venison jerky back, and I thought you might like to try it." He opened a sack and gave them each a piece.

"It's good," said Matt.

"Did you do the same thing with fish?" asked Rick.

"We smoked some fish."

"Have you thought about college?" asked Matt.

"I have," answered Rick, "but I don't think that I can afford go to a university. I'm planning to go to a business college at night and take some accounting courses."

Jack said, "Louie really wants me to quit school now, but he's letting me finish high school."

"Did you use the library during the summer?" asked Matt.

"I read four or five good books," said Rick.

"I got interested in rivers, and I studied about the Mississippi," added Jack. "Did you know that it starts small in Minnesota and continues to get wider as it passes St. Louis and flows to the Gulf of Mexico?"

Rick asked, "Why does it keep getting bigger?"

"Most all of the rivers in America flow into it," answered Jack.

"No wonder it keeps flooding," Rick replied as he turned to Matt. "What did you read, Matt?"

"In Gladesville we didn't have any books or a library, but we did read the Bible every night. I especially liked one verse in Proverbs: 'Trust in the Lord with all thine heart; and lean not unto thine own understanding.'"

As the boys grew into men, their lives became quite different. Each of them worked hard and learned what they could from their unique experiences. They still found time to continue their close friendship.

8

1939-40: Jack, Rick, Matt

JACK

During the school year, Louie and Blackjack did not see much of each other, but in the summer they worked together once again. When the Clydesdales went on tour in the summer of 1939, Louie and Blackjack returned to the Ozarks. Louie thrived in the primitive life in the mountains.

A week after they had set up camp on the St. Francis River, Louie told Blackjack, "I'll be gone a few days."

"Where are you going?"

"I'll tell you when I get back," said Louie mysteriously.

"Okay," said Jack, frustrated by Louie's unusual behavior. Although Jack knew how to fish and hunt and collect berries and herbs, he didn't like being left out of Louie's plans.

*　　*　　*

Louie climbed the rugged Ozark Mountain rocks and walked through the heavy underbrush until he reached a cornfield on the plateau. He walked through the waist-high corn that led up to the hog barn and hollered, "Hi, Jimmy! It's Louie LeGault. Do ya remember me?"

Jimmy shielded the setting sun from his eyes, "It's been a long time, Louie. I heard that you left the river. Come inside."

They talked and traded stories into the night over coffee, ham, and cornbread.

The next morning Louie said, "Jimmy, if you don't need the mountain below your farm, I'd like to buy it. I've got a thousand dollars from my veteran's bonus and other savings."

"Let me think about it," answered Jimmy as they walked around his farm through the cornfield into a wooded area to a gravel road. "The last time I climbed down to the river, I fell and broke my arm and never went down again. I've always wanted to buy this small piece of land that separates my farm from the county road, but I've never had the money. If I can work out a deal to buy this land for a thousand dollars, I'll sell the mountain acreage to you."

"Jimmy, here's fifty dollars to work out the deal."

"Okay, when will you be back?" said Jimmy as he took the money and shook Louie's hand.

"Next summer."

*   *   *

Louie got back to the river on the fourth day and told Blackjack what he had done. Louie felt sure that the mountain would become his. Blackjack was amazed by how much more aggressive Louie was when he was in the mountains. Jack had done well by himself and was now confident that he could survive in the forest alone.

That winter Louie talked about the mountain all the time. He waited impatiently for next summer, like a child expecting a puppy for Christmas.

*   *   *

The summer of 1940 did come, and the horses went on tour. Louie and Blackjack left for the Ozarks and arrived at their campsite near dark. Louie had a restless night's sleep. At daybreak he left for Jimmy's farm with his life savings.

He was gone five days before he came running into their river camp shouting, "Blackjack! Blackjack!"

"Are you okay, Louie?"

"I bought the mountain!"

"You what?"

"I bought the mountain!"

"I can't believe it."

"It's true," reaffirmed Louie proudly.

"Tell me how you did it."

Louie told Jack how he and Jimmy had walked to Fredericktown where they completed the sales. Now Louie owned the mountain, and Jimmy owned the acreage along the county road. Both had achieved their dreams.

RICK

In 1939 Rick planted his cabbage plants with help from Jack and Matt, but Rick was not looking forward to hoeing and harvesting them again by himself. His secret idea of farming the land across the alley began to look impossible.

Once again Rick squarely faced the limitation of working with one hand. It wasn't going away. He would have to get help to do things that he could not do himself and concentrate on what he could do best. But how? Rick could not find the answer.

Rick continued working with his cabbages and visiting with Mr. Sarno whenever he had free time. Mr. Sarno seemed to have recovered from his illness and was able to work in his garden again. After Rick helped park cars for ball games, they enjoyed visiting on the porch.

Mr. Sarno would tell Rick about growing up in Italy before he came to America. Rick would tell Mr. Sarno about his secret plans to raise cabbages in the lot across the alley from his home.

Mr. Sarno expressed his concern about Mussolini's war plans. "They say that he has the trains running on time and that he's building an army. He should use his army to defend Italy and stay out of other countries. I don't trust him."

"My father says the same thing about Hitler."

*　　*　　*

Rick had practiced driving in the alley and had asked questions as he watched his father drive. On Rick's sixteenth birthday, Emil took him to get a driver's license and said, "Let's celebrate, Rick."

"How, Papa?"

"Why not take Mama out to meet Mr. Sarno?"

"Swell. He always said he wanted to meet her."

Maria made some cabbage soup to take, and Rick drove them over to Mr. Sarno's house. They had a good visit.

As they started home, Rick asked, "Papa, could I drive you to a special place?"

"Sure."

Rick took them on a drive through Forest Park and stopped at the boys' park bench by the lake with the swans. They got out of the car and sat on the bench long enough for Emil and Maria to appreciate their son's favorite place.

"It's beautiful, Rick," said Maria softly.

Emil smiled, knowing his son was a man . . . a good man.

*　　*　　*

In August Rick took two cabbages to Scott. He was home, but he looked troubled. "Thanks for the cabbages, Rick. I'll give them to Mama. Let's go to the levee and talk."

"Okay."

Seeing how serious Scott was, they walked to the levee without talking. When they sat down, Scott's voice broke as he said, "Papa was killed in an accident two weeks ago loading some stuff onto a barge. He'd been getting paid better the last two years because he was doing more dangerous work on the docks that others wouldn't do."

"I'm sorry," said Rick, not knowing anything else to say.

"The company paid for Papa's funeral, but we don't have Papa anymore. Papa always worked hard and did the right thing. Last week I quit school to start working."

"What kind of work are you doing, Scott?"

"Loading barges, but most days I don't get work."

"How's your family going to live?"

"It's going to be hard, especially since Nadine brought her baby back to live with us after her husband left her. We already have Mabel and her baby; Mabel never had a husband. Mama has a job working three days a week at a house at the end of the streetcar line in Clayton. Nadine has a job on Saturday cooking in a restaurant, and Mabel mostly cares for the babies. What's going on with you, Rick?"

"About the same, except for one thing. I have a driver's license. My father lets me drive his car sometimes when he's with me. I'll bring sauerkraut for your family next month."

"What's sauerkraut?"

"We make it from our cabbages."

On his way home, Rick wrote in his notebook that maybe he could pay Scott to help him with his cabbages next year.

After selling all of his cabbages at the end of the summer, Rick went to the filling station where his father bought gasoline. He got a St. Louis map and took it to the park bench in Forest Park, so he could study certain locations around St. Louis. He discovered that Mr. Marcus, who owned the land across the alley from Rick's home, lived on the other side of Forest Park.

Rick walked to the Marcus home and was surprised to see brick and stone buildings that looked more like apartments than homes. He almost lost his nerve but decided that he wouldn't get his answer unless he went to the front door and rang the bell.

A man came to the door and asked, "What do you want?"

"I'm Rick Bauman, and I've come to see Mr. Marcus."

"Mr. Marcus is busy and won't have time for you."

Rick was persistent and said politely, "Please ask him if he can see me for a few minutes? It's important."

The man closed the door, and Rick stayed on the front porch and waited, not sure that anyone would come. After what seemed like a long time, the door opened, and a small elderly man with a bald head and a well-trimmed white beard said, "What can I do for you?"

"Thank you for coming to the door, Mr. Marcus. I'm Rick Bauman, and I grow cabbages on the property across from your clothing factory. I'd like to talk to you about renting the old horse lot next to your factory."

"What would you do if you rented the lot?"

"Grow more cabbages."

"I'll be glad to talk with you, Rick. Go to the bench in back of the house and wait for me."

Rick went to the back of the house and sat down on a bench located in a brick patio inside a stone wall edged with flowers. He sat nervously on the bench and waited until Mr. Marcus came out through the back door and sat down. Rick explained how he could double his sales if he could plant cabbages on the lot that Mr. Marcus owned.

Mr. Marcus asked a number of questions, and Rick told him how he made crocks of sauerkraut each year in addition to selling the cabbages. Mr. Marcus seemed interested in the fact that Rick was carrying the cabbages out to where he could sell them at a higher price than at the Farmer's Market.

"When you graduate from high school next year, what do you plan to do besides grow cabbages?"

I'll be going to business college at night to study accounting."

"What is your secret goal, Rick? You must have one."

"To own and manage a parking lot, but I haven't figured out how to do it."

Mr. Marcus surprised Rick by saying, "When I was a boy living in Germany, I'd eat fresh sauerkraut, and I miss it. You may rent my lot this year for a crock of sauerkraut. When you bring the sauerkraut to me, I'll decide what to do the following year."

"Thanks, Mr. Marcus."

"You have quite a challenge finishing school and getting all those cabbages grown and sold, but I believe you'll do it." He glanced at Rick's missing hand without mentioning it. "I'll look forward to seeing you next August."

Rick told his mother about his visit to Mr. Marcus. Maria was concerned and said, "You'll have to figure out how to get all that plowing done. Can you do it by yourself?"

"Scott needs work, and I think he'll come over and help me when he isn't working on the dock. I'll give him a crock of sauerkraut and pay him from my savings."

"Have you talked to Scott?"

"No, but he needs work and can't get it every day."

"Ask Papa to let you drive to Central Hardware and see if you can buy a better plow."

*　　*　　*

Rick talked to Scott, who was pleased to have a chance for extra work. In the spring of 1941 they got all of the little cabbages planted in the two lots. Having purchased the new plow that his mother had suggested, Rick wrote in his notebook, "Better equipment can reduce work time."

When Rick had planted all his cabbages, he went to see Mr. Sarno. Finding the door unlocked, he went inside.

"Is that you, Rick?"

"Yes, Mr. Sarno."

"I've been sick again."

"Can you get to the back porch, Mr. Sarno?"

"I think so. That would be nice."

Rick helped Mr. Sarno into his wheel chair and wheeled him to the porch. After Rick got the garden ready for planting, he joined his friend on the porch to talk.

"I've planted twice as many cabbages this year."

"How could you do that?"

Rick explained about his visit with Mr. Marcus and about having Scott's help.

Rick asked, "Have you seen your doctor?"

"Yes, he came by and said that I should just take it easy because he couldn't help anymore."

As he left, Rick said, "I'll be back to help."

MATT

Matt returned to Gladesville to help his grandparents again in the summer of 1939. This time his mother came with him to visit her parents for a week.

It was a memorable reunion. Grandma McClaren and her daughter told stories as they fried chicken, made noodles, and baked pies. They opened some of the jars of vegetables and watermelon rinds that Matt and Grandma had canned the previous summer. Matt could help Grandpa to a table under the oak tree, which made their meals more festive.

In the evenings Grandpa and Grandma McClaren told stories about growing up in the nineteenth century. They told how Grandma had been orphaned at sixteen and married Grandpa who was thirty years old. Their marriage seemed ordained. Grandpa had fourteen acres of land and his two-room house. Later he bought two more acres and added a chicken coop and a shed for a cow. They had two children, Elizabeth and Mary Lou. All of them worked every day on the farm until it was too dark to see.

Tragedy came to the family when Mary Lou got pneumonia. They all had taken turns sitting with her, keeping cool cloths on her forehead day and night until she died.

Matt learned that when his mother was seventeen, her teacher had helped her to get a scholarship to the University of Illinois. The McClarens had used cash from egg and butter sales to assist her, but after two years Elizabeth left the university to marry Matt's father.

After the evening story telling and Bible reading, Matt and his mother would fall asleep in their beds of blankets and chicken-feather pillows on the floor.

*   *   *

When Elizabeth returned to work after her trip to Gladesville, her friend, Calley Carr, told her that Mrs. O'Hare had died. She had been doing quite well after her release from the hospital the year before, so Elizabeth was shocked to hear the unexpected news. Elizabeth and Calley rode to the funeral service with Mr. and Mrs. Flarity. With Mrs. O'Hare's sudden death, Elizabeth couldn't help thinking just how important her recent visit with her parents was.

*   *   *

Later in the summer Matt helped his grandparents move to Effingham. After everything was moved, Matt helped Grandma unpack boxes and arrange the furniture in the room where they would live. Finally, it was time to move Grandpa. Matt and Ben Turnbull lifted him in his chair into the back of the truck. As they drove away, Grandma McClaren looked back and sobbed. Grandpa McClaren sat stoically and did not look back. Matt left for St. Louis the next day.

*   *   *

In January 1940 Elizabeth received word that her father had just had a heart attack. She and Matt left immediately on the next train to Effingham, but when they arrived at the station, Grandma McClaren met them tearfully with the news that Grandpa had died that morning. With the help of friends, she had already made the funeral arrangements.

A rain storm on the day of the funeral created an almost impossible situation. Just before the hearse carrying the casket arrived at the cemetery, the front wheel got stuck in the muddy road. Horses had to be brought from a nearby farm to pull the hearse out of the mud and up the hill to the Gladesville Methodist Church and Cemetery. After more than an hour had passed, the procession could proceed.

Family and friends had gathered inside the church and had been singing hymns while they waited for the funeral to begin. As the hearse neared the church, a young boy, who had been impatiently waiting for over an hour, tugged the rope to toll the bell in the church steeple. The McClarens had worshiped in this little wood church for decades with eight to ten other families.

When the time came for Elizabeth and Matt to leave, Grandma McClaren assured Elizabeth at the train station, "I'll be missing John, but don't worry; I'll make do."

*   *   *

Business in the Rathskeller Restaurant had been increasing, and both Calley Carr and Elizabeth had received pay increases in the fall of 1940. Mr. O'Hare began to come to the Rathskeller each afternoon and ask, "Ready for coffee, Elizabeth?"

"Most certainly," Elizabeth would respond, and they would visit for ten or fifteen minutes.

"How's Matt's football team doing?"

"The team is winning; Matt loves it, and I worry," answered Elizabeth. "How's your daughter doing in California?"

"She loves California, but she's never found a man she'd marry," answered Mr. O'Hare. "She's been promoted to buyer for Wilson's Department Store. I think she married the store."

One day Mr. O'Hare asked, "Do you ever go to the outdoor Municipal Opera in Forest Park?"

"I've taken Matt and two of his friends a couple of times."

"Would you go with me on Saturday night? I'm sure that you can trade some work hours with Calley."

"I'd love to go."

They had such a good time that he asked her out again and insisted that she call him "Pat."

At the end of the football season in 1940, Matt was selected by the sportswriters to be on the All Missouri Team. Washington University in St. Louis and The University of Missouri had offered him four-year scholarships.

"What university should I take, Mom?"

Elizabeth could not hide her pride or anxiety. "Matt, it's your decision."

"Then I think it will be the University of Missouri."

*　　*　　*

Elizabeth had to make a crucial decision in May 1941. She and Pat had been talking about marriage. Elizabeth reviewed her thoughts, 'I want to marry Pat, but why is life so doggone complicated? With Pat's new hotel in New Orleans, we'd need to leave by the end of June. I'm thirty-seven, and Pat is fifty-one. Matt'll only be seventeen in June. Pat's Catholic, and I'm not.'

They had previously considered these concerns one by one. Pat had commented, "Matt has already proven that he's a man and able to take care of himself. Age doesn't make a man."

"I know you're right, Pat, but he seems so young to me."

Pat spoke to the other concerns. "We can work out our religious differences by respecting each other's beliefs, but you must make the decision about moving."

Elizabeth sensed that tonight she would have to make her decision. She was right. After going out to dinner, she and Pat drove to the top of Art Hill in Forest Park. He parked the car, and turning to her, he whispered in her ear, "Do you love me?"

"More than I believed possible." Elizabeth kissed him in a way that left no doubt.

"Then marry me and come to New Orleans with me."

"Yes, Pat. I'll marry you, and we'll go to New Orleans."

Elizabeth's body quivered and pulsated in a way that she had not felt since Bill was alive. They held each other tightly and eased the anxiety of their decision.

"You've made me so happy, Elizabeth."

"I love you, Pat."

Elizabeth talked to Matt later that evening, and he relieved her doubts. "I like Mr. O'Hare, Mom. He's a fine man."

"Thank you, Matt. I'll miss you so much."

"I'll miss you too, but I'll be going to the University of Missouri and not living here, anyway."

"We'll always find ways to visit and be together, Matt."

The next day Elizabeth set the wedding date for June 14. She and Pat would have their honeymoon at the Lake of the Ozarks and then drive on to New Orleans to the Hotel Du Jardin that Pat had purchased. The hotel had twenty-one rooms to rent by the day or by the week. They'd live in the top floor suite. Pat would manage the hotel, and Elizabeth would be in charge of the courtyard restaurant.

Matt faced the fact that life wasn't static. He'd always need to adjust to dramatic changes in life, good and bad. Events were often out of his control.

AT THE LEVEE

After high school graduation in May 1941, the boys met at the levee to discuss their future plans.

Jack said, "I've got a full time job with Louie at the horse barn starting tomorrow. Together we'll be making twenty dollars a week. We're going to build a cabin on the St. Francis River."

Matt asked, "How are you going to get your building supplies through the rugged terrain that you described to us?"

"We'll float it. Louie said he did that once before, with his Grandpa Piney."

"Matt, when's your Mom leaving?" Jack went on to ask.

"In a couple of weeks," Matt answered. "Rick, have you and Scott planted all the cabbages in both your lots?"

"Yes, I should have almost 800 big cabbages this year."

They sat quietly for awhile, enjoying the same Mississippi River scene that kept them coming back. Life seemed wonderful.

Matt broke the silence. "Life is so strange. I'm going to be at the University of Missouri for four years, but I sometimes wonder what might happen to change things."

Rick said, "When plans don't work out, you get new ones."

Jack said, "I'd give a dollar to anyone who could tell me that everything was going to work out the way we think it will."

"Do you have a dollar, Jack?"

"Yes, and a few more. I've decided to try to save what money I can. Taking care of the Clydesdales is good for now, but I'll want to do something else later."

"We'll miss you next fall, Matt," said Rick. "Hope you have a good football year and learn a lot."

"Do you think you can sell all your cabbages this year?" asked Matt.

"I think so, now that Papa lets me use his car to carry my cabbages.""What's Louie going to do with his mountain, Jack?"

"Louie's determined to keep the forest the way it's always been. He's not going to cut a trail from the River Ranch Lodge to our camp like Derk wants him to. He thinks people will use it and ruin the place."

"He's probably right."

"We're going to the Ozarks each time the Clydesdales go on tour. It's getting harder to get on a barge, so we're going to take a bus to Ste. Genevieve this year."

"I'm glad that Louie has his mountain," said Rick thoughtfully. "A good man should see his dreams come true."

"Can we make St. Louis better like we said?" asked Jack.

"Sure we can," the other two boys replied.

"I think so too," said Jack. "I wonder how?"

Reinforced by each other's friendship, they started home quite confident about the years ahead.

9

Fall 1941: Jack, Rick, Matt

JACK

The LeGaults felt the excitement of living more affluently now that they had two salaries. Louie did something very unusual. He bought new Levi Strauss clothes: a shirt, pants, and hat. The pants were khaki and would be good in the woods as well as in the city. He had looked at the hat for several years in a gun store but could not afford to buy it. Louie planned to buy Blackjack a Levi jacket with a wool lining for his Christmas gift.

After wearing worn and tattered clothes for so many years, Louie felt uncomfortable wearing his new clothes that even smelled strange. Gradually, after wearing each of the items separately a few times, he wore all the clothes together and felt fine. Louie stood straighter, walked more briskly, and even started to whistle. Having Blackjack with him and having more income gave Louie self assurance.

Blackjack was also excited. He decided to fix up their flat. He thoroughly swept and mopped the floors, and washed their one sooty window. After a few weeks of shopping, he found an old icebox at a junkyard and bought it for two dollars. Although no one delivered ice anymore, at a place nearby he could buy a fifteen-pound piece of ice and carry it in a gunny sack to their flat.

Their best times together were in the Ozark Mountains. Louie had close, personal friends that respected him, and Blackjack, who had never known people like Jimmy and Derk, would listen and learn from them. And, Jack was always eager to learn more about the forest.

When they climbed the mountain to visit Jimmy, Louie would remind his son about the dangers of climbing. "Ya gotta ignore bruises or any bramble scratches. Only concentrate on the climb. Check each rock for firmness before grabbin' it with yer hand or plantin' a boot."

When they reached the plateau and walked through the cornfield, Jimmy'd see them and call, "Good to see ya!"

"Jimmy, we got some fresh fish and venison."

"How about fryin' them fish with some bacon?" Jimmy would tease, knowing how Louie liked fried fish. When Louie and Blackjack would stay over to visit Jimmy, the three of them would talk about everything from how Jimmy butchered hogs to how he harvested corn.

On cool fall mornings Jimmy would have a crackling fire in the fireplace. Bean and coffee pots hanging near the fire filled the house with a pleasant aroma. Blackjack would study the warm expressions on the faces of Jimmy and Louie as they told stories of their first years in the Ozark Mountains. When Louie and Blackjack would reluctantly leave, Jimmy would always send them off with some eggs and a friendly warning.

"Come back again, Louie, and don't break them eggs on your climb down!"

"I might break a rib, but not them eggs!"

The LeGaults would make at least one trip to visit Derk. Louie and Blackjack would take fish and venison, and Derk in return would give them bread. Derk still wanted Louie to come to the forest to live and guide his ranch visitors, but Louie stood firm about keeping his mountain the way his ancestors had found it.

Blackjack and Louie liked to swim in the river too. They would strip off their clothes and play their game of "last one in the water cooks." They would splash and play like muskrats. When they finished their swim, they would lay on their backs and watch the upper branches of the tall walnut trees blowing to and fro in the wind, as though the trees were waving to them. The sun's rays would slip through the trees to warm them, and turning their faces, they could smell the lush ferns that grew in the silt left by years of spring floods.

In the late fall they would bravely splash cold water on their faces and chests and consider themselves bathed. The Ozark mountain air was fresh with morning dew glistening on beautiful wild flowers. Jack thought, 'People living in the smoky air of the city don't know what they're missing.'

"Why'd you ever leave here, Louie?"

Louie explained in his simple way, with a sadness in his voice, "The city folks came and the animals left." Jack began to understand how hard leaving the forest had been for Louie.

When they returned to St. Louis, Blackjack found a book on how to build a radio. He bought the simple parts needed for a crystal set that used a crystal detector instead of radio tubes. His radio didn't look like expensive commercial radios, but with earphones they could listen to Eddie Cantor and to baseball games. Their life was good.

On December 7, 1941, the LeGaults were listening to a radio program that was suddenly interrupted by President Roosevelt's somber voice announcing the infamous treachery of the Japanese bombing of Pearl Harbor. America was at war! The LeGaults were shocked. They took off their earphones and tried to comprehend fully what had happened.

Blackjack spoke, "What's it mean to us, Louie?"

"I don't know," Louie answered as though he had been

betrayed. "General Pershing told us that if we won the war in France, there'd be no more wars. I believed him."

Blackjack anxiously said, "This war will be the worst ever."

"It's gonna be bad. We won't talk about it tonight,"

RICK

Rick continued to learn more about business. Doubling the number of cabbages he grew and employing Scott proved to be good decisions. At first he thought that he would make $600 in profit, but he had forgotten that there would be expenses. After he had paid Scott, bought his plow, and paid other minor expenses, he would have only $400 left. Rick was discouraged until he realized that he would be making more than the dollar a day that his friends were making.

Rick took a crock of sauerkraut to Mr. Marcus in August. Sitting on the backyard bench, Mr. Marcus asked, "Did you make a profit on your cabbages, Rick?"

"My cabbage business is doing great, but my expenses are higher than I thought they'd be."

"They usually are, Rick. Learn to allow for unanticipated expenses when you plan a business venture."

"Excuse me while I write in my notebook."

"What are you writing?"

"Allow for unanticipated expenses."

Then Rick explained how he used shorthand to write down new ideas and plans in his business notebook.

"Would you read me a page?"

Rick read a page, and they talked some more. They agreed on the same rental agreement for the 1942 year.

*   *   *

Rick took the streetcar to Mr. Sarno's house to let him know that soon he would be bringing the last of his cabbages to sell. Carrying some cabbage soup that his mother had made, he walked up to Mr. Sarno's front porch to find his door padlocked. He knocked but did not get an answer. Looking in the window, he saw an empty wheel chair.

Rick was frightened. He went to a neighbor and asked, "Mrs. Sanders, have you seen Mr. Sarno?"

"When I didn't see him yesterday, I asked my son to go over and check on him. Mr. Sarno died in his sleep."

Rick was confused and shaking. He smelled cabbage soup that had spilled on his trousers. Awkwardly, he handed the soup to Mrs. Sanders, "Mama made this soup. Will you take it?"

"Yes, Rick. I know that you'll miss Mr. Sarno. He told me many times how much your friendship meant to him."

Rick was devastated.

When he got home, Maria consoled him. "You always like to think that you can help someone all the time, but you can't."

"I think I'll go over to see Matt."

Maria wanted to lean down and kiss her son, but he was a head taller than she was. Instead, she put her arms around him and held him before he left to see Matt.

With emotion in his voice, Rick told Matt what had happened.

"Rick, you did everything that you could have done. Now you have to think about what to do with the rest of your cabbages now that you can't sell them at Mr. Sarno's house."

"I'd forgotten about the cabbages."

"I'm still working at the Farmer's Market, and I'll talk to some of the men and see if they can help you."

Not knowing what else to do, Rick went home and started weeding his cabbages. That evening Maria said, "Emil, you and Rick need to sit in the chairs in the back lot and talk."

Emil took two chairs out back and called Rick from his garden. They did not eat at eight o'clock that night.

Emil concluded their talk, "Sometimes it's better; sometimes it's worse, but a man can't quit."

"Thanks, Papa, I won't."

They quietly ate a late supper and went to bed. Rick lay awake for a long time thinking of good memories he had with Mr. Sarno.

*   *   *

A few weeks after Mr. Sarno's death, a man came to the house and asked, "Does Emil Ulrick Bauman live here?"

Maria was startled but answered, "Yes, Rick lives here."

She thought something had happened to Rick but couldn't imagine what. She rushed outside and was relieved to see him hoeing. She called for him to come before realizing how abruptly she had left the stranger.

"Rick is coming," Maria told their visitor. "Please come in and sit down, and I'll get you a cup of coffee."

"Mrs. Bauman, my name is Anthony Mareno, and I'm the attorney responsible for Mr. Sarno's estate."

Rick came into the house dirty and sweaty from his work. Mr. Mareno greeted him, "Rick, you must have been a good friend to Mr. Sarno."

"I tried to be. I miss him."

The lawyer continued, "Mr. Sarno came to me two years ago and asked me to prepare his Last Will and Testament. I'm not going to read the entire will, but I'll tell you what it says. Later you and your parents should come to my office to help me carry out Mr. Sarno's wishes."

Rick didn't understand. Maria thought she did but wasn't sure.

Mr. Mareno continued, "Briefly, Rick, the will states that Mr. Sarno's house, his savings account, and all his personal belongings are to be held in trust for you until you reach the age of twenty-one. Your parents, who are to be trustees for the estate, will have the authority to make transactions helpful to you."

Rick was confused and asked, "Does that mean that I can sell my cabbages at Mr. Sarno's house?"

"Yes, the house and the garden belong to you."

"Mr. Sarno did that for me, Mr. Mareno?"

"Yes, Rick. Mr. Sarno told me that he had grown up with fine parents in Italy who died years ago. Since then, no one had meant as much to him as you. He wanted everything that he had to be yours."

Rick rushed out into the yard, leaned against the wall of the house, and wept. It was the first time that he had cried since Mary Ellen died.

Observing that Rick was disturbed with the loss of his friend and stunned by the contents of the will, the lawyer turned to Maria. "When Mr. Bauman comes home, ask him to bring Rick to my office. Here's a card with my address."

When the Baumans went to the attorney's office, he read the will and explained that it would be a few months before the final legal requirements were met. He had made arrangements for Rick to use the Sarno house and to sell his vegetables.

In September, as the Baumans were eating supper, they discussed Rick's latest plans.

"Papa, I start business college tomorrow night, and I'll go each Tuesday and Thursday night."

"School is good. Do you have enough money?"

"Yes, from my cabbages. After ball games I'll have to go straight to the college, and I'll need to take a sandwich."

"I'll make your sandwich," said Maria, anxious to help.

*   *   *

One afternoon waiting for the ball game to be over, Rick had an idea. The wooden planters that Mr. Sarno had built to work in his garden from his wheelchair were no longer needed, so he could break the wooden sides off the planters and plow the entire back yard for next year's garden. He'd use the boards to build a bigger vegetable stand.

After paying for his night classes at business college, Rick used the rest of his savings to buy paint and supplies. He cleaned the house and painted the inside walls and woodwork, and when he had completed his renovations, Rick drove his parents to his newly painted house. They were excited by Rick's fine work and his prospects for the coming year.

Their elation was suddenly dampened that evening when Emil turned on the radio in time to hear that the United States was at war.

MATT

For eleven years Matt and his mother had lived in their cold-water flat. His mother had left in June, and now it was his turn to leave. He'd put everything he owned into his suitcase and had it ready to go to the bus station. Matt had an empty feeling as he stared at the paint-flecked walls and the one light bulb hanging from the ceiling in the empty room. Sitting on the floor by the only window, he marveled at how God could guide each life. He had faith that God knew the right way for him and was upbeat about going to the University of Missouri.

Matt tried to understand the past that had come and gone. He had enjoyed his life with his mother and with Jack and Rick, who seemed more like brothers. He would always be grateful for Miss Goerner, who had taught him to read and know the value of the St. Louis Library.

During the summer he had spent most of his free time reading about history, health, sex, first-aid, and aeronautics. Because his eleven years living in his river front neighborhood seemed so important, he wanted to learn about the history of previous centuries.

Earlier in the week, Matt and Jack had taken his two beds and tied them to the top of the Bauman car and driven them to the LeGault home. Then they'd taken the cots that Jack and Louie had been using to Scott for his sisters' children, who had been sleeping on the floor.

Matt remembered how he had cried when he and his mother had first moved from Webster Groves to the slums on the Mississippi River front. At that time he never considered the possibility that he would feel sad when he left; but he did. He went over to the wash basin, splashed water on his face, and took a drink from his cupped hands. After drying his hands on his pants, he started for the bus.

When Matt got off the bus in Columbia, Missouri, he took his suitcase to the front of the bus station to look at the city where he would be living. His scholarship provided tuition, books, room, and board. He would sweep a gymnasium each day to earn money for personal expenses.

Since football players had been instructed to come early for practice, the bus station was nearly empty, as regular students had not yet arrived. While he was standing outside the bus station, an eager cab driver asked, "Do you want a ride?"

"I'll walk. What direction is the athletic dormitory?"

"It's about two miles," the cab driver said. "Do you really think you want to walk that far with your suitcase?"

"Yes, I think I will," answered Matt as he started to walk.

"Are you one of the freshman football players? Football players ride free in my cab," said the cab driver.

"Are you sure?"

The cab driver introduced himself and said, "Give me your name for my boss, and he'll reimburse me."

He took Matt for a ride around the campus before he let him off at the athletic dorm. Matt entered the large lobby--the football players paid no attention to him. He went to his room and found that his roommate, Spud Jones, was already there. Matt and Spud were both freshmen and needed each other's support. Spud was listed as the state's fastest high school running back.

Matt worked hard at both football and his studies. Since the athletic dormitory had too many distractions, he went to the library each night. He found football competition was tougher than he had anticipated. He learned early to study the opposing players to anticipate their moves, and in their last game, Matt caught a long pass and ran for his first touchdown.

*   *   *

From an announcement over the loud speaker in the dining room, the football players heard the news that the Japanese had bombed Pearl Harbor. The athletes had mixed reactions. Some remained silent; others cursed loudly, while others insisted that they would join the military and kill the bastards.

Spud reacted differently. He nudged Matt, "Come up to the room. I need to talk to you."

When they got to the room, Spud said, "My brother is a sailor on the battleship *Oklahoma*. Will you listen to the news reports with me?"

"Maybe your brother's ship was out of the harbor."

In their room, a radio report confirmed that the Japanese had destroyed airplanes on the ground and had sunk navy ships that were in the harbor, including the *USS Oklahoma*.

Later Spud heard from his parents that his brother had been killed.

PART TWO

WAR YEARS 1942-1945

NEVER THINK THAT WAR, NO MATTER
HOW NECESSARY, NOR HOW
JUSTIFIED, IS NOT A CRIME.
ASK THE INFANTRY AND ASK THE DEAD.

Earnest Hemingway

10

Spring 1942

Rick had written a letter to Matt inviting him to stay in Mr. Sarno's house during Christmas break. Matt's mother had also written and sent him a train ticket to New Orleans. Matt decided to go directly to New Orleans and spend a day in St. Louis on his way back to the university.

As his bus pulled into the St. Louis station from New Orleans in January 1942, Matt scanned the crowd to find Rick and Jack. There they were, running and waving.

"It's great to see you," Matt yelled.

"How was the university?" asked Jack.

"Just like going into Jefferson Elementary School for the first time, but I got over that feeling." Matt stepped on the running board of Rick's car and climbed in.

Rick said, "It's a little cold, but we're going straight to the park. Mama made us a picnic lunch."

When they reached their park bench, they talked rapidly about what each of them had been doing. When the last sandwich was gone, the conversation changed to war. Countries were already involved in a death struggle for world dominance.

Germany had conquered most of Europe and was fighting

a two-front war with Russia and England. Italy had conquered Ethiopia. Japan had conquered Korea and much of China. If the free world was to survive, it would have to destroy the German, Italian, and Japanese military powers.

Then the conversation got personal. Matt said, "My best friend and roommate at the university quit school and joined the navy last week. His brother was killed at Pearl Harbor. I've decided to enlist in the Navy Air Force next June when I'm eighteen. I've always wanted to fly an airplane. When I told Mom, she cried and wanted me to delay as long as I could."

"I'm going to enlist in the Marine Corps in June," added Jack. "According to books I've read, they're the best fighters. I want a marine beside me when I fight. I don't want to kill people or be killed, but I don't see that we have a choice. If he had his way, Louie would hide me in the Ozark Mountains."

"What did Louie say about your enlisting in the marines?"

He said, 'It'll be a miserable, stinking war. Why do you want to hurry to hell? Then he got drunker than I've ever seen him, and he passed out. He stayed off work the next day."

Rick's voice was shaking, "I heard Mama and Papa talking after they thought I was asleep. Mama said that she now knew why God had given me only one hand. Papa agreed and told her that it's a blessing when a man doesn't have to go to war because it is hell on earth."

Rick stood up and spit, then kicked some dirt. "It doesn't seem right for me to stay here when you have to fight."

Matt got up from the bench and put his arm on Rick's shoulder, "Jack and I don't really have a choice, and you don't either. Maybe you can help us when we get back."

"Thanks, Matt, it helps just to know you feel that way."

*   *   *

Emil and Rick arrived home cold and covered with a January snow. Maria greeted them, "We've got three letters."

Emil said, "We'll eat first."

After clearing the table and washing the dishes, they sat down together to read their three letters.

First, a letter from Mr. Sarno's attorney:

> Rick, the Probate Court has released all of Mr. Sarno's property to you with your parents as trustees.
>
> Arrange to come to my office with your parents to review the legal documents.

Second, a letter from Herman Marcus:

> I returned to active management of my clothing factory to do everything in my power to help stop the German and Japanese atrocities.
>
> Rick, please arrange for you and your father to meet me in my office at the Marcus Clothing Factory next Monday.

The third letter, from the Anheuser-Busch Personnel Supervisor. Emil read quietly, almost to himself:

> When we reviewed our retirement policy with you last week, you asked to have your retirement delayed until March. Your request has been approved.

Maria knew that Emil had not fully understood mandatory retirement at age sixty-five. She encouraged him, "Maybe it's best you retire."

Emil shrugged his shoulders, "It's not good."

The frigid January weather continued. The next morning wind blew falling snow into Rick's face as he shoveled the drifts that had piled high against the garage door during the night. Emil was wearing his boots and all of the heavy clothes he owned as he left for work.

*   *   *

When the Baumans went to see Mr. Mareno, he answered all their questions before concluding, "Rick, all expenses have been paid; you own Mr. Sarno's house and this check for $602. Your parents will be trustees until you're twenty-one."

Driving home, Rick suggested ideas for his new house. "We could either move into the house or rent it."

Maria was visibly upset and said, "We wouldn't want to leave our home. It's the only home I've ever had."

Emil ended further talk, "Now is not the time to decide."

*   *   *

The next day Rick and Emil went to the Marcus Clothing Factory. They sat in upholstered chairs in a waiting room and admired the attractive wall paper with pictures of sunrises that seemed to Rick to suggest optimism. The white carpets were thick and soft and made the Baumans wish that they had scraped and shined their shoes that morning. Being there was an awesome experience for both of them.

Mr. Marcus invited them into his office. "Thank you for coming."

"How can Rick and I help?" asked Emil, a bit bewildered.

Mr. Marcus continued, "Vice President Truman was familiar with my clothing factory when he was a Missouri Senator. He called me last week and urged me to double my factory output by June. The military needs uniform clothing as soon as possible."

Rick was beginning to understand. He could not raise cabbages on the Marcus property if it was needed for the factory expansion. His disappointment showed in his face.

Mr. Marcus immediately assured him, "Rick, the property you've been using to grow cabbages is needed to expand the factory, but you'll be paid for the cabbages that you would have grown this year."

"Thank you, Mr. Marcus, and I'll still have enough cabbages to bring you a crock of sauerkraut this fall."

Then Mr. Marcus gave them a real jolt. "Mr. Bauman, your property is also needed for the factory expansion."

The horrified facial expressions of both Emil and Rick were so apparent that Mr. Marcus felt it necessary to put them at ease quickly. "Mr. Bauman, I've prepared a generous offer for the purchase of your home. Do you have an attorney?"

"Here is Mr. Mareno's card; he has helped us before. My wife loves her home, but I'll talk to her."

"Why don't I have my proposal made available to your attorney? He can advise you before we talk again."

"That would be good."

The Baumans went directly to Mr. Mareno's office. Emil made arrangements for him to represent them with Mr. Marcus and went home to explain to Maria what was happening.

Maria said lovingly, "Emil, you've always known what to do, and you will now." Emil kissed her gently.

Within a week their attorney, Mr. Mareno, had the Baumans back in his office and told them, "You have some important offers to consider. When we finish reviewing them, you will need to go home and think about them before you decide what to do."

"Two independent appraisers valued your property at about $3,000, and Mr. Marcus has made a cash offer of $9,000. If that amount of money isn't acceptable, Mr. Marcus won't pursue the matter further. He'll purchase property on the other side of his factory. He'd be disappointed, as it would require two extra months for the expansion."

Emil said, "I'll accept the cash offer."

Mr. Mareno continued without responding to Emil's hasty

decision, "Mr. Marcus seems to like you, Rick, and thought you wanted to own a parking lot."

"I do, but I've never talked to Papa about it."

Seeing Rick's keen interest, Emil said, "I'll listen."

Mr. Mareno continued, "Mr. Marcus is selling his parking business and is willing to have one or more of the lots become part of the purchase price. There are four parking lots with different appraisals and business considerations. You must decide what is best for your family, cash or parking lots."

"Thank you," said Emil sincerely. "Now, I understand. We'll take the proposals home and study them."

Mr. Mareno handed them a summary sheet of the four parking lots to consider:

> A lot (70 feet by 200 feet) located at Walnut Street is appraised at $3,600. It is fully developed and parks 20 cars.

> A lot (70 feet by 200 feet) located near Sportsman's Park is appraised at $800. It parks up to 20 cars for ball games.

> An undeveloped lot (160 feet by 400 feet) at Broadway is appraised at $5,100. If fully developed, it could park 150 cars.

> A lot (200 feet by 300 feet) located at Union Station is appraised at $9,000. It is fully developed and parks 120 cars.

When they got home, Maria was anxiously waiting with lots of questions.

"It's best we talk in the morning," Emil assured her.

They ate supper quietly and went to bed.

In the morning Emil told Maria what Mr. Mareno had told them.

"What will you do, Emil?" asked Maria.

"We'll move to Rick's house. Rick has to decide whether he wants a parking business or something else for his life's work."

"I've studied the idea for a long time, Papa. I think parking cars can be a good business, but I'm not sure which lots are best."

"Rick, drive to the lots and study them before we talk."

The next morning Rick drove to Walnut Street and spoke to an old man, "I'm Rick Bauman. I may buy this parking lot."

"I'm Billy Mills; I've been operating this lot for fourteen years. I don't care who owns it, as long as I have my job."

Rick could see that the lot had been a busy one.

Next, Rick went to the lot that was nearer to the ballpark than Mr. Sarno's property was. A neighbor told him about a rumor circulating that someone was going to buy and tear down more houses.

When Rick drove to the Broadway lot, he was surprised to see that the tenement buildings that were there a few months ago were gone. He thought they should be torn down, but he remembered that folks had been living in them. One old house remained, and a few cars were parked on the vacant lot. Rick asked the drivers where they were going. One said to the bus station; another said to the Farmer's Market.

Last on Rick's list was the large Union Station lot. Rick found the parking attendant and introduced himself. "I'm Rick Bauman. Can I talk with you?"

"I'm Charlie Johnson. Wait until rush hour is over."

Rick watched and studied the parking procedure. When fewer cars were entering the lot, Charlie spoke to a young man who had just arrived. "Sunny, this fellow wants to talk to you."

Sunny Williams had flaming red hair, freckles, and a big smile. He introduced himself to Rick and said, "When I finish my business with Charlie, we can go over to Nellie's Coffee Shop across the street and talk."

Rick seemed to understand less and less about Mr. Marcus' parking business. Ten minutes later Rick went with Sunny to Nellie's, and they ordered coffee.

Sunny said, "I'm graduating from the College of Engineering at Washington University in May. For the last two years, I've worked part-time for Mr. Marcus. He was developing and buying parking lots, but now he's selling out."

"What do you do for him?"

"I collect the money and keep the records on the Walnut Street lot where Mills is and also here at the Union Station lot. Mr. Marcus had me contracting to demolish or move buildings. We moved a house near the ballpark and tore down a bunch of dilapidated tenement buildings at Broadway. One tenement house is left."

"I saw it."

"I was to demolish that building next month and have the lot cleared and graveled. Then Mr. Marcus told me that he was selling the lots and wouldn't need me after February.

"What would it cost to clear the lot and spread the rock?"

"My time would be about a hundred dollars. It'd cost you about two hundred dollars to remove the remaining rubble and to buy and spread rock."

"I could probably afford that much." said Rick.

"Rick, the house ought to be torn down, but you wouldn't have to do it right away. There's another problem--no curbs, and cars can enter the lot from any direction. Mr. Marcus had planned to ask the city to put curbs on the streets and have only one entrance to the lot."

"Curbs would cost a lot of money. Would the city do it?"

"Mr. Marcus thought he could get the city to do it. You'd need to have an attorney talk to the city officials."

"If I buy the lot, would you finish the work you planned to do for Mr. Marcus?"

"Sure."

"Where can I reach you on the first of March?"

"Here's my card, Rick. To look at it, you'd think that I'd been in business for a hundred years. I'm going to the Army Engineer Corps in June. They tell me that I'll be blowing up bridges and rebuilding them."

As he started to leave, Sunny broke into song, "Wherever you go, I'll follow . . . "

"Follow who?" asked Rick.

"The Lord, of course. Where He leads, I'll go and do my best. Let me know if I can help."

"Thanks, Sunny, I may be in touch with you."

Rick stayed for another cup of coffee. Looking out the window, he watched Sunny walking happily down the sidewalk, and a thought crossed his mind, 'No wonder his name is Sunny.'

Then Rick got serious and wrote in his notebook: "business cards, telephone, and engineer." He would study these things later. Rick now knew how Mr. Marcus had succeeded in the parking business. You hire people to do what you can't do.

That night he told his father what he had learned.

"What do you want to do?"

"There's more to learn. I'm going to study everything tomorrow."

"Good. Tomorrow you'll know what to do."

"Thanks, Papa."

The next morning Rick drove to the St. Louis Public Library where he would have a quiet, warm place to work. Using what he had learned from his bookkeeping and accounting studies, he considered probable income and expense for each different combination of parking lots. He sat quietly for awhile to relax and prepare himself to be objective. He wanted to take the parking lots, but he wanted to make the right decision. He knew that accurate accounting records could guide decisions better than emotions.

First, Rick considered his father. 'Since Papa isn't working now, maybe he could go into business with me to help get the business started. Mama and Papa can raise the vegetables in the backyard and sell them, and Papa can park cars at our house and at the ballpark lot.'

His thoughts continued. 'I can only handle one parking lot myself. Maybe I should take the lot by the Union Station and forget about the other lots. Right now the trains carry the most passengers, but in the future it looks to me as if more people will drive. I'll bet Mr. Marcus was thinking of the future when he bought downtown lots.'

Finally, Rick decided that the best thing for him to do would be to take the ballpark lot because his father could help. Rick could attend the Walnut Street lot and still have time to take the La Salle Correspondence School courses from Chicago that his accounting teacher had suggested.

Then an important thought disturbed him, 'I'd have to fire that nice old man. Since he has been doing such a good job all these years, why not let him continue? I'd have a profit without too much of my time. I could develop the Broadway lot, and in a few years I'd have a larger income.'

Rick went back to his appraisal sheet. I'd be short $500 if I took the three lots. I need the money in my savings account for unanticipated expenses, but maybe Mr. Marcus might let me pay the $500 in fifty-dollar payments from parking income.

As they sat in the backyard that night, Rick explained to his father what he had decided.

"Good. You'll have a hard time the first year. Do you really want that big, unfinished lot?"

"Yes, Papa."

"You can do it."

When Rick and his father explained their proposal to Mr. Mareno, he called Mr. Marcus' attorney. Mr. Mareno then told them, "Your proposal is satisfactory, but you must move in thirty days."

"We'll start moving right away," Emil replied.

When they got home, Emil kissed Maria and said, "It's decided. Rick is going into parking business. We'll help him."

Neither Rick, nor his parents slept well that night. They were taking a risk, and their lives would change dramatically. Maria was happy for Emil. He had always told her that he would like to go into a business with his son.

The next day Rick went over to see Jack to tell him what was happening.

"WOW!" Jack expressed himself in the same way that he had when the three friends walked into the Union Station for the first time.

"What are your plans, Jack?"

"I'll enlist on my birthday in June. Louie won't agree to sign enlistment papers before then."

"I'm glad. The longer that you and Matt wait to go into military service, the happier I'll be."

While Rick was gone, Maria asked Emil, "Is Rick ready to handle such a big business?"

"He's strong, and he's learning in school. He's ready."

"It'll be nice to have you home more, Emil."

Later in the evening Rick quietly climbed into the loft thinking that he would soon have a room of his own. He was happy and slept well.

*   *   *

Rick started his day by arranging to have Mr. Mareno obtain curbs for the Broadway lot from the city. Rick was told that things sometimes go slowly at city hall, so he would contact city officials right away.

That afternoon Rick went to see Sunny Williams. He found Sunny in his "office" in a storeroom behind a grocery store. He was sitting in a chair behind a desk with a two-drawer file and a telephone. Rick told Sunny that he'd like him to take charge of the removal of debris from the Broadway lot and have rock spread on it the following week. Sunny agreed to do it.

As Rick was going over to his Broadway lot, he envisioned having a business card and an office like Sunny's on the first floor of the old tenement building. He'd have Scott attend the lot and live on the second floor. He began to feel both pressure and excitement.

Arriving at the Broadway lot, he opened the door to inspect the house. In a quick glance, he saw a greasy pot belly stove and a filthy porcelain sink with the faucet rusted shut. Opening the toilet door, he jumped back from the putrid odor and the ugly sight of a cracked commode used as a toilet without water. Rick was completely unnerved and fought off nausea.

Rick rushed home to talk with his father. When he arrived, his parents were on the back porch planting the small cabbage seeds that would grow into small plants for transplanting to their garden.

Maria looked up. "Rick, you're home early."

Emil asked, "You can help us plant seeds?"

"Papa, can you come to the Broadway lot with me?"

"Can't we go tomorrow morning?"

"Yes, but I'd really like for you to come now."

"All right." Emil did not ask questions. He needed to discover what traumatic situation was bothering his son.

When they arrived at the rubble-filled lot, they got out of the car and walked back to the old building where squatters had lived. Rick opened the door saying, "Papa, will you walk through this house and tell me if it's possible to fix it to use."

They walked silently through both the downstairs and upstairs before they sat down on the steps facing the parking lot.

"It's really bad, Rick."

"Can we fix it?"

"How long do you have before the truck removes rubble?"

"About a week."

"It can be done, but it's an awful mess. We'll need help."

"What can be done, Papa?"

"City officials won't approve people living here, but you can fix it for your office. We'll start by cleaning the house and installing a faucet. You'll need water."

"How do we get the sinks and commodes out?"

"We'll get tools and come back in the morning. It has to be done before the rubble is removed."

"What about the toilet, Papa?" asked Rick as they left.

"You'll have to remove the fixtures and get the savings from your business before you get toilets, electricity, and telephone. Use the toilet in bus station for now."

"Okay. I'll be glad just to have a table and a filing cabinet where I can do my work and keep my records."

"Your office is good idea. You need a place to work, but you have to be patient in a new business and get savings."

"Thanks, Papa. I didn't know what to do."

The next morning Emil and Rick carried tools to the old house. Emil knocked the walls out in the sink and toilet areas and found where the plumbing entered the building.

"Rick, let's go talk to Louie. Maybe we can work together like we did in the carriage house making the toilet for Maria."

They drove to the LeGault home.

Emil said, "I need ya, Louie."

"Sure, Blackjack and I can work a few hours with ya today."

Emil and Louie struggled for five hours. They managed to disconnect the plumbing fixtures on both floors and attach a new piece of pipe and a faucet onto the water pipe from the street. Rick and Jack worked with a broom and an old coal shovel. They cleared the debris off both floors and carried the junk and filthy fixtures out of the house to the pile of rubble.

As they worked, Rick had an idea, "Do you remember, Jack, when we were boys and used milk bottle caps for free rides on St. Louis Dairy Day at Forest Park Highlands?"

"I remember."

"Last night the boy who lives next door asked me if I had

junk aluminum. Apparently, boys can get free rides next week at Forest Park Highlands if they bring in junk aluminum for building war planes. I've seen some broken aluminum pans in that rubble pile. Let's pile them into the car for him."

Late that afternoon the Baumans drove the LeGaults back to their home and thanked them.

"Pleased to help ya, Emil."

"Wash up, Louie. We'll wait and drive you to work."

Emil and Rick went to the city water department the next morning and paid to connect water for the first floor faucet. The city would install the water meter on March 14.

A few days later Rick went to see Scott. His mother told Rick that Scott wasn't home, but he'd be back tomorrow.

"Mrs. Lincoln, would you please ask Scott to meet me at the Greyhound Bus Station at ten tomorrow morning?"

"I'll tell him. I'm sure he can be there."

The following day Rick met Scott at the bus station, and they walked to the Broadway parking lot. Sitting down on the wooden steps of the old tenement house, Rick told Scott the whole story of how he had gotten into the parking business.

"Scott, would you be willing to attend this parking lot seven days a week? When the lot is ready for cars, I can collect enough money to pay you ten dollars each week. If I can get this house repaired, you can live upstairs."

"I'd like working with you. It'd be better than working on the dock and getting hurt like Papa did. Are you sure you could pay me every Friday?"

"I'm sure I can when I get the lot finished. Now I can only pay you for three half days a week."

"Living here someday sure would be nice. When can I start working?"

"I don't know yet."

"I hope it works out," Scott added. "I've been counting on working in your cabbage patch again this year too."

*   *   *

One day, Jack came out on a streetcar to see Rick unexpectedly but found him gone. Jack and Emil sat down to visit. In the conversation, Emil suggested that he could teach Jack to drive. Jack was so excited. He figured he could sleep in the morning, take his driving lesson in the afternoon, and still get to work on time. Usually Rick used the car, but with gasoline rationed, he sometimes took streetcars. On those days Jack could take his driving lessons with Emil.

Rick was willing to work ten hours a day, seven days a week to learn his new business. He thought about dropping his spring accounting course but decided to stick with it because he knew how important keeping financial records were to any business. Rick soon realized how much he needed his father to talk with him about problems.

Rick was discouraged one afternoon in May and drove by to see Jack. "Can you ride out to the park bench?"

"Let's go," answered Jack as he climbed into Rick's car.

As they sat on the park bench, Rick felt better just relaxing and enjoying the pleasant park scene. They missed Matt, but they knew he would be arriving soon.

Jack asked, "How's your business coming along, Rick?"

"It's not like parking nine cars in Mr. Sarno's front yard."

"Rick, you'll struggle for awhile, but you'll make it."

"Thanks, Jack. I'll try to be patient. Since you've learned to drive, why don't you drive the car back to your house?"

"Swell. Your father's a good teacher. He doesn't talk much, but what he says is important."

Rick was pleased to see that Jack had become a competent driver.

*   *   *

On the bus to St. Louis, Matt reflected on who he was and where he was going. He had the same hollow feeling that he'd had when he left St. Louis. Matt had been living at the University of Missouri for only a year, but he enjoyed the campus environment with all the vibrant young students. Now, all that was gone.

Matt thought, 'Everything is going so fast. I'll soon be in St. Louis, and I'll only have one day before I get on the train to New Orleans. On my eighteenth birthday I'll be on a navy bus.'

Matt had given the recruiting officer his home address as New Orleans, but the truth was he didn't have a home. The recruiting officer had told Matt that he had the physical and mental qualifications to be an excellent navy pilot. Matt knew that he'd have to work hard to master the training, but for now he would focus on today.

Jack warmly greeted Matt at the bus station.

Matt asked, "Where's Rick?"

"He's been as busy as a barge captain landing at the levee in a Mississippi River flood. We'll see him in a minute."

Jack got Matt's suitcase and walked with him to the Broadway lot and visited with Scott before Rick arrived.

"Hey, Matt!" Rick called. "I have some sandwiches for us, and I'm going to celebrate your arrival by taking the afternoon off."

On their way to Forest Park, Rick stopped at the Walnut Street lot to pick up the morning collection. When they finally were sitting on their park bench, Rick sighed his relief, "Fortunately, this place never changes."

Matt suggested, "Let's just sit for awhile."

After a couple of minutes, they laughed as they all started talking at once. They had a lot of catching up to do. Matt told them all about Columbia, Missouri, and about the good year he'd had.

"What about the marines?" asked Matt turning to Jack.

"On my birthday I'll be on a train to South Carolina, and then on a bus to Parris Island."

Matt asked, "What kind of an assignment do you expect?"

"The recruiting sergeant told me that I'd probably be trained for combat infantry."

Matt turned to Rick and asked, "How in the world did you get into such a big business?"

Over the next twenty minutes, Rick explained what had happened in the past few months. Matt commented, "It seems impossible that all that could have happened in such a short time."

"It seems real to me," Rick explained. "I'm having a hard time keeping my head above water. It's like when we learned to swim at Fairgrounds Park. Going into deep water for the first time, we weren't sure we could stay on top."

"Tell me about AP, Inc."

"I don't know much about corporations, but I'll take a correspondence course this fall to learn more."

"What's your most serious problem?"

"The cash in my savings account is almost gone, and I have to pay Mr. Marcus, Scott, and Mr. Mills on a regular basis, even though my income isn't always the same from week to week. I've got to get a larger cash account."

"You will, Rick. By the way, I have a gift for both of you," said Matt as he handed each of them a photo.

"I'll be damned," Jack said.

"Thanks, Matt," Rick said softly. He looked strangely sad and pleased at the same time.

Matt explained, "I found the negative of this picture that the guy took of the three of us on our park bench when we were thirteen, and I decided to get these prints for us to keep while the war separates us."

Goodbye was not easy for them. Matt was leaving tonight, and Jack would follow in two weeks.

Jack said, "Louie and I don't have much, but we have each other. At first I didn't worry about joining the Marine Corps. Now I'm getting scared about leaving, and I'll miss Louie. No telling when the three of us will be together again either."

"I feel that way too, Jack," said Matt.

Rick added, "I feel like I'm losing two brothers. I'm determined to make a success of my parking business while you're gone. Hopefully, I'll be able to help you when you get back."

Matt asked, "Rick, does your family have enough income now that your father isn't working on a regular job?"

"Being poor all our lives has taught us to learn how to live in tough times. My family doesn't really need much more than the house and the garden. Until the business grows, my first priority is to meet my obligations."

Rick drove Jack home. Then he took Matt for a short visit with his parents before leaving him at Union Station later that evening.

*   *   *

Before leaving for Parris Island, Jack visited the Baumans. He gave Emil a lightweight folding chair to use when he worked at the ballpark lot. Their evening together was ominous, like a dark cloud covering the sun, predicting a terrible storm. The Baumans tried unsuccessfully to bury their thoughts that they might not see Jack again.

The next day Rick drove Louie and Jack to Union Station and waited while they had their time alone. Just two weeks ago he'd told Matt goodbye. Rick felt a feeling of abandonment that was indescribable.

11

June 1942-August 1945: Jack

As Louie and Blackjack stood beside the train, they were traumatized, not knowing what to say to each other. They had each gone over in their minds things they wanted to say when it was time to leave. Those words disappeared in the passion of the moment. They just held each other tightly until the train moved and Jack jumped on, waving goodbye to Louie.

Three months at Parris Island stretched a man to the limits of his breaking point, both physically and mentally. Some men broke and left the marines for other services; most did not. They had been recruited to handle the treacherous, humiliating training, and they did.

Jack left Parris Island a different person. He was confident that he could do what was needed to be done when he had to do it. Marines expected to be sent into the most dangerous battles and into the worst fighting conditions. He was glad he would be with dedicated, well-trained fighting men.

Shortly after arriving at Camp Pendleton, California, Sergeant Baer called Jack and six other privates who had been on guard duty with him into his office. He told them that they would be going to the firing range. That morning they fired their rifles from all positions. In the afternoon they fired other hand weapons and then threw grenades. Toward the end of the day, they took their rifles apart, cleaned them, and put them back together. In the background they kept hearing:

> READY FROM THE RIGHT;
>
> READY FROM THE LEFT;
>
> READY ON THE FIRING LINE;
>
> FIRE!

They heard that command all night in their sleep.

The next morning Sergeant Baer gave orders for Jack and three other privates of the seven who had been with him on the firing line to report to his office. They entered and stood at attention, but Sergeant Baer put them at ease. "No more chicken shit. Call me 'Wooly' when we're alone."

The tough kid from New Jersey, Tony Lucassi, said, "Okay, Wooly Baer, what's going on?"

Sergeant Bear responded quickly, "Keep your fuckin' pants on, and you'll find out; if you don't, you'll be assigned to KP every weekend you're in this camp."

The privates got the message. Sergeant Baer was one of them, but he was in command. They'd better respect him.

"The seven of you I sent to the firing line were rated 'exceptional' at Parris Island. You four scored best."

'WOW!' thought Jack.

"You're going to work with me learning to be scouts. Jack and Bo will be partners. Tony you'll partner with Danny."

"What are scouts expected to do?" asked Tony.

"Scouting teams are trained to search out enemy locations and to shoot snipers. You'll learn more about that, starting now. Study these field reports and procedure manuals."

Bo Johnson from Mississippi said, "I don't read good."

"Work at it. Your life and the lives of other marines depend on it. Jack'll help you."

They studied hard, and Sergeant Baer came by to answer questions. Later they were tested verbally. All four did well and Wooly said, "Rifle scouts are important, and you're each being promoted to corporal. Congratulations."

Jack and his new friends finally got their first weekend passes. They headed for a beautiful Pacific Ocean beach to enjoy swimming and girl-watching, which was often part of barrack talk. Having lived on rivers, Jack couldn't imagine walking into the ocean without being swept downstream.

The next weekend Jack and his friends went to the USO in La Jolla, near where his company had taken twenty-five mile hikes. The USO club and local volunteers provided military personnel something to eat and a nice place to visit.

Jack left the USO and walked a few blocks to a city park on a cliff overlooking the ocean. He saw a ledge a little way down the cliff and climbed down to watch the white-capped waves surging into shore and to think about Louie.

Louie did not write letters, but once Rick had addressed a postcard of the Mississippi River to Jack and had Louie write on it in carefully drawn letters: "Blackjack, I miss you. Don't get killed. Louie." Jack always carried that postcard with him.

One weekend Jack got separated from his friends. Marines on a truck to San Diego invited him to come with them, so Jack followed along as they checked into a dollar-a-night hotel before going to a crowded bar. A young girl pushed her breasts into Jack's shoulder and temptingly said, "I'm Misty. How about buying me a drink?"

As they finished their drinks, Misty asked, Where're you staying?"

"Around the corner at the Candle Light Hotel."

"Jack, let's go to your room," Misty coaxed.

As Jack left with Misty, he waved to his fellow marines, who gave him a thumbs-up sign. They seemed more confident about his decision to leave with Misty than he did.

The Candle Light Hotel was dirty and run down but gave special, hourly or all-night rates to marines. An old church pew was in the small lobby. Jack's room had a bed and two wooden chairs that showed two colors where the paint had peeled. A small closet had two twisted wire hangers.

When they got to the room, Jack was confused and strangely excited. Misty tossed off her shoes, fluffed a pillow, and jumped onto the bed. Before Jack could say anything, Misty said, "Got any two dollar bills? I save them, you know."

Marines at the barracks had told stories about situations like this, but Jack was still unsure of himself. He gave Misty two dollars and babbled, "I'm not sure what to do next. I've never been in a room alone with a girl before."

"Oh, shit," said Misty. "The Rabbit Hutch Bar has three dozen or more horny marines, and I draw a virgin."

Before Jack could say another word, Misty said, "You won't have any trouble." Misty was right in her prediction.

*   *   *

The day before Christmas, Jack, Bo, Tony, and Danny got orders to prepare to ship out with a thousand other marines from Camp Pendleton. All leaves were canceled. A Pacific Ocean fog engulfed the camp, adding to the eerie feeling of heading into the unknown. Marines were writing last letters.

Bo asked, "Jack, will you come to chapel to pray with me?"

"Yes, but I don't pray very well."

"I'll pray for us both."

Jack and the other marines were given a big meal before being taken to the port of embarkation, where they marched up the ship's gangplank and down into a hold well below the water line. A set of bunks for ten men took about four feet by eight feet of scarce space. Each bunk had a strip of canvas eighteen inches wide roped to the bunk frame that was folded up in the daytime and down at night. Jack's bunk was a bottom one next to the latrine.

As Jack lay in his bunk, he saw an exit light at the end of the hold moving slowly up and down. He shut his eyes; it helped. Then, as a marine said later, "The shit hit the fan." Men were "puking" in all directions. Some tried to slip and slide their way to the latrine, but most did not get past Jack's bottom bunk. Two of the four men on the bunks directly above him just leaned over and didn't try to get out of their bunks. Late that night, Jack wanted to die, but instead, he just passed out.

A few of the hundred men sharing Jack's hold drew cleanup duty the next morning. Jack didn't, but he couldn't eat for two days while recovering from his seasickness. Daily routine called for being on deck in daylight hours and staying in the hold at night.

Jack had no idea where the ship was going. Rumors were flying fast when the speaker blasted:

NOW HEAR THIS! NOW HEAR THIS!

WE ARE UNDER LOCKED ORDERS.

OUR DESTINATION IS UNKNOWN.

The troops settled in for a long trip. They had two meals each day. Salt water showers were available when a man decided that he had to use one. They kept a man from stinking, but they did not leave him refreshed.

Weeks later the speaker blasted:

NOW HEAR THIS! NOW HEAR THIS!

OUR ORDERS HAVE BEEN RELEASED.

WE WILL DEBARK TOMORROW AT NEW ZEALAND.

The ship docked, and the marines were settled in camp. Jack

and Bo met Sergeant Dan "Sly" Burton, who had been recovering from wounds he had received in the early fighting at Guadalcanal. He was expecting them.

Sly said, "I'm glad you two corporals are assigned to me. You must be excellent scouts, or Wooly wouldn't have sent you to me. I saved his life once, and he never forgot it."

GUADALCANAL

In the late spring of 1943 the Third Marine Division was sent to Guadalcanal to relieve the exhausted First Marine Division. The First was being sent to Australia for rest and recuperation. Jack came down the side of the ship on a rope ladder and crowded into a landing craft.

Tokyo Rose in her radio broadcast reminded them that there were still Japanese remaining on Guadalcanal, and occasionally a Japanese plane, referred to as "Washing Machine Charlie," would fly over at night from Bougainville to disturb the area. Even so, the First Marine Division had successfully fought the last major battle on Guadalcanal.

On their third scouting mission, Sly spotted a sniper and motioned Jack and Bo to head back. Sly made his report to Captain McNally who ordered, "Get six days of food and water and be ready to lead two platoons. You knock off the snipers, and the platoons will attack the camp the snipers are protecting."

Close to the place where they had been a few days before, Sly shot a sniper and instantly rolled over twice before a shot hit near him. Bo shot the second sniper, who'd given away his cover. The platoons, not far behind them, moved forward with the scout team to the enemy's fortified camp. The marines surrounded and killed twelve Japanese soldiers defending their base. The dead enemy soldiers looked as though they'd had little to eat. One marine was wounded in the attack.

Day after day the scouts and patrols would search the jungle and find nothing. Staying alert was hard, but Jack remembered Wooly's warning about the dangers of boredom. In the fall their division went through amphibious training. Their full routine was over.

BOUGAINVILLE

On November 1, 1943 Jack made his first amphibious landing on the shores of Empress Augusta Bay. Bougainville was an island about 150 miles long at the north end of the chain of Solomon Islands. Jack was told that the Japanese had prepared to defend an assault with 35,000 troops and six airfields at Choiseul.

Japanese officers were surprised and unprepared when the Third Marine Division landed on a swampy shore on the opposite side of the island. The Japanese beach defense, although fortified, was without adequate manpower, ammunition, or heavy equipment. Navy and marine fighter planes turned back Japanese Zeros trying to reach the landing marines.

Time was crucial; rain was coming. No time to think! Just do something! Jack flattened himself before moving forward. Sly lobbed grenades over a coconut log barrier, while Jack and Bo readied themselves to shoot the soldiers running from the grenades. The Americans soon secured the area.

Marines were unloading tons of supplies from LSTs (Landing Ship Transports). LCIs (Landing Craft Infantry) were bringing in more marines. The Seabees were frantically trying to construct a landing strip for marine aircraft, but they had to drain the swamp first, which was causing dangerous delays. Building this airstrip seemed an impossible task, but the Seabees finally did it in record time.

After the infantry had secured the beach, they went into the jungle to find hidden or approaching enemy. Knowing that there were thousands of Japanese troops moving across the mountainous jungle in their direction was not comforting. After marine patrols located a Japanese base camp near a trail being used to move soldiers and supplies, Captain McNally's company was assigned the responsibility of finding the camp and destroying it.

Sly, Jack, and Bo led their company deeper and deeper into the jungle. They wondered if they would ever get out. As they sloshed through the stench and decay, they realized that the dense rain forest was more of a threat to them than the Japanese were. Pressing forward, the marines fought off leeches, fire ants, and thick clouds of malaria-infested mosquitoes. The scouts were no longer able to spot a sniper fifty yards ahead.

On the second day into the jungle, a lone sniper killed Sly. Jack killed the enemy soldier who'd fired the shot, but it was too late to help their friend. Sergeant Dan "Sly" Burton had survived wounds in so many bloody battles before, but now he was dead.

The marines moved on, and a day later, Jack and Bo found the Japanese camp. They gave Captain McNally the information he needed. His company surrounded the camp and killed the platoon of Japanese soldiers defending it. One marine was killed and four were wounded.

After the battle, Jack was with Captain McNally searching bodies for possible information about troop movements. Jack kicked the head of each dead soldier before searching his body. Out of the corner of his eye, Jack spotted a slight movement from a soldier that Captain McNally had leaned over to search. Instantly lunging forward, Jack rolled the seemingly dead soldier over on a grenade with the pin pulled. Shrapnel hit Captain McNally in the arm and hit Jack in the foot, but they were alive. Five days later the exhausted marines managed to get their dead and wounded back to the beach.

Tents with cots protected by mosquito nets served as a field hospital for sick and wounded marines. Patients could rest and stay clean, but medical care was limited. Men with malaria or dysentery outnumbered those with gunshot wounds.

After two days in the field hospital, the doctor in charge gave orders to have forty-six of the more seriously sick and wounded, including Jack and Captain McNally, put on a destroyer transport and returned to Guadalcanal. When Jack and Captain McNally arrived at the base hospital, doctors removed pieces of shrapnel, treated infections, set broken bones, and stitched up their wounds.

After Captain McNally was able to get up and around, he came to see Jack. "Thanks for saving my life. I'll search the next dead Jap differently."

"Sir, I was taught that there are no dead Japs."

"You were taught well."

"How soon will we get back to our company, Captain?"

"The doctor says that it will take six or more weeks for us to heal and go through rehab. I've been promoted to major and reassigned to the Fourth Marine Division in Hawaii on maneuvers. At my request, you've been promoted to sergeant and reassigned to me as a lead scout."

"Thank you, sir. I'll be proud to scout for you."

"We'll be leaving with a load of sick and wounded marines tomorrow. We'll join the Fourth Division as soon as we get a medical release." As Major McNally left, he smiled. "By the way, Sergeant, you've been awarded the Silver Star." Jack was stunned and could not reply.

In March 1944 Jack was ready for active duty with the Fourth Marine Division. Corporal Mike Smith from Newton, Illinois, and Corporal Will Besterfield from St. Claire, Missouri, were Jack's scouts. Will knew the St. Francis River area in Missouri, but he had done most of his hunting along the Meramec River with his younger brother, Josh.

Jack taught Mike and Will the things that Wooly and Sly had taught him. They listened carefully and learned. Training was intense, and Jack knew from their amphibious training that their next battle would be quite different from the jungles of Guadalcanal and Bougainville.

SAIPAN

Operation Forager was reportedly made up of ships carrying 127,000 men. This American assault force was to secure the Mariana Islands, specifically Guam, Saipan, and Tinian. Airstrips on these islands were essential for later assaults closer to the Japanese mainland.

On June 15, 1944, wave after wave of fighting men came onto the shores of Saipan and landed along an eight-mile strip of beach. Before the first day was over, more than 20,000 marine and army men were ashore with their weapons and supplies.

Jack was with the second wave, and his LCI slowly moved toward the beach. He heard the thunderous shelling from American battleships attempting to destroy Japanese fortifications. Planes from aircraft carriers were successfully fighting Japanese Zero fighters and Judy bombers to prevent them from strafing and bombing landing troops.

As Jack's landing craft hit the beach, he and other marines jumped out and quickly moved forward into the sand dunes. They adjusted their equipment and looked along the shore, seeing the scattered bodies of the dead and dying. They could hear exploding Japanese artillery shells. Realizing that the American battleships hadn't knocked out Japanese fortifications as expected, Jack was terrified.

Major McNally ordered Jack to move ahead with Will and Mike and then to report back. Moving forward and keeping his eyes focused on the terrain ahead for snipers, he heard Will's voice. Reaching his hand back to signal, he pushed against the still bleeding stump of the leg of a dead marine. Jack quickly checked. It wasn't Will or Mike. They dug in and waited for Major McNally.

When Major McNally arrived, Jack reported. "Major, one Jap machine gun two hundred yards ahead is causing most of the casualties around us." Major McNally told Jack to guide Lt.

Jackson's platoon to a place where they could get in position to capture the machine gun.

The platoon succeeded but paid the price of three dead and six wounded. The battalion caught up and spent the night in the vicinity of the captured machine gun, which was now being used to protect the exhausted marines while they slept.

Battalion commanders reported casualties and received instructions from Lt. Colonel Jeb Williams. At dawn marines were moving forward on an eight-mile front. A report came that a banzai assault had occurred three miles down the line.

Jack instructed Mike and Will, "We are to protect advancing marines. Shoot any Japanese sniper in range who shows himself." To avoid giving away their location after each shot, they rolled and waited two minutes before firing again.

Jack, Will, and Mike moved forward slowly all day and then waited. Major McNally caught up with them with new instructions, "Battalions in our regiment are to take the town of Garapan and then join other regiments to take the airfield at Aslito on the north end of the island."

By July American troops had killed or captured almost all of the 30,000 well-armed and trained Japanese soldiers. Many of the 3,000 native Chamorros and 20,000 Japanese civilians had surrendered, and the soldiers were giving them food and water. Battlefields were being cleared of the dead and wounded.

The vicious land battle for Saipan was reportedly won at a cost of 13,000 American marine and army casualties, but it was a major step in getting closer to the Japanese mainland.

*   *   *

On July 9 Jack was riding in the front seat of a jeep guarding Lt. Colonel Williams and Major McNally in the back seat. The officers' assignment was to tour the island to help develop a plan for occupation troops. Since his earlier fighting had not included civilians, Jack was observing a side of war that he had not seen before. In Garapan he saw confused civilians walking aimlessly in the streets.

As Colonel Williams stopped the jeep occasionally to obtain information, Jack saw exhausted marines using flame throwers and explosives to burn or blast the remaining resisting Japanese out of their fortified caves. The stench of burning flesh defied description.

At one stop a marine officer told them of a reported banzai charge ending in Tantapon Harbor. Japanese soldiers and some civilians had charged with swords and bayonets as their ammunition ran out. Two thousand Japanese and 500 marines had died.

Riding through that battlefield, Jack saw a dead marine with a knife in his neck and a dead man on top of him. The marine must have shot the Japanese soldier as he'd lunged with his knife. That picture burned a memory into Jack's mind, reminding him forever of the brutality of hand-to-hand combat.

Some time later they came upon a mass burial. Seabees dug pits with their large, dirt-moving equipment and buried thousands of Japanese bodies. Trucks were continually bringing bodies to be bulldozed into the pit.

Suddenly, at the side of their jeep, Jack shot a woman pulling a grenade from her loose dress. Jack's shot rang out just as she pulled the pin of the grenade. It exploded in her hand as she fell.

Major McNally calmly said, "Thanks, Jack. Stay alert."

Jack needed to be alert. There were other incidents along the way when he had to use his rifle. They drove by soldiers taking Japanese prisoners, wearing only G-strings, to a prison camp in trucks to be fed, sheltered, and interrogated. As they continued their tour, Colonel Williams spoke to some wounded men who had been in the vicious battle for the 1,554-foot-high Mt. Tapotchau. One battalion had nearly a hundred percent casualties from a night banzai assault.

As their jeep approached the Morubi Bluffs, they heard

Japanese interpreters broadcasting that persons surrendering to American troops would be treated well. This assurance did not attract many of the Japanese civilians who chose Gyokusaii, or "death with honor for their emperor," rather than surrender. Men, women, and children of all ages were throwing themselves off the 800-foot cliffs. Seeing a mother jump off the bluff holding her child's hand was among Jack's recurring nightmares. They drove back and reported to general officers what they had heard and observed.

TINIAN

After the major battle of Saipan, the military gave Jack his issue of a case of beer and a carton of cigarettes and gave him time to rest. Two weeks later he boarded an LCI with new rations of ammunition, food, and water. He was ready for the invasion of Tinian Island, just a few miles from Saipan.

On July 24, without early opposition, the marines landed on the beach and moved rapidly into the sugar cane fields of Tinian. The attack strategy was completely successful. Some of the marines drew Japanese troops south while other marines landed on the north side. This time the heavy air strike and battleship artillery shells had successfully softened defenses.

Marines killed or captured a reported 10,000 Japanese soldiers defending the island, with only 400 marine casualties. Jack had gone through the bloody battle of Saipan without a scratch, but at Tinian he had been hit in the butt by a piece of shrapnel. The wound was painful, requiring sixteen stitches, but he remained on active duty.

IWO JIMA

On February 19, 1945 the Fourth and Fifth Marine Divisions, with the Third Division behind them in reserve, were moving toward Iwo Jima. They had reached the shore in fleets of different kinds of landing ships. Battleships fired heavy artillery shells over them in a continuing attempt to soften Japanese fortifications.

Major McNally had told Jack before the landing, "Iwo Jima will be well fortified and manned with suicidal defenders who know the strategic importance of this battle. Landing strips on the island are necessary to enable American B-29's to bomb the Japanese mainland more safely and accurately."

Iwo Jima was a narrow island of eight square miles of volcanic rock defended by 23,000 Japanese soldiers. Mt. Suribachi, the 550-foot-high point of the island, was a volcanic fortress filled with deep caves and tunnels that the Japanese had spent months building. Navy carrier planes had turned back the enemy planes, but Japanese defenses had not been destroyed by the heavy bombardment of battleship artillery shells.

Jack splashed into the shallow water and onto the shore. Japanese were firing heavy artillery shells from their Mt. Suribachi fortress onto the landing American soldiers. The beach was cluttered with shattered equipment and bodies from earlier landings.

Jack moved forward with Will and Mike. Others were landing, and they had to get off the beach. He moved forward a hundred yards, sometimes sinking to his knees in volcanic ash. He stopped behind the body of a dead marine whose open eyes stared blankly and directly into the sun.

Jack finally got out of the volcanic ash and crawled and ran on the barren, volcanic rock that defied digging. As they moved forward out of the direct target of the artillery shells, they were met by holed-up snipers and later by machine guns and mortars from caves.

American and Japanese soldiers were given the same command:

"kill or be killed." No civility, just the sheer power of men against men until one side didn't have a man left.

Jack moved relentlessly forward for hours that seemed like days. A sniper rose to fire from a hole in the lava rock directly in front of Jack. Will killed the sniper before he could shoot. Jack turned his head in time to watch in horror as Will's face and part of his head disappeared. Mike lunged forward and jabbed his bayonet into the sniper that had shot Will. Jack had seen enough. Major McNally was not far behind him, so he and Mike waited and reported that Will was dead.

Major McNally said, "Stay close to me for now. The only command we have is to move forward."

Marines moved forward courageously, taking fortifications one at a time. Tanks and infantrymen directed flame throwers into the caves. As burning Japanese soldiers rushed out of the caves, Jack and other riflemen killed them. Their enemy fought to the death with no thought of surrender.

As Major McNally crawled by each Japanese body, he rubbed the face into the volcanic rock. His men nicknamed him "Rub McNally." No more second chances for "dead Japs."

The concussion of an exploding shell knocked Jack unconscious. He recovered in time to watch a marine platoon off in the distance make the final climb to the top of Mt. Suribachi and raise the American Flag.

Heavy fighting continued. On what was named "Bloody March 5," thousands of marines died, including Colonel Jeb Williams. Major McNally was promoted to lieutenant colonel and assigned to reorganize two regiments into one with surviving marines. He promoted Jack to lieutenant and assigned him to lead a search and burial detail.

Jack's men were to locate wounded marines on the battlefield and carry them to vehicles that would take them to evacuation ships waiting at the beach. They were to take dead marines and body parts on trucks to a burial site.

Jack led his platoon through the battlefield while the mortars and artillery shells were still landing in the area. They had only a few hours of sleep a night and kept the mission going nonstop. As a result, many of the wounded men lived. On the second day Jack found Mike who had disappeared on "Bloody March 5." Mike had an arm missing and was dead, but his open eyes seemed to beg Jack for help.

On the third day a mortar round exploded near Jack, riddling his body with shrapnel. Colonel McNally, seeing Jack unconscious on a litter, scribbled a note recommending a Bronze Star and stuffed it into Jack's bloody shirt pocket.

Combat was over for Marine Lieutenant Blackjack Pershing LeGault.

12

June 1942-August 1945: Matt

The conductor called out, "All aboard."

"Where are the Pullman cars?" Matt asked the conductor. His parents had surprised him with a Pullman ticket.

"Seven cars forward."

Matt walked through the coaches carrying his well-worn cardboard suitcase strapped shut with a leather belt. When he reached his Pullman car, the porter said, "You have Upper Berth 29. It's ready for you, sir."

Matt stopped at a toilet before climbing into his berth. Shutting the door behind him, he looked into the mirror and said aloud to himself, "What's next, Matthew?"

He went to his berth and climbed up the ladder, rolled in, pulled the curtain shut, and lay down. All he wanted to do was sleep. He pulled off his shirt and pants, placed them neatly in the corner of the berth, and slipped under the sheet. He went to sleep thinking, 'Mom and Dad were sure nice to get this sleeper ticket for me.'

In the morning Matt was awakened by noise and lights. He peered through the curtains and saw passengers climbing out of berths. He dressed quickly, ruffled his hair, climbed down from his berth, and got in line for the toilet. The porter was closing berths and assisting people to their seats. When he returned to his seat, Matt looked out the window. Daylight was breaking through the fog over the Mississippi River.

The conductor called, "New Orleans, twenty minutes."

Stepping off the train in New Orleans, Matt saw his mother hurrying toward him. Matt gave her an emotional hug and put his arm around her as they walked to a taxi that took them to the Du Jardin Hotel.

They entered through an archway with a hanging lantern that the hotel kept lit as an invitation to guests. Wrought iron gates formerly had opened to allow the entrance of magnificent horse-drawn carriages. Matt and his mother walked along the passageway on the edge of a beautiful courtyard garden with a fountain in the center.

Meeting them, Pat said, "I'll bet you're tired, Matt."

"I had a good night's sleep thanks to you."

Elizabeth smiled. "I'll walk with you to your room."

At Matt's room, Elizabeth said, "I'll get back to work now. Come down for breakfast when you're ready."

"Thanks, Mom," said Matt, giving her a hug.

Matt had a wonderful time in New Orleans. Every morning before the restaurant opened he came down to the flagstone courtyard for coffee and French pastry with his mother and Pat. The flowering plantings around the courtyard had a restful beauty.

Elizabeth wanted to know about Matt's year at the university, and Matt wanted to know everything about the hotel business. When the restaurant was not too busy, Elizabeth walked with Matt through the French Quarter. Other days he usually rode the St. Charles streetcar to Audubon Park to run.

Pat extended his daily coffee time when visiting with Matt. They talked about the historical influence of the French, Spanish, and English that provided the unique, rich heritage of New Orleans and Louisiana. This common interest helped them to know each other better as Matt asked questions and Pat talked about New Orleans.

"Why did you want to come here?" asked Matt.

"New Orleans has always been home to me, like St. Louis is to you. I lived here until I was thirty-four. My Irish father came to New Orleans as a young man, and my mother and my first wife, Angela, were both Creole and grew up here."

"How did you happen to leave?"

"I'd worked in hotels here and had no intention of leaving. But, when I was offered the position of assistant manager of a Statler Hotel in California, I took the job. My daughter, Mary, loved California and still lives there."

"When did you go to St. Louis?"

"In 1923 when I was promoted to manager of the Jefferson Hotel. I always liked St. Louis, but I jumped at the chance to buy the Du Jardin Hotel and return to New Orleans. A wealthy shipping family built the Du Jardin in 1798. It was formerly known as the Le Faisen Mansion before the owners converted it into a hotel in 1873. On special days my father used to take our family here to eat."

Matt understood why his parents were so happy here.

When Matt and Pat were talking together one afternoon, Pat said, "Elizabeth tells me that you have an interest in history. You might like this book about New Orleans."

Pat continued, "Our hotel was built after a fire burned most of the wooden buildings in the *Vieux Carre*, as the French Quarter was called then. After 1794 multistory buildings had to be built of cement stucco-covered brick and have tile roofs."

Matt nodded, "St. Louis had a fire like that in 1849."

"The Du Jardin construction is *briquette entre poteaux*, or 'brick between post'," explained Pat. "The town house building design is French, and courtyards, arches, and wrought-iron balconies are Spanish."

"When did Louisiana become a state?"

"In 1812 after General Andrew Jackson defeated the British.

There was political opposition by Massachusetts and a few other states that thought they'd lose too much political power to the southern states. Others were concerned that the state language might be French rather than English."

Matt asked, "Did the people of New Orleans speak French in 1812?"

"French was more popular than English."

The days Matt had for his visit went by quickly, and all too soon it was time for him to leave. Elizabeth sighed, "Matt, please be careful; I worry about you. I'll pray for you every day."

Matt held her in his arms to comfort her. "I'll work hard to be a good pilot, and I'll be back, Mom."

The navy bus pulled out of New Orleans leaving an odd assortment of tearful wives, mothers, and sisters. Most fathers and younger brothers fought back their tears.

Sitting next to Matt on the bus was a young man who quickly showed his enthusiasm. "I'm Buster Adams, and I'm going to be a fighter pilot. What do you want to do?"

"I'm Matt Simmons, and I just want to be a good pilot."

"Where are you from?"

"St. Louis, but my parents live in New Orleans."

"I've never been out of New Orleans and never wanted to be until now," said Buster with provincial pride.

"Did you go to a university here?"

"I had a football scholarship and graduated from Tulane University this year," answered Buster. "You?"

"I finished my freshman year on a football scholarship at the University of Missouri."

"I was a running back," said Buster. "You?"

"Left end."

Passengers could see the beautiful gulf coast beaches on the other side of the bus, but Matt and Buster were too busy developing their friendship to notice. Both were glad to have the support of a friend to share an unknown future.

PENSACOLA NAVAL AIR STATION

After rolling slowly past the guard station, down a road lined with live oaks and cabbage palms, the bus finally stopped. A bus ahead of them was already unloading. They got off their bus and started bunching and talking to each other. The marine drill sergeant quickly got their attention with a loud command, "Line up! You're here to become navy officers. Some of you will; some won't."

Buster said to Matt, "I forgot that we have to get through basic training before we see an airplane."

The sergeant spoke before Matt could reply, "Unless you're asked to speak, don't. You belong to me for now. Listen up! I don't repeat! Follow me; stay in line."

Barbers gave the new recruits uniform haircuts, and medical personnel gave them inoculations. After receiving uniform clothing, Matt and the other men were then marched to their barracks.

Buster asked Matt, "You want the top or bottom bunk?"

"Right now I couldn't care less."

Preflight Training started immediately. Words and actions told cadets that time was short and lives were at stake. Army, navy, and marine personnel were dying, and they would keep dying until the German and Japanese military forces were defeated. All of the cadets would be fighting. Those who kept up with the intense wartime training schedule would be flying navy or marine aircraft, and the rest would receive other navy assignments.

Calisthenics, drilling, small arms firing, five-mile runs, and twenty-five-mile marches with full pack filled the weeks ahead. Neither Buster nor Matt had envisioned the discipline and physical training that they were experiencing. They worked hard.

Matt was concerned about the water survival test. He had learned to swim with Jack and Rick at Fairgrounds Park when they were children, but navy flyers had to swim well. Matt asked Buster if he would meet him at off hours at the pool, and Buster readily agreed. He'd had the benefit of a swimming coach and a pool in his backyard as a child. He helped Matt learn and practice the swimming techniques needed to pass the water survival tests.

The time for the survival test came. During the endurance test, Matt swallowed a lot of water but persevered and swam the required distance. He demonstrated his ability to fall off backwards into the gulf, tread water while inflating his life jacket, inflate a raft, climb into it, and paddle across the water. He couldn't have passed without Buster's help.

The members of the class who passed the required tests advanced to Primary Flight Training. They continued to work seven days and nights a week. Unscheduled time was used for study because initial training of fleet pilots included theory of flight, silhouettes of ships and planes, parachuting, and Morse code.

The Morse code requirement washed out a lot of the cadets, but it came almost naturally to Matt. Since Buster had trouble learning the Morse code in the time allotted, he helped Buster practice the code and rhythm until he could pass his test.

Cadets learned to fly in the N3N plane known at the air base as the "yellow peril." Using a gosport speaking tube, the instructor could communicate in the air with the student. They learned about techniques of aerobatics and formation flying. A few midair collisions and casualties from landings made cadets more aware of the dangers of flying. They completed their Primary Flight Training with a solo flight.

Cadets who passed Primary Flight Training requirements advanced to Intermediate Flight Training. They now flew the SNJ plane and had additional gunnery and night navigation training. At the end of this training, most cadets had logged over 250 hours of flying time and had an opportunity to fly fleet-type aircraft. Matt and Buster enjoyed flying and planned to be commercial pilots after their discharge from the navy.

They advanced to Operational Flight Training and were assigned to the type of aircraft they would fly in combat. Matt was assigned to the SBD Dauntless Dive Bomber, and Buster was assigned to the Hellcat Fighter. They had gunnery and ordinance training and learned more about combat strategies. When their training was complete, they had logged about 350 hours of flying time.

Matt had military orders to report to the Naval Air Station at Glenview, Illinois, near Chicago, for carrier flight training. Buster had orders to report to Quantico, Virginia for marine fighter training. Matt could not imagine landing a plane on a ship in Lake Michigan, but he was eager to learn.

*   *   *

The newly-winged ensigns were given ten-day leaves before departing for their new assignments. On the bus ride to New Orleans, Buster said, "I'm going to show you a New Orleans that you've never seen."

After a day of family visiting, Buster came to the Du Jardin Hotel dressed in navy shorts driving his green convertible with white strips that made his loyalty to Tulane University very clear.

"Where are we going?" asked Matt.

"Fishing. Change your clothes."

"I've never fished before," confessed Matt.

"It's time you learned."

Matt changed his clothes quickly. As they crossed the bridge, Buster explained the layout of New Orleans and Algiers. When they reached the swamp area, they got into a small boat with one of Buster's old friends and motored out to a fishing area.

Buster said, "Chape, help Matt while I start fishing."

Matt watched Buster cast his fly and decided it didn't look too hard. But, even though Chape showed Matt the casting motion and how to handle the line, Matt was throwing the fly out like he would a football, with an embarrassing result. He finally did get the hang of fly fishing, though, and caught his first fish as Buster and Chape cheered. Buster caught five before they headed back.

"Chape, these fish are for you," Buster said as they guided the boat back to the dock. Buster opened his drink cooler and took out a couple of beers. Matt took a coke.

"Never saw a navy man turn down a beer before."

Matt shrugged his shoulders in reply.

Buster commented to Chape with sincerity, "Matt's special but hard to figure."

"You guys are both special," said Chape. "Those Jap bastards won't last long when you get after 'em."

As they were leaving, Chape had a final word, "Good to see you again, Buster. It's been a year since you've been out here, and I miss our times together."

"It's been fun."

"Thanks for putting up with me," Matt called back.

The next night, Buster and Matt had a wonderful time going to all the night spots, good and bad. Of everything they experienced, Matt enjoyed the music at Preservation Hall better than anything.

At breakfast the next morning, Elizabeth asked wistfully, "Can't you stay around more, Matt?"

Matt explained, "Buster's getting married in two days, and I'll be his best man. Tonight we want go to Lake Pontchartrain to get oyster loafs. He's taking his fiancé, and I'm taking his cousin."

After Matt had left, Pat privately consoled Elizabeth, "Matt needs to let off steam. He's got some tough times ahead of him."

*   *   *

Buster's wedding was quite a celebration. Tulane football players and classmates all came to the wedding and to the reception afterward. Bands, dancing, drinking all added to the

152

merriment. Family and friends enjoyed the biggest event in all of New Orleans that evening, until the newly weds finally left for their honeymoon to an unannounced hide-a-way.

As Matt had spent more and more time with Buster and his fiancé and their families, he realized that he was falling hopelessly in love with Buster's eighteen-year-old cousin, Marguerite Leone, whom they affectionately called "Marcie."

Marcie was tall and slender. Her slow, graceful walk reminded Matt of the swans in Forest Park. Her long black hair fell softly to her shoulders, and her dark eyes and soft smile seemed to beg Matt to come close. She wore loose, colorful clothing that gracefully draped her lovely body. When Matt held her, she cuddled into him like a kitten.

For the next few days, Matt and Marcie took walks along the river, ate beignets at Cafe Du Monde and rode the paddle wheel steamer. One day they drove out to the plantation country to see Marcie's grandmother. Now all they wanted was to be alone.

Time was running out. Matt asked nervously, "Will you marry me, Marcie? I love you so much."

"Oh, Matt! Yes, yes, yes."

After long kisses, they realized the importance of their decision. Marcie said, "Let's go tell Daddy and Mama. They'll be surprised."

Matt fearfully thought, 'What will our parents think?'

As Marcie and Matt entered the living room where Mr. and Mrs. Leone were playing cribbage, Marcie blurted out, "Guess what! We're getting married."

Mr. Leone pushed his chair back and said, "Would you please repeat what you just said . . . slowly?"

Matt answered, "Marcie and I would like to get married, sir."

Mrs. Leone looked stunned, "Married?"

Marcie's father took charge. "Marcie, tell your mother all about it. Matt and I'll go out by the pool to talk." At the conclusion of their talk, the plan was to postpone the wedding until Matt's next leave.

When he returned to the hotel that evening, Matt was glad that his parents were there to greet him. As the three sat down to coffee in the courtyard, Matt held back his excitement as he said solemnly, "Marcie and I are engaged to be married. We talked to her parents earlier tonight."

Matt's mother was visibly shaken. "You've only known Marcie a few days. Are you sure about marriage, Matt?"

When Matt and Marcie had lunched with Pat and Elizabeth earlier in the week, the conversation had been pleasant and casual. Now everything had changed.

"Quite sure," answered Matt firmly.

"When do you plan to get married?" asked Pat.

"On my next leave."

"This is so sudden," said Elizabeth. "You leave for Pensacola tomorrow morning."

"With the war going on, things have to be done quickly or not at all," defended Matt. "Leaving tomorrow will be difficult."

The next morning Matt called Marcie and made arrangements for his trip back. Elizabeth would drive over to meet Mr. and Mrs. Leone, and then she and Marcie would drive Matt to Pensacola.

GLENVIEW NAVAL AIR STATION

Matt was upset when he left Marcie and his parents but was eager to get on with his training. He knew that Carrier Qualification Training would be the toughest of all his training, so he had to stay focused. The pressure of war was all around the young pilots.

The navy had purchased two old, coal-fired, side-paddle cruise ships and had removed everything above the lower deck almost to the waterline. Seabees had installed five-hundred-foot carrier decks with catapult and arresting gear. These ships, named *Wolverine* and *Sable*, qualified over 15,000 pilots, including Matt Simmons. The navy had selected the inland Lake Michigan for training to avoid the need for radio restriction and the possibility of German submarine attacks.

Matt was a highly rated pilot and made his required qualifying launchings and landings without a mishap. Although he had learned to swim adequately, he was relieved that he had never had a faulty launch and had his plane sink into Lake Michigan as some pilots had experienced.

JACKSONVILLE NAVAL AIR STATION

Matt and Marcie exchanged letters regularly and longed for the day when they could get married. They were disappointed when he and other graduating pilots were flown to Jacksonville, Florida. He'd expected a leave when he had completed his carrier training in the summer of 1943. The navy assigned the new pilots to new aircraft carriers that were coming off the east coast production lines for the Southwest Pacific Command.

Matt faced the reality of his delayed marriage and forced himself to concentrate on a whole new learning experience: living aboard a carrier on her shakedown cruise. The larger deck on the new carrier made his launchings and landings easier, but the rough Atlantic Ocean caused the deck to roll, providing a new landing challenge.

Because rumors were circulating that there would be leaves before their carrier fleet headed for combat, Matt wrote to tell Marcie to get ready for their wedding. Matt received Marcie's letter of spectacular plans on the same day that orders came that all leaves had been canceled and men were confined to the ship.

Matt's first thought was how to tell Marcie. He stayed awake that night thinking of what he could say. By morning he realized his only choice was to be as blunt with her as the navy had been with him. He sent a wire saying, "Leave canceled. Will explain later. Love, Matt." His ship sailed for the Panama Canal in September 1943 to an unknown destination in the Pacific Ocean.

*   *   *

For a year and a half, Matt's home had been his aircraft carrier. Today he was in a reflective mood. He looked at the calendar on his writing desk: February 7, 1945, and began to look back on his life at sea. He was trying to get over his let-down mood after his recent exhaustive battle experiences in support of the Leyte landings. His aircraft carrier was now in the China Sea heading for the next battles on Okinawa and mainland Japan.

Matt thought back to his first few months after he had joined the fleet when his early missions were limited to scouting. Most flights were scheduled to prevent unexpected attacks by the Japanese. Usually a pilot and his gunner/radioman would fly out a few hundred miles looking for Japanese ships and would see nothing but ocean. Their greatest excitement began with launching and later landing on a rolling deck.

After those first few months, the primary role of his SBD Bomber had shifted from scouting to bombing support for the hundreds of thousands of American assault troops. Matt thought about the times he had made his dives through enemy antiaircraft fire to drop his 1,000-pound bombs. He would reload and return again and again, until all the troops were securely on shore.

Antiaircraft flak had damaged Matt's plane four times. His friends kidded him about having a charmed life. Matt was alive and well but scarred by memories that kept flashing back in his mind. He remembered the bombing mission when his Texas gunner/radioman, Billy Joe Weldy, had been hit.

"What a beautiful day for flying!" Billy Joe had teased. He believed that his job included keeping his pilot happy.

"Couldn't be nicer," was Matt's reply.

Billy Joe was older than Matt and prematurely bald. His friend loved to talk about his wife, Betty Ann, and their children, Sandra Lee and Billy. As Matt listened, he had envisioned the time when he and Marcie would have children.

As Matt had started his dive with the other bomber pilots in the squadron, he'd yelled, "Ready, Billy Joe?"

"Ready, Matt."

No more talk. The plane shook as it had approached the Japanese destroyer. Matt had returned fire as he flew through machine gun and cannon fire. After he had dropped his bomb and pulled the plane out of the dive, he had called out to Billy Joe, who was not firing his machine gun. "Something wrong, Billy Joe?" Matt could still remember the sick feeling he had when Billy made no response.

Matt was convinced that Billy Joe was the best. He'd saved their lives several times, like the time he'd shot down a Zero on their tail. Matt kept thinking how Betty Ann and her children would have to face this news, and he really missed Billy Joe too.

Matt's thoughts turned to Robby, Billy Joe's replacement. Robby Esposito from New Jersey had joined Matt a week after antiaircraft fire had hit Robby's plane. His critically wounded pilot had been able to ditch their plane near the carrier before he died, so Robby had been picked up safely. There always seemed to be someone to replace a lost pilot, gunner, or sailor. More would be lost in the future, but the Japanese knew by now that replacements of men, ships, and planes were already on their way. Matt had found Robby to be as capable as Billy Joe.

Matt thought about the excitement and fearful anticipation he'd felt when his first major battle with Japanese battleships and aircraft carriers (the second naval battle of the Philippines) had finally come.

The Japanese were gambling most of their navy in an effort to prevent MacArthur's return to the Philippines. Their strategy was to let over a 100,000 American soldiers and their equipment land safely. Through a surprise attack, the Japanese Northern Fleet, in a pincher movement, would meet their Southern Fleet at Leyte beaches. The American Fleet would face an all-out assault by "Divine Wind Kamikaze" suicide planes. Japanese battleships and aircraft carriers were to get close enough to the beach to annihilate the American landing force.

The American ships were already facing typhoon winds that exceeded 100 miles an hour, causing mountainous waves. The storm had obliterated three American destroyers and cost the lives of 800 men. Other ships were so badly damaged that they had to be taken out of action. Because of the typhoon, the Army Air Corps fighters and bombers were based too far away to join the fight in the Battle of Leyte and, therefore, could not protect army assault landings.

The Japanese naval strategy was to use a decoy to take away the American task force that was guarding the San Barnandino Strait. The decoy worked. The Japanese Northern Fleet got through the strait and headed south toward the now vulnerable soldiers on the Leyte beaches.

A small group of American light-aircraft carriers and their escort ships courageously waged a vicious "David versus Goliath" attack. The Japanese admiral, believing he was fighting the entire United States Seventh Fleet, turned back in retreat. This unwise and unnecessary action of the Japanese Northern Fleet made it possible for the United States Seventh Fleet to attack the Japanese Southern Fleet that had been sighted at the Surigeo Strait moving toward Leyte.

If the strategy of the Japanese Naval Forces had been successful, the 100,000 American soldiers on Leyte beaches could have been annihilated. Instead, American battleships and aircraft carriers destroyed most of the Japanese Southern Naval Force.

Matt vividly remembered starting his roll with other bomber pilots at about 12,000 feet. Their planes were diving at a Japanese battleship that his squadron had been directed to attack. Although he had felt his plane shake from exploding heavy antiaircraft shells nearby, he had held his dive. When the Japanese began firing at his plane with their lighter forty-millimeter ack-ack, he had returned the fire almost instantaneously with his wing guns. Finally, he was able to let his 1,000-pound bomb go at about 2,000 feet before starting his gradual pullout at low altitude with maximum speed. He remembered hearing Robby's twin thirty-caliber machine guns firing into the antiaircraft gunners on the battleship. Matt's bomb had made a direct hit.

In November and December 1944 Matt continued to support the Leyte invasion. He was concerned for the soldiers who'd be fighting the more than 100,000 Japanese soldiers waiting in the hills for them, but Matt had the satisfaction of knowing that the Japanese navy would not be killing any of these American soldiers.

American carrier planes also sank Japanese troop ships with a reported 10,000 soldiers that the American ground troops would not have to fight. Seeing thousands of men floating and swimming hopelessly in the high seas was a terrible sight that he could not forget.

When Matt later read the damage report for the Naval Battle of the Leyte Gulf, he learned that the Japanese had lost four carriers, three battleships, six cruisers, twelve destroyers, troop ships, and most of their planes from Luzon. The United States Navy had lost less than 200 aircraft, a light carrier, two escort carriers, and three destroyers.

Carrier pilots kept count of their landings as an indirect way of reminding themselves that complacency or loss of concentration could cost them their lives or the lives of landing-signal personnel. Matt had made 249 successful landings.

*   *   *

Matt didn't live on memories. Today was mail day, and after retrieving three letters, he headed back to his quarters to read them. He saved the letter that smelled of Marcie's perfume until last. He tucked it under his T-shirt while he read the other two letters.

First, he read the letter from Rick:

> Dear Matt,
> You probably thought I'd forgotten you, but I haven't. I've been working hard developing the business. Please be careful.

Matt smiled and thought, 'Rick's as dependable a friend as anyone could have.'

Then he read the letter from his mother:

> Dear Matt,
> I've sad news for you. Grandma died last week. I went to Gladesville for the funeral. Her friends asked about you. I was proud to tell them where you are.

Matt thought back to the summers when he had lived with his grandparents. He remembered the sad time when his grandfather was in his wheelchair in the truck, leaving his farm forever. Matt felt terrible that he would not see them again, but he would never forget their wonderful times together.

Then he opened Marcie's letter. Her letters always inspired him because she knew just what to say to make him feel good. She was the most important person in his life. Matt was still upset when he thought about how the navy had caused their wedding plans to be postponed when his aircraft carrier received secret orders to depart from Jacksonville for the southwest Pacific.

When he was able to take his attention away from flying, he always thought of Marcie and their future together. She kept him going when combat pressed him to the limit.

He read Marcie's letter:

> Dear Matt,
>
> The weather here is wonderful for this time of year. It's been more than two years since we've seen each other, and I've been lonely. I don't know how to say this, but I will. I married a man who works for a congressman. He was lucky and got a draft deferment. Matt, you're a special person and deserve someone better than me.

Matt stood dazed in disbelief, holding his hands over his face as if to hide the news. He was devastated. His dreams were gone. All he could think about was, 'What's the purpose in going on?'

Just then, an urgent announcement came over the loud speaker: PILOTS REPORT TO THE READY ROOM.

Instinctively by disciplined training, Matt fought off the trauma of Marcie's letter and rushed to the Ready Room to await his briefing with the other pilots:

> One of our planes spotted an oil tanker with three escort vessels. Our assignment is to take them out. You must also take out any enemy planes that might show up unexpectedly. You'll have the usual antiaircraft fire from ships you attack. The Japanese can't continue the war without fuel.
>
> Report to your planes.

As the elevator moved the planes to the top deck, Matt fought off the fog in his mind. He wanted to crawl into a black hole; instead, he climbed into his plane.

Matt's plane flew off the carrier and joined the other planes in search of the tanker. After about an hour, on the vast horizon, several dark spots emerged as their target. Without enemy carriers in the area, no fighter planes would be there to meet them. They had received no losses or hits in a similar tanker sinking a week before.

Commander Dutch Mueller knew that their mission was to sink the oil tanker. He also knew that the two escort destroyers needed to be diverted. He assigned Matt to attack a destroyer.

As Matt rolled over at 11,000 feet and started his descent, his plane shook as he felt the pressure of the dive. He met the antiaircraft fire with the machine guns in the wings of his plane, and his dive speed reduced his enemy's accuracy. At just the right moment, he released his bomb and started to pull out of his dive. Robby's machine guns fired back at the antiaircraft gunners.

He heard Robby say, "You hit 'em, Matt."

The exhilarating moment changed to fear as Matt realized that his plane had been hit and his left hand was hurt. He was unable to pull out at the usual thirty-degree angle, but he did manage to pull out of the dive and out of antiaircraft range. The enemy gunners had hit the fuselage, and the blow had forced a jagged piece of metal into the cockpit, severely cutting Matt's left hand and wrist. He yanked a scarf from his neck to wrap his hand and slow the bleeding.

"What happened?" shouted Robby. "You barely got the plane off the water."

"I'm hit."

"Where?"

"Left hand."

"Can you fly?"

"Yes, but I'm losing blood."

Matt managed to reach the rendezvous altitude and join the other planes. Robby radioed, "Dutch, we've been hit. The plane can fly, but Matt's left hand is badly hurt."

Dutch asked frantically, "Matt, can you hold out until we get to the carrier?"

"I think so."

"Stay close. You'll land first."

Matt's mind drifted into a trance as he thought, 'How could Marcie do that? I love her so much.'

"Matt, wake up!" shouted Robby. "You're losing altitude."

Matt pulled himself together. His wound continued bleeding profusely in spite of the wrap. He prayed that they'd be back soon. He felt weaker and weaker. . .

They finally approached the carrier, ready to land. Sheer tenacity kept Matt alert. He knew exactly what he was supposed to do. He'd done it 249 times.

"You okay, Matt?" shouted Robby.

"Can you make it, Matt?" Dutch asked .

"I'll make it."

"Then go," said Dutch.

"You can do it, Matt," urged Robby.

Matt knew he would have to make the landing the first time in spite of the dizziness engulfing him. There'd be no second try. His plane hit the deck hard, but the tailhook caught. He'd landed his plane safely. The last thing he remembered was a sailor pulling him out of his plane, muttering, "I can't believe what I'm seeing."

After Robby and Dutch had each given Matt a direct blood transfusion, the ship's doctor took care of Matt's hand as best he could. Matt was conscious the next day long enough to ask a corpsman, "What happened?"

"You're lucky to be alive, sir."

Matt faded back into unconsciousness. When he became conscious again, he was being moved by stretcher. Dutch and Robby were walking beside him.

"What's happening, Dutch?" asked Matt.

"They're flying you to Hawaii for surgery by an excellent surgeon that the doc knows personally. You did a hellava job landing your plane before you passed out."

"Is Robby okay?" asked Matt not seeing him.

"I'm fine, " answered Robby a step behind him.

Combat was over for Navy Lieutenant Matthew William Simmons, Jr.

13

1943-45: RICK

Rick had made his last fifty-dollar payment to Mr. Marcus and was standing in front of the Marcus Clothing factory. He had worked and studied fourteen hours a day all year to earn enough income from his parking business to meet expenses. Now things should be less arduous.

He looked at the new factory addition that had replaced his childhood home and felt depressed. Jack and Matt were fighting for the country. Even though he had his business, it didn't seem enough. There must be more to life.

He sat on the curb and spit on a rock. It didn't help.

A voice above him spoke softly, "Is that really you, Rick?"

Rick thought he was dreaming. He was not--this was real . . . pretty Ruth Alger was standing right beside him.

He jumped up and questioned in disbelief, "Ruth?"

"Yes, it's me. You look unhappy. What's wrong?"

"Nothing now," answered Rick as he stared at Ruth Alger, whose lovely brown hair and magic smile were the same as when they were together in first grade.

"I'm late for work, Rick."

"When can I see you again?"

"Tomorrow's my day off. Here is my address. Come by in the afternoon if you can."

"Swell, I'll see you tomorrow about two."

They hugged briefly, and Ruth rushed off to work.

When Rick got home that evening for supper, Maria greeted him as he ran up the back steps into the kitchen, "I didn't know how important your last payment was to you."

"A man can celebrate when he pays his last debt," said Emil as he quit reading his newspaper.

"You're right, Papa, but something even more important happened to me today."

"What could that be?" asked Maria.

"I found my friend, Ruth, or I should say, she found me."

"Where, Rick?"

"Ruth was going to work at the Marcus Clothing factory and recognized me. I'll see her tomorrow."

"Where does she live?"

"In a boarding house a mile from the factory. Mama, she is so pretty and nice, just like I remembered her."

Rick rushed to work the next day and made arrangements with Scott to adjust their Sunday work schedules. When he knocked nervously at the door of Ruth's boarding house, she was waiting. They drove to Forest Park and stopped in front of the Art Museum where they could see the beautiful scene below them. The car was cold, so they went into the museum. It was a restful place where they could visit quietly.

"Where did your family move when you left the river?"

"To southwest St. Louis."

"Where did you go to school?"

"I never went back to school. Both my parents worked long hours with no free time, so I took care of Joy and Joey and did most of the cooking and housekeeping. How did you get into the parking business, Rick?"

"I was growing cabbages on the land where Mr. Marcus

expanded his factory. He traded my father part of his parking business for our home and my cabbage field."

"It sounds complicated."

"How are Joey and Joy?"

Ruth started to cry, and Rick put his arm around her and asked what was wrong. Ruth was shaking when she answered, "Joy died of typhoid fever a few days after we moved from the river. She kept getting weaker and died in my arms, just before Mama and Dad got home."

Rick held Ruth close and whispered, "I felt like that when Mr. Sarno and Mary Ellen died."

"Joy was so sweet," sobbed Ruth, reliving her tragedy.

After a long pause, Rick asked about Ruth's brother, Joey.

"Joey started school when he was seven and always studied hard. He's now in the army, driving a truck in Africa."

They didn't talk much the rest of the day but huddled together, thankful for having found each other.

They continued their pleasant Sunday visits. Rick was flushed with excitement and desperately in love. He didn't yet understand that their friendly weekly meetings were evolving into something more serious.

When the weather got warmer, they'd go to the park bench in Forest Park. They never seemed to have enough time together.

Over the next few months, Rick told Ruth all the things that he had done with Matt and Jack. Ruth told Rick that her mother had bought her a sewing machine and taught her how to use it when she was twelve. Her mother had read directions on patterns for her, and later Ruth began designing her clothes without using patterns.

Ruth's parents moved to California after her father had been drafted. She didn't go with them because she needed her job at the Marcus Clothing Factory. Her supervisor recognized her ability as a seamstress and had her teach nightshift workers how to improve their cutting and sewing skills. She worked six days a week, eight hours a day, with Sundays off. She'd saved almost a hundred dollars from her twenty-dollars-a-week pay.

Rick explained to Ruth how difficult his first year in business had been. But now he was expecting income to increase in his second year since startup expenses were finished and the city had constructed curbs for the Broadway lot. Rick and Ruth were becoming more involved in each other's lives.

One Sunday, Rick drove Ruth over to the Broadway lot and introduced her to Scott.

"Hi, Scott. Rick says that you work about as many hours as he does."

"Almost," answered Scott. "Rick never took an hour off until he found you."

Rick showed Ruth his office and explained, "Scott and I are patching the roof of this old building and painting the walls. When we're finished, Scott'll move into the upstairs. Papa and Jack's father installed the toilet on the first floor."

"Rick, how can you park cars and still do extra work."

"The improvements will make our lives better."

"Our lives are already better," added Scott. Rick had been able to increase Scott's pay and still pay for building materials.

When Rick came home early one evening, his mother asked, "What are your plans with Ruth ?"

"I'm not sure."

"If you love Ruth, why is your decision hard?"

"I want to marry her, but I'm afraid she won't marry me."

"Why would you be afraid?"

"Mama, do you think a girl would want to marry someone with only one hand?"

Maria answered quickly and firmly, "That's a silly excuse for being afraid to ask her. Have Ruth come to dinner next Sunday and visit with Papa and me."

Ruth came to the Bauman home the next Sunday. She visited with Maria in the kitchen and helped her serve. Then after dinner

they all sat on the porch and talked for a long time before Rick
drove Ruth home.

Sitting on the park bench the following Sunday, Rick got the
courage to ask Ruth to marry him. She said yes right away. They
held each other and kissed, feeling sensations that only the love
of a man and a woman can create. The sun had gone down before
they drove to the Bauman home and entered holding hands.

One look at their beaming faces and Maria guessed what had
happened, but she innocently said, "You look excited."

"We're going to get married!"

Maria clapped her hands and hugged Ruth.

Emil smiled his approval and asked, "When will you be
married?"

Rick explained, "We'd like to get married as soon as we can.
It'll be sometime in August.

Ruth said, "I've written my parents to tell them."

Not long after Ruth had written her parents, she entered her
boarding house and found a letter in the mailbox from her mother.
Rick had already driven off, so Ruth rushed upstairs to open it. She
was confident that her parents would be pleased with her marriage
but was eager to hear from them. In her room, she threw off her
shoes, sat down and elatedly started reading the letter:

> Dear Ruth,
>
> I've been crying all day. I don't know how it's
> possible to be happy and brokenhearted at the same
> time. Your letter came today, and we were so happy
> to hear about your wedding. An hour later an army
> officer came to the door and told us that Joey had
> been killed while driving an ammunition truck and
> was buried in a military cemetery in North Africa.
> Dad and I cried and held each other.

Ruth cried herself to sleep that night, thinking, 'I wish that I could be in Rick's arms now like Mom was in Dad's arms.' The next day she told Rick about Joey. He held her, and it did help.

Rick and Ruth had grown up in homes where practical considerations took priority. They would have a small, private wedding and would delay having children. Ruth's mother had once told her, "When you get married, postpone your babies for a year or two. Enjoy each other and save your money."

After the wedding Rick and Ruth lived at the Bauman home and worked out a successful routine. Rick drove Ruth to and from her work. They wrote letters to Matt and Jack telling them all about their marriage.

Emil and Maria were asleep each night when they arrived home. It was like having a private home for themselves. Their intimate moments together made them become like one. They searched and explored each other's minds and bodies until there were no secrets between them.

*   *   *

In January 1944 the weather was terrible, making Mr. Mills' and Scott's work outside very difficult. Rick increased their weekly pay and studied other parking lots to find ways to improve his lots. Some had small entrance buildings for attendants. His father agreed to build similar buildings at the Broadway and Walnut lot entrances. Mr. Mills and Scott gladly assisted, knowing they'd be protected from rain and snow.

Rick's parking lots were more successful than he could have imagined; the curbs, signs, and entrance buildings worked well. Cars were parking in the lots throughout the day and evening. Mr. Mills was doing the same steady work that he had been doing for many years. Corporate income was increasing, and Rick had decided to try to buy an unoccupied, two-story building next to his Walnut street lot. The purchase and demolition to extend his lot would cost about $5,000. Rick did not have that amount of cash in the bank.

When Rick talked with his father, his first question was, "Rick, will the additional income from the larger lot pay the loan payments?"

"Probably not."

"Then why would you want to spend that much money?"

"After the war new cars and gasoline will be available, and the enlarged lot could be filled with cars most of the time."

"What savings do you have, Rick?"

"Nine hundred and forty dollars, and no debt."

"Talk to the bank and then decide."

"Okay," replied Rick.

His banker approved his plan and loaned him the money to complete the project. Rick was convinced that the larger lot would be valuable when gas rationing stopped after the war.

*   *   *

Hilga Goerner was reading the *St. Louis Post-Dispatch* in June 1944. Hilga was startled when someone turned the key of her antique doorbell causing a loud CLANG, CLANG. The doorbell was a modern feature when her father built the house in 1898. She straightened her dress and opened the door to an attractive young couple.

"Miss Goerner, do you remember us?"

With only a moment's hesitation, Hilga exclaimed, "Ruth and Rick!"

Hilga's fondest dreams could not have pleased her more. When they said they were married, she was even happier. Hilga's memory went back to 1930, when Matt, Jack, Rick, Ruth, and Mary Ellen had been so special. She knew that if Mary Ellen had lived and Ruth had continued in school, they would have achieved the same success as the boys.

Miss Goerner insisted that they stay for tea and cake.

They talked awhile before Ruth asked, "Would it be possible for you to teach me to read on Sunday afternoons, Miss Goerner? We'd pay you for your help."

"I'd love to teach you, but you don't need to pay me." answered Miss Goerner, who would now have an opportunity to give Ruth something she'd missed all these years.

"We both have good jobs, and we'd be more comfortable if you'd let us pay you."

"All right, Ruth."

As they walked to the door to leave, Miss Goerner encouraged Ruth. "You'll learn quickly," she said. "I have all the books you'll need to start. Later you can get books from the library."

Ruth had a reading lesson every Sunday afternoon, and Rick helped her as she studied and read during the week. Ruth was as exhilarated by reading as a blind person would be seeing for the first time. When she had learned to read well, Miss Goerner taught her to add, subtract, multiply, and divide.

*   *   *

Mr. Mills accepted each day as it came along and seldom showed any emotion. One day Rick came to pick up the collection and found Mr. Mills walking around the parking lot in a cold rain staring blankly at his wet newspaper.

"What's wrong?"

"Read this, Rick."

Rick looked at the *St. Louis Post-Dispatch*'s listing of wounded, missing, and killed military personnel from the St. Louis area. It read:

> Captain Sunny Williams, killed in action. His company of Army Engineers received a Presidential Citation for constructing a bridge across the Rhine

171

River under heavy small arms fire from retreating Germans.

*   *   *

In March 1944 Rick brought Louie a letter from Jack.

Dear Louie,

My friend Bo taught me to pray a little, and I do when it's really bad. You can say a prayer for me--that one you know. Bo says any prayer's a good one. I was wounded in (Censored) but now (Censored) I'm well (Censored). They made me sergeant.

When Rick had finished reading the letter, Louie looked blankly out the window at nothing and asked, "Do ya think he'll ever get home?"

Rick answered softly, "Somehow, I think he will. He's smart and tough."

Rick was concerned about Louie but was determined not to worry Jack. In late February 1945 Rick asked his father to come with him to see if they could help Louie. When they arrived, Louie had been drinking heavily and looked depressed.

"How are ya, Louie?" asked Emil.

"Not good. My drinkin' got me in trouble at Anheuser-Busch, and they don't want me no more. I can't see them beautiful horses again."

"What will you do, Louie?" asked Emil.

"When the weather warms, I'm goin' ta the forest."

"Do you have enough money?"

"Yes, I've saved some, and they gave me two weeks pay when they asked me to leave. Maybe I'll work for Derk."

Emil said, "You can do it, Louie, but you can't drink so much. Blackjack will need you when he gets home. Maybe the war is over this year. I heard that on the radio."

"Thanks, Emil, yer a good friend. Yer right about the drinking, but I don't drink so much when I'm in the forest. Rick, write to Blackjack, and tell him what I'm planning to do, but don't tell him why."

Not knowing what else to say or do, Emil and Rick waved goodbye to Louie and drove home.

In March 1945 Emil read a *St. Louis Post-Dispatch* article that named Jack as "St. Louis Hero of the Month." Rick took a copy and read it to Louie:

> Marine Lieutenant Blackjack Pershing LeGault received a Bronze Star and a Purple Heart for his heroic action as marines captured the Island of Iwo Jima, moving Americans to within 600 miles of the Japanese mainland.
>
> Lieutenant LeGault was seriously wounded as he led a mission on a battlefield to locate and assist wounded marines after the heavy fighting on March 5, 1945. Lieutenant LeGault's platoon found and carried hundreds of wounded marines to a location where trucks took them to a field hospital.
>
> Lieutenant LeGault also fought at Guadalcanal, Bougainville, Saipan, and Tinian where he received a Silver Star and two other Purple Hearts.

Louie listened intently and was quiet for awhile before asking, "Rick, does this mean that he'll get well and fight again."

Rick replied cautiously, "I don't know, but he's going to get well, and I hope he can come home. We'll get a letter from Jack when he's well enough to write. When will you be leaving for the Ozarks, Louie?"

"I was goin' in April, but I'll wait for Blackjack's letter."

*   *   *

Hilga Goerner stared in shock when she read the *St. Louis Post- Dispatch* and saw Jack's picture with the story of the "St. Louis Hero of the Month." She sat back heavily in her chair as tears flowed down her cheeks. She finished reading the story thinking, 'I remember that pathetic child who entered my first grade class in 1930. He had so much to learn before he could fit into the world in a normal way. I couldn't give him all the things he needed, but I did teach him to read.'

She thanked God that Jack had not been killed. Hilga did not sleep well that night because she dreamed of an undernourished little boy who stood in front of her class with ill-fitting clothes, holes in his shoes, and no socks, saying, "My name is Blackjack Pershing LeGault, and I ain't got nobody but Louie."

*   *   *

In May 1945 Rick received a letter from Jack for Louie and read it to him:

> Dear Louie,
> I'll be coming home. I can't believe it. I got wounded pretty bad at Iwo Jima, but I'm going to be okay. The doctor says I'm through fighting. I still have the postcard you sent me of the Mississippi River, even though it's torn and bloody.

"Rick, wait for me. I wanna be alone for a little while," said Louie as he went into his bedroom and shut the door.

When he came back, he said, "When Blackjack asked me ta say my prayer that I learned from the Sisters of St. Joseph when I was a boy, I did every day, and I must'a done it right. I just went ta my room now to try ta thank God for keepin' Blackjack safe."

"He'll be coming home soon," Rick comforted him. "You can go to the Ozarks now. He'll find you there."

"Thanks, Rick. I'll go ta the forest tomorrow. I still worry about Blackjack, though, 'cause he's been wounded before. A man can't take too much without breaking."

*   *   *

Rick and Ruth reread letters from Matt and Jack. Early letters had shown their confidence and hard-earned pride in their accomplishments. As years went by, their letters revealed other feelings . . . fear, pain, dread.

February 1945, from Matt:

Dear Rick and Ruth,

My hand is hurt, and I'll be coming home. Grandma died. Marcie got married and didn't wait for me. I just wanted you to know. Your last letter reached me at a time when I really needed a friend. I'm so tired.

May 1945, from Jack:

Dear Rick and Ruth,

Don't read this letter to Louie yet. I've enclosed one for him. The doctor told me that my surgery is complete. I don't know exactly what they did, but my upper arm was broken in two places and is in traction. My ribs were broken—they removed one, and the other two are healing. My smaller wounds are fixed but still draining. I hurt!

It's terrible how many marines are dead, and how many thousands more will die when they fight on the Japanese mainland.

Rick thought, 'Maybe I can help Matt and Jack in some way when they return.' He was determined to do this.

175

*   *   *

In the summer of 1945 Rick noticed that his father was not well and would get out of breath quickly. Maria finally talked him into letting Rick drive him to see the doctor.

On the way home, Rick asked, "What did he say?"

"My heart is not good. He told me to quit gardening, but I can still park cars and sell vegetables."

When they were home, Emil was tired and went to bed. By the end of July, Emil had become much weaker and was unable to get out of bed. Rick decided to bring the doctor out to the house. After the doctor talked to Emil, he then spoke to the family, "I can do nothing more for Emil. The pills I gave him should make him more comfortable."

After the doctor left, Rick went to talk with his father.

"Rick, the doctor says I won't be better."

"I'm sorry, Papa. I'll take good care of Mama and Ruth."

"I'm tired now. We'll talk later. I'm proud to have a son like you."

The next morning Emil was no better or worse. Maria said, "I want you to help me today, Rick. Take me by St. Vincent's Church so that I can try to talk with Father Schmitz. After I talk with him, I want you to bring him back with us to visit Papa."

"Years ago both Papa and I had some bad experiences that turned us away from the church. We haven't had confession since. It is important to me, and I know it will be to Papa to have a time of confession."

Rick was confused and had lots of questions for his mother, but simply said, "Yes, Mama."

On their way to see Father Schmitz, Maria confided in Rick for the first time how difficult life had been for them before they came to America. He had always wondered about their lives in Germany and Poland, but when he had questioned them, neither of his parents would talk to him about their past. Until now he had not realized how severe his parents' hardships had been. Waiting in the car, he thought, 'I'm so thankful that they overcame those hardships and made a home for me.'

Maria made her confession to Father Schmitz:

> When I was a girl in Poland, soldiers raped me. I was going to have a baby, but the soldiers made me have an abortion. I was sick a long time. I didn't think that the church wanted me, so I never went back. I left Poland for America to start life over. Forgive me, Father, for my sins.

Father Schmitz then rode with Maria and Rick to see Emil, and he made his confession:

> My younger brothers were killed in the first war. I had to be soldier and kill. Mama and Papa died while I was fighting. I blamed God and left Germany and didn't go back to church. Forgive me, Father.

Rick took Father Schmitz back to St. Vincent's church and thanked him for helping his parents.

When Rick and Ruth came home that night, Maria was sitting at the kitchen table with her face in her hands sobbing.

"Are you all right, Mama?"

"Papa died in his sleep, Rick."

*   *   *

JACK'S RETURN

The Third, Fourth, and Fifth Marine Divisions made their Iwo Jima landings on February 19, 1945, and fought valiantly in one of the bloodiest battles in Marine Corps history. After twenty-six days of fighting, reports came back that not a Japanese soldier was left who was able to fight. Nearly 20,000 Japanese soldiers had died, at a cost of 17,000 marine casualties and nearly 6,000 marine deaths.

After Jack was wounded and received first aid, a truck had carried him to a field hospital while he was still unconscious. When he later regained consciousness, the doctors had already cleaned his wounds and strapped his badly injured arm and ribs tightly to his body. Medical staff evacuated him with other wounded marines to a base hospital in Guam. Doctors in Guam listed Jack's condition as "critical." Five days after an emergency operation, his condition was changed to "serious," and they flew him to a hospital in Hawaii for additional surgery.

After intensive care and surgery, Jack's body healed enough for him to be able to travel by hospital ship to the Naval Hospital in San Diego for rehabilitation. He arrived on his twenty-first birthday, June 19, 1945, exactly three years after he had enlisted.

Jack's physical therapist, Charlie Wilson, took one look at Jack's chart and body and shrugged in dismay, "Your scars tell me that you shouldn't be alive and that we've got a lot of work to do."

"Let's get started, Charlie. I won't get my strength back by talking," said Jack, eager to begin his therapy.

"You're right. Can you raise your arm?"

"A little, but it hurts like hell when I do."

"How much walking have you done?" Charlie asked, trying to determine where to begin Jack's rehabilitation program.

"Only up and down corridors."

"Before you leave, I want you doing two push ups and running a half mile. After you leave here, you've got to work out five times a week," said Charlie.

"How long will I be here?"

"A couple of months or more."

"What do I do now?"

"Walk a mile slowly each day this week." said Charlie. "We'll start working on your arm and chest muscles. Your chart says you had some bones broken in your foot. Is that right?"

"Yes, but that was almost two years ago in Bougainville."

"Let's see it, Lieutenant," said Charlie as he moved the foot in several directions. "We'll work on the foot too. We'd better start your walk with a half mile." After six painful weeks of hard work, Charlie was astonished but agreed that Jack was ready to leave.

While going through rehab programs together in San Diego, Jack had become friends with a fellow marine, Bur Chapman. When Pearl Harbor was bombed, Bur was living with his wife and two children on a small farm home near Cape Girardeau, Missouri. He'd enlisted in the Marine Corps shortly before his name was to come up for the draft.

Bur had been wounded at Guadalcanal but recovered and stayed with his division. In the fall of 1944 he was shot again while fighting at Pelelin. Doctors had told Bur not to expect to have full use of his arm, but Bur's response had been, "I'm a farmer, and I'll need my arm." After months of alternate healing and painful surgery, he had gained back much of the use of his arm, but he would have to wear a protective brace and avoid heavy lifting.

Since Jack and Bur were ready to go back to Missouri at the same time, together they hitched a ride on a navy plane that had a stop at Lambert Field, St. Louis. Bur asked Jack, "Do you have someone meeting you when we get to St. Louis?"

"No, I'm going to take a taxi to the nearest bus stop. How will you get to Cape Girardeau?"

"It seems unbelievable, but my wife Rachel and my children, Dusty and Susie, and our dog, Sam, will meet me in my old Ford pickup."

"How old are your children?" asked Jack.

"Here's a picture that I got from Rachel last week. When I left, Dusty was two, and Susie was six. Now Dusty is six and Susie is ten. Where do you get off the bus?"

"Ste. Genevieve is the closest bus stop to the River Ranch Lodge. My father lives in a cabin about fifteen miles south of the lodge. I'll stay with him this month and then go to school at Washington University."

"I know the River Ranch Lodge. I used to take hay to Derk once or twice each winter. You can ride in the back of the truck with Sam and Dusty, and we'll drop you off at the lodge."

"Swell, that'll get me there a day sooner. What are you going to do when you get back, Bur?"

"Use the money we've saved to trade my 1932 truck for a newer model and get a tractor to replace my horses."

When they reached the terminal, Jack took his duffel bag a respectful distance away and watched Bur's reunion with his family. There was not much talk, just long hugs, kisses, and tears. Bur embraced Rachel for several minutes as the children stood back, looking a little bewildered. After everyone had regained their composure, Bur brought his family over to meet Jack.

As they rode slowly along the winding Ozark Mountain roads, Jack felt as though he was dreaming. He wondered, 'Am I really going to see Louie after all these years?' He didn't notice the sweating through his shirt in the hot August sun.

Dusty broke into his dreams, "Sir, can you tell me something about my Daddy? Mama always read all his letters to me and Susie, but I don't really know him."

"Your Daddy'll take good care of you."

"Mama takes good care of us," defended Dusty, unsure of the changes ahead.

"That's right, but your Mama and Daddy need each other. He loves you, Dusty. You need to help him learn what's happened in the past four years while you were growing up," said Jack, as Sam and Dusty both moved closer to him.

"Do you think he'll like my pet raccoon?"

"Your Daddy likes animals. Tell me about your raccoon."

When the truck turned onto the gravel road to the lodge, Dusty was anxious to get out of the truck and hug his Daddy.

Derk was surprised and pleased to see all of them. They ate

and visited for a half hour before Bur and his family started the second half of their trip home.

When they were alone, Jack asked Derk, "Is Louie okay?"

"He needs you, Jack. He's tired and lonely. He was here last week, and I asked him to stay as a guest until you got here. He only nodded his thanks and told me that he wanted to be in the forest when you got back. Louie expects you tomorrow so why not stay here tonight?"

"Thanks, but I don't want to wait a day longer to be with Louie. I'd like to change this uniform for fatigues and leave my duffel bag here. I need to buy some food to take with me."

"Okay, but the food is on me. I've always felt like a draft dodger, even though the draft board wasn't drafting fifty-year-old men," said Derk sensitive to Jack's years of self-sacrifice.

"When I was in the trenches at night, Derk, I was glad to know that you were here for Louie."

Jack knew that the miles of walking along the river would be difficult for him, so he was soon on his way. He was tired and hurting from the long trip but determined to see Louie. When Jack finally approached Louie's camp, it was already dark. He walked up to the small cabin and called, "Hey Louie! It's me, Blackjack."

No answer. Jack shined his flashlight across the dirt floor and onto the cot where Louie always slept, but he was not in the cabin. There was no evidence of a campfire that evening, and Jack was worried. He reasoned, 'Louie's probably just slow in catching his fish for supper.' Jack walked to Louie's favorite fishing spot, but he was not there.

Jack had been hardened not to overreact. He searched the area in a semicircle, a hundred yards from the camp. Searching farther seemed hopeless, even though a full moon was shining light through the trees. Then he remembered the spot on the ridge where Louie had buried his Grandpa Piney. Jack knew it would be hard to get up there as tired as he was, but he decided to try.

In about twenty minutes, Jack neared the ridge and called as loud as he could, "Hey, Louie!"

A call came back, "Over here."

Their long separation had hovered over each of their lives like a buzzard waiting for an injured animal to die. Now they were safely together. They said Louie's prayer together before returning to their campsite.

The next morning, almost in disbelief, Louie looked at his son sleeping peacefully. He lit a fire with the sticks piled up in anticipation of Blackjack's arrival. The river sparkled flashes of color from the sun that was straight above him shining through the gap in the trees. He went over to the spring where he'd put eggs to stay cool. Blackjack woke to the pleasant aroma of coffee brewing over a burning fire.

Louie and Blackjack spent their first week trading stories about some of the things that had happened to them. They never seemed to finish. The first time they took their clothes off to take a swim, Louie was shocked, "Blackjack, yer more shot up than ya let on in yer letters. How'd they keep ya alive?"

"Good marines, doctors, nurses, and rehab people," answered Jack, showing his appreciation for people who had cared for him.

"You wouldn't have lived with those wounds in my war."

Blackjack explained to Louie that his rehab wasn't over, "I have to do special exercises every day for at least a year. I get out of breath easily and need to walk more."

"If ya need to walk, let's go down the river ta where ya shot yer first deer."

"I'd like that."

Blackjack shot a young deer the next morning. They cleaned it and carried the carcass back to camp. They arrived worn out but still had to salt and smoke the meat. When they finally finished, they sipped some bourbon and slept soundly for ten hours.

The next day Louie said, "Maybe I can get back into condition if we walk and both do yer exercises. I've been sittin' and drinkin' too much."

"That's a good idea, Louie. Our swim each day helps, but we need to walk, and my arm needs special work."

"Jimmy asked me to bring ya to see him when ya got back. I haven't been there this year, 'cause I didn't like goin' alone. Do ya think you could climb up the mountain?"

"Let's walk and swim a lot this week, and then we'll be ready to go to Jimmy's next week."

Their long walks and swims did help. At the end of the week they started for Jimmy's. When they reached an old trail used by animals for centuries, Blackjack had an idea. "Louie, why not walk down the ridge trail to see if we can find an easier way to the top."

"Yep, there might be one. Piney and I only went to the top of the cliff when we were really hungry and couldn't find deer or rabbits near the river. Animals must've had a better way."

Neither Blackjack nor Louie admitted to each other that they weren't sure they could climb up the cliff. After walking almost a mile, Louie saw what might have been an overgrown trail. They pushed through high grass and brush and followed a little-used trail that did wind to the top. Following the new trail took twice as long as the shorter cliff route but was much less treacherous. They were worn out when they finally reached Jimmy's corn field, but they were glad they'd gone the safer way.

When they sat down together, Jimmy told them that he had heard on his radio that American forces had dropped an atomic bomb, causing the Japanese to surrender. Blackjack was overwhelmed by the news and walked out into the woods alone. This meant that there would be no assault on the mainland of Japan. He'd had nightmares of having to kill suicidal women and children. He also remembered battles in which his friends had been killed or wounded.

Louie, Blackjack, and Jimmy had enjoyable days together. They could have recorded their stories as chapters in Missouri history. Before the LeGaults were to leave, Jimmy got serious. "You've been kind not to say so, but I'm gettin' feeble. I had to have someone do my farming this summer. I hate it, but I hav'ta sell my farm and move to town."

"Ya sure, Jimmy?"

"I'm sure."

"How much can you get when you sell it?" asked Jack.

"My neighbors ain't got the money, but the man in town that sells farms thinks I can sell it for about $3,000."

Jack continued his questions, "I know you have frontage on the road, but I never did know about the size of your farm."

"It's about thirty acres. I reckon it's a couple of miles long, but it's less than a hundred yards wide in most places."

While Louie and Jimmy sat and talked, Blackjack was deep in thought. Then he interrupted them, "Jimmy, if you'd sell your farm to me for $2,500, I'll buy it, and you can live here with Louie and not have to go to town."

Jimmy and Louie were startled by the idea. Louie went to the window, and Jimmy scooted his chair noisily. After a pause, Jimmy asked, "Would that be okay with you, Louie?"

"Never thought about it, but I'd sure be pleased to be here with you. I wondered how I'd do on the river this winter. Do you have that much money, Blackjack?"

"Yes. When I was in combat, they issued me everything I needed including cases of cigarettes and beer. In the hospital I just worked to get well. I have a money order with me for $2,776 that includes my mustering-out pay. I'll need the $276 for personal expenses this year."

Jimmy got out of his rocker and walked over to the window where Louie was standing and said, "If you're sure it's right for you, Louie, I'll do it. I don't want to move into town, and I wouldn't have to if you're with me."

The next morning the three friends rode with a neighbor into Fredericktown to see Jimmy's lawyer, who had been holding the documents on Jimmy's property for him. Blackjack opened a joint bank account and wrote the $2,500 check to Jimmy. When they got back to the house, Jimmy and Louie just looked at each other in happy disbelief. Blackjack went to sleep early, but the two old friends talked and made plans late into the night.

In the morning the LeGaults went back down to the river. Jack thought, 'Now, I'll have nerve enough to tell Louie that I'm going to enroll in Washington University.'

Louie's and Jack's days together started with exercises and then swimming and splashing in the river. Afterward, they would climb out of the river and lie on the bank to dry. Trees above them hid the morning sun but not the sunbeams slivering through the tree tops. The sun's filtered rays highlighted glistening drops of water that clung to the leaves after the night rain. Lush marsh ferns grew beside the river in the rich soil left from centuries of spring floods. Each bird had a unique song, except the mockingbird that stole its song from other birds. The river, too, had its own musical sound as it moved rapidly over its stone bed.

Lying by the river, listening to the sounds of the forest, and enjoying the smell of the warm, wet grass, the LeGaults would lazily search out small patches of blue sky through tree tops that waved greetings as their branches swayed in the breeze. A fading crescent of white reminded them, though, that the full moon they had admired on the night Blackjack had arrived would soon be back.

For two centuries LeGaults had lived and preserved this beautiful part of the forest. Blackjack and Louie were resolute about protecting this spot in the Ozark Mountains.

When the time came for Blackjack to leave, he and Louie walked to the River Ranch Lodge. Derk drove them to Ste. Genevieve where Blackjack caught a bus to St. Louis. After the bus was out of sight, Derk drove Louie back to be with Jimmy.

*   *   *

MATT'S RETURN

Matt rode in a plane from his aircraft carrier to an army airfield where he was transferred to a C-47 air transport. Even though the doctor had tightly strapped Matt's hand and arm to his chest, the throbbing pain never stopped during the rough, bumpy ride.

When Matt arrived in a hospital in Hawaii, a surgeon came to see him immediately.

"I'm Max Feldman, Matt," said the doctor. "I have a brief description of the condition of your injured hand from your ship's doctor, my friend Charlie Means. He and I went to medical school together at Johns Hopkins University. His note says that you're a remarkable young man."

"No one will tell me what is wrong with my hand," complained Matt, expressing his concern.

"It is badly injured, but I'm going to try and save it."

"What do you mean, save it?"

"I won't know what I can do until I see your hand. I do know that time is important. I've instructed your nurse to have you ready for surgery in the next half hour."

The orderlies wheeled Matt into the operating room where he was anesthetized. The next thing he knew, he was awake in his hospital room with his heavily bandaged hand and arm in traction. A pretty nurse standing over him smiled. She was the first gentle person that Matt had seen for a long time. Her smile cheered him until he thought of Marcie.

"What's with my hand, nurse?"

"Dr. Feldman will talk to you in the morning. I'm giving you something to reduce your pain and make you sleep."

The next morning Dr. Feldman explained the surgery, "I was able to save your thumb, index and middle fingers, and most of your hand. Your thumb will get back to normal in a short time, and after a lengthy rehabilitation you should get the use of your two fingers."

"How can I fly a plane or play football?"

"You can't, Matt. It's time for you to start thinking about how to meet new challenges."

"You're right, of course, but it's hard to accept."

"Are you right or left handed?"

"Right."

"Good."

"What happens now?"

"I'll check on you once a week. When your hand heals and the stitches are out, you'll be sent stateside."

In May 1945 Matt was on a hospital ship headed for San Diego. During his short stay in San Diego, he was depressed and wanted to be left alone. It wasn't long before other men gladly avoided him.

Matt wrote three short letters:

> Dear Marcie,
>   Your letter came. I'm sorry. You almost waited long enough because I'm on my way home.

> Dear Mom and Pat,
>   I hurt my hand and can't fly any more. I'm coming home like I promised you.

> Dear Rick,
>   My hand's hurt. The war is over for me, and I'm coming home.

In June Matt arrived at the Pensacola Naval Hospital for his rehabilitation program. The therapist introduced herself, "I'm Nancy Barnes, Matt. How are you doing?"

"How do you think?" answered Matt sarcastically.

"I think that you are pretty upset, demoralized, and you hurt. What are we going to do about it?"

"As far as I'm concerned, not much."

Nancy challenged, "Do you want to use your two fingers again, or have them stay stiff as a board the rest of your life?"

"I'd like to use them again, but I'm not really in the mood to work on them today."

"You're assigned to me. Neither you nor I have a choice. We're going to work on your hand together," said Nancy firmly. "Let me look at your fingers."

"Real ugly, don't you think," said Matt dejectedly.

Nancy gently held what was left of Matt's hand and studied it before she spoke, "Your surgeon did a remarkable job to save your two fingers and most of your hand. If you feel sorry for yourself, just look around this room."

Matt glanced up and looked around the room. He saw some men learning to walk with artificial legs, others learning to talk with jaws damaged or missing, and paralyzed men learning to use wheel chairs.

"I don't feel lucky, Nancy, but these guys have plenty of reason to think I am. You made your point, so let's get to work."

"Good. You start by running with those men by the door. I'll start on your fingers when you get back."

When he returned from his run, Nancy tried to move Matt's two fingers.

"Ow!" said Matt, pulling his hand back.

"It's going to have to hurt, but if it hurts too much, tell me, and I'll ease up. It's the only way you'll get the use of them."

Elizabeth visited Matt as soon as she knew that he was in Pensacola. As she entered the waiting room and saw Matt, her tears flowed. As they hugged each other, they were overcome with emotion.

"I love you, Mom," said Matt.

"Oh, Matt. I can't believe you're really here."

"It's me. Let's go outside and find a bench."

They walked outside into the warm sunshine, found a bench and sat down. Matt said, "You look wonderful, Mom."

"You look tired, Matt. Are you all right?"

"I'm fine."

"Let me see your hand."

"You don't want to see it; it's not pretty."

"Matt, I'm your mother," insisted Elizabeth.

"Okay."

"Thanks, Matt," said Elizabeth, carefully holding and examining her son's injured hand.

Matt refused to talk about his war experiences or about Marcie but encouraged his mother to tell him about things that had happened when he was gone. Elizabeth knew that Matt needed time to heal and restore his self confidence.

She remembered the complex emotions that she had felt when her husband had shot himself. Wisely, she didn't try to offer simple answers and said, "I won't try to visit here at the hospital again, but please spend some time in New Orleans before you go to St. Louis."

"I will, Mom."

For six weeks Matt ran each morning, and twice a day Nancy Barnes worked on his fingers and thumb. He didn't believe that there was any hope of ever using his fingers, but after four weeks he was amazed that he felt some mobility in each finger. His thumb felt normal but was weak. In only six weeks, he could close his two fingers into a loose fist.

Nancy challenged him, "Work with your two fingers and thumb daily for a year or so. They'll continue to improve."

"Thanks, Nancy," Matt replied with new confidence. "I didn't think you could do anything with them."

"I've done all I can for you, Matt. The rest is up to you."

Matt was discharged after serving more than three years in the navy and joined other surviving veterans who'd had a part in destroying the German, Italian, and Japanese military powers. These veterans would have to rethink their future. A grateful nation warmly welcomed them home and provided generous benefits as they entered civilian life, but their physical and emotional scars would have to heal slowly.

Matt returned to New Orleans in a navy bus like the one he had taken to Pensacola a little over three years before. He'd been full of enthusiasm, but now it seemed as if it had all been a bad dream. Matt questioned the truth of the old saying "time heals."

Pat and Elizabeth were eagerly looking forward to having Matt with them and thought they were prepared for his arrival. But they were overpowered with emotion when he walked into the courtyard in his white uniform.

Elizabeth broke into tears. Pat jumped up from his chair and rushed over to Matt to shake his hand, without realizing that Elizabeth was right behind him. Customers in the courtyard stopped eating and clapped spontaneously for the returning veteran. Matt was embarrassed by the attention but relieved to be home at last. Pat had Matt's bag taken to his room, and they went together to the O'Hare suite.

On the bus ride from Pensacola, Matt had conjured up an illusion that everything would be normal when he got home. It was good to be back, but after an hour of conversation, Matt realized that his parents could not comprehend his combat experience . . . day after day on the edge of danger with no assurance that he'd live through the next hour.

Elizabeth and Pat were disappointed when Matt said, "I'd like to go to my room for the rest of the day. I need to do some serious thinking about what it means to be out of the navy. It's been my home for over three years. I'll be down for an early breakfast, and we can talk then."

Pat asked, "Don't you want to eat something now?"

"No, thanks."

As Pat started to speak again, Elizabeth interrupted, "Matt needs some time to himself. We'll talk tomorrow."

Understanding that Elizabeth was right, Pat said, "I'll have a waitress bring some sandwiches and coffee for you later, Matt. We'll look forward to a visit tomorrow."

When Matt was alone in his room, he rested for an hour and then thought about his future. 'How could he make up for what seemed to him to be three lost years?'

At breakfast the next morning, Pat said, "You have every reason to feel depressed, Matt. We can't possibly know what your war experiences were like, but your mother and I both know the loss of someone we loved. It isn't easy."

"You're right, Pat. I've decided on a routine that I'll follow while I'm here. At six each morning I'm going to run like I did at Pensacola. Running helped to clear my mind. Between meals I'll rest, exercise my fingers, and do some reading. In the evening I'm going to walk around the French Quarter. Please call on your coffee breaks, and I'll come down to visit."

One morning while they were having coffee, Pat asked, "Why did you decide to go to Washington University instead of going back to the University of Missouri?"

"It was too hard for me to think of being in Columbia and not playing football. In St. Louis I'll be with Jack and Rick."

"Are you still planning to study law?" asked Elizabeth.

"Yes, no use studying aeronautical engineering if I can't be a pilot for TWA."

Matt went by to see Buster's parents. He thought Buster might be coming home since the Japanese had surrendered. Buster's mother came to the door when Matt knocked. She broke into tears when she saw Matt and rushed away without speaking. Buster's father came to the door and welcomed Matt. "Please come in, and sit down."

"Thank you, Mr. Adams."

"I've got bad news for you. Buster was killed in action in the Solomon Islands two years ago."

"Not Buster!" said Matt in shock and disbelief.

Mr. Adams proudly added, "He shot down four Jap planes before he was killed."

"He was the best pilot in our class, Mr. Adams."

191

"Matt, I try to face reality, but Buster's mother will never recover from losing her son."

Matt wondered, 'Can scars left by war ever be wholly overcome?'

"Thanks for coming," said Mr. Adams, who had noticed Matt's hand but said nothing about it.

"Buster was a good friend, and I'll miss him."

At the end of August Matt read a letter from Rick:

> Dear Matt,
> Enclosed is the university application you wanted. I have a place for you and Jack to stay. Did you know that Jack was wounded in March and is home in the Ozarks with Louie?
>
> Matt tried again to get comfortable thinking about his future. It seemed so empty without Marcie, football, and flying. Though he was depressed, he was looking forward to being with Rick and Jack again.

PART THREE

1945-1961: THE CORPORATIONS

THOSE FRIENDS THOU HAST AND
THEIR ADOPTION TRIED,
GRAPPLE THEM TO THY SOUL
WITH HOOPS OF STEEL.

Hamlet, Act I, Scene III
William Shakespeare

THERE IS A TIDE IN THE AFFAIRS OF MEN,
WHICH TAKEN AT THE FLOOD,
LEADS ON TO FORTUNE:
OMITTED, ALL THE VOYAGE OF THEIR LIFE
IS BOUND IN SHADOWS AND IN MISERIES.

Julius Caesar, Act IV, Scene III
William Shakespeare

14

Peacetime Economy

Everyone in America was euphoric as soldiers and sailors returned home at the end of the war, but now these returning veterans would need jobs and reeducation. Wartime industries would have to be shutdown or converted into other businesses. A rapidly growing peacetime economy was sweeping across St. Louis.

Mr. Marcus retired and sold his business, and the new management rushed to have civilian work clothes ready to sell by 1946. Employers discontinued night shifts, but Ruth and some of the more highly skilled seamstresses were reassigned to a temporary design team.

Gasoline was no longer rationed, and companies were manufacturing new cars again. As Rick had predicted, there were not enough parking spaces. The city had renovated Sportsman Park, and the Cardinals were on their way to winning the National League Pennant. The Cardinal management was purchasing properties around the ballpark. Rick had been given an offer for his small lot but decided to wait for a better one.

Rick had savings and wanted to buy an additional parking lot. He'd decided to buy a lot near Washington University, so Matt and Jack could park cars for additional income. With veterans going to college, he knew that university enrollments would increase. Parking would be inadequate.

Rick contacted a realtor and told him what he wanted to buy to help his friends. The agent showed him a house and an empty lot across from the university campus.

Rick said, "I'm not interested in buying a house."

"Why don't you come in anyway?" insisted the real estate agent.

Rick reluctantly agreed, and when he saw that the house was fully furnished, he asked, "Who lives here?"

"No one. The house is to be sold 'as is' to settle an estate."

"You said that the house had four bedrooms and two baths, but I've never seen a house so long and narrow."

"This narrow house allows for a side yard that you can use as a parking lot. I have instructions to sell the house this month for $9,500, including the side lot."

"How long has the property been available for sale?"

"Two months. Could you afford this property?"

"Yes, and it may meet my objective, but I'll need to talk to my friends."

"To hold the property, I'll need $1,000 in escrow that goes to the owners if you decide not to buy the property."

"I'll think about it and call you."

When he arrived home that night, Rick said, "Ruth, we need to talk."

"What about?"

"We've some savings, and the parking income is increasing each month. I think that I can expand my parking business and help Jack and Matt at the same time." Rick explained his plan and asked, "What do you think?"

"You want to be careful not to over extend your business," Ruth cautioned, remembering the painful times her family had on the river. "Would they like the house?"

"I can't find out until they get back, but I think they might even want to buy into my parking business."

"It'd be nice if you could help them. I think the three of you would be good partners. Enough business. Let's go to bed; I want you to hold me tight and tell me how much you love me."

*   *   *

After getting two appraisals the next day, one for $11,500 and another for $10,500, Rick talked to his banker, who assured him that he could obtain a loan. Rick negotiated a price of $8,750 with $1,000 in escrow.

When he explained the purchase to Ruth, she responded, "I hope Jack and Matt realize what a good friend they have. I'm glad that you didn't have to go to war, Rick. I don't know what I'd do without you."

"I couldn't stand losing you either, Ruth. I didn't know that I could love anyone so much."

*   *   *

These were good days for Rick. Corporate income had tripled since he started the business. He had increased Scott's and Billy's pay for the third time. Now he could offer Jack and Matt a nice place to live.

As Rick drove into the Broadway lot, he saw a crowd gathering. A policeman was talking to a sailor with a bleeding cut over his eye. A few drunk sailors were cursing loudly.

"What's going on?" asked Rick to no one in particular.

"A nigger hit Jon Paul in the eye," said one of the sailors.

Rick asked a policeman who was walking Scott to the police car, "Where are you taking Scott?"

"He's under arrest and charged with assault."

"Can I talk with him?"

"Go over to the bus station. I'll come over and talk with you after the crowd is gone."

Rick impatiently waited for ten minutes. When the policeman arrived at the bus station, Rick told him, "I'm Rick Bauman. I own the parking lot where the trouble occurred."

"My name is Flanagan, Rick. I'm glad to meet you. I've watched how you've improved the neighborhood. There's never been enough parking on the streets. The sailors were drunk and bullied Scott. He hit one of them. This is a hell of a time for a black man or anyone else to hit a returning veteran."

"What can I do?"

"You'd better get a lawyer. Scott is at the Second Precinct."

Rick went to his office and telephoned Mr. Mareno, who said, "I'll call the precinct now and find out what's going on."

"Whatever it costs, take care of Scott!"

That afternoon Mr. Mareno brought Scott back to the Broadway lot to take over his parking duties. Then Mr. Mareno went to Rick's office and explained, "One of the sailors cursed Scott and told him that he wanted to 'rub his fuzzy head for luck.' Scott walked away, and then the other three grabbed him, calling him a 'dumb nigger.' Each of them insisted on rubbing his head and wouldn't quit. Scott hit one of them hard enough to knock him down."

"No wonder Scott hit the sailor; I'd have hit him too!"

Mr. Mareno continued, "I was able to get Scott out of jail and taken to the City Court. The city judge had over a dozen people lined up, mostly drunks and vagrants. When it was our turn, I convinced the judge to drop the assault and battery charge. Scott was convicted of a misdemeanor charge and given a choice of ten-day jail sentence or a $100 fine. I paid the fine, and you owe me an additional $200 for legal services."

"Thanks for all you've done," said Rick, as he wrote a check that left his business with only a $210 cash reserve. Rick had over extended his business and would not have enough cash to meet weekly expenses. He thought, 'Insurance doesn't cover everything. I must keep more cash savings.'

He called Mr. Mareno again. "When I bought the house recently, I left myself short of cash. I've got to sell the ballpark lot. The Cardinal management offered me $2,500 last June, so please negotiate between $3,000 and $5,000."

Mr. Mareno called back ten days later, "You hit them at the right time, Rick. They want their new lot ready for the expected World Series games. We'll close the deal on August 30 in the Cardinal management office for $4,300 cash."

Rick began to have second thoughts about purchasing the house and lot at Washington University. He asked himself, 'What if Matt and Jack don't want to live in the house?'

15

Partners

When Jack and Matt arrived in St. Louis, Rick drove them to his home. As they rode, Jack asked, "How's your hand, Matt?"

Matt had kept his hand hidden, but now he held his hand up for them to see, "What's left of it is doing much better. I wanted to write and tell you, Rick, but I just couldn't."

Jack said, "That's why you didn't go back to the University of Missouri. I couldn't believe that you didn't want to play football. I'm sorry, Matt. I'm messed up too."

Rick was stunned and expressed his sympathy to Matt but hid his deeper feelings. He knew it would be especially hard for Matt because he had always had two hands.

When they reached the Bauman home, Maria and Ruth eagerly hugged and kissed Matt and Jack. Ruth said, "It's unbelievable that we're together again."

When their visit was over, Rick drove Matt and Jack to the house that he had bought across from Washington University. Rick proudly said, "Here is the place where you're going to stay."

Matt and Jack were confused.

"What's this all about, Rick?" asked Matt.

"I'll tell you when we get inside."

They walked slowly around the outside of the house and then up on the front porch where Rick opened the door.

"Who lives here?" asked Jack as they walked inside.

"You do for now."

Matt said, "This is quite a place, Rick, but you must be planning more than just having the two of us stay here tonight."

"I am."

"What are your plans?" asked Jack.

"First let's walk through the house."

When they finished their tour and sat down in the living room, Rick explained why he had bought the house. He gave them copies of possible plans that he had written earlier.

> First plan: You each pay low rent and live in this house while you attend the university.

> Second plan: You buy this house and lot from me for the $9,000 it cost me; live in it for four years; get income from parking cars on the lot, and sell it when you graduate.

> Third plan: You buy stock in the AP Corporation and go into business with me. You live in the house without rent. Parking income would help pay the mortgage.

> Fourth plan: You live some place else. I will rent the house and sell it later for a capital gain.

"Wow!" said Jack, showing his respect as he read the written plans. "It's been over three years since I thought of anything but killing or being killed. To be honest, I don't know what you're talking about."

Matt said, "How do you expect us to react?"

"Don't try to react or make any decisions now. Talk about it together, and then later with me."

Matt was concerned for Rick. "What happens to you if we stay at a dormitory and don't use your house?"

"I'll be disappointed, but you won't need to feel badly. I'll sell it in a few years and buy a downtown lot."

Jack was worried for Rick too. "This is a big house, Rick. I doubt that I've got enough money for any of your plans."

"Maybe not. How much do you have?"

"Almost $3,000 when I left California." Jack did not mention that he had already used his money to take care of Louie and Jimmy.

"I've got almost $6,000," said Matt. "If you don't gamble, you don't spend much money on an aircraft carrier. I didn't feel like celebrating when I got back. I'd been saving to get married, but you know how that fell through."

"You have enough money to make any of the plans work."

Rick had thought about the house for so long, he did not realize how confusing his plans might be to his friends. He remembered his bewilderment when Mr. Marcus offered his father different parking lots as an alternative to cash.

Rick got up from his chair in the living room and said, "Right now get some rest, and start your university. Ruth and I want you to stay here for a month as our guests."

"You couldn't have done anything nicer," said Matt.

Jack agreed.

Rick handed them the keys and said, "I'll be back in two weeks after you've learned your way around."

When Rick left, Jack asked, "What do you think, Matt?"

"I'm too tired to talk tonight."

"Okay, I'm going to walk around before I go to bed."

When Rick got home, Maria was sleeping, and Ruth was reading in the living room, "How did things go, Rick?"

"Let me wash up before we talk."

"Sure. Do you want something to eat?"

"No, thanks, I'm just tired and thirsty."

Ruth went to the refrigerator for lemonade and waited.

Rick returned and sat down, "I gave Matt and Jack my plans. They were confused. I told them they'd be our guests this month, and I'd be back in two weeks."

"What do you think they'll do?"

"I don't know."

Ruth said thoughtfully, "My Grandpa Alger was in World War I when horses pulled the artillery equipment. When the soldiers found water, they tried to make the horses drink, and some wouldn't. They were in trouble later. Grandpa's sergeant told him that you can lead a horse to water, but you can't make him drink."

"I wish I knew what they'll do."

"You told Matt and Jack to think about it for two weeks, so I guess you'll have to be patient."

*   *   *

The campus was beautiful and restful like Forest Park. At first Matt and Jack thought they wanted to share a dormitory room on the campus. After thousands of young students arrived, however, they knew they didn't want to live in a dormitory.

One evening they had a long talk about Rick's plans and agreed that they'd be better off staying in his house. They had more questions than answers about whether to buy or become part of the parking business. The rent plan was more logical, but they agreed that they should take Rick's other plans seriously. They liked the idea of working together.

Matt and Jack greeted Rick warmly when he came to see them in mid-September. "You'll have a hard time moving us out of this house. We really feel at home here."

"I'm glad. I felt sure you'd be better off here."

Jack said, "We're thinking of renting your house. We don't think that we'd fit into your other plans."

"Let's get a cup of coffee and talk," Matt suggested as he headed for the kitchen.

When they had settled down with their coffee, questions came faster than Rick could answer them.

"What's a stock? What's a capital gain?"

"Please, only one question at a time. Stock is a part ownership in a corporation. Capital gain is when you sell something for more than you paid for it."

"How do you know that you'll have a capital gain?"

"I don't."

"When do you buy and when do you sell?"

"You buy when you have the cash, and the price is right. You sell when you can do something better with your money."

"How do you know the price is right?" asked Matt.

"Professional appraisers."

Jack asked, "Why are you so sure that you'll have a capital gain on this house, and how long would you have to wait?"

"A few years. The university will have to buy more property with the expected enrollment increase."

The questions and answers continued over a second cup of coffee, and Rick said, "Let's quit the questions now. Get started in your classes. I'll be back at the end of the month."

"One more question, Rick," asked Matt. "Where the hell did you learn all this stuff?"

"The same way you learned to fly. One step at a time. I studied at the library and took night classes at a business college."

"One last question, Rick," Jack asked. "How do we get people to park in the lot next to the house?"

"I'll get a sign up tomorrow. You collect the money."

Rick was back two weeks later. Matt said, "We're ready to rent or buy the house. What would be best for you?"

Before Rick could answer, Jack added, "We don't see how we could relate to your corporation."

"We've got all evening to talk about the house and the AP Corporation. First tell me about yourselves. Do you think that Washington University is right for you?"

Matt said, "It really is a fine university."

Jack told Rick about their first few weeks and explained the G.I. Bill of Rights, "We'll have free college tuition and a living allowance of $50 a month. Because of our wounds, we're classified as disabled veterans and get extra money. I'll only get my disability checks until I get fully healed, but Matt'll get his checks as long as he lives."

"I'd rather have a hand," Matt said bitterly.

"You're alive, and you've got two fingers and a thumb. I'm glad you really didn't lose your hand," said Rick softly.

"I'm sorry, Rick. You've learned to live without a hand all these years, so I can live with only part of a hand."

"I know you miss flying and football, and it'll be awhile before you adjust to your hurt hand, but you will," said Rick sympathetically. "Someday I'll give you a few suggestions."

Jack decided it was time to change the subject. "What about the parking business, Rick?"

"It's a good business."

"Why?" Matt asked.

"What's important in business is income over expense. You'll learn about the complexities of business in your university courses. If we go into business together, I can help you now, and when you graduate you'll be able to help me."

"How much of the business would $5,000 buy?"

"AP has been appraised at $58,000, so I should be able to sell it for that amount, pay the $8,000 bank loan and have $50,000 left. AP has 1,000 shares of stock. If you disregard the intangibles, which would be in your favor, the price for a share of stock should be fifty dollars."

Jack whistled, "That's better than growing cabbages."

"What does all this boil down to?" asked Matt.

"You and Jack could buy the house, or each of you could buy stock and own part of AP."

"What would you do with the money?"

"Probably pay off the bank loan or buy another lot."

"What else do we need to know?" asked Jack.

"I bought a new car. If you come into the business, I'll put a telephone here and leave the corporation's 1936 Ford for you to use. You'll collect money for cars that park next to this house, and deposit it into the AP account each month. You won't have to pay rent."

"We can't stand out on the street and wave cars in as we did at the ballpark," laughed Jack.

"Last week I put up a sign about monthly rent, and the dentist, who has his office next to the lot, called and offered to pay $50 a month for ten parking spaces for his patients. You get customers for the other ten spaces."

"What do you get out of the corporation, Rick?"

"I'll pay myself a salary of $500 a month to manage the corporation. Income over expense will accumulate cash reserves for purchasing new lots."

"What's next?" asked Matt.

"Talk it over together and study this balance sheet. Call me when you decide what to do."

"How do we know that you won't mess up?" kidded Jack.

"You don't."

"You've done amazingly well so far, Rick," said Matt.

After Rick left, Matt said, "You didn't mention to Rick that you spent all your money to buy a home for Louie."

"Louie has forty-seven gold coins in our bank box, and I'll get a coin appraised. Louie got $150 for two coins in 1934."

"How can you talk to Louie?"

"Drive out to see him in the car Rick's giving us?"

The next afternoon Jack and Matt took the streetcar to see Rick. After they got their driver's licenses, Rick gave them the 1936 Ford. They drove to the bank where Jack took one of Louie's gold coins out of the safety deposit box and took it to a nearby coin dealer to determine its value.

"I've only seen a few of these quarter eagle gold coins in all the years that I've been in this business. I can sell it for about $500, with a ten percent commission," the dealer advised.

"Thanks for the information. That's all I need now."

As Jack and Matt walked down the street, Jack showed the elation that he had held back when he was with the coin dealer. "Can you believe it, Matt?"

"I can't believe it, but I did hear it."

The next weekend Matt and Jack drove out to see Louie. He had been down to the river and had brought back several fish that Jimmy cooked for dinner. Jack told them about the house, the AP Corporation, and the visit to the coin dealer.

Louie turned to Jimmy. "Young city kids today get me all mixed up. Maybe going ta high school and college these days is a good idea, but me and you belong in the country."

"What do you think, Louie?" asked Jack.

"Do what you think is right, Blackjack. I'm just glad you boys are home and together."

"Thanks for the great dinner."

"Bye, boys," Louie and Jimmy said, "Come again."

Jack sold twelve coins. He and Matt each bought shares of AP stock and were in business with Rick.

16

Civilian Life

Matt and Jack had trouble returning to civilian life. Matt was bitter, and Jack drank too much. They had conflicts about how to handle their parking responsibilities and whose turn it was to cook. Matt objected to Jack's smoking and leaving cigarettes around the house. Jack complained about Matt's griping and being depressed all the time.

One day in early November, they had a serious quarrel. Matt was upset because he had not done well on an exam. That evening Jack came home drunk and announced, "I met an Army Air Force B-17 tail gunner at the VFW. Claude Mulot flew on twenty-nine bombing missions over Germany. He has a wife and a nine-year-old son. They're paying high rent and having a tough time, so I asked him if they'd like to live with us."

Matt was angry. "What the hell are you thinking about? All you want is a drinking partner."

"That's crap, and you know it."

"Bring 'em over, and I go out," said Matt defiantly.

"They're coming on Saturday to look over the house. I was over to Claude's place for dinner once. His wife is a great cook. She's willing to do all of the cooking, cleaning, and washing instead of paying rent. The sloppy way we've been living is no good. You can get the hell out now as far as I'm concerned."

Matt stormed out of the house.

That night Jack felt terrible and continued to drink until he finally passed out on the living room couch. He woke at eleven the next morning and missed all of his Friday classes. He went to Matt's room to see if his stuff was still there. It was, but Matt had not come back.

When the Mulots came over on Saturday to visit the house where they expected to live, Matt had not returned.

Claude took Jack aside while his wife and son walked through the house and asked, "Where's your friend, Matt?"

"The truth is that he's pissed off."

"Why?"

"He's was feeling sorry for himself, and I didn't handle him right Thursday night."

"What bothers him?" Claude asked, trying to understand.

"He lost half of his hand in the war, and the girl that he was to marry didn't wait and married a draft dodger."

"He's alive, isn't he?" commented Claude sarcastically.

"Hardly. He's not the way he was before the war."

"None of us are," said Claude.

"It was really my fault. Come over Monday evening as we planned, and I'm sure I can straighten things out."

"Okay. Debra's all excited about having a dinner for you here on Monday evening. I don't want her disappointed."

"I'll expect you Monday about five."

Matt showed up late Sunday evening in a rotten mood.

"Where the hell have you been, Matt?"

"None of your damn business," growled Matt.

"Are you staying or going?"

"I don't much care."

"Well, I care."

"What are you going to do about it?"

"What do you want me to do?"

Matt got serious and said, "Quit smoking and drinking in the house and take me into consideration when you decide to do something that affects me."

"Your friendship means a lot to me, Matt. I won't smoke in the house anymore except in my room, and if I get drunk, I won't come home. I apologize for not talking to you before I asked the Mulot family to come here."

"Thanks, Jack. I shouldn't have lost control of myself. I don't know what's wrong with me. If I'd acted like that in an airplane, I'd have killed someone besides Japs."

"It'll be awhile before the war will be over for us, Matt. It wouldn't hurt you to go out and get drunk some weekend."

"I'll work it out, but not that way."

"Matt, now that we're friends again, you have to do something that's important for me."

"What?"

"The Mulots are fine people. They're coming over tomorrow, and Debra is cooking a dinner for you and me. Be polite to them like you've been to people all your life, or so help me, I'll hit you in the head with a brick!"

"You've got your problems, Jack, but you're no fool. Your plan may be the best thing for us. It'll be nice to sit down with a family for dinner."

Monday evening Claude, Debra, and Pierre came promptly at five. Debra headed for the kitchen, and Matt and Claude started talking about airplanes. Jack listened.

Pierre asked, "Mr. Simmons, my Daddy says that you landed airplanes on ships in the ocean. Is that true?"

"Yes, Pierre."

"How could you do that?"

"It took a lot of hard work and practice."

"It's a wonder that you didn't get killed practicing."

From the dining room, Debra called, "You men wash up; we'll be eating in a few minutes."

When they sat down, Claude thanked God for their food and

friendship. After the dinner was over and the kitchen was cleaned, Debra and Pierre came to the living room.

Matt took the initiative, "That was a fine dinner, Debra. Jack says you're going to move into this big house with us. I'm glad."

Jack smiled as Debra gave Matt a kiss on the cheek.

"Are you sure, Matt?" asked Claude.

"Quite sure."

"God bless you, Matt. We'll move in next Saturday."

On Thanksgiving weekend, Jack and Matt drove out to see Louie. The Ozark Mountains were beautiful, glistening with a light snow. Jack stopped at a gasoline station in the town of St. Claire and asked a man sitting on an old Coke machine, "Can you tell me where the Besterfield family live?"

The man looked Jack over carefully and then answered, "Turn right at the next corner, cross the bridge over the Meramec River. Then turn left and drive until you see a white house."

"Where are we going, Jack?"

"When I was on Iwo Jima, Will Besterfield was killed saving my life. I want to tell the family what a brave marine he was."

"How'd he get killed?"

"Will was protecting me as I was moving forward on Iwo Jima. He exposed himself, killing a sniper who had his rifle aimed at me. Out of the corner of my eye, I saw another sniper jump out of a trench a few feet in front of Will and shoot him right in the face. Will's face and head just disappeared. My other scout killed that Jap."

As they drove up to the house, a young boy had just placed his rifle and two squirrels on the porch where his parents were sitting. They were quietly watching the falling snow, seemingly waiting for someone else who had not arrived.

When Jack reached the porch, he said, "You must be Josh."

"How'd ya know?"

"Your brother Will told me all about you."

Mrs. Besterfield shuddered emotionally, "You knew Will?"

"Yes, Ma'am. I'm Jack LeGualt. Will was a brave marine who saved my life once. I was with him when he was killed."

Mr. Besterfield got to his feet and hugged Jack, "He told us about you in a letter. He was proud to scout with you."

"He missed all of you and loved to talk about you," Jack replied.

"We keep thinking he'll come walking out of the woods with Josh one day, but we know he won't," sobbed Will's mother as she turned and went into the house.

Mr. Besterfield looked anxiously at Jack and asked, "Did Will have to suffer?"

"He died instantly, sir."

"God bless you, Jack. I'll sleep better knowing he didn't have to suffer. At the right time, I'll let Will's Mama know."

Jack and Matt had a nice weekend with Louie and Jimmy, but that night Jack had a haunting dream: Will's face and head kept disappearing in front of him.

17

Rick and Ruth

In November 1945 the Baumans had just finished their Sunday dinner. Ruth and Maria cleaned the kitchen, and Maria went to her room to take a nap.

Ruth came over and sat on the couch beside Rick where he was reading and said, "Can we go to the park?"

"Why not? It's a beautiful day."

When they got to the park bench, Ruth snuggled against Rick and said, "I'd like to talk about something important, but I don't know where to start."

"That's easy. Just start."

Ruth sat up straight, "Let's start with work and babies."

"What in the world are you talking about?"

"In January they don't need a design team, and I go back on the factory line. I'll be worth more doing something else."

"What?"

"I want to have a baby."

Rick was caught off guard and said, "When we got married, I thought that we agreed to have a baby later."

"It's later now, Rick. We've been married two years,"

"You said you had some other things to talk about."

"There are a lot of things I could study and learn."

"Like what?"

"If I work another year with Miss Goerner on Sundays, I could learn more about mathematics and language."

"Okay, if that's what you really want to do."

"Learning to read was wonderful, but I'd like to learn more. I missed so much by being out of school as a child."

"You could still work at the factory."

"That would be okay in the winter, but your mother needs help in the garden. I could handle the parking and the vegetable stand. Mama would have more time to work around the house and cook as she likes to do."

"You're right about not working at the factory next spring after baseball starts and the garden needs planting."

"Can we see Miss Goerner this afternoon?"

"Sure," answered Rick as he pulled Ruth close to him.

Ruth kissed him on the ear and whispered, "Now, about the baby."

"I'll have to think about that a little longer."

"You have until tonight, Sweetheart. Think hard."

They took a walk around the lake and then drove to Miss Goerner's house. She was happy to see them and was eager to teach Ruth again.

In bed that night, Ruth convinced Rick with extraordinary loving passion that it was time to have a baby. After Ruth had gone to sleep, Rick thought quietly to himself, over and over, as though he could solve the age-old mystery: 'How does a woman have so much influence over a man?' He went to sleep, without finding an answer.

18

1946-49

Rick had just stepped out of his car at the Broadway lot on a cold January day. Scott was sick in bed with the flu. It was still dark, and cars had not started to arrive. Sleet covered the parking lot. Suddenly Rick froze with terror as he felt the point of a knife pressing into his ribs.

"Give me the money bag!" demanded a tall, skinny man with a mask on his face.

"What are you talking about?" asked Rick defensively.

The robber responded by ripping Rick's jacket open and slashing a deep cut in his side. Blood flowed profusely as the money bag fell to the ground. A heavy blow to his head caused Rick to black out.

Scott heard Rick scream with pain and came to the window in time to see what had happened. He called the police and an ambulance and ran to Rick who was unconscious and bleeding badly.

For two days and nights, Jack, Matt, and Ruth took turns sitting with Rick at the hospital. Matt provided blood for a transfusion, but Rick lay unconscious in critical condition. Jack was beside him when he opened his eyes.

"Are you okay, Rick?" Jack asked.

"Where am I?"

"In the hospital. They put thirty stitches in the cuts on your head and side. What happened, Rick?"

"I was robbed. The guy took my money belt."

While they were talking, Ruth walked in the door. When Rick spoke to her, she knelt down at his bed to thank God even before she kissed him.

The next day Matt drove Rick home and insisted he stay there for a day before going back to work. Jack and Matt gladly took over his responsibilities while he was unable to work.

When Rick returned to work, he sat down in front of the desk that his father had made for him. He missed his father who had been gone six months now. The early morning attack, news that Ruth was pregnant, and the first AP Board Meeting brought Rick's life into sharp focus. His business success or failure was not just a personal thing any more. If the business went bankrupt, he could not feed his family; Scott and Billy would lose their jobs; Jack and Matt would lose their savings.

Rick always wanted to have a bigger business. He still did, but he was forced to face the fact that an expanded business would mean that he would be responsible for the welfare of more people. He thought back to the time when his father lost his coal and ice business. Until now, he had not realized the heavy burden that his father had carried by himself.

*   *   *

In February 1946 Rick opened their first AP Board meeting with a plan to use some of the $10,000 that Matt and Jack had paid for their stock. He suggested that they asphalt the Walnut Street lot and paint lines. They could park more cars and increase the hourly charge.

Matt asked, "Why not just pay off the bank loan?"

"The business wouldn't grow that way."

Jack asked, "How big should the corporation be?"

"Good corporations have no limit. They grow continuously by improvements and expansions."

After they agreed to improve the Walnut Street lot, Rick proposed that they offer to sell their side lot to the dentist. They all agreed and adjourned the meeting.

In March Jack received a letter from Colonel McNally asking him to return to the Marine Corps. Jack wrote back and told him that he was attending Washington University and would not reenlist.

*   *   *

In May 1946 Matt, Jack, and Rick sat on their bench in Forest Park enjoying the coming of spring.

Rick asked, "How are your university courses going?"

Matt answered, "I've changed from history to aeronautics and economics courses."

"What kind of work do you want to do as a lawyer?"

"When I was in New Orleans, Pat suggested that I consider doing legal work for one of the aircraft corporations, and I think it's a pretty good idea."

"How about you, Jack?" asked Rick.

"I'm majoring in management."

Matt asked, "Are you still studying, Rick?"

"I have books on insurance from the library."

Jack changed the subject, "How did the asphalt at Walnut Street turn out?"

"We're getting a lot more cars. Even though I increased charges for short-term parking by twenty percent, our customers seem satisfied to pay the higher rates. I expect to recover the improvement costs within two years."

"When are you going to talk to the dentist?" asked Matt.

"In August. When do you leave for New Orleans?"

"On Tuesday."

"I'll go back to the Ozarks for the summer," added Jack.

Rick asked, "How's your hand, Matt?"

"I'm getting more strength in my hand and more flexibility in my two fingers. I still have trouble doing some things."

"What's worrying you most?"

"Law students need typed briefs. In high school I spent a year learning to type, but it won't help me now."

"When I have a problem because of my missing hand, I study the situation and usually find a solution."

"What about typing?"

"I learned shorthand. Why don't you take a shorthand course this summer at a business college?"

"Are you sure that I could ever read it?"

"I've learned to read shorthand. You've enough money to pay somebody to type your shorthand notes."

"Gee, that could be the right answer."

They enjoyed some quiet time, and then the three friends walked around the lake and headed home.

*   *   *

When Matt arrived in New Orleans for the summer, he told Pat and Elizabeth about Rick's idea of taking shorthand. They both thought it was a good plan.

Matt said, "I'll go for my run every day, but I'd like to work at the hotel if you can use me. I'll go to school at night."

"That sounds like a pretty big load," said Pat.

"I seem to do better with a big load."

The next week Matt found a business college that offered a summer course in shorthand. He would work at the hotel registration desk at night when he returned from his class, so he would have time to practice shorthand between required duties.

*   *   *

Jack had the car to himself after Matt left and was able to help Jimmy and Louie get supplies from Fredericktown. Jimmy was weaker than when Jack had last seen him, but he was strong enough to stay alone some of the time. Jack and Louie went to the river for two or three days at a time. Although Louie didn't hunt anymore, he did fish.

When they went to see Derk, he told them that the Federal Government and the State of Missouri had authorized the establishment of a national forest and wilderness area.

"Where will it be?"

"Part of it will be along the St. Francis River in this area."

Louie frowned.

"It's a means of saving this area and not changing it."

"If they wouldn't change it, why would they buy it?"

Derk answered, "I didn't mean that they wouldn't change it. They'd have trails and lodges on the edge of the forest area. In fact, they've talked with me about buying my property. They'll probably want to buy your mountain."

"I'm not interested. I think they'd mess it up."

*   *   *

When Jack and Matt returned in September, Rick telephoned and said, "The dentist bought our lot for $3,000."

"That's great," said Jack.

"When is your baby due?" asked Matt.

"Soon. Ruth'll go to a hospital instead of having the baby at home like they used to do in the old neighborhood."

When Rick arrived home that evening, Ruth met him, "I just called the doctor. He'll meet us at the hospital."

"What's wrong, Ruth, are you sick?"

"No, silly, I'm going to have our baby."

"Tonight?"

"Tonight!"

Maria interrupted nervously, "Quit talking and go, Rick."

That night Ruth had a baby girl, and they named her Joy. When they brought Joy home, they put her in the crib that Rick had slept in as a baby. Maria said, "I wish Emil were here to see Joy. He'd be so proud."

*   *   *

In November 1946 Rick, Jack, and Matt met in the living room for their board meeting. They glanced at the agenda as they sipped their coffee.

Rick opened the meeting and shared his good news, "Even with my $500 monthly salary and the $100 a piece we each receive for our board meetings, net income this year was fifteen percent higher than last year."

"That's the good news. Any bad news?"

"Not bad news, Matt. Just a problem to solve. In any business, things don't always work out the way you think they will. You have to look for alternatives."

Conceding the point, Matt said, "What's the problem?"

"Since we asphalted and lined the lot at Walnut Street, it has gotten too busy for Billy to handle. He's really not well."

"Can you replace Billy with a younger person?"

"Yes."

"Do you want to?"

"No."

"What are you thinking?"

"I'm thinking that a corporation is built on integrity and appreciation. It needs to work both ways. When I needed Billy, he was loyal and dependable. Now, Billy needs me."

"Can you hire someone to work part-time?"

"Yes, I've worked out a way to give Billy extra help, but when he suddenly gets sick and can't show up for work, I don't know what to do."

Jack said, "Matt and I could substitute part of the time, but I have another idea."

"What?"

"Some of the students at the university aren't rich and would be happy to get part-time work. We could get some students to work."

"Good idea."

Matt asked, "Will you asphalt the Broadway lot?"

"When a lot is only sixty percent full, it isn't nearly as important to have lined spaces. I've heard rumors that they're going to tear down some more of the tenement buildings. I'd like to know what's going to happen to the area before I spend much money on the lot."

"You'll have your hands full resolving the problems at Walnut Street in the next six months and continuing to maintain your profit," said Jack.

"You guys are beginning to talk like real businessmen," Rick said with a grin.

As they started for the car, Rick asked, "If you are going away for Christmas this year, would it be all right for Ruth's parents to stay here when they come to visit?"

"Sure," said Jack. "Claude told me the other night that they're going to Memphis to see their parents over the holidays. Matt's going to New Orleans, and I'm going to be with Louie."

*   *   *

The next years went by quickly. Matt's application to the Washington University Law School was approved in the summer of 1948. During the Christmas and summer breaks, Matt went to New Orleans, and Jack went to the Ozarks. Corporate income continued to increase, but the three business partners were making no major decisions until they paid off the bank loan.

In the summer of 1948 Jimmy became very weak. Jack and Louie took him to the hospital where he died peacefully in his sleep a week later. Jimmy's death was quite a shock to Louie. Jack wanted Louie to come to St. Louis and stay with him, but Louie was determined to stay on his mountain.

Jack and Claude both graduated in June 1949. Claude went into management training at Holiday Inn, so the Mulots moved . to Memphis.

In late spring 1949, before Matt and Jack would leave for the summer, Rick called a special meeting of the AP Corporation.

Rick opened the meeting. "We have a major decision to make that could change the corporation for years to come."

"What's it about?" asked Jack.

"I have an opportunity to buy the SUN Corporation."

"What's the SUN Corporation?" Matt voiced the first of many questions he and Jack had.

"It's a parking company like ours."

"What would it do for us?"

"It would double the size of our corporation."

Matt thoughtfully interjected, "That would create both opportunities and problems."

"That's why we need to talk about it."

Jack asked, "How many parking lots does SUN have?"

"Eight lots and some other property."

"Why buy a corporation?" asked Jack. "Why not just buy land and start another lot?"

"There'd be a lot of work and expense in starting up another lot. If you buy a corporation, all that startup work has already been tested. And, I'd sell our nonprofitable lots."

"But it isn't that simple," Matt pointed out. "If you buy too much at one time, you can jeopardize the entire business."

"Yes, and we'd have to protect against that possibility, if we go ahead with this plan."

"Why is the SUN Corporation for sale?" asked Jack.

"The owners had a fight about management policy, but neither one has the money to buy the other out."

"Are you getting current appraisals?"

"I will this summer."

"Are you ready to tell us what you recommend?"

"No, but I'm going to work on it all summer. When you come back in the fall, I'll have all the facts we need."

"Good luck," encouraged Matt. "You've expanded the business several times. I'll bet you can do it again. I recommend a fifty percent salary increase for Rick."

"Agreed," said Jack. "You're doing a great job, Rick."

Rick responded, "Thanks, I appreciate your confidence."

19

Blackjack and Louie

Blackjack was in an unusually pensive mood when he drove out of St. Louis on his way to the Ozarks. He should have been confident about life ahead of him now that he had graduated from Washington University. Instead, he thought, 'I feel like I'm back on a landing craft bobbing around like a cork on the Pacific Ocean before landing on some unknown beach.'

On an impulse, Blackjack turned onto State Highway 21. Maybe the drive off the main highway would help him focus his future. South of the town of Potosi, he crossed Big River which was closer to Ste. Genevieve than the St. Francis River was. One time Jack had asked Louie why he and Piney had always gone farther south to the St. Francis River to trap rather than to Big River. Louie had just shrugged his shoulders, as he often did when he did not know or want to say. Jack always thought that they wanted to be in a wilder place.

At Arcadia he turned off the state road onto a gravel county road that wound its way through the forest. When he arrived at Louie's house late in the afternoon, he drove off the road up to the porch where Louie was sitting in a rocking chair. It seemed strange that Jimmy was gone.

Blackjack jumped onto the porch and said affectionately, "Hi, Louie." Blackjack sat in the empty rocker next to Louie.

"I hope ya finally got enough schoolin' Blackjack."

"I've got enough."

"What are ya gonna do with it?" challenged Louie.

"Just sit and rock with you."

"Good, I miss Jimmy. We always sat on the porch in the evenin' as the sun set, before the mosquitoes came out."

"You okay, Louie?"

"Fine, but I'm glad yer here. I get lonely and drink too much now that Jimmy is gone."

That evening they ate food from tin cans; Louie liked to call it city food. They talked a long time over a few drinks.

Louie warned Blackjack, "This bottle seems like a good friend when yer lonely or mixed up. Good friends shouldn't hurt ya, but if ya ain't careful this bottle will."

That was a long speech for Louie, and Blackjack did not try to respond. They were both ready to turn in.

At breakfast Louie said, "Let's live on the river this summer."

"You sure?"

"I'm sure."

"It'd be tough on you coming back and forth."

"You can get supplies. How are yer shot-up parts now?"

Blackjack answered with twenty quick push ups.

"I didn't think ya'd ever do that again."

"Matt and I made a deal that we'd do our exercises together, then neither of us would goof off and skip them."

Later that day Blackjack put a pack of supplies and their sleeping bags on his back, and they headed for the river. As they worked their way down the trail, he noticed that Louie was picking each step with total concentration, even on easy parts of the trail. When they reached the river, Blackjack thought, 'Louie will never make it up again. I'll have to get a car for him at the Lodge.'

Blackjack did the hunting, fishing, and berry picking. Louie stayed in camp where he built the fire, smoked their meat, and did most of their cooking. Once every week, Blackjack visited Derk. He took venison and smoked fish to Derk and returned with eggs, bread, and basic supplies.

Louie and Blackjack enjoyed kidding each other. Once when Blackjack was going hunting for their supper, Louie teased, "Take only one shell, and see if ya can bring back a squirrel."

Jack took one shell and brought back a squirrel.

In August Louie got out of breath with almost any effort. One evening, he said, "Let's go up to Piney's Ridge."

"You can't make it up there, Louie," warned Blackjack.

"I'll make it."

Louie did make it, but after the climb he was breathing heavily. Blackjack had brought sleeping bags because he was sure that they would stay until morning. It was a good decision.

"Don't talk to me now, Blackjack. Just listen. I've got some things to say to ya."

"All right, Louie."

"Yer a good son, and I'm proud of ya. Please protect this forest and the animals. God made this mountain, and it shouldn't be torn up. Remember, Blackjack, there is a God. Believe that, if you don't believe nothin' else. God has always been good to me. He gave me Piney, Monet, and you. What more could a man want?"

Louie fell over on his side, and Blackjack lifted him into his arms and asked, "Can you make it, Louie?"

"Not this time."

"What can I do for you?"

"Rest with me. Don't never take me from this spot."

"I won't."

"This is where I buried Piney. I'll be with him tonight."

Louie died in peace as the sun set with sparkling reflections on the river below.

Blackjack sadly said parts of the prayer that Louie had taught him from the Sisters of St. Joseph, "Holy Mother, pray for us sinners now. . . ." Then Blackjack put Louie's body into his sleeping bag and slept beside it.

The sun was up when Blackjack woke. He carefully dragged and lifted Louie's body in the sleeping bag down to their cabin on the river. He then went to get a horse from Derk. When he returned to the campsite, Blackjack lifted Louie onto the horse in his sleeping bag and led the horse back to the lodge.

Derk drove them to a funeral home where Blackjack gave strict instructions, "Do what is legally required, and give me the ashes. There'll be no ceremonies."

Two days later Blackjack was on Piney's Ridge again. He scattered Louie's ashes over Piney's grave site and said their prayer once more. Then, standing ramrod straight, he sucked in his gut and walked away.

*   *   *

After two days of drinking and four days recovering, Jack drove to St. Louis. He did not tell anyone that he was returning because he wanted to be alone for awhile before Matt arrived.

Jack phoned Rub and asked, "Is your offer still open?"

"Yes, it is."

"My father died, and I've completed my degree at Washington University. I've decided to return to the marines. That seems to be where I belong."

"I know you do, Jack. After I've made the proper contacts, I'll mail instructions. When can you start your reenlistment?"

"I've got some work to do here, but I could report any time."

"We need your combat experience, Jack. You and I know how difficult it is for new recruits to go into battle for the first time. No war's going on now, but North Korean communists are positioned to attack South Korea. Politicians don't agree, and they're pulling out our troops and equipment."

"I'm not looking forward to another battle, Rub, but I'm prepared to fight if there is one."

"How's your health, Jack? Can you pass a physical?"

"I'm sure I can. I've worked hard at rehabilitation, and I'm able to do almost everything that I could do before my injuries."

"I need you as a company commander, Jack. I can bring you in as a lieutenant and then have you promoted to captain to fill a vacancy in my battalion. The Commandant has asked Battalion Commanders to recruit men like you."

Jack knew that the bureaucracy would need time to complete the procedure that Rub had proposed. He hoped he could be of help to Rick while he was waiting.

A few days later Jack met Matt at the train station and drove him home. Jack asked, "How was your summer?"

"Really great. I'm beginning to understand the hotel business a lot better. How about your summer?"

"The best and worst that I've had in the Ozarks."

"What happened?"

"Louie and I had a wonderful summer together, but he was weak. One night he had a hard time breathing but insisted that we climb to a favorite place of his. I didn't think that he'd make the climb, but he did. We talked, and then he just closed his eyes and died in my arms."

"It must have been hard. I didn't know he was sick."

"I knew he was getting weaker, but somehow I guess I believed that Louie'd never die."

"How are you doing?"

"I haven't really adjusted to it yet."

"I'm sorry, Jack."

"I can't really think of life without Louie."

After they drove home and unpacked, Matt asked, "Have you talked with Rick."

"Yes, briefly, about Louie. He's coming over tomorrow for our meeting, and he'll explain the work that he's done this summer.

Reading between the lines, he seemed to have some pretty heavy stuff. We'd better get some sleep."

Jack had decided not to say anything about his decision to reenlist. He would wait and see what Rick presented the next day and try to find the right time. Probably neither Matt nor Rick would think it was a good idea.

20

SUN Corporation

When Rick gave Matt and Jack his formal proposal on the SUN purchase, he looked like he had the future of the world on his shoulders. "I've been working all summer on the SUN Corporation purchase. Here are the results."

"When you bought into the business in 1945, AP was appraised at $58,000 and had a bank loan of $8,000. In the 1949 appraisal that I received last month, AP is appraised at $100,000 and our bank loan is fully paid."

"You've really done well, Rick," Jack complimented him.

"What was the appraisal of SUN?" asked Matt.

"$307,000 with a $99,000 bank loan."

"That's big bank loan."

"It's a real concern, and one of the reasons that I was able to negotiate a low purchase price."

After Matt and Jack had read the report, Jack said, "This report indicates that our bank would loan us $121,000. after you sell the Broadway lot and pay the negotiated purchase price. Is that correct?"

"Yes, but there are other things to consider. I'm going to be short of cash reserves. The bank loan is dependent upon having a $20,000 cash reserve at the time of the sale, and I'm not sure that's enough."

"Can you borrow more?"

"Not easily."

"You've certainly done your homework," said Matt. "Can you stay in business with a bank loan of $121,000 even if you obtain the cash reserves you need?"

"We'd have to sell six Sun properties and pay off half the loan."

"If we sell most of the lots, why buy SUN?" asked Jack.

"My goal is to keep the three large lots that are real money makers. They have good people attending them, and I wouldn't change the way they're run."

Matt asked, "What happens to Scott if you sell the Broadway lot?"

"Billy said that he wants to retire soon. He'd be happy to work part-time for Scott with less pay. The real problem is that Scott'll lose his living quarters."

"Where will Scott live?"

"You'll note in the report that I don't plan to sell the house owned by SUN. If everything else could work out, I'd move my family into the SUN house. It's located near Tower Grove Park where Ruth lived as a child. Then I could let Scott move his family into the house by the ballpark where I live now."

"Wow!" said Jack.

"My house near the ballpark has a large attic space with a window at each end. Scott's sister and her children could sleep up there."

"What else should we know, Rick?"

"Scott's getting married."

"You're kidding!"

"No. Sometimes it just seems that it's time for the whole world to change. It happened to us several times when we were growing up, and I guess it will be the same way the rest of our lives. Just about the time things get settled, things change."

"You could sell the house where Jack and I have been living," offered Matt. "I could move to a dorm."

"Thanks, Matt, but I'd rather sell my house and rent a place for Scott."

"You've thrown a lot at us, Rick," said Matt. "We'd better think about it and then talk again."

"I'll be back tomorrow after you think about the purchase. Jack, you could work for AP and sell properties to help pay the bank loan."

"I'll be glad to try."

After Rick left, they talked over Rick's proposal.

"I believe Rick's plan will work," said Matt.

Jack agreed and added, "I didn't want to tell Rick until I knew what you were thinking, but I'm going down to the bank tomorrow and sell the rest of Louie's coins and buy some more stock. Scott could move his family into Rick's house."

"If you could, it'd sure take a lot of pressure off Rick."

"Call Rick in the morning and ask him to come over in the evening, instead of earlier in the day to give me time."

The next morning Jack went down to see the coin dealer and asked, "Do you remember when I was here four years ago and sold you some gold coins?"

"Yes, I do," the coin dealer answered. "I still have two of the coins."

"Would you be interested in buying any more of the coins like the ones I sold you?"

The coin dealer took off his eye shade and answered, "My problem is that it would take me too long to sell them. You surprised me the day you walked in with twelve of these rare coins. How many coins do you have?"

"I have thirty coins, and I want to sell them for six hundred dollars a piece."

"The price is okay, but I can't handle that many coins at one time. It would take me years to sell them. I'll pay you $6,000 for ten coins, if they are in good condition."

Jack said, "I've talked to other coin dealers who will buy the coins, but I don't want to go to New York or Chicago to sell them."

The coin dealer looked at Jack and knew he had been talking with someone who had studied the business and said, "Come back this afternoon. Maybe I can buy all the coins."

Jack was confident that the dealer would accept the offer, so he went back that afternoon with the coins.

The dealer said, "I've found someone who will buy half of the coins. I'll pay $18,000 for your thirty coins if they're in good condition."

Jack showed him the coins, and he checked them carefully and said, "Five of these coins are not in satisfactory condition. I'll only be able to give you $15,000 for the coins."

Jack accepted the offer.

After depositing his check at the bank, he went home and told Matt.

Matt was pleased and said, "I'm glad you could do that for Rick. He's done so much for us."

That evening Jack gave Rick a check for $15,000, "Here's a check for a few shares of stock. Matt and I agree that you should buy the SUN Corporation. You can move your family into the house over by Tower Grove Park, and Scott can move into your house."

"I can't believe this," said Rick. He was stunned.

Jack continued, "Matt can stay here in this house until he finishes law school, and then you can sell it."

Rick couldn't sit still any longer. He stood and walked around the room before regaining his composure.

"I have one suggestion, Rick," suggested Matt. "Keep the two corporations separate, so if one is in trouble, we'll still have the other one. Also, having a corporation that might be used differently in the future is valuable."

"A good idea," Rick agreed. "Jack, the corporation can pay

you $300 a week while you sell the non-profitable properties. What are your future plans?"

Jack knew his time had come to reveal his personal plans, "I'm reenlisting in the marines."

Both Matt and Rick were caught off guard, and since they were slow to respond, Jack told them about his talk with Colonel McNally.

Rick didn't try to hide his disappointment. "Why?"

"I feel at home in the marines," said Jack. "It's something I can't describe."

"I think I understand," said Matt.

"I don't," argued Rick.

"I believe that I'll be able to save lives of young recruits."

"Where will you be stationed?" asked Matt.

"Camp Pendleton, California."

"When will you leave?" asked Rick.

"In about three months, so I can still sell the SUN properties."

Then Jack surprised Rick again by saying, "I've thought of a strategy to sell the small lots. How long will it take you to complete all of your purchase transactions?"

"Everything must be completed by October 15."

Jack poured some hot coffee, and Matt asked, "What is your plan to sell the properties?"

"Each small lot is next to an office building. I'll tell the owners that the monthly fee for parking cars will have to double, but we'll give them an opportunity to buy the lot before we proceed to sell to developers."

"You did learn something at Washington University," said Rick. "Why not change your mind about the marines?"

Jack ignored Rick's last remark and said, "October 15 will come fast, so I'll have to hurry to get proposals ready. Is there anything I can do to help you now, Rick?"

"Can you take over my collection duties?"

"Sure."

"Can I help you move?" asked Matt.

"Thanks, I'll need some help

Before Jack left for the Marine Corps, he sold five unprofitable lots for more than their appraised value. The bank loan had been reduced by $48,000.

*   *   *

In December Jack received a letter from Colonel McNally:

> Report to the recruiting station in downtown St. Louis. Show them this letter. They will complete your reenlistment as a lieutenant after you pass the physical.

Jack visited the Ozarks once more before he left for the Marine Corps. Derk told him that he had sold the River Ranch Lodge and would be moving soon. It'll be part of the Mark Twain National Forest and Wilderness Area. He asked Jack what he planned to do with his house.

"I'm not sure."

"Jack, would you be interested in letting me rent your house? I'd rather not move into town."

"Sure. Don't pay me rent. Lease the farm land, and use the crop payment to pay for maintenance and improvements."

"Thanks, Jack. I'll take good care of the place."

21

Matt: Flying Again

Nostalgia flooded Matt's mind as he walked into the Rathskeller Restaurant at the Jefferson Hotel in June 1950. Ten years had gone by since his mother had worked there, but he almost expected to see her. Matt's law professor had invited him to dinner to talk about working on a law case. In the lobby Matt's thoughts were abruptly interrupted by a handsome, fifty-year-old man with prematurely gray hair.

Matt spoke first, "Hello, Professor Walters."

"Hi, Matt. While we're off campus, please call me Steve."

"All right, Steve."

When they were seated and had ordered, Steve Walters explained the purpose of their meeting. Matt listened intently.

"During the summer I work as a counsel for a firm in Arlington, Virginia. They do military work. I read your resume and saw that you had been a navy pilot and have taken some science and engineering courses."

"That's right," Matt replied.

"My assignment on this trip is to determine whether a commercial airline has a legal case against the navy."

"Will you try the case?"

"No, my responsibility is to determine facts."

"How do I fit in?" asked Matt, excited about the idea of actually being involved in a law case.

"Most lawyers don't know anything about flying airplanes or engineering problems. You have the background to discover facts that others might miss. I'd like you to help me with a navy accident case. Can you work all summer?"

"Sure. When do you want to leave?"

"Seven tomorrow morning. I usually fly my own plane. Maybe you'd like to do some of the flying?"

Matt was shocked at the idea. "I didn't think I'd be able to fly again after my hand was injured."

"You can't fly navy or commercial flights, but you can get a civilian pilot's license. You didn't ask about your pay."

"I was too excited about the thought of flying to ask."

"How about seventy-five dollars a day and expenses?"

"That'd be fine with me."

The next morning as they climbed into Steve's plane at Lambert Airport, he handed Matt the trip plan to study. When the plane was in the air and reached the proper altitude, Steve said, "I want you to get acquainted with personnel in the law firm and at the Pentagon. I'll work directly with principals of the firm and involve you later."

"How long will we be there?"

"Probably two weeks, and then we'll go back to St. Louis to do some research."

"Where will we stay?"

"At the J. W. Marriott Hotel in Arlington."

The two weeks flew by, and Matt was swamped with information and contacts that he had carefully recorded in his shorthand notes. Two days after they returned, Steve showed Matt a list of questions concerning technical details.

"After you read these documents, Matt, decide where you want to go for information. If you have access problems, let me know, and I'll help you."

Matt worked hard in several libraries and on phone calls to the contacts that he had made in Washington. In July he went to Parks Air School in East St. Louis and had an instructor give him flying time on a Cessna. He was pleased at how easy it was to fly a small plane.

Noticing how Matt's confidence shifted from anxiety to excitement, his instructor commented, "Your missing fingers may keep you from navy flying, but you're a thousand times better than most pilots that I've checked out."

"Thanks. You don't know how good that makes me feel."

Before they went to Washington again, Matt had his civilian pilot's license.

By August Matt had completed his research of the technical aspects of the accident between the navy flier and the commercial plane. He concluded that the commercial pilot had made some minor, identifiable mistakes, but the navy pilot had made a serious error that could have caused fatalities.

Matt gave his report to Steve, who had come to similar conclusions. They agreed that the navy should try to negotiate and avoid trial. They flew to Washington and presented their facts and recommendations.

That evening at their hotel, Steve suggested, "Make a New Orleans flight plan for our return, and you can visit your parents."

Matt was ecstatic as he flew the plane to New Orleans. The two men had dinner with Elizabeth and Pat in the airport terminal before Steve flew his plane on to St. Louis. Matt stayed for a short visit and then took the train to St. Louis.

When he returned, he told Rick about his experience and thanked him for suggesting shorthand, "The notes that I took this summer improved my final report."

"Do you have trouble reading them?"

"Not any more."

Rick hesitated, "I've another suggestion for you."

"What?"

"Do you remember telling Jack and me about how you got excited dating girls at the University of Missouri?"

"Yes, why?"

"Do you date girls here at Washington University?"

"No."

"Why don't you, Matt? You shouldn't live alone forever."

"You're right, Rick, but every time I meet a girl that I'd like to be with, I remember Marcie. It still hurts."

"Take more time then. Remember, you didn't think you'd fly an airplane again."

After their discussion Rick pulled out a letter from Jack. He had completed the Command and Staff Training Program and had been assigned as a captain in Colonel McNally's battalion.

A few days later the *St. Louis Post-Dispatch* reported that the First Marine Division had sailed for Japan.

22

JACK: Korean War, 1950-1953

Every marine in the First Division knew that this was the Marine Corps and that they would get the job done, whatever the cost. War is brutal. Instructions must be clear, and discipline strict.

Jack spoke to his platoon leaders, "We're not getting the intensity that we need. Yesterday, I saw men doing what they were told, but you'd have thought they were playing a game. Keep the joking and horsing around for the barracks and not for maneuvers. Also, I saw some men drop out of our double-time marches and then try to catch up. Let them know that nobody drops out. If they have a problem, they have to learn to overcome it. We haven't assigned anything to these men that they can't do. You're marines."

He looked squarely at his lieutenants. They learned to respect his toughness. He wanted to know the truth, and they were trained to tell it. He expected loyalty and got it. They learned to work with their noncommissioned officers in the same way, and now the company was becoming a highly motivated unit.

Jack had confidence in his platoon leaders.

Peter Olson weighed 200 pounds and was over six feet tall.

"Ole" was 22, the youngest of the group. His blond hair, blue eyes, and gentle personality gave a misleading appearance of softness. He had grown up in International Falls, Minnesota, where he had shipped out on Great Lakes steamers for weeks at a time before he had decided to join the marines.

Gaylon Smith had been a Kentucky coal miner for four years before volunteering for the Marine Corps in World War II. Marines called him "Sooty." He had fought in Guadalcanal and other battles as the Japanese were pushed north. He was a six-foot-four, 240-pound brawler with black hair and brown eyes.

Davy Alexander was six feet tall, 185 pounds, and hard as steel. He had grown up in North Carolina and joined the marines during World War II. He had fought in Saipan and had been wounded, but he had recovered in time to fight at Iwo Jima. On his return to the United States, he served as a drill sergeant before he was commissioned.

Sam Gonzales was the same size as Jack, five feet ten inches tall, and weighed 165 pounds. He was smart and quick, a second generation American who was proud of his Mexican heritage. He had grown up in Santa Fe, New Mexico, where his father was a successful merchant. Sam had not known hard times until he had made assault landings on Guam and Okinawa in World War II. He had reenlisted after the war.

Colonel McNally briefed his captains, "We're ready to ship out, and my greatest regret is that we're taking recruits to Korea without the benefit of amphibious training. Drive home the conditions they will face in assault landings. MacArthur's not bringing marines to Korea without an assault landing in mind."

Jack relayed these instructions to his lieutenants. Two days later they boarded a ship for Japan, and in August 1950, they were transported to Pusan, Korea.

*   *   *

Colonel McNally briefed him, and then Jack told his lieutenants, "We have stopped North Korean Army advances at Pusan and have prevented them from being able to force the United Nations troops to withdraw into ships."

"How does the South Korean Army rate as a fighting force?" asked Sam.

"The report we have is that they are dedicated to their cause and are willing and able to fight, now that they have the support of American planes and tanks."

"What's our mission?" asked Sooty, impatient to know when and how his marines would enter the fight.

"Our initial mission is to search out and kill North Korean Army soldiers while they're disorganized. They're dispersed, and many have intermingled with civilians. There'll be few casualties if your men are alert."

Davy asked, "Are they well supplied?"

"The North Korean soldier is tough and brutal. He can live on very little food with no interest in anything except to kill you. He'll put civilians in front of him as a shield. He'll slip through your lines and kill you while you sleep, even though he faces almost certain death."

Ole asked, "How do we handle the South Korean civilians?"

"Help civilians when you can, but don't risk your life doing it. You're here to kill NKA soldiers before they kill you. Don't let one of your marines forget it."

Sam asked, "How disorganized are they?"

"The North Korean Army soldiers have lost the battle to break through the Pusan perimeter, but they're regrouping for the next fight. They're equipped and supplied for their type of warfare."

In the weeks ahead, Jack's company fought well and had minor casualties but no deaths. All of his men were healthy for major battles ahead.

*   *   *

"Condition and prepare your men; check and recheck all equipment, and be 'on the ready.' Expect special orders," Jack instructed his lieutenants.

A few days later the First Division loaded onto amphibious ships. Jack explained their destination and mission as he had been briefed: "We're on the Yellow Sea, and we'll land at Inchon, north of the main communist forces. Our landing will be on a wall rather than on a beach. You'll get over the wall by climbing a ladder with your gear."

Davy Alexander asked, "Will we go in at high tide?"

"Yes, but the tides are not like those in North Carolina."

"What's the difference?"

"Have you seen tide change four or five feet in an hour?"

"Hell, no!"

"You will tomorrow, so have your men ready. If we're lucky, we'll hit the wall at the peak of high tide, but our time to get off the landing craft will be short."

"What kind of reception do you expect?" asked Sooty.

"Our landing should catch the enemy off guard. We should have no heavy fighting during the landing, but be prepared to fight as soon as you're over the wall."

"What's the object of our mission?" asked Sam.

"Land safely and move to take back the city of Seoul. We'll be north of most of the communist forces, but thousands of enemy troops will meet us at Seoul."

"Sounds impossible," said Sooty, "but my men will be ready."

Jack commented, "When you fight for MacArthur, you do the impossible. Sometimes you have remarkable success, and other times you experience dismal failure. We're committed. No changing minds; be prepared for anything."

On September 15 the marines climbed over the wall prepared to fight. The huge LSTs managed to get tanks and cargo to shore farther north on the rocky coast. An army division landed next to the marines. All together there were 18,000 troops ashore in a short period of time with minimal casualties. Within hours, they were moving toward Seoul. The dangerous and surprise landing had been a remarkable military achievement. Marine and army troops reached Seoul and took back the city.

*   *   *

After the fighting in Seoul, the First Marines moved onto amphibious ships that transported them through the Yellow Sea back around the tip of Korea into the Sea of Japan. They were headed toward Wonsan, North Korea, where they expected to land and fight a retreating North Korean Army.

The operation proved to be a debacle. After their three weeks on rough water, marines arrived suffering from seasickness and dysentery. They found the Wonsan Harbor so heavily mined that they were forced to go north to debark. By the time the marines reached Wonson, the United Nations army divisions had already occupied the city.

*   *   *

Colonel McNally briefed his company commanders, "We'll enter the Chosin Reservoir Valley between two mountain ranges and move to the Yalu River on the Chinese border. Get all of the winter gear that you can from supply, and prepare for a tough time. We'll be vulnerable to surprise attacks. With only one road in and out, there'll be no support on either flank."

Jack asked, "Have the bridges over the Yalu River been bombed?"

"No, the Joint Chiefs of Staff have instructed MacArthur not to bomb the bridges or the Chinese Communist divisions gathered on the other side of the Yalu. Intelligence reports indicate that only a small number of Chinese have crossed the Yalu River into Korea on these bridges."

For the next ten days the First Marine Division marched toward the Yalu River, deep into Chosin Reservoir Valley. It was November 10, and they had not seen one enemy soldier. Suddenly, they encountered an enemy that intelligence had only casually reported to them--the weather. Although marines had brought all their heavy winter gear, they weren't prepared for the sudden turn in the weather, now twenty degrees below zero with a wind chill of minus seventy degrees. Men were freezing; weapons wouldn't fire, and vehicles wouldn't start.

Marines improvised. They set up warming tents with coffee and soup for returning patrols. They learned to fire their weapons and start their vehicles at periodic intervals to keep them from freezing. Men were told not to let their hand weapons go unfired during the night or to let the vehicles stand all night without starting them. Conditions got worse.

Unknown to the marines, Chinese Communist divisions dressed in white-quilted uniforms had swarmed across the Yalu River bridges into North Korea. These elite Chinese troops had come directly from defeating the Chinese Nationalists, forcing them to retreat to the island of Formosa.

Chinese troops had confronted army divisions on the other side of the mountain range. Heavily outnumbered, the army divisions were given instructions to retreat south. By the time the marines received the same orders, Chinese divisions had already surrounded them with a command to annihilate the famous First Marine Division at any cost.

The First Division had orders to fight through the Chinese, attacking from the south. Tanks were turned around to block Chinese forces attacking them from the north. Marines had orders not to give up any weapons, kill as many Chinese as possible, and move south.

Colonel McNally and the other battalion commanders instructed infantry troops to move into the mountains to confront the Chinese directly and protect marines who were moving their vehicles and heavy equipment on the only road south.

The marines did everything they could to defend themselves against the weather. Still their faces and feet were freezing. The Chinese would attack at night with their bugles and whistles blowing. They would scatter in the hills in the daytime when marine pilots could provide air support. Marines were dying, but every morning there would also be piles of dead Chinese soldiers. Night after night, attacks continued. Some Chinese got through and used their rifles, bayonets, knives, and grenades to kill and wound marines. A squad was assigned to carry the dead and wounded to trucks on the road below.

Jack went from platoon to platoon encouraging his men. Having a sidearm instead of leading the way with his rifle was a new combat experience for him. Casualties were heavy. An enemy soldier seriously wounded Lieutenant Davy Alexander with his bayonet. Jack happened to be close enough to kill the soldier and pull Davy to where he could be carried to a truck on the road below. Jack's company now had casualties above fifty percent. Jack himself had only received one flesh wound, but his feet had frost damage.

The First Marine Division fought courageously until December 15 when they finally got out of the Chosin Reservoir trap and onto ships at Wonsan. The Chinese Communists had not succeeded in their mission to annihilate the First Marines, and they had paid a high price for trying.

Later reports of the Chosin Reservoir Valley battle indicated 4,500 marine casualties, including 700 killed. Many in the First Division suffered severe frost damage to hands, feet, and faces. Over half of the First Division Marines returned to the States, either dead, wounded, or exhausted. History would report that the Chinese had 37,000 casualties, including 15,000 killed, 10,000 by marine ground troops and 5,000 by marine air support.

*   *   *

The remainder of the First Division went by ship back to Pusan where they had started their Korean ordeal only five months before. The division was reorganized, and new troops filled in the ranks of the dead and wounded. Jack was promoted to major.

As the marines moved north again from Pusan, they went through what they referred to as "Massacre Valley," where the Second Army Division had fought so valiantly.

In April the marines moved north to Chunchon. On June 4, 1951, army and marine divisions established a defense line during what became known as the "Battle of the Punch Bowl." By then General MacArthur had been fired for public clashes with President Truman and the Joint Chiefs of Staff. MacArthur insisted that he was fighting a war not a defensive police action. His goal was to unite Korea by defeating the Chinese, who were in direct combat with his armies.

For two years the bloody fighting continued. Orders were not to go beyond the defined defense line but to hold that line at any cost. Jack was wounded twice. In 1952 after Colonel McNally was shot in the chest and returned to the United States, Jack was promoted to lieutenant colonel.

Fighting ended when the Armistice of Panmunjam was signed on July 27, 1953. The First Marine Division returned to the United States by ship, giving them a chance to recover and reflect on their three horrible years.

At the end of the war, Jack received a letter from his friend, Rub McNally, who had recovered from his wounds and had been promoted to brigadier general. He asked Jack to call after his leave about a new assignment, but he did not mention what it was.

23

Matt and Marcie

It was New Year's Day 1951. Matt was having coffee and pastries with Pat while his mother was still in her room resting from New Year's Eve.

"We had quite a night, Matt."

"Imagine having a night like that 365 days a year."

"I'd retire at the end of that year."

"Do you have plans for retirement?"

"No, Matt. I thought about it once a few years ago, but the telephone rang, and I forgot about it."

"Today is so nice that I'm going to get on the St. Charles Streetcar and take my run at Audubon Park."

"You could take a shorter run here in the Quarter?"

"For some reason, I have a strong urge to go to the park."

"Okay, I'll tell Elizabeth that you'll have a late lunch."

Matt stepped out into a typically cool New Orleans winter day with the noonday sun shining bright and warm, the kind of day when hound dogs search out a sunny spot and lay down in a stretched-out position unconcerned about last summer's flies and sweat bees.

Matt had finished his run down International Drive and

around Audubon Park to the end of the footpath near Tulane and Loyola Universities. He was in a reflective mood and decided to walk around the lake before catching the streetcar back. He had tied his navy sweatshirt around his waist.

Matt's mind was blank as he just enjoyed absorbing the surroundings. The grass in the park had browned for its winter rest; white cumulus clouds floated lazily overhead. Matt was startled by a little girl chasing her black and white Sheltie puppy. When she finally caught up with it, the puppy was chewing on Matt's sweat pants.

"What's your puppy's name?"

"Pup," answered the girl, as she picked him up and turned to her mother who was hurrying to catch up.

Her mother, trying to catch her breath, stopped abruptly, as if she were coming to the edge of a high cliff.

"Matt!" she exclaimed in disbelief.

Matt looked down at Marcie's face as she unsuccessfully fought to hold back tears. "Is it really you, Marcie?"

"It's me." They embraced and moved to a nearby bench as Marcie called to her daughter, "Stay close, Andrea."

"Yes, Mama."

Dumbfounded at seeing Marcie for the first time in nine years, Matt blurted out, "What happened, Marcie?"

"I never wanted it to happen. It just did! All I ever wanted was you, Matt." Marcie's first attempt to explain failed as she rushed to tell Matt what had happened seven years ago. Tears were now streaming down her face.

"It's okay, Marcie," consoled Matt. "Take your time."

"I went to a wedding party for a close friend of mine, Matt, and it just happened."

"What?"

For years Marcie had wanted to tell Matt her story, and now she couldn't get it out fast enough. "The girl who brought me to the wedding party had to go home early. Tommy Ryan offered to drive me home later. He was a family friend for many years, so I stayed."

"What happened?"

"A lot."

"Please go on, Marcie; I need to know."

"Well, on the way home, Tommy asked, 'Why not stop at the Roosevelt Hotel Lounge and catch up on old times?'"

"Did you stop?"

"I was lonely and hadn't seen Tommy for a long time, so I went with him. We had a drink and talked, and then I told him it was time for me to leave."

"Did you?"

"No."

"Why not?"

"Tommy was always a smooth talker, and I reluctantly agreed to stay for a second drink. On the way to the lobby, Tommy said that he wanted to say goodbye to a friend who was staying at the hotel. Like a fool, I went with him."

"Was his friend there?"

"Yes, but he left while I was in the bathroom."

"Then?"

"Tommy took my arm, and we started for the door. But he yanked me around and kissed me. I can't go on Matt."

"You don't need to, Marcie, but why did you marry him when you knew I loved you and would have understood."

"A month later, I found I was pregnant."

"Andrea?"

"Yes. I didn't know what to do, Matt. I had terrible thoughts, and couldn't talk to you. I kept thinking you'd be killed like Buster. I didn't want an abortion."

"What did you do?"

"I cried for days and then told Mother. Tommy married me and was good to me, but he was always a playboy."

"Where's Tommy now, Marcie?"

"He was killed, Matt."

"Killed! How?"

"Two months after we were married, Tommy and one of his friends got drunk and ran their speed boat into a pier. They both died before they got to a hospital."

"Why didn't you write me, Marcie?"

"I was too ashamed. I considered that part of my life over and decided never to marry again. Instead, I decided to spend all of my time being a good mother and helping girls in trouble. I went to Tulane University and got a degree in education, and now I'm teaching in a literacy program. I'm not really happy, but I'm content with my life."

"You're still beautiful, Marcie."

"What about you, Matt? Did you get married? I always thought that you'd be a wonderful father."

"After losing you, I never wanted anyone else. In June I'll graduate from Washington University Law School in St. Louis."

Matt held Marcie and kissed her as she cried softly. They embraced without speaking until they saw that Andrea had the leash on Pup and was walking toward them.

"Pup seems to like you, Andrea."

"Yes, sir. He does."

Marcie asked, "Andrea, do you see that big tree?"

"Yes, Mama."

"Please take Pup over there to play until I call you."

As Andrea left, Matt noticed for the first time how much she looked like Marcie.

Matt became recklessly urgent and to the point, "Marcie, I love you. Please marry me."

"Oh, Matt. Things are happening so fast that I'm dizzy."

"Too fast to answer my question?"

"Of course, I'll marry you, Matt. That's all I ever wanted."

Matt held Marcie close and whispered in her ear, "Now we can forget our scars. The war is finally over for us."

*   *   *

Matt and Marcie did not allow anything to slow their marriage plans. They had a private wedding a few days later. After a short honeymoon, they packed everything into Marcie's car and started their drive to St. Louis. As he drove his family into the driveway of his home, Matt Simmons felt like a whole person again. Andrea and Pup ran to the porch swing.

Matt kissed Marcie and whispered, "We're home."

Marcie got out of her 1948 green Studebaker Champion and looked at Matt with affection, "I can't believe so much has happened in such a wonderful way in two weeks."

After Marcie and Andrea had walked through their new home exploring every nook and cranny, Marcie commented, "A New Orleans shotgun home. What a pleasant place to live."

When they were rested from their trip, Matt said, "I want to take the two of you to my favorite place."

At Forest Park they got out of the car, walked to the park bench, and sat down. A light snow was beginning to fall. Andrea, who had never seen snow, ran around in circles with Pup. Matt put his arm around Marcie.

"This is a lovely place, Matt. Let's come here often."

"We will."

When Marcie tucked Andrea into her new bed that night, she said with a big smile, "Mama, this is the nicest Christmas that I've had in my whole life. I have a puppy and a daddy, just like my friends."

Matt telephoned Rick the next day, "Since tomorrow is Sunday, can you come over for dinner about noon and bring your family?"

"Sure, if it's important, Matt."

Matt went out to greet the Baumans when they arrived, and Marcie and Andrea waited in the living room.

"Matt, did you have all of us come over here just to see your new car? You've never been known to be a great cook."

"The surprise is in the living room."

As they entered the living room, Matt said, "I want you to meet my family. This is Marcie and Andrea."

The Baumans were speechless, waiting for an explanation.

The children broke the silence. Andrea asked, "How old are you, Joy?"

"Five."

"Me too."

"Come with me, Joy, and see my puppy and my doll."

After the hugs and confusion, they sat down while Matt and Marcie explained what had happened. Later Marcie served a dinner of red beans and rice with a salad. They finished the meal with chicory coffee.

As the Baumans drove home, Maria said to Ruth, "I liked Marcie's dinner, but I've never eaten that kind of food."

Rick added thoughtfully to the family conversation, "Only a compassionate God could do something like that for Matt."

24

Matt and Rick

In 1951 Matt graduated from law school and was working with Steve Walters again in the summer. Steve described their next case as they were flying to Washington, "A navy flyer bailed out, and his plane went down in the Virginia mountains. The pilot survived with a broken leg and managed to drag himself to a nearby farm house for help."

"I read a little about it on a back page of the *St. Louis-Post Dispatch*. Wasn't it a routine training flight with no unusual weather conditions?"

Steve answered, "Yes, the manufacturer and military personnel investigating the accident found no failure on the part of the plane, and maintenance records were complete and seemed accurate. Preliminary navy findings point to pilot error."

Matt responded, "Pilots do make errors, but sometimes I get upset when the preliminary findings always seems to be probable pilot error. Where is the pilot now?"

"In the Bethesda Hospital in Maryland. He's unmarried, and newspapers haven't shown much interest in the story because there were no fatalities. This is probably a routine investigation, but the firm wants facts in their file."

"Where do you want me to start?"

"Interview the admiral assigned to the investigation, the pilot, and personnel where the plane was manufactured. Since you've graduated, your pay will be $300 a day. Did you know how much more valuable you are this year?"

"Not really, but I'm happy that somebody thinks so."

At the end of the week, Steve reviewed his notes with Matt. Their conclusions were in direct conflict. They were both disturbed and talked about it.

"The evidence seems to be pretty compelling, Matt. This particular model plane had flown five years without an accident, and inspectors found no maintenance or technical problems."

Matt interjected his position, "I'm convinced that Pentagon personnel drew their conclusion without a thorough review. I interviewed the pilot on events from the time the plane left the ground until the accident. He told me that his plane had been descending rapidly, and he was unable to pull it up. He concluded that his only choice was to eject."

"What else did you learn?"

"I telephoned Pensacola where the pilot had been trained and got a copy of all of his flight records. He was at the top of his class, and all of his immediate superiors reported that he was an excellent pilot."

"We'll stay over a week and let the firm know that we need to check more carefully."

"Steve, I'll call you when I get back after my interviews with corporate personnel. If the plane has a defect that isn't found, a pilot could be killed and another plane lost."

After his interviews Matt was convinced that there should be further investigation, so he asked for technical personnel to check out subcontractors' records.

"The firm is skeptical of your concern, Matt. They think you're biased, but they'll give you the technical staff you need to investigate more thoroughly."

An important discovery gave reason for even further

investigation. After the first fifty planes were manufactured, some parts were used from a new subcontractor. The plane involved in the accident was one of the planes manufactured last. The finding was significant enough that the firm authorized Matt to continue working with his technical staff.

The investigation narrowed to the part that could have affected the plane in the way the pilot had described. Military maintenance personnel removed the questionable part from two of their planes and checked them carefully; they found defects. Planes manufactured with that defective part were grounded until the part was replaced.

The firm quietly negotiated a settlement between the navy and the manufacturer. Matt was pleased because the action would save lives. The firm was pleased because they had obtained a large financial settlement.

In August Matt was still trying to decide his future plans when the president of Sunburst Pilots Union in St. Louis called Matt to ask if he would meet with their officers.

When Matt sat down with them a few days later, they asked him if he would consider being their legal counsel in a paid staff position. "We heard how you handled the accident case in Virginia and were impressed. Most of our work involves working conditions and pay negotiations, but our pilots prefer an attorney who's an experienced pilot."

They worked out a contract with a priority for half of Matt's time, which would allow him to do other legal work. When Matt talked with Rick about his agreement with the pilots' union, he asked Matt to be the AP/SUN legal counsel, paid on a case-by-case basis.

They located an office in the same downtown building where Sunburst Pilots Union had their offices and meeting rooms. Rick had learned that location and time are valuable assets. In addition to working for Sunburst Pilots Union and for the AP and SUN Corporations, Matt had now become a legal consultant to Washington University.

*   *   *

Three baby boys were born in the fall of 1951: Dred Scott Lincoln, called "Abe;" Matthew William Simmons, Jr. called "Billy," and Emil Ulrick Bauman, Jr. called "Emil." During the rest of 1951, and all through 1952, the children and the AP and SUN Corporations grew.

*   *   *

Rick explained to Matt that while he was getting a cost estimate to remove the tenements on the SUN property, a development corporation from Boston contacted him and offered him $70,000 for their city block of tenement buildings. He had tried to sell the block in 1949, but there were no serious buyers. Rick rejected the Boston offer and asked Matt to discover why the SUN property value had changed.

A few weeks later Matt reported his findings to Rick. "After being delayed by the Depression and war years, the Jefferson National Exposition Memorial Committee is now active. When we were kids living on the river front, we laughed about these tenements ever becoming a park."

"I'd forgotten all about that talk," mused Rick.

"President Roosevelt's executive order in 1935 designated a thirty-six-block area as a unit of the National Park System."

"Is the SUN property to be part of the proposed park?"

"No, but I found in studying property transactions that a corporation from Boston has been quietly buying all of the land within a mile of the park. Our block is in that area."

"When will the city complete the park?"

"Some people who should know say five to ten years."

"Good job, Matt. I think we should keep the property."

"I agree."

*   *   *

Rick decided to walk across the SUN property, building by building, instead of driving by as he had always done. The area was almost unrecognizable to him. His living standard had improved so much that he could hardly believe that he and his friends had ever lived and played in these slums.

As he walked from building to building, his memories returned. He stopped abruptly at one building that he vaguely recalled and climbed the broken wooden steps. He entered the door of a three-room, cold-water flat. As Rick walked, he tripped on an old washtub and stumbled across the room. He was startled by a sudden wretched memory. This was where his childhood friend Mary Ellen had lived.

Rick's energy drained out of him, and he had trouble breathing. He rushed out and almost collapsed on the top step. Tears came to his eyes as he thought over and over, 'Mary Ellen didn't have a chance living in this place and having polio, measles, and then scarlet fever.'

Rick left resolved to demolish all of the tenements on his property. He never wanted to see them again.

25

Jack's Return

"Where to, Colonel?" asked the cab driver.

"To the highest hotel in St. Louis."

Arriving at the hotel, Jack was able to get the room he wanted on the top floor. Tonight Jack wanted to reflect privately on the mystic Mississippi river front and block out his excruciating memories of his three years of combat in Korea.

After checking the room and handing Jack his key, the bellman showed his elation when Jack gave him the largest tip he had probably ever received. Jack knew how the bellman felt, remembering the half dollar the lady had given him at Union Station years ago.

To have an evening alone, Jack had arrived a day earlier than he had told Rick and Matt he would. He took two small bottles of bourbon out of the bag that the stewardess had given him on the flight to St. Louis. He poured the bourbon into a glass of ice and let it cool while he slipped off his medal-covered jacket, loosened his tie, and kicked off his shoes.

Jack lit a cigarette and pulled the drapes all the way back. Pulling two chairs over to the window wall, he sat down in one and placed his shoeless feet on the other. As he smoked his cigarette, he sipped his drink and dozed off.

When Jack woke an hour later, night had fallen and the lights of the river front sparkled below him. He got up slowly and walked to the phone. He called room service and ordered a steak dinner and a cold bottle of Budweiser beer.

When the service cart was wheeled into the room, Jack noticed that the cart included flowers and a bowl of fruit. Thinking that there'd been a mix-up in the order, Jack asked, "Why are there flowers and fruit?"

"Compliments of the hotel manager who spotted you in the lobby. He was a marine in World War II."

"This is a special night for me. Please thank him."

As Jack started to eat, he reflected on the lights of the city below and the stars twinkling at him in the sky above. He wistfully thought, 'I'll bet Louie's watching me now.' Jack ate his dinner slowly, relishing every moment. When he finished eating, he slept soundly until ten the next morning.

Matt had invited Jack to stay with his family before going to his house in the Ozarks. As Jack took a cold shower and washed his battle-scared body, he thought to himself, 'No one will ever know why some men live in battles, and some men don't.' When he finished his shower and dressed, Jack telephoned Rick to let him know that he was on his way to Matt's.

"Welcome home, Jack. Marcie will have lunch for you, and Ruth and Mother will have dinner for you this evening. Can you handle that much?"

"You bet I can. Thanks, Rick. It's great to be home."

"We've waited three long years for you."

*   *   *

Jack arrived at the Simmons' home and sat down in the living room with Matt, Marcie, Andrea, and Billy. He thought, 'Matt has a wonderful family and is acting like his old self. It's incredible how his world has changed so much in a few short years.'

Matt and Jack did not have time to catch up on what had happened in the years that Jack was gone, but there would be time later for longer visits. Corporate business had been postponed until the end of Jack's leave. His visits in Matt's and Rick's homes reminded him how he felt when he found Louie after World War II. This feeling is uniquely known to combat veterans coming home alive.

On Sunday the Bauman, Simmons, and Lincoln families had planned a picnic for Jack at the park bench in Forest Park. Ruth arrived after the others with Miss Goerner, whose hair was now completely gray but nothing else about her seemed to have changed. She went straight to Jack and hugged him. As soon as she had said hello to everyone and had been introduced to Scott and his wife, Laura, she turned to the children.

"Please come over here a moment children. I'm Miss Hilga, and I'd like you to tell me your names."

Their response was like chirping birds, "Joy, Andrea, Abe, Billy, Emil."

"I hear that you boys each have your second birthday this month, and I have a special party just for you. Andrea and Joy would you please open this box and put candles on the cake."

As the girls fixed the cake, Hilga turned to the boys, "How many fingers make two?" The boys, giggling and jumping, proudly showed two fingers as did Miss Hilga.

Marcie lit the candles, and everyone sang "Happy Birthday." When the five children had blown out all the candles, they headed for the lake with their fathers and Jack after them. The ladies put the food on card tables--sandwiches, apples, lemonade, deviled eggs, and Hilga's cake. It was a wonderful reunion party.

"Thanks for everything. It's great to be home with friends," Jack said when they were ready to leave. "I'm going to my home in the mountains tomorrow, but I'll be back in St. Louis before leaving for my new assignment."

As they left for their cars, the children all chirped happily, "Bye, Uncle Jack. Bye, Miss Hilga." They all sensed that they had two new friends who loved them.

Jack's next stop on his leave would be an emotional visit to Louie's mountain. As Jack drove up to the house, Derk got up from his porch chair and waved. Jack waved back.

"The marines have landed," laughed Derk.

"The place looks nice with the new roof and paint. How've you been, Derk?"

"Okay, except for a little interference in my walking," answered Derk, pointing to a newly carved cane.

"What happened? Did you twist an ankle or something?"

"No, Doc says that I had a stroke last year, and my left leg doesn't work quite right. Are you all in one piece?"

"Yes, except for a couple of new scratches and one foot that got too cold."

"I'll bet that's an understatement."

Jack and Derk visited for the next few days and shared each other's experiences of the past three years.

One afternoon Derk said, "Jack, I hate to bring this up, but we'd better have another talk about the Mark Twain National Forest and Wilderness Area."

"Something new happening?"

"Not really, but a government agent came by a few weeks ago wanting to buy your property. I told him that you didn't want to sell your land, but I promised him I'd give you his card and have you call him."

"I haven't changed my mind."

"You'd better call him. He'll find you anyway."

"You're probably right."

"He also left this map of the land that has been purchased for the forest and an information packet," continued Derk.

"What's the purpose of this Mark Twain Forest and Wilderness Area?"

"To protect vast acres of natural forest from developers."

"Louie thought they'd mess it up. I think he was right."

"They'll mess up parts of the forest but save most of it."

Jack changed the subject and said, "I'm going down to the river for a few days."

"I don't think anything's changed."

When Jack started down the mountain, he found the trail grown over, but he didn't have trouble finding his way down to Piney's Ridge. Jack moved slowly along the old animal trail because he wanted to prepare himself for the emotional moment when he would reach the unmarked LeGault grave site where he had scattered Louie's ashes.

The LeGaults had always respected the natural beauty of this rugged area in the Ozark Mountains. Jack felt that he had inherited the responsibility to protect the forest for his ancestors, but he was living in a different time in history when nature's balanced way of protecting its plants and animals and river basins was no longer adequate against human beings.

When he had reached a large boulder embedded in the side of the mountain on the edge of the trail, Jack knew he was at the grave site. He put down his back pack and searched the area for any changes. 'Everything is at peace on Louie's mountain. How can I keep it this way?'

He lay flat on the rough ground with his head on his pack. After the frightening experiences that he'd had in Korea, he just bathed in the warm feeling of being at home with Louie. Jack thought, 'Now I know why Louie felt better after his visits here.' Suddenly Jack was overcome by a strange vision of Louie beside him and their ancestors sitting on the rocks nearby looking at him, as though they expected something from him.

Jack was startled by a whole new thought, 'I can't save this place by myself. I need the right lawyer, one who knew Louie and knows how desperate I am to meet my responsibility. I'll talk to Matt; he'll find an answer.'

As Jack stood and lifted his pack, he felt a gust of wind that rustled the leaves and berry bushes nearby. The images of Louie and the other LeGault ancestors seemed to fade away with smiles of satisfaction, and Jack's spirit felt strangely renewed.

Colonel Blackjack Pershing LeGault enjoyed the pleasures that Louie had taught him living in the Ozark wilderness along the St. Francis River. He picked berries, fished, hunted, splashed like an otter in the river, and bathed in the warm sun that slipped through the trees.

Jack arrived back at his house with fresh fish and a quart of berries. He called ahead to Derk, who greeted him.

"What happened to you, Jack? Could a short time on the river make you into a new person?"

"I think it did."

*   *   *

When Jack returned to St. Louis, he called Matt and told him that he needed to have a long talk. Matt said, "We can meet at the Missouri Athletic Club for lunch."

Jack arrived early, drove his car into the Missouri Athletic Club garage off Washington Street, and took the elevator to the lobby level. He wandered around in the lobby looking at paintings.

When Matt arrived, he asked, "What's on your mind, Jack?"

"Let's go to the dining room first."

They ordered, and Matt repeated, "What's bothering you?"

"I must keep a promise, but I don't know how."

"What's the promise all about?"

"The federal government is establishing a National Forest and Wilderness Area in the Ozark Mountains. They want to buy Louie's mountain that I promised to protect," answered Jack without revealing his supernatural experience.

"You told me that you weren't going to sell it."

"There's a government agent who doesn't want to take 'no' for an answer," said Jack. "Can they force me to sell?"

"Probably."

"Matt, you're the only one I trust to do the right thing."

"Jack, let's enjoy our steaks and then go out to our park bench. We'll review your options and personal priorities."

"Thanks, Matt."

When they got to the park bench, Matt started asking questions, "Are you interested in using the mountain yourself? Do you want to protect the property after your death?"

"Yes to both."

"That's a starting point."

A half hour of questions and answers later, Matt concluded, "You'd better negotiate. Don't even let them consider condemnation of the property for their use. Going to court should be your last resort."

"Go ahead and start the negotiation."

" First we'll negotiate your priorities, moving slowly to resolve one issue at a time."

"Time is my lowest priority. Bill me for your time and expenses."

"I'll keep in touch with you as I address each issue."

"It's nice to have a friend and an attorney I can trust," smiled Jack.

26

The Corporations

Matt brought a pot of coffee and a box of donuts from his adjoining office. He and Jack could sense Rick's ideas coming like the flooding of the Mississippi River in the spring--Rick must have something extraordinary to discuss.

Before they started on corporate business, Rick asked, "What are you going to be doing this year, Jack?"

"I'll report to the marine base at Quantico, Virginia."

Matt asked, "What will your assignment be?"

"I'll be an instructor at the Command and Staff College."

"Teaching what?" asked Rick.

"The science of battle tactics in combat situations."

Matt commented, "It's time, Jack, that the marines assign you to something other than actual combat."

Then Matt turned to Rick and asked, "What's the agenda?"

"It's hard for me to describe quickly, but I believe it's time to restructure the corporations."

"What do you mean?" asked Jack.

"Determine clear and separate goals for the AP and SUN Corporations and make adjustments to meet those goals."

Rick briefed Jack on what had happened in the past three

years and concluded, "Corporate income has increased fifty-eight percent, and we have fewer properties."

"Have you bought any other properties?" asked Jack.

"No."

"Do you have a current appraisal?"

"Our present combined appraisal is $366,000, and the debt has been reduced to $19,000."

"Rick, do you have a major goal to accomplish in this meeting," asked Matt, guessing that he did.

"Yes, that AP become exclusively a parking business and SUN become exclusively a development corporation."

"What needs to be done?" asked Jack.

"Have SUN parking lots transferred to AP, and leave only the downtown block of tenements in the SUN corporation."

"Sounds sensible," responded Jack. "Just go ahead and get those problems corrected, Matt."

"Okay," Matt said. Then he suggested, "We could transfer ownership of your house where Scott's been living to him as a gift. Then transfer the house that you're living in near Tower Grove from the SUN Corporation to your name."

"That's a good idea, Matt," said Jack.

Matt continued, "I'm purchasing a new home in Webster Groves. You can sell the house at Washington University where I live."

"What kind of a house is it?" asked Rick, pleased that Matt was a step ahead of him.

"It's larger than we need, but Marcie likes it, and there's a park across the street for the children."

Rick then suggested, "Matt, why don't you brief Jack on the river front and downtown development activities near our SUN properties?"

"Okay. Do you remember, Jack, when we were kids, around 1935, when there was a lot of crazy talk about demolishing our neighborhood on the river front for a park?"

"I kind of remember, but nothing happened."

"Well, it's happening now," said Matt.

"Is that what all the vacant land and rubble is down near the levee that I saw out of my hotel window?"

"That's it," said Rick.

Matt continued, "Thirty-six city blocks, including twelve along the river front and others three blocks back, are being cleared for a park."

"How big will the park be?" asked Jack.

"Eighty-six acres," answered Rick. "About the only buildings left where we lived and played will be the Old Church and the Old Courthouse. History may speak about it, but our children and grandchildren will never see the old downtown river front neighborhood where we lived."

"Wow!" said Jack.

"The plan started in 1935."

"What stopped them from building the park?"

"The Depression and World War II."

"What makes you think they'll develop it now?"

"A Jefferson National Expansion Memorial Committee was established in 1947. The architectural design that they selected was a giant arch located in a river front park. The Gateway Arch and the memorial park will be a reminder that St. Louis was the gateway to the West for thousands of 19th century pioneers who settled land west of the Mississippi River. Also, the Lewis and Clark Expedition started here in 1804."

"It doesn't seem real to most people, including me. It's to be higher than the Washington Monument, and people will ride to a viewing platform and see thirty miles in all directions."

"Do you believe that, Rick?" asked Jack.

"In 1876 they didn't believe that James Eads could build a bridge for carriages on one level and trains on another level to cross the Mississippi River at the same time, but he did."

"They completed that bridge in 1894, and it will be there forever," said Jack.

Rick added, "A man's idea is usually limited only by his faith and determination. If St. Louis planners and Eero Saarinen, the architect, have these qualities, they'll succeed."

"It could revitalize St. Louis more than anything since the 1904 World's Fair," said Matt.

"Is anything else going on downtown?" asked Jack.

"August Busch is building a huge new stadium not far from the new park to replace Sportsman's Park.

Rick went on to explain more about what was happening around their block of tenements before suggesting that they take a break.

"We didn't get donuts on our breaks in Korea, Rick."

"What's Korea like, Jack?" asked Matt as he opened the box of donuts and passed them around.

"The real difference is the geography and the culture," answered Jack. "A lot of marines disliked South Koreans because they look like the North Koreans that were killing us. But I visited in some South Korean homes, and they're nice people with thousands of years of history."

Matt said, "Navy flying is different because you usually don't see people while you're fighting."

Jack continued, "What demoralized us in Korea was that President Truman and his Joint Chiefs of Staff in Washington insisted that we weren't fighting a war. We felt that we had nothing to win, like unifying Korea. We were only there to keep North Korean and Chinese Communists out of South Korea."

Matt added, "I feel sorry for the Koreans. When the Japanese invaded Korea in the 1930s, they ravaged the whole country, imprisoning, enslaving, raping, torturing, you name it. When we defeated Japan, we allowed Korea to be politically and arbitrarily divided. Now, after three years of bloody war, Korea is still divided."

"Matt, we'd better get back to work, or Rick will reduce our pay," Jack laughed, as he pushed the empty donut box aside and lit a cigarette.

Rick started the meeting again, "Matt is going to buy some

lots near our SUN property at an auction for back taxes. They are small lots, and each of them has a deteriorated building. Properties of this kind are not usually attractive to home owners and are too small to attract developers."

"Do you need these properties as parking lots, Rick?"

"Not now, but someday they'll be worth a lot of money."

"Anything else?" asked Matt.

"Why don't we have one two-day annual meeting?" said Rick. "We can have special meetings if we need them."

"That would help me," said Jack.

"Each of us should receive $2,000 for participating in the annual meeting, and in Jack's case, expenses."

Sounds good to me, Jack laughed, "I move we adjourn."

Rick had not told Matt or Jack his private wish to develop their city block as his personal memorial to Mary Ellen. Rick was forthright in everything he did, but this was private. He could hardly wait to see the tenements gone.

27

Louie's Mountain, 1957

Jack opened their discussion of Louie's Mountain. "Matt, when I heard that Derk had died last spring, I couldn't picture living here in the Ozark Mountains in this house without Louie, Jimmy, or Derk. But since you were able to sell Louie's Mountain for me, I've decided to keep the farm for myself and my children."

"What children?"

"None. But I do have a future; I'm only thirty-three."

"Sure you have a future, Jack, and a good one," assured Matt more seriously as he opened a survey map.

After they had studied the map and finished lunch, Matt suggested, "Let's walk along the edge of the farm and look at the markers that divide your farm from Louie's Mountain."

They walked from marker to marker before sitting down on the trunk of a tree that had fallen in a storm. Matt started to explain the legal terms of the contract, "The land as marked by the St. Francis River on the west and the permanent markers on the south, east and north as recorded . . . "

"Matt, explain the agreement in your own words."

"Okay. The mountain acreage covers about a square mile with

271

almost a mile of river front. It's classified as a wilderness area and referred to as "Louie's Mountain" on all publications.

"What's a wilderness area?"

"It means that neither you nor anyone else can change Louie's Mountain in any way, including tree cutting, roads, building construction, or almost anything."

"Can I keep Louie's cabin?"

"Yes, but you can't build another one."

"That's what Louie wanted."

"You and your immediate family members are authorized to hunt on Louie's Mountain and to fish in the river for fifty years, subject to laws of the State of Missouri. I hope it's all right."

"It's an excellent contract. How did you do it?"

"Four years of patient negotiations."

Jack had no reservation and signed the contract. "How much will the check be?"

"The sale price is $99,400. My time and expenses came to $12,700, leaving you a check for $86,700. How do you plan to invest your money?"

"My friends say, 'Invest in Coca Cola.' They were right in 1953 when they told me to invest my $5,000 that I brought back from Korea in IBM. That stock's worth $19,000 now."

"Why Coca Cola?"

"You drink it instead of beer, don't you, Matt?"

"Yes."

"Well, people are beginning to drink it all over the world. In many countries the water isn't safe to drink."

Watching the sun setting below Louie's Mountain, Matt said, "It's time to go back for supper and get some sleep. Rick will be here early in the morning for our board meeting."

The next morning as the sun was rising, they heard a horn honking loudly. They looked out the window and saw Rick driving up to the house. Jack was making coffee, and Matt was frying eggs and bacon. As Rick came in the door, Jack greeted him, "Sit down and have some breakfast."

"Smells good, but you really don't seem properly dressed for a board meeting," Rick joked, observing them in their undershorts and bare feet.

"We'll dress as AP/SUN Corporate Directors later," said Matt. "Now it's time to eat. I put another egg in the skillet when you honked to let us know that our president had arrived."

"Enough of that," said Rick with an embarrassed smile.

After breakfast they went out to the porch rockers for their meeting. It was a pleasant day, a little cool and windy, but the sun was up and felt good to the men sitting on the sheltered porch. Matt and Jack both were thinking that the day was too perfect to spoil with serious business.

Rick spoke the words they had hoped to hear, "No momentous decisions to make today, unless you fellows have some earthshaking ideas."

"Not me," Matt and Jack said simultaneously.

Knowing that nothing important was expected of them, they relaxed. The tree limbs in front of them were swaying and shaking their multicolored fall leaves, causing them to flutter aimlessly to the ground. Crows were noisily cawing as they ate the remains of the harvested corn field.

Jack broke the silence. "Why don't you both tell me what's been happening in St. Louis. Your letters and phone calls help, but they don't tell the whole story."

"You start first, Jack. How is teaching men to fight compared to fighting?" Matt asked.

"Safer."

"Seriously," encouraged Rick.

"I learn from officers' questions about as much as they learn from me. It was a good assignment. Last summer, my friend Rub McNally was promoted to major general, and he gave me a chance to visit with other senior officers, including the marine commandant, a couple of times."

"What do you mean, it 'was' a good assignment?"

"I've been promoted to full colonel and given a new assignment, effective on my return from leave."

"Congratulations, Colonel. What's the assignment?"

Jack answered, "Navy Liaison to the Senate Armed Forces Committee."

"That's a big responsibility," said Matt as he got up and slapped Jack on the back. "It'll be good news to the navy."

"What are we talking about," asked Rick, who didn't understand what Jack would be doing.

Jack explained, "As a staff officer, I'll be expected to insure proper communication and coordination between navy requirements and the Senate Armed Forces Committee."

Rick was confused, "I thought you were in the marines."

Matt interjected, "Marines are a component of the navy."

"Why don't admirals or the marine commandant talk directly to the committee?" asked Rick.

"They do, at public hearings, but in politics much of the communication is subtle. My job is to see that conflicts are worked out privately. If a serious public conflict occurs, the marine commandant, admirals, and senators must be in a position to plausibly disassociate themselves from it."

"Who gets blamed?" asked Rick.

"I'd accept responsibility for failures."

"I'd rather be in the parking business."

"Enough of me, guys."

Matt said, "Jack, you're not the only one changing jobs. I accepted a position as Associate Professor at the Washington University Law School, specializing in Real Estate and Negotiations. I'll drop my work with the pilots' union, but I'll be able to continue to work with Rick and Steve."

"Congratulations, Matt. You'll enjoy teaching," said Jack.

Rick spoke up, "You fellows don't have all the good news. I sold my Tower Grove house and lot to a pharmacy last month and bought a four-bedroom, three-bath house near Fontbonne College, not far from Forest Park."

"Did you get a good price?" asked Matt.

"Enough to buy our new home and furnish it."

"Does your family like the move?" asked Jack.

"It's a beautiful house in a nice neighborhood on an acre lot with trees. They love it."

Rick started the business meeting by reviewing actions over the past few years, "Washington University bought the house where Matt's family had been living for $21,000. We've completed the demolition work on our SUN property."

Jack asked, "How about debt, cash reserve, and net worth."

"No debt, and $91,000 cash reserves. Our net worth is over $500,000 and annual income continues to increase. There are more cars in downtown St. Louis and not enough lots to meet the demand. Most of our business is hourly parking."

"You've really done well," Jack complimented.

"If we're finished, Rick, why not take a short walk to work up an appetite for lunch?" suggested Matt.

"We're finished, unless you have questions."

"I'll show you the trail down to the river," said Jack.

When they saw the trail, Matt and Rick agreed that nature had not planned the climb down for a man with one hand. They returned to the house, and Jack fried fresh fish for lunch.

When Matt and Rick had gone, Jack was rocking on the porch thinking how lonely he was without Louie, Jimmy, or Derk, even though he did like spending his military leave on Louie's Mountain.

28

Senate Armed Forces Committee: Jack

Sitting on a leather sofa in Rub's office with their jackets off and ties loosened, Jack and Major General McNally counted votes needed to guarantee that the Senate Armed Forces Committee would approve the navy and Marine Corps budgets. With the flags, plaques, and Marine Corps colors all around, this clearly this was the office of a man who had given his life to the Marine Corps.

Rub had decided that Jack should assist Senator Bennie Benson in buying property on the Gulf of Mexico. A navy plane would fly them to the Pensacola Airport, and from there they would drive to Gulf Shores, Alabama.

As they finished their drinks, Rub said, "Jack, your plane will be ready for you and the Senator on Tuesday."

Jack made final arrangements for Senator Benson to inspect the property that he had expected to buy at a good price. After arriving at the Pensacola Naval Air Base, they drove to Pleasure Island, passing miles of sand dunes, family-owned motels, and scattered beach homes. The beach property had impressed the Senator, and he wanted to buy it. On the drive back to Pensacola,

Jack worked out details with Senator Benson, assuring him that he would get the contract through the usual sources.

A week later Senator Benson gave his unequivocal commitment to support the navy appropriations request. The next day Jack called the Senator to be sure that he was properly pleased with the Gulf Shores property.

"Senator, do you have the Gulf Shores contract?"

"Yes, but Merry Lou tells me she wants a more glamorous vacation retreat on the Grand Cayman Island, with the bars, night life, and shops."

Somewhat taken aback, Jack recovered quickly and said, "Why don't we go to dinner some night next week and discuss property at Grand Cayman?"

"Fine," replied the Senator.

"Could we meet at the cocktail lounge at the Mayflower Hotel at seven Wednesday evening?"

"Excellent choice, Jack. I'll be there."

At their Wednesday dinner, they talked about Grand Cayman Island. Finishing their second after-dinner drink, Jack handed the Senator a privately prepared prospectus and said, "Senator, take a quick look at this property."

"This is interesting. Let me review it with Merry Lou. Could you get us down there during the Senate recess?"

"I'll go to work on it right away, and I'll pick up the Gulf Shores documents tomorrow and return them."

Jack complemented Senator Benson, "Your comments to the committee clarified the navy and Marine Corps requirements. We're getting positive vibes from the press."

When Jack picked up the Gulf Shores contract, he decided to buy the property himself, if Rub had no objections and could arrange it. He went to Rub's office and briefed him on his meeting with the Senator.

"The old bastard's speech gave us the boost we needed, but I wish to hell that he'd make up his mind. He must think he's a real stud to divorce his wife and marry that young filly. He'll be eighty in a couple of years. She'll wear him out."

"She's a beautiful girl, Rub," Jack said, reflecting on the time he'd taken Merry Lou to a reception and introduced her to the Senator. "How do we get them to Grand Cayman?"

"Work it out and brief me."

"Rub, I'd like to buy the Gulf Shores property myself. Could you arrange it without any flack?"

"I'll give it a shot."

Rub made a few calls the next day, including a call to Hal Parsons, who had been a Marine Corps fighter pilot. They were both injured in the Solomon Islands and had become friends while recovering in a hospital in Hawaii.

"Hal, how about golf Saturday at the Pensacola Air Base?"

"Sure."

"Get a tee time in my name and bring two of your business acquaintances to round out a foursome."

While Rub and Hal Parsons were riding in the golf cart the next Saturday, Rub said, "Senator Benson's wife talked him out of buying the Gulf Shores property, but he appreciated your help and strongly supported our appropriation request."

Rub continued, "Colonel Jack LeGault, on my staff, would like to buy the Gulf Shores property through a development corporation in which he's invested some money. Jack saved my life several times. I'd like to help him."

"It can be done, Rub, since the owner just asked me to help you, but he doesn't want his name used. The property is in the name of my company for sixty days and then reverts back to the owner's company. The time is about to run out, so tell the Colonel he'll need to get right down here."

"Okay. Let me know when south Alabama can use some help from Washington, and I'll get the right people on it."

"We'd better concentrate on our game now," said Hal with a smile. "These guys are getting ahead of us."

*   *   *

It was morning but still dark outside. Matt had finished his shower, slipped on his shorts and had started to shave. Marcie came up behind him in her flimsy, silk nightgown and put her arms around him. She pulled her sensual body tightly against his bare back and purred in his ear, "Matt, you really don't want to fly to Pensacola this morning, do you? I've got better things for you to do."

"Don't tempt me, Marcie," Matt responded. "This isn't fair play when you know that I don't have a choice."

Seeing that Matt couldn't be deterred, Marcie gave in and asked, "What's Jack up to, asking you and Rick to be in Pensacola with less than twenty-four hours notice?"

"I honestly don't know, but if it's important to Jack, it's important to me," answered Matt as he hurriedly put on his shirt and trousers. "I need to pick up Rick in thirty minutes. Be nice and fix some coffee and toast."

"Okay, but you'd have more fun if you stayed home with me," Marcie teased and started for the kitchen.

When they had finished breakfast, Matt gave Marcie a nicer than usual goodbye kiss and a friendly pat on a tender spot as he left for the car. "Tell the children goodbye for me."

"Be careful, Matt."

Matt picked up Rick who was waiting on his front porch. Riding to the airport, Rick asked, "What does Jack want?"

"He told me that he had an opportunity to buy some property and had to complete the transaction tomorrow."

"Is that all he'd tell you?"

"For some reason, he didn't want to talk over the phone." They stopped guessing and started talking about their families. Rick observed, "Watching children grow let's you know how fast time flies."

Matt said, "Each year they're in a new stage of maturity, and I never seem ready for the change."

"It seems impossible that Andrea and Joy are teenagers."

"Can you keep Joy off the telephone?"

"Not really. Ruth talks to her about trying to keep her conversations shorter."

"We didn't even think about telephones and televisions when we were that age. We wouldn't have heard a radio if it hadn't been for the Farmer's Market," reflected Matt. "Has Joy started to flutter around the house trying out new ways to look?"

"Does she ever." Rick agreed, "First it's clothes, then facial expressions, then hair, and then, she forgets herself and just has fun."

Matt turned his attention to his flight plan, but asked, "Can you change with them fast enough?"

"I try to let Ruth keep up with Joy's mood changes. When Joy confuses me, I go out in the yard and play with Emil."

"My parental ego is better when I play ball with Billy."

Forgetting about the children, Matt pointed, "Do you see how the Mississippi River gets wider as we fly south?"

"I've been trying not to look down," answered Rick. "I'm not comfortable in an airplane."

"This Cessna is a safe airplane."

"Matt, do you really feel safe flying?"

"Safer and happier than in an automobile."

"This is my first plane ride, and I'm nervous."

Rick forced himself to look down and became fascinated with the limitless expanse of rivers, roads, and towns.

"Matt, you haven't convinced me that flying is safe, but I can certainly understand the beauty and value of flight."

"When were you on the river front last?"

"Two days ago, and the acreage is almost all cleared for the park. We'll need to think about a plan for our land."

"Sometimes a plan will emerge on its own," suggested Matt. "I think we should sit tight and do nothing until we see how the Arch and Busch Memorial Stadium change St. Louis."

"You're probably right, Matt, but I get impatient waiting. Do you have any information on timetables for completion?"

"I'll get all the factual information I can by our fall meeting. Gossip I've heard can't be considered reliable."

When they landed in Pensacola, Matt taxied the plane over to the hanger and left it with instructions for the return flight. Jack was at the terminal to meet them.

"What the hell is going on, Jack?" asked Matt, greeting him with a hand shake. "No one else but you could've talked us into coming down here with less than a day's notice."

"We've got the rest of the day to talk. Let's get you settled in your rooms and have lunch first."

By the time they had finished their lunch, they knew Jack's entire story. They would be buying a property at a price that was about half of its probable value and would be introduced as president and attorney for the SUN Development Corporation and not as Jack's lifelong friends.

"What are you using for money, Jack?" asked Rick.

"I'd like you to write a check today for $20,000 as a down payment on the purchase. I'll sell some stock and send you my check for the full purchase price of $80,000, and you can send your $60,000 check to Parsons Realty."

"What is your plan for the land, Jack?" asked Rick.

"Nothing now."

"How long would you hold the land?"

"Five to ten years."

"I'll write the check today, and we can discuss ownership and future plans at our fall meeting."

Matt agreed, and Jack thanked them for coming.

The next morning they drove about thirty miles to Parson's Realty Office in Gulf Shores where Hal greeted Jack, "Hi, Colonel. Are these the gentlemen that you told me about?"

"Yes, this is Rick Bauman, president of the SUN Development Corporation, and attorney, Matt Simmons."

"Good to meet you folks. Welcome to Pleasure Island, one of

the nicest white sand barrier islands on the Gulf of Mexico. Have you been here before?"

"I learned to fly at the Pensacola Air Base, but this is my first time in Gulf Shores."

Rick answered, "This is my first visit to the Gulf."

"You'll find the water glassy smooth today, but next week it could have six-foot waves. It changes rapidly when the storms come and go," Hal explained.

"Our Mississippi River can rise fifty feet in the spring floods," said Rick. "How do your tides change?"

"Gulf tides rise and fall daily, but serious flooding is limited to the occasional hurricane."

A few minutes later they left the car and walked across sand dunes to the water that was rolling softly onto the shore. Rick did not say anything, but he was amazed that there were mounds of sand with tall grass as far as he could see. Houses were built on posts above ground.

Hal said, "This property has 600 feet of beach front and goes back to the road. The view is especially beautiful at sunrise and sunset."

Matt asked, "What trees and plants grow in this sand?"

"If they get the proper care, a great variety of tropical trees and plants can grow here. You'll see a few landscaped properties, but most folks just let nature take its course. They know the importance of the dunes and native grasses in a storm."

"Development seems limited," Rick observed.

Hal gave his projection of the island's future, "When developers discover Pleasure Island, it will become like the lower coast of Florida. It won't happen this year, but as sure as the sun rises tomorrow morning, it'll happen."

As they drove back, Hal asked Rick, "Have you had time to study the contract?"

Rick answered, "Yes, Matt and I studied the contract, and the SUN Corporation will buy the property."

"We can complete the purchase at my office in a few minutes. Are you going to be here a few days?"

"We'll sign the contract, give you the initial check and head back to St. Louis."

"You corporate people never seem to have time to play. I would have enjoyed taking you fishing."

On their way back to Pensacola, Rick asked Matt, "Do the waters in the Gulf really get as rough as Hal told us?"

"They sure do."

"Was the tide in or out when we walked to the water?"

"The tide was in. There could be another hundred feet more or less of beach when the tide is out."

Matt cut off questions that he and Rick could have asked and kidded Jack, "You're pretty mysterious, Colonel. If you bankrupt our business, I'll sue you."

"Stay friendly. I'll answer all your questions in October."

When Matt had the plane in the air on the way back to St. Louis, Rick said, "Matt, do you think Jack knows what he's doing? That's a lot of money to pay for sand."

"We're not buying sand. We're investing in the future of Gulf Shores. It's an excellent long-term capital investment."

Rick said, "Jack made the expansion of AP in 1945 and later the purchase of SUN possible. I unequivocally trust his judgment now."

Matt changed the subject, "Rick, my approved flight plan takes us directly over places that you should see."

As they flew over Pleasure Island, Rick commented, "Our property looks different from the air. Jack's probably right; it'll be valuable when its natural beauty is discovered."

"Rick, soon we'll be flying over New Orleans, and we'll follow the Mississippi River north to St. Louis."

The different perspective that he had from the air fascinated Rick. As they came over St. Louis, Rick had a view of the river front area and was pleased to see the SUN property so well located. Rick thought of the infinite opportunities for development that went well beyond parking. He envisioned the St. Louis Gateway Arch and Busch Stadium completed. Amazing! The synergy of the architect, contractors, city and federal officials who had been working together for ten years on these projects was so impressive. Their work would have a huge impact on St. Louis.

As they left the plane at Lambert Field and drove home, Rick asked, "What'll you tell Marcie about this deal?"

Matt answered with a smile, "As little as possible."

"Good advice, Counselor."

*　　*　　*

The week after Jack returned from Pensacola, he arranged to have Senator Benson and his wife flown to Grand Cayman. Jack met them at the airport and took them to a lovely condominium with a view of the beach and pool. The special price pleased the Senator, and Merry Lou was pleased to be near her friends.

Major General McNally reported to the Marine Corps Commandant that the Senator Benson matter was settled. Personally, Rub was pleased to have had an excuse to spend a day with his Marine Corps buddy, Hal Parsons, and to have had an opportunity to help Jack. Rub McNally was not one to forget men with whom he'd shared life and death struggles.

*　　*　　*

At the October AP/SUN Board Meeting, Jack explained to Matt and Rick how politicians could sometimes obtain votes in the United States Senate.

Jack told them, "I had set up a 'sweetheart deal' for a senator to buy the Gulf Shores property, but he rejected it. That property was such a good investment that I told Rub that if he could arrange it, I'd like to buy it. Even though Rub's friends were glad to do him a favor, not to have me make the purchase myself was better for appearances."

Rick and Matt both agreed that since Jack was willing to put $80,000 into the corporations to buy the property in Gulf Shores, his share of the corporation ownership should be increased accordingly. Rick would now own sixty, Jack thirty, and Matt ten percent of their corporations, now valued at nearly a million dollars. They proudly agreed that they had done pretty well toward achieving the goal they had set for themselves when they were thirteen years old.

29

Blackjack and Sandy

"We're almost there," said Davy Alexander. Jack did not reply. He was deep in thought, reflecting on the conversation he'd had with Davy the night before. Two years ago Davy had married and now had a son. Davy had always planned to return to his father's tobacco farm after he retired from the marines, but he had intended to raise cattle instead of growing tobacco. In the past ten years, he had purchased three tobacco farms adjacent to his father's farm.

A month ago, July 1960, Davy's father had died, leaving his sister alone to take care of the farm and their fishing camp. His sister needed help, and Davy thought he would have to leave the marines three years before his twenty-year retirement.

Since their combat days together in Korea, Davy had always admired Jack and respected his opinions. He asked Jack to give him some business advice, and Jack agreed to go to North Carolina to analyze Davy's business plan. Jack warned him, though, that he knew nothing about ranching. Somehow Jack knew that going to North Carolina to try to help Davy was something he should do. When Jack felt strongly about something that he couldn't logically understand, he'd learned to follow his instinct. Doing this had saved his life on more than one occasion.

"How far is it from here?"

"This is it," said Davy in an excited voice as he turned onto a narrow gravel road marked by a weather-beaten sign hanging crooked from a tree limb, "ALEX FISH CAMP."

"Isn't working by herself in a men's fishing camp a tough life for your sister?"

"Yes, but she handles it okay. When Dad was alive, he did the heavy work, and my sister did the cleaning and cooking. If we sell the fish camp, life will be better for her."

Jack's eyes swiftly scouted the place as he'd been trained to do on the battlefield. Long grass in front of an old privy suggested that no one had used it in recent years. Farther south he saw a creek in a patch of woods behind an odd-shaped building, badly in need of paint. Three boats were fastened to a pier. Outboard motors hung on a sheltered wall rack. Glancing north, he saw several attractive lake front homes.

Davy opened a wooden screen door and walked up behind his sister and gave her a hug. She was cleaning a couple of fish and did not turn around.

"Hey, Davy. Great to see you. Get washed up, and I'll have supper ready for you."

Davy said, "Sandy, turn around and meet my friend, Jack LeGault. Jack, this is Mary Ann."

"Hi, Mary Ann. I thought Davy called you Sandy."

"Hi, Jack. Only Davy calls me Sandy. Glad you can help us."

"I'm not sure that I can, but Davy thinks so."

"Davy respects your opinion, Jack, or he wouldn't have had you come. He's used to making his own decisions."

"You do well to handle both the fishing camp and the farm, Mary Ann," said Jack in admiration.

"I miss Dad. This place isn't fancy, but we've always kept

expenses low by doing our own work. We have a couple of fishermen at a time, usually on weekends."

After they had finished eating, Davy said, "Sandy, I'm going to take one of the boats and show Jack some places where we fish. We'll be about an hour."

"I won't hold my breath."

"Thanks for the great meal," Jack added. " I've never eaten better biscuits."

"Glad you liked 'em," answered Mary Ann. "I've had it for the day. I'm going to shower and get to bed. All the bunk beds in the back room are made up. Take any one you want."

When they returned and hung their motor on the rack, Davy told Jack, "Tomorrow I want Sandy to drive you out to the farm while I look after the fishing camp. Walk over the farms, so you can give me your ideas while we drive back."

"Are you sure you want to give up on tobacco?"

"I've had it up to here with tobacco," answered Davy as he held his hand up to his chin.

"I know that feeling. I had it with potatoes once."

Knowing that they had to get up early, they didn't talk long.

When Jack and Davy woke, they smelled ham and eggs frying. It didn't take them long to wash and dress. Sitting down at a picnic table near the kitchen, Jack could see that Mary Ann was ready for them, like a mother bird who had babies in a nest hungry for food. After they had eaten, Mary Ann and Jack waved goodbye to Davy, leaving him to clean the kitchen and be ready for the two fishermen who were due to arrive.

As Mary Ann drove the car out of the camp drive, she said, "You must be a good friend of Davy's to put up with me."

"You're underselling yourself, Mary Ann. I'm looking forward to spending a day with you on your farm."

"Me too. I'm overdue for a day off."

While Mary Ann answered Jack's questions about North Carolina, he took time to observe her. She was dressed in a red and white checked shirt, well-worn levy pants and boots. Her red hair was tied behind her head, but not fully hidden under the ball cap she was wearing. Her face had a few freckles left from childhood. Jack liked her easy smile.

Three hours later, they drove by a sign that read, "CROCKETT, NORTH CAROLINA, POPULATION 498."

Mary Ann joked, "This is our town; it'll grow to over five hundred when Davy and his family move back."

"It's a nice little town," said Jack thoughtfully.

Mary Ann pointed to a small church as they drove out of town toward the farm, "That's the Oak Grove Baptist Church where Davy and I were baptized. Dad and Mom are buried in the cemetery behind the church. You should go to church with me sometime. That's when I pretty-up and wear my one dress," she laughed.

"You look pretty now," said Jack sincerely.

Mary Ann blushed.

Three miles farther they turned into a long, tree-lined drive to a two-story frame house with a large front porch. A tobacco barn and a small shed for tools stood alone in the back. No signs of flowers or vegetable gardens revealed that the family had apparently been fully occupied with tobacco and working at the fishing camp.

Mary Ann told Jack that there were three bedrooms and a full bathroom upstairs with living quarters and a lavatory downstairs. They walked out and looked over the barn and the tool shed before returning to the front porch to talk.

Jack asked, "How many acres do you have including the farms that Davy bought?"

"One hundred and eighty."

"That's enough for Davy's cattle, but he could probably use some more land for winter hay when he can afford to buy it. Is any of the land fenced?"

"Not really. There are fences, but they're in bad shape."

"What do you think of Davy's idea of selling the fish camp and substituting cattle for tobacco?"

"Davy should decide, since he has the family. I'd still have plenty to do, and I'm not in love with tobacco."

At lunch time Mary Ann went to the refrigerator for a basket of sandwiches that she had made that morning while Davy and Jack were still asleep and placed them on the table.

Jack asked politely, "Do you have a can of beer?"

"I get along without beer. Can you?"

"I can get by for a few days without it, but I wouldn't want to be without it too long," answered Jack honestly, a little taken back at Mary Ann's direct question.

"Davy says that you have two bad habits, otherwise you're the finest man he's ever met," said Mary Ann.

"What habits?" asked Jack, who had decided to be as direct with Mary Ann as she was with him.

"He says that you smoke and drink too much. He didn't put it that way, but that's what he meant."

"I live alone and don't think much about it, but Davy's probably right. I started drinking when I was a boy and started smoking with the issue of cigarettes in combat."

"Either of those habits can kill you."

"I've been more concerned about mortar shells."

After lunch Mary Ann said, "We'll take a walk through the woods to the river and to the farms that Davy bought."

After walking 400 yards into the woods, Mary Ann showed Jack a deep part of the otherwise shallow river and said, "This is my favorite place. Davy and I came here to swim when we were children. I'd come here by myself to sit on this raised bank and think of any nice thing I could."

"I see why you like this spot."

"I don't know about you, Jack, but I'm going to cool my feet," said Mary Ann pulling off her boots and rolling up her pants.

"Good idea," said Jack, as he did the same. "Any fish in this shallow pool?"

"Only minnows and fish too small to eat. A few good fish are always here in the spring after the floods."

"What about deer?"

"A few. Davy used to hunt, but Dad never did."

"Davy calls you Sandy. What's your real name?"

"Mary Ann. What's your real name, Jack?"

"Blackjack Pershing LeGault, after the general of the army in World War I. Louie, my father, always thought that General Pershing was the greatest man he'd ever known. Louie always called me Blackjack, but everyone else calls me Jack."

"Was General Pershing's real name Blackjack?"

"That's what his soldiers called him. I read that he got that name when he was a new lieutenant out of West Point assigned to lead black soldiers in the Spanish American War."

"Dad named me Mary Ann after his favorite beauty queen, but he told Mom that the name came from her aunt. Dad named Davy too. Since our town was named after Davy Crockett, he named his son Davy Crockett Alexander."

"Your father was right about one thing. You're pretty enough to be a beauty queen."

Mary Ann blushed. This time she smiled and said, "I'd like to call you Blackjack as Louie did, and you can call me Sandy."

"I'd like that, Sandy," said Blackjack who was still trying to understand the girl who was sitting beside him.

"Why didn't you ever get married, Blackjack?"

Blackjack felt that Sandy wouldn't be satisfied with a partial answer, so he said, "While I was growing up, I didn't have time or money to be with girls. I spent almost six years of my adult life in combat conditions. At Washington University I dated girls, but they seemed to me like immature children."

"Davy told me that you're stationed in Virginia and have an active social life."

"Davy's right. My work requires me to be at social events where I've been with women. One was interested in marriage, but I backed away . . . all she wanted was a social life. We didn't have much else in common."

Sandy pressed on, "What about your mother, Blackjack?"

"Louie met and married a young girl in France after World War I. We lived in Paris until I was three years old when my mother left us. My father took me back to St. Louis."

Blackjack thought that if Sandy could be that direct, he would be just as direct. "Why didn't you get married?"

"I almost did. I was engaged to a boy in town, but he got drafted. We were going to get married when he got his leave. He didn't get the leave; he was killed on Normandy Beach on D-day. He was a wonderful person. I decided that if I couldn't marry Danny, I wouldn't marry anyone."

"Do you still feel that way, Sandy?"

"No one has ever made me want to change my mind."

They sat quietly for a few minutes, without realizing that they had crossed their feet together under the water. As they became conscience of the intimacy of their entangled bare legs and feet, Sandy abruptly said, "I don't feel like it, but it's time to go if you want to see all of Davy's farms."

They put on their socks and shoes and started walking toward some of the old fence lines. Blackjack suggested, "Let's cross the river and walk to the property line on the other side. How much of your property fronts on the river?"

"Nearly 1,500 feet on this side and about 600 feet on the other side. Davy's last purchase was a farm on the other side of the river."

"How far does the river flood over in the spring, Sandy?"

"Not too much. Usually fifty feet on the low side and fifteen on this side. It's more like a river in the spring but more like a creek now. Some folks call it a creek."

They crossed the river stepping on stones in a shallow spot. Blackjack thought to himself, 'Sandy was right about the fences; they'll have to be replaced.'

On their way back, Sandy slipped on the last stone crossing the river, and Blackjack jumped into the water to catch her as she fell and held her a little longer than necessary. The impulses of their bodies were telling them something that they were not ready to admit.

At the house Blackjack took off his shoes and hung his socks to dry. He had brought a small bag with him but had left his uniform trousers at the fishing camp in Davy's car.

"Did you bring another pair of trousers, Blackjack?"

"No. These can dry on me."

"Davy's pants are too big for you, but I think you can squeeze into a pair of mine. Go upstairs and try them on," said Sandy, as she tossed him a pair of levy pants from the laundry room. The pants were tight, but he could wear them. When he returned, Sandy had a can of beer for him and held a Coke for herself, saying, "I found this lone can of beer that Davy left in the bottom of the refrigerator."

"Thanks."

When they finished their drinks, Sandy said, "Read our Raleigh newspaper while I get supper."

After they had eaten, they talked for several hours about anything each of them could think to ask. By the end of the evening, they thought they knew all about each other's life experiences.

Sandy said, "You'll have to start early, so you'd better get some sleep. You can sleep in Davy's room."

When Blackjack started to turn into his room, Sandy could not resist giving him the kiss she had wanted to give him all day and broke away, whispering, "Blackjack, you're the first man since Danny died that made me think I could love again."

At breakfast the next morning, Blackjack took the initiative and said, "Sandy, I'd like to come back and see you again on my October leave. How would you feel about that?"

"I was hoping that you might."

They quickly cleaned the kitchen and were ready when Davy drove up. Blackjack hugged and kissed Sandy before they went out to meet Davy. The three of them talked a few minutes until Davy and Jack had to leave.

"Bye, Sandy," said Davy.

"Bye, Davy," said Sandy kissing him on the cheek and then kissing Blackjack on the mouth slowly.

"Bye, Sandy," said Blackjack. "I'll write."

"Bye," returned Sandy, brushing a tear from her eye.

As they drove out the drive, Davy said, "You had quite an influence on Sandy. It's been a long time since I've seen her show her emotions. What do you think of her?"

"She's remarkable," answered Jack. "I've never met a girl like her or had a girl affect me the way she does."

"What are you going to do about it?" challenged Davy.

"I asked her if I could come back and visit on my leave."

"Good for you," said Davy, pleased. "What did she say?"

"Yes."

"Good for her."

The subject changed, and Davy asked, "What do you think about my plan of switching from tobacco to cattle?"

"You can be successful with cattle, but I think you may want to reconsider your timing."

"What do you mean?"

"You'll have a lot of startup expense that you may not have thought about, and my friend, Rick, always warns about unanticipated expenses."

"I have money saved to buy a bull and some cows," Davy said, defending his plan.

"If you start next January, you'll have more expenses than income," continued Jack.

"But I plan to sell the fishing camp to get more cash."

"What price can you get for the fishing camp?"

"A neighbor is interested in buying it for about $5,000."

"I think that I can show you how to get a better price, but I don't think it would be enough for you to get started."

"What are you trying to tell me?"

"I'm suggesting that you spend three more years in the Marine

Corps, so you'll have your pension. You'll need that income for your family while you get your ranch started."

Davy was not expecting this answer and thought a minute before he asked, "Are you sure you're right?"

"No one can be sure they're right. It's like preparing young marines for battle: better preparation increases their chances of coming back alive."

"What else?" asked Davy, realizing that Jack was serious and probably right.

"In these three years, you have three leaves that you can use to prepare your farm for raising cattle."

"Like doing what?"

"Build fences, prepare hay fields, buy additional equipment, convert the tobacco barn to a cattle barn, and bulldoze several water holes in your river, so there'll be plenty of water for cattle in dry years and for fish in wet years."

Davy hesitated and then said, "I see what you mean. Those are things that I hadn't thought about. You said earlier that I might get a higher price for the fish camp. How?"

"Get appraisals and talk to realtors in Raleigh."

Davy looked discouraged.

Aware of Davy's disappointment, Jack said, "Be patient, read books on raising cattle, and talk to cattlemen."

"What would you do first, Jack?"

"With your father gone, I'd sell the fishing camp to get the money needed to prepare your ranch for cattle."

Later, as they drove into the Quantico Marine Base, Davy thanked Jack for coming and asked him to be kind to his sister. Jack promised that he would.

During the next few weeks, Jack telephoned Sandy regularly. Their conversations became longer and more intimate. Jack's October leave seemed a long way off to them. Jack decided it was too long, so he changed it from October to September and then called her about his new plan.

"I thought you were coming in October, Blackjack."

"I didn't want to wait that long," Blackjack said with some concern. "Is September okay?"

"Of course, but I can't believe this is happening to me."

"Me either, but it is," said Blackjack. "I love you, Sandy."

"I love you, too, Blackjack."

Later that evening, Jack called Davy who was surprised and pleased that Jack was returning to see Sandy so soon.

*   *   *

When Jack drove down the long, tree-lined drive to the Alexander home, he saw Sandy waiting for him on the porch. As he walked up the steps, she met him with a hug and a kiss. He could not believe his eyes. Sandy had her red hair combed carefully to her shoulders and was wearing the dress that she had said she only wore on Sundays.

They still had their arms around each other when Blackjack said impatiently, "I have something for you."

Jack reached in his pocket and handed her a white box with a ribbon tied around it. Blackjack was not much for ribbons and fancy wrappings. He had not planned on having the box wrapped, but the lady at the jewelry store told him that women liked things wrapped. She was right.

"What a beautiful box, Blackjack. I've never had such a pretty gift in my whole life. Can I open it now?" asked Sandy, looking up with a smile that reduced his anxiety.

"Yes, it's for you."

Sandy opened the package and sat back in her rocker gasping for a quick breath. Then she kissed Blackjack and whispered in his ear, "It's such a beautiful ring. Does it mean what I want it to mean?"

Blackjack put the ring on her finger and gave her another box, "If you'll marry me, this one's for the wedding."

"Oh, yes, Blackjack, as soon as we can."

They sat on the porch step and hugged and kissed without saying anything. Then Blackjack asked what seemed like a silly question to Sandy, "How do you get married around here?"

"When do you plan for us to get married?"

"As soon as we can."

"I'll call Reverend Smallwood."

Blackjack waited in the living room, while Sandy telephoned Reverend Smallwood. When she returned, Sandy explained, "He'll marry us tonight."

"Tonight!"

"Reverend Smallwood said, 'If you're both in the house alone, I'd rather marry you this evening.'"

"Don't you need a marriage license?"

"Yes. We'll need to drive to the court house."

"We'd better get started then."

They nervously held hands as they walked to the car. They drove to the court house, got their license and returned as quickly as they could. Each of them had hopefully anticipated a wedding, but it hadn't occurred to either of them that it would be today. They rushed to get ready.

Marines shower and dress quickly, and Blackjack was downstairs waiting for Sandy at ten after six. He had dressed in marine dress uniform with his chest full of colorful medals that he'd brought, hoping that they might marry on his leave. He waited nervously for an hour before he heard Sandy coming down the steps. Blackjack was overcome with emotion when Sandy came down the stairs wearing a beautiful white, silk wedding dress with a veil that could not hide her red hair.

"Sandy, you're gorgeous!"

"I wanted you to think so."

"Where did you get the lovely dress?"

"Mom made it for me years ago. It was to have been for my wedding to Danny. Now it'll be for you."

"I'm glad you saved it."

"You look so handsome," said Sandy. "Davy wore his dress

uniform at the church when he and Ginny got married. People at the church will be proud of you like they are of Davy."

"What people?' asked Jack startled.

"I forgot to tell you that Reverend Smallwood said he'd get the word out that we're getting married this evening."

When they arrived at the church, they saw trucks and cars parked all over the area in front of the church and along the road. Davy met them in his marine dress uniform.

"Davy!" exclaimed both Blackjack and Sandy.

"When I heard you were coming, I decided that Sandy would either need a chaperon or someone to give her away."

Reverend Smallwood greeted them at the door. "We've got a lot of anxious townsfolk and church members inside. Colonel LeGault, you walk to the front with me, and Mary Ann and Davy, you stay back until the piano starts playing and then start walking slowly down the aisle together. We haven't had the benefit of rehearsal, so just watch me and do what I tell you."

Jack could not have guessed how much the town of Crockett loved Sandy. The church seated eighty members comfortably. Today, with children on the laps of parents, a hundred were seated. In addition, fifty or more folks were standing in the back of the church and on both side isles. Many had come straight from tobacco fields in their bib overalls.

People in the church almost drowned out the piano with their "Oh's and Ah's" that spontaneously accompanied Sandy's walk down the aisle. They could not believe that it was their Mary Ann, who had done so much to comfort them at different times when they had needed help.

People left the church after the ceremony and waited outside for the bride and groom. As the newly married couple walked out the door, children had fun throwing rice over their heads, and adults were in a long line to greet them. One older couple remained at the end of the line. Sandy introduced them, "Jack, these are Danny's parents, Mr. and Mrs. Wilson."

Danny's mother was crying as she bravely and sincerely said,

"Jack, I know you'll take care of Mary Ann, just like Danny would have done. We're so happy for both of you."

"God bless you both," agreed Mr. Wilson. "I'm glad Mary Ann won't be alone any more."

"I'll take good care of her."

After the wedding they visited with Davy's family. Then Sandy packed her things, and she and Blackjack went to a hotel in Raleigh. For three days they relaxed and loved. They began to comprehend how their lives would be better than they had dared to imagine.

They each made a request of the other before flying to St. Louis to meet Blackjack's friends and go to his Ozark home.

Sandy cautiously asked, "Do you love me enough to do one very hard thing for me, Blackjack."

"What?"

"Mom and Dad smoked, and I watched each of them die from lung cancer, suffering terribly for years before they died. I couldn't stand to see you suffer. Please quit smoking."

Blackjack was stunned. He walked away from the window where he had been standing and sat down in a chair. He put his hands on his face with his head down and was silent for a full minute that seemed like an hour to Sandy. Then he took a pack of cigarettes out of his pocket, slowly dropped them into the wastebasket, and said, "I've done hard things before, so if it's that important to you, I'll stop smoking. Please, try not to ask me to do something that difficult again."

"You'll never know how much I love you, Blackjack, but I'm going to try awfully hard to show you."

When Blackjack recovered from the shock of Sandy's request he said, "Now I have a request of you, Sandy."

"What?"

"When you start living in the city, don't change from the honest, beautiful country girl that you are now."

Jack called Matt and Rick to tell them the news. Matt insisted that they stay at his home when they were not at their own home in the Ozark Mountains. Sandy made a goodbye call to Davy.

Jack kidded Davy about reading his mind because Jack still had not gotten over his surprise in seeing Davy in front of the church. Davy and his family had stayed with friends until the word came to them about wedding plans.

*   *   *

When Jack and Sandy arrived at the Simmons' home, Marcie came running out of the house to welcome them, "Hi Sandy! I'm Marcie. Come inside, and rest after your trip."

"Thanks, Marcie," replied Sandy. "I feel like I'm on a cloud in Never Never Land, and I need to find some reality."

Marcie understood. "Come with me to your room where you can wash up and change your clothes if you'd like."

"This is my only dress," Sandy replied apologetically. "On the farm, I always wore work clothes."

"Get on your work clothes for now. You'll be more comfortable and come down for lunch when you're ready."

The children joined them for lunch. They still had unanswered questions by the time lunch was over, but Marcie assured them that they would have more time with Aunt Sandy and Uncle Jack later.

Marcie turned to Matt and said softly but firmly, "You and Jack rinse and stack the dishes before you go to your meeting. Sandy and I are going shopping to find some new clothes."

Matt saw that Marcie was serious and started to clear the table. Sandy started to object, but she saw Marcie's finger to her lips indicating to her that she should say nothing.

*   *   *

Later at the board meeting in Rick's office, Rick reported that the business was in good shape. Then he added, "You need to know that Scott is going into business for himself."

"What kind of business?" asked Jack.

"He's found some property for sale that he plans to buy and develop into a parking lot."

"Has he the money to buy it?" asked Matt.

"He's been saving for the past ten years," answered Rick. "He has money to buy the property, but not enough to develop it. He asked me to recommend him to our banker."

"Did you?"

"Yes."

"Could he get the loan?"

"The bank will loan Scott $6,000."

"What's the problem, besides losing your most loyal employee?" asked Matt.

"To start a business he needs cash reserves to operate, and he'll have unanticipated expenses."

"How much more would he need?" asked Jack.

"I'd estimate $5,000 more than the bank will lend."

"What are you going to tell Scott?" asked Matt.

"If you agree, I'd like to encourage him to go ahead with his plan by giving him a $10,000 bonus because of his special contribution to our business."

Jack and Matt quickly agreed.

"I'm glad you share my feelings," said Rick. "I'll never forget how Scott helped me when I desperately needed him."

*   *   *

That evening after their meeting, Blackjack and Sandy drove to the Bauman home in a car that Matt had loaned them. Ruth took Sandy to her sewing room after dinner where they had a long private visit.

After a while Ruth said, "I'd like to design and make a dress for you as a wedding present."

"Are you sure? Wouldn't it be too much for you to do?"

"Not at all. Let me measure you. Do you want to pick a pattern or have me make a dress that I think you'd like?"

"You decide, please. I don't know much about dresses."

When they had finished, they went back to the living room and visited with Jack, Rick, and the children until it was time for the LeGaults to return to the Simmons' home for the night.

In the morning as they were driving to Jack's home in the Ozarks, Sandy could no longer contain her excitement, "I can't wait to see our home."

"Don't get your expectations too high, Sandy. The place is plain like most homesteads built a hundred years ago, but you'll enjoy the big porch and the old fireplace."

They drove up to the house and parked the car in the front yard.

"Blackjack, you're right about the front porch."

"I've had some wonderful times here with Louie, Jimmy, and Derk. Now we can share our home together."

Sandy said thoughtfully, "It's nice to be with people, but I'm glad to have private time, just you and me."

For the next week they carefully explored the house, the farm, and each other. In between times, they took turns cooking interesting meals. Once they went into Fredericktown.

"I didn't know that we lived so close to town, Blackjack."

"It didn't seem close when Jimmy and Louie walked."

"Let's walk around the square and look at the courthouse."

Blackjack told Sandy some history, "Fredericktown was first established in 1799. During the next century, the town grew into a mining and farming town, mining in the mountains and farming in the valleys. After the Iron Mountain Railroad came to Fredericktown from St. Louis in 1869, the town became known as a banking and trading center. The Madison County Courthouse was built about 1900. My ancestors seldom came here. They trapped on the river and traded their fur pelts at Ste. Genevieve."

"When can I see the river?"

"We'll climb down tomorrow."

At daybreak Blackjack and Sandy put on their full backpacks and started the climb down. As they reached the river, Sandy exclaimed with delight, "What a beautiful river! This area looks just like it must have looked hundreds of years ago. I love it."

"Like all rivers, in some places you'll find it's shallow with rapidly running water. In other places, deep holes slow the movement of the water. This bend in the St. Francis River seldom gets below five feet."

Sandy was so euphoric that she took her boots, socks, and jeans off and waded into the river.

"How cold is it?"

"Just right," answered Sandy, as she playfully splashed water on Blackjack. "Come on in."

Before Blackjack had his boots off, Sandy had all her clothes off. She was swimming and splashing as she had as a child in the river on her father's farm. Jack quickly finished undressing and jumped into the river. Before he knew what was happening, Sandy pulled him under water."

"Louie and I used to swim like this."

"Davy and I'd swim in our river like this when we were children. I'd forgotten how much fun it is."

"I haven't been swimming here since Louie died. I love this place, and I love you, Sandy."

When they finished splashing and hugging each other, they went up on the bank where Jack had laid a blanket. After they made love, Jack went to sleep. Sandy lay awake in the warm sun, listening to the river and smelling moist fresh air. Her prayers had finally been answered. She would always cherish this moment.

When Jack awoke from his nap, he turned to Sandy and said, "This is one of the two happiest times of my life."

"What was the other one?"

"It was on this mountain. Seeing Louie for the first time on my return after World War ll."

Sandy said, "My other happiest time was when Davy got

home from World War II, and also the saddest when Danny didn't get home."

"No one knows why some soldiers live and others die."

"Davy told me you saved his life in Korea. Is that true?"

"It takes a lot of men to save a marine's life. I did the first part. I got him to the truck where he received first aid. Good doctors saved him--I thought his wound was fatal."

Sandy ran her hand over the scars on Blackjack's body, "I don't see how you were kept alive for me. I'm so thankful."

"It's time to eat," said Blackjack, as they got dressed, folded their blanket, and started back to camp.

"Are we going to eat the eggs and smoked sausage we brought?" asked Sandy. "What about water?"

"We'll eat a fresh fish if we can catch one," said Blackjack as he reached in his pack for hooks and line. "There's a good spring near here for water."

"Where do you fish?"

"My favorite spot is upstream."

"Where's your pole?"

"Louie showed me that you can catch a fish faster with a hand-held line with a few hooks."

"That makes sense."

"Louie'd never catch a fish unless he was going to eat it."

"I wish I could've known Louie."

"Louie was an unusual person like you are, one of a kind. You'd have liked him."

They caught their fish, built a fire, and cooked a delicious supper. That night they slept like babies, and in the morning they picked berries in the hills while Blackjack explained how Louie and his ancestors had trapped animals and tanned their pelts for sale.

Blackjack woke Sandy early one morning before daylight and said, "Come with me; I'll show you some deer."

"You don't have your rifle."

"We're just looking now. When we live here someday, we'll shoot a deer to smoke or put in the freezer."

They went upstream and waited until almost daylight when a buck and two does came down to drink.

Their week on the river went fast. Blackjack had even forgotten how much he missed his cigarettes. When they were climbing up Louie's Mountain, Blackjack stopped at the spot on Piney's trail that was sacred to him. He told Sandy how his ancestors were buried at this unmarked spot.

When they reached the house, they cleaned and packed their things. They stopped at Ste. Genevieve for lunch on their drive back to the Bauman's home.

When the LeGaults arrived, Ruth said, "Sandy, come to my sewing room. I have something to show you."

In the sewing room Ruth held out a beautiful green silk dress that complemented Sandy's fair skin and red hair.

"Ruth, how could you make a dress like that in the short time that we've been gone? It's so pretty."

"I work carefully but fast. I'm glad you like it."

Sandy held the dress to her excitedly, "Can I try it on?"

"I've been waiting to see you wear it."

The dress fit perfectly, showing off Sandy's slim waist and full breasts. Looking into a mirror, she thought, 'Maybe I am as pretty as Blackjack says I am.' After years of living and dressing like the men, she especially liked looking like a girl.

"Thank you, Ruth. What a lovely wedding present."

When they went into the living room, both Jack and Rick were startled and stood up to admire the dress. Jack was grateful to Ruth for unmasking Sandy's beauty and said, "Sandy, I fell in love with you because you were a country girl, but with Marcie's shopping help and now Ruth's beautiful dress, you'll be at ease in your new social life in Virginia and Washington D.C."

"I may not be at ease, but my confidence is raised."

After fun, good food, hugs, and goodbyes, Jack and Sandy returned to the Simmons' home for the night. The next morning Matt took them to the airport.

PART FOUR

1961-1994: THE FOUNDATION

YOU ARE THE FELLOW
WHO HAS TO DECIDE
WHETHER YOU'LL DO IT OR TOSS IT ASIDE.
YOU ARE THE FELLOW WHO HAS
TO MAKE UP HIS MIND
WHETHER YOU'LL LEAD OR
WILL LINGER BEHIND.

"You" from *The Light Of Faith*
Edgar Guest

30

1975: Matt, Rick, Jack

Matt, Rick, and Jack sat on their park bench on a fall day in 1975, reflecting on generational changes that had taken place in their lives since 1960. These changes were as ordained in life as the Mississippi River was ordained to flow into the Gulf of Mexico and be replenished by winter snows and spring rains.

The day was perfect for sitting in the sun and pondering past years. The leaves were at their peak of multicolored beauty, tenaciously staying on the trees as long as possible before fluttering to the ground. Squirrels scurried to store food for the winter, and birds were ready to fly south.

In the intervening fifteen years, the three men had become wealthy entrepreneurs, no longer feeling financial pressure in supporting their families. They had talked about selling their corporations and retiring, but they were only fifty-one years old and could expect many more productive years. Their future plans had yet to be resolved.

Matt, Rick, and Jack still remained close friends and continued working together as business partners. Today they had come to their park bench to reflect quietly on their lives and then decide together whether to expand their business enterprises or to sell out and retire.

RICK: 1960-1975

Rick felt the generational changes going on in his life. In 1966 his mother had died peacefully in her sleep; she was eighty years old. Shortly after Maria's death, Ruth's father had died, and her mother came to live with the Baumans.

Rick was beginning to accept that his children were capable of handling their own lives and were no longer dependent on him. Joy had graduated from The University of Missouri and was now living in Columbia, Missouri, with her husband and two children. Emil had graduated from Washington University and had scored in the upper one percent on the CPA exam. He was now studying computer science at Stanford University.

The AP Corporation continued to be profitable. In 1965 the corporation constructed a multistory parking garage on one of the expanded downtown lots. St. Louis needed additional parking, and Rick was pleased to be able to help. Two years after completing the construction, Rick sold the parking garage to a business group for $1.5 million. Their corporation invested the money from the sale in stock that was now worth $2 million.

Rick thought about Scott and his family. He was pleased that Scott had been able to buy a second parking lot and had increased his income in ten of the last fifteen years. Abe had received a football scholarship from the University of Missouri. His two younger sisters were proud of him, and they had enjoyed the special status of being seen with him. After graduating from the university, Abe had gone on to law school and was just about to finish.

An agent of a hotel chain had offered Rick $2.5 million for the SUN Corporation's vacant downtown properties between the

Jefferson Memorial National Park and Busch Stadium. Today the three entrepreneurs needed to decide whether to sell or to develop the property themselves.

MATT: 1960-1975

Matt thought about his children and how their lives had changed. Andrea had graduated from Tulane University and had moved to Monroe, Louisiana, with her husband and two children. Billy had graduated from Washington University and was now an ensign on a battleship.

Matt remembered the early morning call from Pat in 1961. Pat's daughter, Mary, was critically ill, and he was going to be with her in Ontario, California. Pat had asked Matt if he would come to New Orleans and help Elizabeth while he was gone. Matt had flown to New Orleans that morning and worked at the hotel until Pat returned after Mary's death.

Matt enjoyed teaching and now had a full professorship. He was challenged by questions from law students who were eager to learn. When he had shown Marcie his first published book, he was rewarded with a big hug and kiss.

Marcie's grandmother and father had died within three months of each other in the spring of 1963, and Matt remembered how distressed Marcie had been. That summer they closed their house in Webster Groves and lived with Marcie's mother. Matt worked as executor of the estates.

Matt thought back to when Pat had died of a heart attack in 1971. Matt encouraged his mother to sell the Du Jardin Hotel and come to Webster Groves to live. She insisted that the Du Jardin Hotel was her home, and that she would continue to manage it, just as she and Pat had done for twenty-eight years.

Recently, Elizabeth was beginning to realize how difficult running the hotel alone really was, and now she was ready to sell it. Matt had obtained appraisals for the Du Jardin Hotel, one at $1.7 million and a second at $2.3 million. Elizabeth was discussing possible reinvestment strategies with Matt but had made no decisions.

JACK: 1960-1975

Jack thought back to 1960 when the newly elected president made political changes. Rub and he had been transferred to Camp Pendleton, California, where Jack bought a home with a swimming pool in La Jolla. Years earlier, in 1943, he had gazed in awe at the La Jolla homes that he had passed on his training marches.

Sandy and Blackjack had two children and loved being part of a family after their years alone. Their son, Alex, had red hair and blue eyes like Sandy. He'd go down to the St. Francis River and take pictures of the birds and animals, but he had no interest in hunting. He certainly would never volunteer for the marines as his father and his Uncle Davy had done.

Their daughter, Monet, had wavy, blond hair and brown eyes. She always reminded Blackjack of his mother as Louie had described her, "Monet was as gentle as a fawn in the forest." Jack marveled at how generational characteristics and features are never completely lost. His own straight, coal-black hair could easily be traced to his Grandpa Piney's mother, Morning Star.

After completing twenty years in the Marine Corps, Sandy's brother Davy had retired and become a successful cattle rancher. When Jack was in Vietnam in 1968, Sandy and the children had traveled to North Carolina to stay with Davy's family.

After he was promoted to brigadier general, Jack had been sent to Vietnam for a second tour, working with his lifelong friend Major General McNally. He shuddered at the memory of Vietnam. His mind flashed back to Khe Sanh and the shout from the helicopter pilot, "We've been hit! Prepare to crash!" His first realization after the crash was that the dead body of the pilot was on top of him. In his semiconscious condition, unable to move, he scanned the scene. Rub was next to him with his head crushed beyond recognition, and a helicopter was landing nearby. Jack lost consciousness again. The next thing he remembered was recovering on a navy ship with his leg in traction, a cast to the hip.

Jack felt an urgency to leave his friends on the park bench. Without a word, he walked toward the lake. When he came to the lake shore, he took off his shoes and socks, rolled up his pants and put his feet in the water. He looked at his crippled leg and remembered the repeated comment, 'You're lucky to be alive, Jack.'

He didn't feel lucky. He had been injured once too often and was forced to accept a disability retirement. As a Vietnam veteran, it was degrading to be confronted by folks who treated him and his profession with disrespect for carrying out a responsibility given to military personnel by an elected president and congress.

As a swan glided by, he relaxed, put on his socks and shoes, straightened his trousers, and walked back to the park bench. He would try to remember happier times.

After he had been released from the naval hospital in 1969, Rick and Matt suggested to Jack that he build a beach house on the SUN property in Gulf Shores. Since then, his family had lived in Gulf Shores in the winter while the children were in school and on Louie's Mountain in the summer.

"Are you okay, Jack?" Matt asked as Jack sat down beside him.

"Yes."

"Good."

Hoping his friends would not retire, Rick asked, "Do we sell out and retire?"

"No," came the firm and simultaneous answer. Shaking hands,

they agreed to meet the next morning to work out a development strategy for the SUN property.

When Matt and Rick started to walk to their cars to go home, Jack made no move to leave and said, "I'll stay awhile longer."

Matt looked concerned, "Are you sure you're okay, Jack?"

"I'm okay, Matt."

"Then we'll go ahead."

*　　*　　*

When Jack was alone, he reflected on his drinking problem. He'd known for years that he had had a problem with his "friend," bourbon, but he had denied being an alcoholic. He would say, "It's just my way of releasing tension." When he returned from his second tour in Vietnam, he had begun drinking more heavily to get to sleep at night, and then he would need a drink to get started in the morning.

He remembered when Sandy had said, "Blackjack, I was so proud of you when you quit smoking for me, and I promised you that I wouldn't ask you to do something that hard again, and I won't. But your children adore you, and I can't stand seeing them hurt. Tomorrow I'm taking them to live in North Carolina for awhile. Fighting in three wars is too much of a burden for any man. Few people could overcome what you've had to endure, but I honestly believe you can."

At Sandy's personal request, Matt and Rick had flown to Gulf Shores to talk to Jack. After two days of talking about old times, Matt had told him bluntly, "Jack, you're an alcoholic. If you don't stop drinking, you'll kill yourself and hurt your family even more."

Jack remembered Rick's challenge, "Spend what time you need here by yourself, days or weeks. You know you can't continue the way you are. You've always had the courage to do the impossible to survive; you can now. Make your own decision, but we'll only be a phone call away."

When Matt and Rick had left him that night in Gulf Shores, Jack remembered how deathly tired he felt. There had been times on the battlefield when he had believed that death might have been a better answer, but Louie had depended on him to come back. Then his family was depending on him. But that night he had realized that his former courage was gone. Sandy and his two boyhood friends had always stuck by him, but he knew then that their attitudes had shifted from disappointment to fear for him. At that point in his life, he had to admit that he had become a hopeless alcoholic.

That night, when he had finished a bottle of bourbon, just before he had passed out into a drunken sleep, he remembered thinking about what Louie had told him, "Bourbon seems like a good friend when yer lonely or mixed up about somethin'. Good friends don't hurt ya, but bourbon will. Remember, Blackjack, there is a God. Believe that, if you don't believe nothin' else."

He remembered waking up late that night in a chair on the deck. It was after midnight. Storm waves were crashing against the shore, and there was no moon, just darkness and his drunken dreams. Like a humming bird hovering over the sweet, liquid nectar of a flower, Jack desperately tried to focus his thoughts. In his mind he pictured three six-year-old boys meeting for the first time in Miss Goerner's class at Jefferson Elementary.

On the deck the next morning, Jack had opened his eyes in time to see the last of the dark storm clouds disappearing, leaving a bright blue tinge on the Gulf horizon. Tempered by the disappearing storm and the falling tide, the waves were gently lapping the shore. A brilliant orange glow had appeared through a hole in the last dark cloud. The sunrise had colored the billowing white clouds to look like a carefully designed tapestry.

Almost as quickly as the storm had moved in the night before, with its lightning and crashing waves, the Gulf waters had become calm and quiet. Seagulls were returning. Cranes came out of hiding and gracefully strolled along the shore. Porpoises were surfacing, rolling smoothly, and returning to the depths to feed. Pelicans broke the silence with their splashing dives to catch their fill of fish. God had made the world right again, and Jack knew what to do next. He had called Matt.

Matt had given him the answer he needed. "Jack, I'll make arrangements for a limousine to pick you up and take you to the Pensacola Naval Hospital. I'll tell Sandy where you'll be. She'll be relieved and proud of you. . . ."

As his memories faded, Jack got up from the Forest Park Bench to drive home to his family. With beads of sweat emerging on his forehead, he realized again that his fight against alcohol would never really be over--but he had no intention of losing a battle that he had fought so hard to win.

31

River Front Hotel

A sense of urgency to begin developing investment plans filled Rick's office the next morning, along with the aroma of coffee.

Matt said, "Mom has sold the Du Jardin Hotel and is ready to invest in our hotel."

Jack asked, "Should we negotiate part ownership in a hotel with the Helms Hotel Group on our SUN property?"

"If they agree to favorable terms, okay; if not, I'd rather build our own hotel," Rick answered.

"There's a financial risk either way," Matt pointed out.

Rick summarized their potential financial assets, "We can accumulate between $4 million and $5 million. If the Helms Group isn't willing to work on our terms, we can get a large enough bank loan to construct the hotel ourselves."

"Then it's settled," said Matt. "I'll talk to the Helms Hotel Group and report back."

*   *   *

For several months in 1975, Matt tried to negotiate a partnership agreement with the Helms Hotel Group. They rejected his proposal for the SUN Corporation to have majority ownership, and the Helms attorney insisted on loopholes that eliminated any meaningful participation of the SUN Corporation in policy decisions.

Matt reported to Jack and Rick, "The Helms Group wants to buy our property, but they don't want a business partner. We have to sell or build the hotel ourselves."

Jack made his position clear, "Let's build it, Rick."

"I'm for going ahead ourselves, but we need to be sure of the financing. Matt, is your mother still willing to invest her money from the sale of the Du Jardin Hotel with us?"

"Yes, and she'd want to manage the restaurant."

Rick said, "She knows the restaurant business, and her hotel experience would help us. I'll manage the parking garage, but what about managing the hotel?"

"Mom and Pat always employed the best person available to manage their hotel. They paid well, so the person was never tempted to leave for a better position."

Rick summarized their financial plan. "With our building site and the $4 million cash that we can raise, we can expect to get a $5 million mortgage loan on the hotel and building site."

"Is that enough, Rick?"

"I think so, but we won't know until an architect finishes his preliminary drawings and cost estimates. We should get the best architect we can find and instruct him to hold the costs for the hotel to $8 million. We'll have a million dollar contingency fund."

They agreed to proceed on that basis. They worked with architects, consultants, and contractors from 1975 until the fall of 1978. The River Front Hotel was finally ready to open.

*   *   *

Rick went by himself to the River Front Hotel the night before the opening. He took the elevator to a fourteenth floor suite. Walking across the plush carpet, he went straight to the window and pulled back the drapes that opened to night scenes above and below him.

A smiling moon among a sea of stars looked down on him in the most majestic way. Boats moored on the levee near Eads Bridge reflected specks of light everywhere. He looked through the 630-foot-high St. Louis Gateway Arch that was now attracting visitors from all over the world.

He scanned Jefferson Memorial National Park that was situated below him above the old cobblestone levee that had protected St. Louis from raging spring floods for more than a century. The park was beautifully landscaped with walks, trees, and lakes. The formerly elevated railroad now went through a tunnel. The river front neighborhood that Rick knew as a boy was gone, except for the Old Cathedral and the Old Courthouse.

Construction of The Old Cathedral on the original site of Pierre Laclede's 1764 log cabin church was completed in 1834. In 1961 the Old Cathedral was proclaimed the Basilica of St. Louis, King of France, by Pope John XXIII and designated as a National Monument by President Kennedy.

The Old Courthouse was built between 1828 and 1862. Its 192-foot cast iron dome had guided steamboat pilots during the nineteenth century. The infamous Dred Scott decision came down from Missouri's Supreme Court in that Old Courthouse.

Rick's time alone in the Mary Ellen Jackson Suite deeply moved him. Tears welled in his eyes as he remembered how Mary Ellen had suffered. He was pleased to have been able to help demolish the tenement where she had died. Risking their fortunes was a small price to pay to participate in the renovation of the St. Louis river front.

*   *   *

On September 8, 1978, the Bauman, Simmons, and LeGault families toured the SUN Corporation's new River Front Hotel with St. Louis dignitaries. They had lunch in the Elizabethan Restaurant on the fourteenth floor. With St. Louis hosting a large convention, and the Cardinals playing the Chicago Cubs in the Busch Memorial Stadium the next day, the hotel would open its doors to customers with no vacancies.

At one point in the tour, Rick, Matt, and Jack left the St. Louis dignitaries to be together a few minutes by themselves. This was a proud moment for these three lifelong friends.

"Amazing!" said Jack, as he looked out at the magnificent view. "Louie should've seen this."

"Mom is pleased that we can contribute to the renovation of the river front," added Matt thoughtfully.

"I wish Mama and Papa could be here," reflected Rick.

To Rick, Matt, and Jack the River Front Hotel would always be a shrine to the past. St. Louis may still have deteriorated housing, but not in their old neighborhood.

32

SUN Foundation

Jack said, "Before we start the regular meeting, I'd like to make a proposal for you to consider."

"What?"

"Scott could not have succeeded with his parking business if we hadn't helped him get started, and I'll bet a lot of men and women need that help."

"What do you have in mind, Jack?" asked Rick.

"What about establishing a foundation to help people get started in business by supplementing inadequate bank loans with grants to individuals with sound business plans?"

"Establishing a foundation like that wouldn't be a problem," Matt agreed. "How much money would you need, Jack?"

"A $100,000 to start, and hopefully it could grow to a million, if our hotel venture is successful. At the beginning we'd only help one or two people a year."

"How would we manage it?" asked Rick.

"I'd volunteer my services to manage the fund and counsel recipients of a grant, like you did for Scott."

"Jack, how would you find the person who could most benefit from help?" asked Matt.

"Our banker could identify a person approved for a bank loan who needs more startup or expansion money than the bank could responsibly loan him. If the business plan is sound, I'd approve a grant to supplement the bank's loan."

"Remember the blood pact we made years ago? We swore that we'd help make St. Louis a better place. This is a way to do it," said Rick enthusiastically.

*　　*　　*

"Matt, can you fly Rick and me to Alabama to see what Hurricane Frederic did to my beach home?" Jack asked.

"Sure, Jack. Would Saturday be okay?"

"I'll call Rick and check on that date."

In 1979 Jack's winter home, built in 1969, was a total loss in Hurricane Frederic. The 150-mile-an-hour winds and huge wave surges had not only broken Jack's home to pieces but had even scattered and destroyed all the furnishings and personal property. The three friends were shocked as they drove through Frederic's devastation of Gulf Shores. Matt was later able to recover $112,000 from their insurance company, and they all agreed to have this money added to their $100,000 SUN Foundation.

"Jack, how many businesses have you been able to start or expand through the SUN Foundation?" asked Matt.

"Five."

"How are they doing?" asked Rick.

"Four are succeeding, but one has failed."

"Why did the one business fail?"

"The fellow couldn't read. After that experience I decided that future non-reading applicants will be given reading instruction and be able to read before we consider them for a grant."

"What's your best success story, Jack," asked Matt.

"The Quick Movers Company that we helped get started in 1975. They move people from one apartment to another on the same day. They provide service for poor families who don't own a car and can't afford to stay any place overnight. Willie Woods started his company with one truck and one employee. Now he has three trucks and ten employees."

"Good work, Jack," Rick complimented him.

33

Facing Bankruptcy

Matt, Jack, and Rick had agreed before their hotel was built that they were not competent to manage day-to-day operations. They interviewed managers from four successful city hotels before hiring Marc Stinson, who had employed his own staff. They thought that they had hired the right man, but as they reviewed the first two years of operations, they had doubts.

"Here's our audit report for 1979-80," said Rick as he handed each of them a copy.

"Still no profit," said Matt visibly upset.

Rick said, "I really didn't expect a profit the first year, but we should have done better this year."

"Last year Marc said that it takes a few years before a new hotel becomes profitable," Jack commented.

"Rick, let's have Marc come up here and answer some of our questions," suggested Matt. "I wasn't concerned last year, but I am now."

"I agree, Matt."

Marc Stinson came into the board room about ten minutes later and asked, "What can I do for you?"

"We're disappointed in the 1979-80 balance sheet."

Marc said, "It takes awhile for a new hotel to be profitable."

"The garage has more cars each year," said Rick.

"Mom thinks the restaurant is doing well."

"Marc, do you expect a profit next year," asked Jack.

"I'm having a consultant analyze the hotel operations this year, and then I can give you a clear picture."

After a series of questions, they excused Marc and continued their meeting.

"Marc's answers didn't satisfy me," said Matt.

"Where does that leave us, Rick?" asked Jack.

"We'll separate the parking and restaurant operations into separate businesses from the hotel as a first step, so we'll know whether they are as profitable as I believe they are."

"Good idea," said Jack.

"I agree," said Matt.

"Until we complete this work and get the report from Marc's consultant, we'll have to be patient," concluded Rick.

*　　*　　*

When they met a year later to review the balance sheets of the three separate businesses that they had established and the report from Marc's consultant, they were horrified and angry. Clearly their hotel was in deep financial trouble. The 1980-81 balance sheets showed that the restaurant and parking businesses had been profitable, but the hotel had a huge loss and was apparently the cause of the previous years' losses.

The consultant's report indicated that it was difficult for an independent hotel to compete with hotel chains, but he believed that the hotel could be sold for $7 million.

"We've got to sell the hotel," concluded Matt.

Rick was silent, but Jack objected strongly.

Matt quickly answered, "Jack, you'll lose the hotel in a bankruptcy court."

"There must be another solution," Jack argued.

"Don't be a damn fool, Jack. Face the facts, our million dollar cash reserve is gone. The bank will own the hotel in a matter of months."

Rick finally joined in the discussion. "In the first six months of this year, the River Front Hotel occupancy has been above average for a hotel of our size, and the rates we charge are about average."

"So what, if we continue to lose money, what difference does it make," Matt replied, getting more and more frustrated.

"Maybe if we get a new management team, we could make a profit next year," defended Jack.

"Stupid, wishful thinking," continued Matt as he stood red-faced in his anger.

Ignoring Matt's remarks, Rick made a recommendation, "We should get a fiscal analysis from a different audit firm before we sell."

"What do you have in mind, Rick?" asked Jack.

"An accounting firm that has a reputation for discovering the weak parts of an unsuccessful business."

"Do you have a firm to recommend?"

"Atkins and Riley, P. C."

"Isn't that the firm where Emil works?"

"Yes, I'd want him to head the audit team and report directly to us."

"How long would it take?"

"A few months."

"I don't want any more delay in selling," said Matt, making his position clear.

Giving the deciding vote, Jack said emphatically, "I'm for the audit."

For the first time in years, the three men could not come to a unanimous agreement. They left upset.

* * *

Three months later Matt, Jack, and Rick waited for the auditors to arrive with their preliminary findings. Matt paced the floor while Jack and Rick sat silently at the table.

When Emil and his assistant entered the room, the three men greeted them politely. Marc Stinson and his staff weren't attending the meeting at Emil's request. The auditors put their brief cases on the table, got out their accounting documents, and handed out preliminary audit reports. The atmosphere in the room reminded Jack of the deadly silence preceding a Japanese banzais charge.

Emil made a request, "Please don't start to read this report until you've heard our opening remarks."

"Why the mystery, Emil?"

"A large amount of money has been embezzled."

"Do you have proof?" asked Matt, shifting his chair.

"Yes, but it's not ready for release. This meeting must be treated as a confidential pre-audit briefing. Our final report is not due for two weeks."

"How much money are we talking about?" asked Jack.

"More than $500,000."

"How did you come to that conclusion?" questioned Matt with a facial expression that clearly showed his doubts.

"Kay and I developed a computer software program while we were at Stanford University that identifies probable fraud, but it doesn't provide the specific embezzlement technique or the employees involved," explained Emil.

Matt asked, "Can you get hard evidence, Emil?"

"Kay can give you that answer," Emil replied as he turned to his coworker.

Kay began by saying, "After we suspected fraud, we made more detailed auditing examinations. We'd like to review the results with you."

After Kay had methodically explained the specific audit examinations they had made of hotel accounting records, Jack asked, "Did one person do this alone, Emil?"

"No, we've identified three participants . . . Marc Stinson, his controller, and an executive assistant."

Matt asked, "Is your evidence enough for a criminal trial?"

"Yes."

"Are you sure, Emil?" asked Rick, concerned for his son.

"Absolutely."

"Where do we go from here?" asked Jack.

"That will be your decision. If you open your reports, we'll review them with you."

An hour later, even Matt was satisfied that a criminal fraud charge could and should be made.

As he was ready to leave, Emil handed them a supplementary finding related to the consultant's report and said, "We had a private investigator check out Marc Stinson's consultant. Apparently, the report was deliberately designed to deflate the true value of your hotel. Did you know that the consultant and his assistants are permanent employees of the Helms Hotel chain, who have wanted to buy your hotel?"

"Certainly not," said Rick.

After the auditors were gone, Matt said, "You have my apology, guys, for some of my remarks a few months ago. Your gut feeling was right all along, Rick. I just hated to think we'd lose any more than it appeared we already had."

* * *

When confronted with hard evidence, the executive assistant pleaded guilty and testified against the hotel manager and the controller. She received a year's suspended sentence and a fine. Marc Stinson and his controller plea bargained for shorter jail sentences by confessing and repaying $489,000.

The River Front Hotel, with a new management team, made a profit of $500,000 the next year.

34

Reinvesting Again

Matt got a phone call from Jack in 1984. "Matt, you and Rick have got to get down here."

"Where?"

"Gulf Shores."

"Why?"

"To see what's going on here."

"What are you doing there?"

"Sandy and the children missed the beach, so I rented a beach house for a month and drove down. I've rented a large beach house next to ours for a week for you and Marcie and Rick and Ruth, to stay here while I show you what's happening."

"You've gone crazy again, Jack."

"It's important, Matt!"

"If you say so, I'll talk to Rick."

The next week the Baumans and the Simmons were neighbors to the LeGaults in Gulf Shores, Alabama. On the first day of their stay, while Sandy, Marcie, and Ruth took a long walk along the beach, Jack drove his friends all over Pleasure Island. High-rise concrete buildings were replacing hurricane-damaged beach houses everywhere.

"Can you believe it?" asked Jack.

"I believe what I see, and I see it," answered Matt.

"How are they using these buildings?" asked Rick.

"As condominiums."

"What are you thinking, Jack?" asked Matt.

"Building a condo on the SUN Corporation beach property."

"We agreed to get out of that kind of business," argued Matt feebly. "What do you think, Rick?"

"Maybe Jack has something."

Matt said, "With inflation and our increasing hotel profits, we should be able to sell the hotel for double what we paid for it. A beach front building might be a wise investment. Jack, do you know what it would cost to build?"

"Probably $7 million."

"Have you appraised the value of the land?"

"No."

"Make a guess."

"A million dollars."

Rick was not convinced. "Explain the condo business."

"A developer will sell or rent the units. Local realtors will manage and rent them for a fee."

"What's a typical sale of a condo unit?" asked Matt.

"About $50,000 to $200,000, depending on size and location."

"Can you build more than one building on our property?"

"Either one or two, depending on the size."

You've done your homework, Jack," said Matt. "I'm interested. How about you, Rick?"

"Jack, talk to an architect and a mortgage company, and bring the information back to St. Louis. We'll make our final decision then. You certainly were right when you talked us into buying this beach property twenty-four years ago."

"Let's forget about business for the rest of the week and enjoy the beach," said Matt.

"Best idea you've had in a long time, Matt."

*   *   *

The three families enjoyed the beach and visited Fort Morgan, Fort Conde, and other interesting places. Matt had a close look at the Battleship *USS Alabama* that reminded him of the Japanese ship he had bombed. One day they visited the small shops in Fairhope.

In the evenings they sat on their deck overlooking the waters of the Gulf of Mexico, listening to the incoming tide lapping the beach with a reassuring melody. They watched the Gulf as schools of small white trout rippled the calm waters while attempting to escape larger fish, which caused a silver glitter in the evening sunset. Porpoises rolled in and out of the water as they passed. A brown pelican occasionally broke away from a fly-by formation to dive ferociously into the water to catch a final fish for the day. As the sun went down, flocks of seagulls began to disappear, and sandpipers scurried to and fro.

In the distance they watched ships gliding through the water toward the Mobile docks. They watched the sun, a round ball of fire, sink into the Gulf water and disappear, leaving brilliant splashes of color across the distant horizon.

Of course, small talk flourished during their relaxing evenings together. One night Ruth asked nobody in particular, "Where do the seagulls and pelicans go at night as they disappear from the beach?"

"To roost for the night like chickens," answered Matt, remembering the chicken coop on his grandparents' farm.

"Where do they roost?" asked Rick.

"On piers, ship markers, or uninhabited small islands," answered Marcie, remembering her father's answer to her question when she was a small child.

"Where do the hermit crabs hide in the daytime?"

"Holes in the sand."

Watching as a grandfather walked by with a small child, signaling the exit and entrance of a generational change--nature in balance--Jack commented almost to himself, "It's at a time like .this when I know Louie was right about God and nature."

After their last evening walk, they talked until the moon was overhead. Marcie was the first to bring everyone back to reality, "The moon moving toward the western horizon tells me it's time to get to bed and be ready for our trip to St. Louis in the morning."

*   *   *

In the fall of 1985 Jack presented the condo information from their architect to Rick and Matt. They decided to build two seven-story buildings on their Gulf Shores beach property. Each condominium would have a swimming pool and three penthouse units on the top floor. The buildings would be on heavy concrete pilings to resist future hurricanes.

If the first condo, to be called "Sea Sand," was successful, they would build the second. Their plan was not as bold as Jack had envisioned, but it made better business sense to Rick and Matt.

In the spring of 1987 their first condo was ready for sale or rent. They turned it over to a real estate management group, but each family kept a penthouse unit for their exclusive use.

*   *   *

In October 1990 Rick, Jack, and Matt were sixty-six years old and again went to the park bench in Forest Park to decide whether they would develop a second condominium. They had sold all the "Sea Sand" condominium units and had accumulated another large cash balance in the SUN Corporation. Matt's mother had died the year before, after a short illness. Jack had some heart trouble, but otherwise they were in good health.

Making their decision did not take long. They would have

their architect prepare plans for their second condominium, which they would name "Porpoise Inn."

Rick said, "SUN Inc. will still have a cash balance of $4 million after we build our second condo."

They left the meeting knowing that their "Sea Sands" condo had been successful and looked forward to the construction of "Porpoise Inn."

35

SUN Foundation

At their next meeting, Jack had good news, "Of the twenty-six businesses that we've helped, twenty-one are doing well. Eight of the grantees took reading courses before they received their grants. They learned to read, and six have profitable businesses."

"Good work, Jack," praised Rick. "Did you ever check to see how many employees these businesses have?"

"Actually, I did. Most of the businesses have less than ten employees, but a couple are growing rapidly. All together the businesses have employed about 310 people."

Matt said enthusiastically, "Imagine the impact on families in St. Louis if our endowment was large enough to reach all the folks that could benefit from this kind of assistance. Can we increase the foundation endowment, Rick?"

"We have the money, Matt, but Jack can't manage a larger program by himself."

"You're right, but I retired from teaching last year and have time to help."

"I can too," Rick offered. "When we sold the hotel, I told the new owner that I would not manage the garage any more."

"Together we can create thousands of jobs for folks in St.

Louis in the same way we added parking lots to the city," added Jack eagerly. "Rick, how much can we add to the endowment?"

"The SUN Corporation cash balance is $10 million with no debt. I suggest that we use $3 million to increase our gift to our SUN Foundation and use the remaining $7 million for the construction of our planned condo in Gulf Shores."

"Get to work on it, Matt," urged Jack.

There was unanimous agreement.

*　　*　　*

Five years later, after they sold their second successful condo, they met to determine the best way to use their accumulated wealth.

Jack suggested, "We could increase the SUN Foundation endowment."

"I have another idea," said Matt. "Why not provide maintenance and replacement support for benches in St. Louis parks."

"We can do both," said Rick. "Let's increase the SUN Foundation endowment to $4 million and establish a $1 million endowment for the parks."

Matt, Jack, and Rick were again adjusting their lives. They chose to assume new leadership responsibilities and turn away from another opportunity for complete retirement.

36

St. Louis Friends

"Did you get a letter from the mayor?" asked Matt.

"Yes," answered Rick, "and so did Jack."

"What do you make of it?"

"I can't imagine. He invited us to his office late tomorrow afternoon, so I guess we'll go and find out."

Rick, Matt, and Jack drove to city hall together and arrived a little early. They took time to look at some pictures in the lobby as they walked toward the mayor's office. There was one of "Lucky Lindy" beside his famous plane, the *Spirit of St. Louis*. There were pictures of the 1904 World's Fair and of the Gas House Gang, who won the 1934 World Series. There were pictures of former mayors and other people whom they didn't recognize without reading the plaques underneath.

When they arrived at the mayor's office, he cordially greeted them and invited them to dinner to talk about some important city business. He kept up a friendly chatter while they were being driven to the River Front Hotel, but he said nothing to clarify why he had invited them. Matt caught Rick's eyes and shrugged his shoulders as an indication of his confusion.

They stopped at the River Front Hotel and took an elevator

to the Elizabethan Room. The mayor led them into the dining room that had been set up for a banquet. As they entered, they were stunned by a big cheer and loud clapping.

The mayor coaxed them to the head table where they saw Marcie, Sandy, and Ruth.

Bill Barnes, spokesman for those attending the banquet, took the microphone. "Now that our honored guests have arrived, we can get on with our program. All of us in this room are recipients of grants from the SUN Foundation. These grants, and the education that went with them, made it possible for us to start or expand our businesses. Some of us got together and felt that we should say thank you. We all have stories we could tell, but I've asked Mrs. Lottie Tarasal to tell hers."

Lottie took the microphone and spoke:

> I remember how disappointed I was when the banker told me that he couldn't lend me the amount of money that I needed to expand my business. Just to go to the bank in the first place had taken all the gumption I could muster. (Everyone laughed with understanding.)
>
> The banker asked me to call Jack LeGault. I did not think it would help, but I did. General LeGault asked me if I could read. I thought that was a silly question, but I answered 'no.' He asked me if I was willing to learn. I was confused, but answered 'yes.'
>
> I went to see him, and the rest is history. That was six years ago, and today most folks around here know about my business Night Magic. We have twelve three-person crews that clean St. Louis office buildings after business folks leave.
>
> Speaking here today has scared me more than going to the banker six years ago, but to be part of thanking these three wonderful men helped me muster up my courage.

Mrs. Tarasal received a well-deserved applause, and Bill Barnes took the microphone again, "Now it's time to eat and enjoy our dinner. Later our mayor will unveil our thank you gift to these men."

When the time came for the unveiling of the gift that was covered from view, Bill Barnes took over again, "It's now my privilege to introduce the mayor of St. Louis, who will help me unveil this oil painting, a token of our appreciation to Mr. Rick Bauman, Mr. Matt Simmons, and General Jack LeGault."

As the canvas cover was pulled away, everyone could see an oil painting of three smiling thirteen-year-old boys sitting on a park bench in rather ragged clothes. Rick, Jack, and Matt each remembered the day that the picture used as a model was taken.

Then the mayor spoke:

A boy's dreams are unlimited and can become his motives as a man. How much greater the force can be when three boys have the same positive fantasies, and later as men share the motivation to fulfill their dreams.

The boys in this painting grew up on the St. Louis river front but refused to let economic depression or wars stop them from fulfilling their dreams.

Through the SUN Foundation, they have given 249 new businesses the extra one-time financial support and guidance needed for success. Over 200 of these businesses have prospered and grown. These businesses have provided more than a thousand jobs to strengthen the St. Louis economy and to enrich the lives of families.

This painting will hang at the St. Louis City Hall. The plaque under the painting reads:

IN HONOR OF
EMIL ULRICK BAUMAN
BLACKJACK PERSHING LEGAULT
MATTHEW WILLIAM SIMMONS,
ST LOUIS BOYS WHO GREW
TO BE OUTSTANDING MEN
AND FULFILLED THEIR
BOYHOOD DREAMS
TO DO GOOD FOR THE CITY OF ST.LOUIS.

Looking at Matt, Jack, and Rick, the mayor asked, "Which of you would like to respond to your friends?"

Matt and Jack quickly turned to Rick, pushing him forward as their spokesman. Rick started to back away, but in response to clapping and cheers he moved to the microphone and began to speak:

> This oil painting of us sitting on our park bench in Forest Park in 1937 is a wonderful gift.
>
> Our business careers started in a cabbage patch at my river front neighborhood home that is now close to the Jefferson Memorial Park. Our close friend, Scott Lincoln, who is here today, worked with us. Our parents gave us love and support, and we had the benefit of some wise and unselfish mentors.
>
> Thank you, mayor, for your kind words and for sharing this occasion with us. Thank you, Bill Barnes, Lottie Tarasal, and all of you businessmen and women who are helping to make St. Louis such a marvelous place to live. Thank you, Ruth, Marcie, and Sandy for your love and encouragement through many happy years of marriage.
>
> I've had many pleasant and wonderful experiences on the park bench in this painting. My wife and I

committed ourselves to marriage at this beautiful spot in Forest Park. I remember the day that I sat on this bench with Matt and Jack when World War II had ended. They had returned home to St. Louis, badly wounded but alive.

Please take your children to visit St. Louis's magnificent parks. Start with the Jefferson Memorial Park, and then encourage them from time to time to sit quietly on a park bench in Forest Park and dream. The future of St. Louis is with her children.

*   *   *

When the Baumans, LeGaults, and Simmons left city hall that evening, they all stopped at the beautiful Jefferson Memorial Park. They went up to the top of the world-famous Gateway Arch in the slow elevator compartments. In the viewing area, they were able to see miles up and down the Mississippi River. They looked down at the Jefferson Memorial Park that was formerly the deteriorated river front neighborhood in which their lives began.

The view from the Arch brought back memories for all of them. Ruth pointed towards a long stretch of river bluff that had been developed in recent decades to serve river and rail traffic. She painfully reflected, "When I was a child, that's where we lived for awhile with other homeless families during the Depression when my Dad lost his job."

Noticing a barge headed south, Jack turned to Sandy and said, "Louie and I used to work on one of those Mississippi River barges for passage to Ste. Genevieve when we spent summers in the Ozark Mountains."

Matt commented to Marcie, "Do you see the tourist boat we took the children on when they were little? When I was a boy, Rick, Jack, and I often sat on top of the levee wishing we could afford a boat ticket."

Marcie's thoughts drifted down the river. "It's hard to imagine that the wide Mississippi River in St. Louis continues to get wider until it is double its size by the time it reaches New Orleans."

Rick marveled at the foresight of men like the French explorer, Pierre Laclede Liquest, in selecting this river bluff to establish the City of St. Louis, and the engineer, James Eads, who constructed the world famous bridge that spanned the wide Mississippi River. They looked with amazement at the impressive Eads Bridge, constructed in the late nineteenth century to expand the gateway to the West.

As Rick, Matt, and Jack surveyed the vast city below, they realized that their accomplishments were now a part of the history of St. Louis. After reminiscing about the past, their thoughts turned to the future. "We've had our turn to make changes in the twentieth century," said Rick. "Now it's our children's turn to make changes in the twenty-first century. I wonder what they will choose do with their lives?"

HISTORY OF ST. LOUIS, MISSOURI: 1763-1930

A French explorer, Pierre Laclede Liquest, recognized the future possibilities of the St. Louis river front bluff when he made his first landing in 1763. He established his fur trading post a few months later, when he and his small band of fur traders poled their boat, loaded with supplies, a thousand miles up the Mississippi River from New Orleans. The spot he selected was on a high bluff, a few miles from of the converging Missouri and Mississippi Rivers. Laclede laid claim to this high land and named it for King Louis IX, patron saint of the French Monarch, Louis XV.

Laclede's trading post soon became the center of the Western fur trade. He predicted that this tiny French village would someday become one of the finest cities in America. Within less than a hundred years, his vision had become a reality. Later, a cobblestone levee was constructed on Laclede's bluff that would be the only barrier between the flooding Mississippi River and the growing City of St. Louis.

Forty years after Laclede's first landing, the Louisiana Purchase Treaty was signed on May 4, 1803. In 1804 the famed Louis and Clark expedition embarked from St. Louis. The West was opened to the newly independent United States of America. Courageous settlers and pioneers moved into and through St. Louis to help establish the western states in the nineteenth and twentieth centuries as the new nation grew.

St. Louis, Missouri, was flourishing in 1843, but it was devastated by three great disasters in the next five years. First, the Great Flood of 1844; then the Great Cholera Epidemic that broke out in 1849; and later in 1849, the Great Fire. Residents hoped that the fire would end the cholera epidemic, but the plague continued. When the cholera epidemic was finally over in 1867, more than one of every ten citizens had died of the dreaded disease. The earlier flood and the later fire had completely destroyed homes on the river front. St. Louis was at a crossroads. City officials and other citizens working together accepted the responsibility of building an even greater city.

Planning commissions were formed to develop new ideas. They decided to bring the East and West together by designing and constructing what would become the most famous bridge in the world at that time, over one of the world's largest rivers. Many engineers scoffed at the design and said it could not be constructed. James Eads told the business leaders that it could be done. They believed him. The bridge was completed in seven years and met the planners' dreams of opening the way for railroads and carriages to replace some of the river commerce being lost to the railroads.

The tide had turned!

Building and revitalization in the next two decades made the city famous again. Excited city leaders were not satisfied. Before the end of the century, there were nearly 3,000 acres of parks including Forest Park, Tower Grove Park, Fairgrounds Park, and O'Fallon Park.

Civic leaders converted the 1,400 acres of Forest Park into the 1904 Louisiana Purchase Exposition, known as the St. Louis World's Fair. The tradition of an Olympic Village dates back to the Games of St. Louis in 1904. New utility systems that improved the quality of life were developed at that time.

Great cities must continue to have new visions. In 1920 St. Louis planners were doing their job. Civic leaders knew that the hurriedly constructed buildings along its historical, Mississippi River levee after the 1849 fire should be considered uninhabitable and be demolished. The planners had a vision to renovate the river front. Future generations would be able to see the beauty and majesty of the Mississippi River and study in museums that would tell of the steamship landings and the city's glorious past.

The Depression in the 1930s and war in the 1940s left new visions abruptly halted and incomplete. These former visions came to life again after World War II.

ABOUT THE AUTHOR

James W. Colmey grew up in Webster Groves, St. Louis County, Missouri during the Depression (1929 – 1940). He served three years in the United States Army during World War II; he was stationed in California, New Jersey, Florida, and Texas before shipping out to the Philippine Islands. After the Japanese surrender in 1945, he remained in Manila and received a Commendation for Outstanding Services for his participation in the establishment of the Philippine Institution for the Armed Forces.

After the war Colmey earned a Bachelor's Degree in Business Administration from the University of Texas in Austin and a Doctor's Degree in Education from Columbia University in New York City.

As an educator, Colmey worked in New York, Florida, Missouri, Tennessee, and Wisconsin from 1948 – 1989. His work included Professor of Education at Peabody College/Vanderbilt University, Director of Educational Research at Memphis University, and Deputy Commissioner of Education in Tennessee. He completed his career as Assistant Chancellor at the University of Wisconsin at Whitewater.

Colmey co-authored three books on educational administration and numerous articles in professional journals. He is past president of the Southeastern Association of School Business Officials. He also served as consultant to the United States Department of Education as well as to many states, making a significant contribution toward the development of state community colleges and educational research.

After retirement Colmey served five years on the Commission for Occupational Education for reviews and accreditation for the Southern Association of Colleges and Schools.